MATANZAS BAY

As an unpublished manuscript, *Matanzas Bay* won the 2007 Josiah W. Bancroft, Sr. Award, and was named a Book of the Year in the 2009 Royal Palm Literary Awards Competition. Author Parker Francis, also known as Victor DiGenti, writes the award-winning *Windrusher* adventure/fantasy series. These books are available as Kindle downloads and as trade paperbacks.

Books by the Author
(Under the name Victor DiGenti)

Windrusher
Windrusher and the Cave of Tho-hoth
Windrusher and the Trail of Fire

MATANZAS BAY
A Novel

Parker Francis

Windrusher Hall Press

Cover design by Greg DiGenti

Published by Windrusher Hall Press
Ponte Vedra Beach, Florida

Acknowledgements

Many thanks to those who helped in the transition of this story from rough draft to finished product. Thanks for their editing, critiques, suggestions, and support. Including Camille Cline, David Poyer, and the Ponte Vedra Writers critique group led by Bill Kerr. To Evanne for her coping skills; to Kay Day for giving voice to the poet, and to all my readers who have waited (along with the author) for this book to be published.

Guilt is the source of sorrow, 'tis the fiend,
Th' avenging fiend that follows us behind,
With whips and stings.

— Nicholas Rowe

People who grumble about life being unfair have it all wrong. It's life's alter ego, death, that isn't fair. Pick up the paper. Turn on any of the twenty-four-hour news channels. See what I mean? Every day we hear of innocent people suffering horrible and senseless deaths. Vacationing prom queens disappear from tropical islands. Drivers rage against one another, ending their commute prematurely. Families slaughtered by homicidal misfits foraging for money, drugs or payback. And I hate to think about the god-awful things perpetrated on innocent children. Not that I don't have personal experience in that area.

I was sitting in the welcoming shade of Trinity Episcopal Church in the nation's oldest city shaking sand from my shoe. My back scraped the rough coquina wall flanking Artillery Lane, one of the narrowest streets in a city known for its challenging roadways. I should be enjoying my sabbatical from the office; instead my mind skewed uncontrollably toward the dark side. Maybe the smell emerging from my sweat-soaked sock was playing tricks with my brain chemistry. Maybe digging up 500-year-old bones gives you a sharper view of life's fragility. More likely, it's my naturally gloomy nature reminding me that in the end we're all history.

In front of me, five other volunteers were mucking around in the shallow pit next to the church. We called ourselves amateur archaeologists, but amateur may be too generous a word. We're just grunts, doing the backbreaking work of digging and screening a fifteen by thirty piece of real estate before progress, in the form of a new parking lot, paved over this particular slice of history.

I didn't know about the others, but I welcomed the grunt work as a distraction from what paid the bills—my regular job as a private investigator. My name is Mitchell, Quint Mitchell. I was enjoying one of my mental health days, sitting here sweating and emptying sand from my size twelve-and-a-half shoe when my cell phone rang.

I checked the Caller ID and took a deep breath. Him again. My dark mood had suddenly become blacker. Slipping the shoe back on my foot, I moved around the corner of the old church away from the others. I didn't say anything. He'd start when he was ready.

"Are you there, you goddamn murderer?"

I wasn't shocked; instead sadness consumed me, nearly taking my breath away. The image of a girl's face convulsed in terror sprang into my head, and I bit my lower lip in an effort to drive away the picture flashing through my brain.

"You should be put down like a mad dog, Mitchell. You're not even worth the breath it takes for me to call and remind you that every day you're alive is one day too long." The man's voice broke; his anguish a serrated blade slicing deep into my chest.

The vision of the doomed girl remained with me, a morbid souvenir of a tragic accident. Consumed by her death, the girl's father called me at all hours of the day and night. Although I was cleared of any blame for my part in the accident, he won't let me forget I was driving the car that killed his daughter. As if I could forget.

I knew I shouldn't answer his calls, save myself the misery. Hearing the utter grief in the poor man's voice, though, I told myself this might be his only comfort. But each call added to the weight I carried, often unleashing darker and bloodier images than that poor girl's death. The slide show in my head, if I let it, would make the leap from last year's traffic accident to a summer's day twenty-three years earlier.

The day my brother was murdered.

"Don't you have anything to say?" The girl's father shouted into my ear, interrupting my morbid train of thought. "Don't you want to explain to me and God why you're alive and ..." He choked back sobs.

I slumped against the church wall, eyes closed, stomach aching. Instinctively, my hand rose to my chest and touched the medallion hanging beneath my shirt. I peered around the corner at the other volunteers. They were still absorbed with their tiny piece of real estate, digging up artifacts from generations past while I dealt with more recent ghosts.

Finally, I found my voice. "I'm sorry." It was all I could say to the man sobbing on the other end. I closed the phone and returned it to my pocket.

"Is everything all right?" Jeffrey Poe's question startled me back to the present. His long face, usually alive with the possibility of discovery each time he supervised these archaeological digs, was set in a serious mask of concern. It made me wonder how I must look to him.

"Just some boring business from the office." I tried to dredge up a tone of lightness I didn't feel. "I'll start on the trash pit now." He watched me step over the twine surrounding the survey area, pick up the trowel and kneel by the depression.

Dr. Jeffrey Poe, St. Augustine's archaeologist, had a sharp eye and didn't miss much. A tall man with perpetually tousled brown hair, a ruddy complexion and a ready smile revealing a gap in his front teeth, Poe took me under his wing after I approached him about volunteering with his archaeological surveys. Over the ensuing months and years, we became close friends.

Seemingly impervious to the searing August heat, Poe wore his standard uniform of long-sleeved denim shirt and floppy, wide-brimmed canvas hat tattooed with the imprint of dozens of digs. As city archaeologist, he followed-up on construction permits within the city limits to determine if the site might add to the knowledge of St. Augustine's storied past. If so, he surveyed the site, retrieved artifacts, and recorded as much data as possible before asphalt obscured the past.

Poe acted as ringmaster of our little circus, directing the six volunteers—four elderly retired professionals, a long-haired Flagler College freshman, and me. Together we're grubbing around in a shallow rectangular pit slightly larger than a boxing ring.

I studied Poe a moment before turning my attention to the trash pit. The city archaeologist walked to the screening table and picked through the scattering of debris searching for anything of value. His face had taken on a nearly beatific look as he lost himself in the pursuit of clues to the old city's past. I couldn't see any hint of the pressure I knew he'd been under since his bitter encounter with William Marrano, St. Augustine's vice mayor. For a while after the two of them clashed over a new development on the San Sebastian River, it looked like Poe might lose his job.

Kneeling in the dirt, I turned my attention to the trash pit. Poe discovered the depression in the corner of the excavation when he arrived today. He explained the heavy weekend rains probably caused the soil to settle. We added it to the collection of other holes dotting the area. The phone call still buzzed inside my head like an angry wasp, but I brushed it aside, concentrating on the task at hand.

I used the trowel to outline the pockmark of recessed soil, then carefully skimmed away the dirt as Poe taught us, one layer at a time. My dig partner, a retired attorney named Rachel, hovered over my shoulder with her grid map and a spiral bound notebook, taking notes as I widened the pit. I shoveled the loose dirt into a five-gallon plastic bucket, surprised to find the soil falling away easily beneath my trowel.

In the branches of a nearby oak shading our site, a mockingbird called, probably searching for female company. I paused a moment to look for the bird and wiped away a trickle of sweat burning my eye.

"This sure looks different from the other trash pits," Rachel said.

"Now that you mention it, I wondered why we weren't seeing the same striations and layers of clay." I'd transferred about eight inches of topsoil from the depression to the bucket, and instead of the hard-packed dirt we found at the other holes, this felt like newly-turned soil.

My trowel scraped against something hard and unyielding. Not surprising. Sometimes when we're lucky, we find intact artifacts like cannon balls or the foundations of ancient structures, usually made from coquina. Poe said this site probably dated back to the first buildings erected in the mid-sixteenth century. I may have found the remains of one of St. Augustine's first homes or a military wall, like the Rosario Line uncovered in 2007. Postholes, trash pits and soil stains are all good indications of early habitation, often leading to the recovery of historically valuable artifacts.

Carefully, I used the edge of my trowel like a brush so as not to damage the buried object hidden below the surface. But there was no telltale sound of metal against rock. Instead something softer, organic.

"What the hell is this?" I asked.

Poe and the others turned around and moved toward me.

"Let me see." Poe leaned down to peer into the hole. "Maybe you've made a real find, Quint." His gray-green eyes sparkled with curiosity.

"I was just saying something seemed different about this pit," Rachel said.

Poe handed me a brush. "Careful now. Careful."

Slowly, I brushed away the last layer of soil covering the object.

"Look at that," Rachel squealed.

Instead of coquina or a corroded cannonball, I'd unearthed the top to what looked like a large wicker hamper. Reed baskets were used by the early settlers, a craft learned from the Indians, but this looked too modern and well-preserved to date back to the 1560s. I'm only an amateur, but I thought it was a good guess since the top of the basket was secured by two brightly-colored bungee cords.

Seeing it wasn't an artifact, but obviously contemporary, Poe lost interest. "Probably somebody's idea of a joke," he grumbled. "Get it out of there."

I tossed the brush aside and took the shovel someone handed me. Tim, the college student, grabbed another shovel and together we cleared more than a foot of dirt from around the hamper. As we dug deeper, I estimated the hamper's dimensions to be at least four feet tall by perhaps two-and-a-half feet wide.

An odor like three-day-old road kill oozed from the basket. Stepping away, my stomach revved into overdrive; my gag reflex fully engaged. The stench brought back memories from my days in the Gulf War, and I pushed away the image of bloated bodies lying in the desert and told myself that the basket contained the remains of someone's old dog.

Wiping the sweat from my face, I thanked Rachel for the water she handed me and took a long swallow.

"God, that smells horrible," Rachel said.

Tim took his cue from me, stabbed his shovel into the ground, accepting the bottled water.

"What do you think it is?" he asked me. His face seemed to have lost some of its summer tan.

"Probably garbage." I took another swallow of water trying to wash down the taste of my cheeseburger lunch working its way into my throat.

Poe shook his head in disgust. He took his work seriously and didn't appreciate anyone corrupting his research. Tim and I bent over the basket intending to pull it out of the ground. The smell was now almost unbearable, and I noticed more color draining from Tim's face.

"Let me see if I can manage it." I'm a fairly big guy, six-one-and-a-half, and I work out regularly, but when I tugged on the basket I barely budged it. Instead of garbage, I decided the basket must contain concrete blocks.

Tim held a handkerchief over his nose and mouth, but bravely leaned over and grabbed one side of the basket with his other hand. "On three," I said between clenched teeth, feeling the cheeseburger making a comeback appearance.

With a series of grunts, we hauled our discovery out of the hole and set it carefully on the ground.

"I have a basket like that at home," Rachel said. "I bought it at Pier One and use it as a clothes hamper."

We all laughed, and I tried to imagine how many dirty clothes would have to be compacted into the basket to weigh what must be well over a hundred pounds.

Poe gestured toward the basket. "It's your discovery, Quint. Why don't you do the honors?"

I fumbled with the bungee cords for a minute. They were stretched to their limits and I strained to disconnect the hooks. As they fell away, I cut my eyes to Poe. He nodded and I reached over to lift the cover from what might be someone's clothes hamper.

My participation in this dig was not a selfless act. I hoped to lose myself in the physical work of scraping and digging as a momentary escape. A form of penitence. Just as Poe reconstructs people's lives by the detritus they left behind, the phone call was a reminder that my life is built on crumbling splinters of guilt still embedded beneath my skin like pieces of shrapnel in a combat veteran. One day there will be a final accounting, but until then I'll have to live with a grieving father's phone calls, with his daughter's death, and, even worse, the terrible knowledge of my responsibility for my brother's murder on a Long Island shore so many years ago.

I breathed deeply through my mouth and heard the mockingbird call again. When I looked up, I saw the bird lift from the tree and fly away. With Poe and the volunteers surrounding me, I removed the lid and stared inside. Immediately the thought occurred to me my search for penitence must have taken a wrong turn somewhere.

Staring back at me was the bloody head of William Marrano

"Holy shit!" I yelled, dropping the lid and jerking back from the open basket. Over my shoulder, Rachel screamed. When I turned away from the gruesome scene I saw Tim retching into one of the plastic buckets.

Poe put a hand on my shoulder and together we examined our find. Marrano's head had a deep indentation over the left temple. Blood had seeped from the wound and caked along the left cheek in dried rivulets. His tongue protruded from his mouth, swollen and discolored like the head of a tree toad. A green garbage bag hung loosely around the lower torso, providing an excellent view of the old Spanish bayonet protruding from Marrano's chest.

I stared at the weapon for a moment before making the connection and looked up at Poe to see if he recognized it. These dagger-like bayonets had been carried by the Spanish arquebusiers or riflemen and were adapted to fit into the bore of the musket. I knew many had been found at various digs throughout St. Augustine, their wooden grips rotted away. This one had a bone handle with a vertical crack running through it—exactly like the one I saw at Jeffrey Poe's house two weeks ago.

One of the volunteers, a retired dermatologist, edged closer to the basket and stared at the corpse. The dead man's head had one eye open and the other closed as if giving us an obscene wink. "Isn't that Bill Marrano?" the doctor asked.

Poe and the others lived in St. Johns County and obviously recognized the vice mayor. Even though I lived in an adjacent county, a client once introduced me to Marrano and I recalled him as a wide-bodied man standing about five-ten. That's when he was standing, of course. And when he had legs. I couldn't be sure because of the garbage bag, but it seemed to me this body was missing those essential parts.

I stepped away from the basket and pulled Poe with me. "Everyone out of the pit," I ordered, reverting back to my Navy Master-at-Arms training. "I'm calling the police, so don't touch anything." I knew the rain, plus our digging and tramping over the site had erased most of the trace evidence, but we didn't need to add to the mess the police would soon find.

A squad car with two young, uniformed officers arrived shortly. They took one look at the basket and ran back to their car. Less than five minutes later, two more cruisers and an unmarked vehicle roared up, sirens wailing, lights flashing. We stood next to the church, out of the glare of the afternoon sun, and watched the police close off the narrow lane. I swatted at a cloud of gnats investigating my ears before moving on toward the corpse.

August in St. Augustine brought with it suffocating humidity, along with throngs of tourists. Dozens of them were now lined up three deep along the yellow police tape gaping at the scene. I saw a boy of around nine or ten perched on his father's shoulders pointing at the dead man's body as if admiring a float at the Macy's Thanksgiving Parade. Finally, one of the uniforms chased them away. A plain clothes detective approached Poe and our knot of volunteers. He identified himself as Detective George Horgan and asked us who found the body. Narrow and bird-like, Horgan's face seemed to have been cobbled together by someone with a wicked sense of humor. His pointed nose and protruding eyes gave him a constant look of surprise.

I answered his question. "That would be me." I described it all for him, from finding the basket in the new depression, to pulling it out of the ground and seeing Marrano inside. Horgan took notes with a silver ballpoint pen, glancing up at me from time to time.

"Can I have your name, address and contact information in case we need to ask you some more questions?" I noticed yellow nicotine stains on Horgan's fingers, and the odor of smoke clinging to him like burrs on wool socks.

"It's Mitchell. Quint Mitchell." I repeated my address and phone number before telling him I was a private investigator from Jacksonville Beach. Horgan's bird-like face grimaced slightly at the words *private investigator* as though he had a bad case of acid reflux. He grunted at me before nodding towards Poe and the others.

"Dr. Poe, I take it these are all volunteers working with you on this project."

"That's right."

"Can you tell me how Mr. Marrano's body *happened* to be buried where you *happened* to be digging?"

Poe licked his lips, eyes darting toward me then back at Horgan before answering. "You're not suggesting I had anything to do with this?"

"I'm not suggesting anything, Dr. Poe. I'm only asking if you knew—"

"I know what you're implying and why you're implying it, but you couldn't be more wrong."

Dots of crimson peppered Poe's cheeks, and I put a hand on his arm to calm him. "Think about it, Detective Horgan," I said. "Would anyone, especially Dr. Poe, be foolish enough to hide the body where it would implicate him? It doesn't make any sense."

Horgan eyed me for a moment then wrote something in his notebook before gesturing toward the other volunteers. "I'll need your names and addresses as well."

While the detective recorded the volunteer's information, a white SUV screeched into the church parking lot. I looked up to see a thick-necked man in street clothes climb out of the Ford Explorer. He had a badge clipped to his belt, and the other officers stepped back as he approached the corner of the dig where the hamper sat.

The cop stood motionless, staring at the corpse. He removed his sunglasses, and ran a hand through curly black hair flecked with gray. From my vantage point, I saw his jaw muscles working furiously, the cords in his neck straining. He stepped over the police tape and walked toward the basket.

"Sarge, maybe you should …" Horgan began, but the sergeant's withering glare made the detective swallow his sentence.

The sergeant stopped in front of the basket and dropped to one knee to look at the dead man's head from eye level. He remained in that position, silent, not touching anything. Finally, he raised a hand toward Marrano's face, but stopped short of touching it. I saw his fingers tremble slightly before he balled them into a fist and turned toward our small group by the church. His eyes immediately drilled into Poe. He popped up and rushed toward the city archaeologist with the fierce resolution of a tiger leaping toward its prey.

"What do you know about this?" he yelled, pushing his face within inches of Poe's. He put a hand on Poe's chest and shoved him against the wall of the church.

Poe wasn't a small man, but the sergeant had surprised him and he fell back, his wide-brimmed hat sliding forward until it touched his nose. The sergeant's face flushed, and his right hand cocked back, the knuckles on his fist wide and white, straining at the taut flesh.

"Hey, wait a minute," I said, foolishly stepping between them. "I'm the one who found the basket, not Dr. Poe."

My gallant gesture had the intended effect of diverting the sergeant's attention, and he stared at me as though I was a cockroach crawling over his Christmas ham. Without a word, he dismissed me and turned his attention back to Poe.

"You hated him, Poe. I know you're behind this somehow. You'd do anything to stop that project." Flecks of spittle flew from his mouth and a little tic worked beneath his left eye. He opened and closed his fingers as if trying to decide whether to slap Poe with an open hand or pound him with his fist.

I'd never seen a police officer lose control of himself in this way, and I considered what the consequences might be if I had to pull him off my friend. I was an inch or two taller, and maybe ten years younger, but the sergeant was broader across the shoulders and chest and had forearms the size of bowling pins.

Before I could do anything, Poe found his voice. "You're wrong, Buck. Sure, Bill and I had our differences, but no way would I harm your brother."

His brother? No wonder he went ballistic. The sergeant leaned in toward Poe, his face a mask of hatred, one huge fist locked in the firing position. Against my better judgment, I spoke up again.

"Listen, sergeant, whatever you may think of Dr. Poe, you can't believe he's capable of murder." I made the mistake of putting a hand on his arm. He whipped it away and gave me his full attention.

"Who the hell are you?" he shouted in my face. "I'll need a name before throwing you in jail for interfering with a criminal investigation."

I raised both hands in a sign of surrender and backed off. Horgan quickly stepped between us. Looking at his notes, he said, "He's the one who found the vict … your brother. His name is Quint Mitchell and he lives in Jacks—"

"Quint Mitchell!" Marrano spit my name out as though it burned his tongue and studied me for a moment before continuing, "I know who you are. You're the Jacksonville Beach PI who's involved with that …" He paused and seemed to search for words. "… with that Howard woman." He sneered and turned away from me.

I felt a wave of heat creeping along my neck and up my cheeks. I fought to control my breathing, my chest tightening, my hands stiff at my sides. "You're out of line, sergeant. I can understand how it feels to lose your brother, but—"

With surprising speed, his left hand shot out, snatched a handful of my shirt, and yanked me toward him. At the same time, his right fist slammed into my stomach just below my ribcage and I doubled over gasping for air.

"You know how it feels, you stupid bastard? How does that feel?"

I struggled to force air into my lungs, to defend myself before he hit me again. He grabbed me by the shoulder and lifted me into position for another punch. Weakly, I raised an arm, but he only smirked and pushed me against the wall next to Poe.

"If you had anything to do with this, Mitchell, I'll make you sorry you ever came into my town."

He raised his fist again, but before he could throw another punch, Horgan grabbed his arm. "Not a good idea, sarge. The chief's here."

Marrano swung toward Horgan who pointed at another squad car pulling into the parking lot. A balding, middle-aged man I recognized as Chief Milo Conover climbed out on the passenger side and approached us. Conover was considered a straight shooter. He'd risen through the ranks of the small St. Augustine Police Department and had been appointed chief last year after his predecessor retired.

Horgan hurried over to the chief and they spoke briefly before Conover surveyed the hamper with its macabre contents. Taking in our little group and the beefy sergeant's threatening stance, Conover strode toward us.

"Buck, I'm so sorry," he said, laying a hand on the officer's shoulder.

Marrano seemed to sag for a moment before the fury returned to his eyes. "We have the bastard who did this right here, chief." He shoved a meaty index finger into Poe's chest. "Everyone knows how much he hated Bill."

The chief toted more than a few extra pounds around his waist, but he carried himself with authority. He grabbed the sergeant by his upper arm and pulled him away from Poe. "You're too close to this, Sergeant Marrano," he said in a stern voice. "I'm asking you to step aside and let us give this case the thorough investigation it deserves."

Marrano tried to pull his arm away from Conover, but the chief held him firmly. "No way. I'm in charge of detectives, and that's my brother over there. This killer has to pay for—"

Conover yanked Marrano's arm, forcing him to turn toward him. "Listen to yourself, Buck." He kept his voice low, under control. "You may be Detective Commander, but you're in no condition to objectively investigate anything at the moment. For your brother's sake, we have to put emotions aside, and I don't think you can do that."

Marrano had been staring over Conover's shoulder at Poe. He looked back at the chief as if he'd just heard him and shook his head vigorously. Before he could respond, Conover said, "I'm putting Detectives Horgan and Thompson in charge of the investigation, Buck, and ordering you to return to headquarters."

Conover held Marrano's icy glare. "Do you hear me, sergeant?"

"I hear you," Marrano murmured. He gave each of us a hard stare before turning and walking briskly to his car, taking one final glance at his brother's head as he passed.

Breathing normally now, I watched Conover and Horgan huddle together, the detective inclining his head in our direction several times before the chief approached us.

"I understand Detective Horgan has taken your statements. This must be very traumatic for you folks, and I apologize for the sergeant's outburst. I'm sure you understand what he must be going through."

Conover puckered his lips and shook his head slowly. "This is a terrible loss for our entire community, but we have to remember the Vice Mayor was Sergeant Marrano's only brother. I hope you can forgive him if his emotions got the better of him." His eyes slid over each of us before settling on me, and I figured Horgan told him Marrano had sucker-punched me.

"Except for Dr. Poe, you're all free to go," Conover said. "Please remember St. Augustine's a small town, folks. We rely almost entirely on tourism. We don't want to frighten anyone, so I'd appreciate it if you kept this to yourself as much as possible while we conduct our investigation."

He turned away and addressed Poe. "Jeffrey, let's go down to my office. We have a few more questions for you."

"But I don't know anything."

"It will be better for everyone if we put this feud business to rest and try to get to the bottom of this terrible crime." Conover studied Poe through hard brown eyes, reminding me of a shark contemplating its next meal.

I stayed in place when the other volunteers departed, thinking I might be of some help to Poe. Offering my most conciliatory smile, I said, "Chief, I'm Quint Mitchell. I found Mr. Marrano's body."

"Yes, Mr. Mitchell, we have your statement and appreciate your cooperation."

"Dr. Poe's a good friend, and if you don't mind, I'd like to accompany—"

"Are you his attorney, Mr. Mitchell?" Conover cut me off.

"Well, no, but I'm a private investigator." Even as I said the words I knew how lame they sounded.

Conover moved closer to me. I smelled peppermint on his breath. "Believe me, Mr. Mitchell, we'll be in touch if we have any more questions for you. Right now, Dr. Poe is the only one we need to speak with. Routine questions, that's all."

With that, he turned his back on me and guided Poe by the elbow toward his squad car.

Three

Poe climbed into the back of Conover's cruiser, and they pulled away leaving me rubbing my aching abdomen and nursing a bruised ego. Yellow police tape had been strung around the entire church parking lot except for a gap to allow official vehicles to enter and exit. While I watched, a man in his late fifties arrived in a white van. He approached Horgan who stood by the excavation site, a clipboard in one hand, an unlit cigarette dangling from his lips.

Horgan greeted the new arrival and passed the clipboard to the man, who wore a limp seersucker jacket that looked like it may have been purchased at a 1978 JC Penney summer sale. He tucked a small black valise under his left arm in order to hold the clipboard and signed in.

As the primary investigating officer on the scene, Horgan was responsible for documenting the chain of evidence. If I was right, the gentleman with the retro coat and black bag was the county medical examiner. They conferred for a minute before Horgan pointed to the hamper where Marrano's remains were now attracting dark clouds of gnats and flies.

The medical examiner's first order of business was to confirm the victim's death. His next task would be to estimate the time and cause of death. The corpse's temperature provided an approximation as to how long the victim had been deceased. But most of the answers would be found during the autopsy.

Standard crime scene investigation procedures call for photographic documentation of the scene in order to create a permanent historical record, collecting of trace evidence and writing a detailed report, including diagrams, of everything found at the scene. But prior to all of this, I knew the police were required to clear all non-essential personnel from the crime scene.

Right on cue, Horgan looked up and spotted me.

"Mitchell, what the hell are you still doing here?" he blared out from his position next to the excavation site. "Even a PI should know a crime scene when he sees one. Now move your ass before I ask one of these officers to escort you to headquarters. If we need you, we know where to find you."

As he yelled, Horgan's eyes bulged to the point I expected to see one of his orbs pop out of his head and roll across the ground like a marble.

"Don't get your tighty-whities in a twist, detective. I was just leaving."

Horgan didn't need to remind me the police were in charge of this investigation, but as I walked away from the church, I worried about my friend. Jeffrey Poe was obviously more than a person of interest. He was at the top of the SAPD's suspect list, and I didn't want to see him railroaded because he and Bill Marrano had disagreed over St. Augustine's future skyline.

I've known Poe for about five years. We've grown increasingly close, particularly after his wife Gail died three years ago. She suffered through an agonizing bout with liver cancer, Poe suffering along with her, a part of his spirit departing when she died. In the weeks following her death, he retreated behind a wall of grief, refusing to answer his phone and ignoring the friends and neighbors who came to check on him. Poe eventually dug himself out of his pit of depression, but now, I worried how he would react to this latest trauma.

After Poe was taken in for questioning I spent an hour sitting on a bench in the Plaza de la Constitución making phone calls and observing the waves of tourists washing over the old city. The Plaza was slung between Cathedral and King Streets. Tourist guides tout it as the oldest public park in the United States, established by Royal Spanish Ordinances in 1573.

From where I sat, across from the Government House, I watched young people playing among the Civil War cannons and running the stairs of the covered pavilion that was once used as a public marketplace. Also known as the Old Slave Market, during the civil rights struggles it had been the gathering place for local demonstrators. During the summer months, the park hosted weekly concerts and an occasional art show. These days, though, homeless men inhabited many of the benches.

If I walked two blocks up King Street, I'd be facing the Casa Monica Hotel. Thinking of the hotel made me remember how Sergeant Marrano had erupted when he heard my name. What did he say? That I was *involved with that Howard woman.* His statement was correct. I just didn't like the way he said it.

Serena Howard is the marketing director for the Casa Monica, and we've been seeing each other for the past three months. Unfortunately, what had begun with a flash of sparks and grew into one of my most meaningful relationships had flickered down to its last embers. Time to pour water over our campfire and declare it officially dead.

I didn't want to think about our crumbling romance now, so I walked the six blocks to the St. Augustine Police Department. I wondered how Poe's interrogation had gone. What could he tell them other than he was completely in the dark about Marrano's murder? But how could he explain away the bayonet?

Poe had a stubborn streak. Sometimes his temper might push common sense aside and he'd say things he later regretted, but in my heart I knew my friend was not a killer. I glanced at the monument sign in the middle of the sidewalk identifying the neat concrete building as the St. Augustine Police Department before climbing the white steps and entering.

A half-dozen plastic chairs hugged the walls inside the small waiting room. In one of the chairs sat a bony woman in a shapeless black dress covered with tiny yellow flowers. Emitting invisible signals of distress, she stared at the massive set of double doors separating the lobby from the rest of the building.

I walked past the woman to the information window on the right side of the lobby. The window was identical to those you see at security-conscious gas stations for after hours' transactions and included a stainless steel tray at the bottom as well as a round aluminum grid in the center for two-way conversation. Behind it, a solidly built woman in a white and green uniform talked animatedly on the telephone, scribbling something in a large three-ring binder.

I waited patiently until she finished her conversation, turned the page in the notebook and finally acknowledged me. She studied me for a moment above a pair of half-frame reading glasses before approaching the window.

"Can I help you?"

"Do you know if Jeffrey Poe is still here?"

Muscles tensed along her fleshy jaw line as she looked down at the notebook still in her hands and back to me. "He's being questioned," she said. "Why don't you have a seat?"

I walked to one of the chairs facing the interior doors. By the time I sat down the receptionist had returned to her desk, leaving me alone with my thoughts and the worried woman who broke the silence with a phlegmy cough.

I gazed at the row of photographic portraits lining the wall directly in front of me. Each member of the St. Augustine City Commission including Mayor Hal Cameron and Vice Mayor William Marrano wore a nearly identical smile. Marrano's face jolted me back to the discovery of his mutilated corpse. I had a little experience with murder cases, but this one didn't seem to fit into the typical patterns of violent crime—escalating domestic abuse, drug-related shootings, or random acts of violence that are more likely to be crimes of opportunity.

Whoever killed Marrano had taken the time to saw off the commissioner's legs, and bury the body at Poe's survey site. This wasn't the work of your average street criminal. A brutal and twisted killer, for sure, but clever enough to know the police would immediately zero in on Poe as their main suspect.

About the time I'd mulled this over, one of the large wooden doors swung open and Poe and Chief Conover walked through. Poe held his wide-brimmed hat in both hands, covering his chest protectively. The archaeologist tried to smile when he saw me waiting for him, but only managed a grimace.

"Thank you for your time, Dr. Poe," Conover said. "I guess I don't have to tell you not to leave town until we get to the bottom of this."

"Yes, yes, I know."

I approached Poe, asking, "Are you okay?"

He pushed past me without a word and scurried out the front door.

His long legs were striding east toward the historic district, when I caught up with him. "How'd it go?"

"I can't believe the bastards suspect me. They asked me the same questions over and over. Where was I yesterday? The day before? Did I own a wicker hamper? Had I ever seen the bayonet?"

"What about that bayonet? It looked like the one you showed us at your house."

"I have half a dozen bayonets in my office and at home. Hell, they're on display at the Visitor's Center and the museum."

Poe stopped at the intersection of King and Riberia Streets and turned toward me, his eyes seeking an answer in mine. "I don't know, Quint. It did look like the same bayonet, but how's that possible?"

"When did you see it last?"

"Not since the night you were there. You saw me leave it in my storage room. I swear I haven't touched it since then." More than a hint of desperation had crept into his voice.

"What happens now?"

"They're getting warrants to search my office, my house, even my truck."

"That's standard procedure, Jeffrey. You don't have anything to worry about if—"

"If I didn't do it? Do you think I'd kill Marrano and bury him at one of my own excavation surveys? How stupid do you think I am?"

"I know you're innocent, and I'm sure the police will come to the same conclusion. But you understand why you're on their radar, don't you?"

"I'm just so damn confused right now. Finding Marrano's body under our noses is too much of a coincidence." He let out a long shuddering breath.

In bed that evening, my mind traversed the day's events, and I tried to make some sense of it all. When I closed my eyes, a succession of images swirled around like dirt caught in the grip of a wind devil, then settled into strange and unnerving forms. I attempted to push away the bloated and discolored face of William Marrano insinuating itself into my thoughts and focus instead on what may have led to his murder.

Poe emerged as the principal suspect because of his heated disagreement with Marrano over the Matanzas Bay project. With St. Augustine's limited tax base, the fifteen-acre Malaga Street site had been trumpeted as the centerpiece of a new downtown renaissance.

Malaga Street was off the beaten path for the tourist trade. The acreage where the development would be built had been used by the City of St. Augustine for its motor pool operations and warehouse storage. Vice Mayor Marrano had proposed selling the property to the private sector hoping it would stimulate development and revitalize the entire area. After a lengthy process and a bidding war among four developers, the St. Johns Group emerged as the winner. Their plan called for a ten-story condominium unit with an adjoining 130-room hotel and a seventy-five-slip marina. A second phase would later add a six-story office building and an upscale spa and health club.

The high-rise condos and commercial buildings were standard stuff for larger cities like Jacksonville and Orlando, but quite a leap for St. Augustine. As the City Archaeologist, Poe considered St. Augustine sacred ground and didn't believe condos were a fitting tribute to the generations of Spanish, British, Indians, Minorcans and others who lived and died to create a unique piece of American history.

Even though the development would front the San Sebastian River, the developer named the project Matanzas Bay, a name with a history of its own. Every school kid in the area knew the story of how Pedro Menendez de Aviles, the settlement's protector and first governor, had massacred several hundred injured and starving shipwrecked Frenchmen. The Spanish found them on a sandbar in the Matanzas Inlet and ferried them to shore in their rowboats. As they collapsed on the sand thinking they'd been rescued, they were greeted by more Spanish soldiers who put them to the sword.

Miles away from the historic heart of St. Augustine, the inlet had been named after the massacre—Matanzas, *Place of Slaughter*. The bay-front of the Matanzas River is in the very heart of the old city, not far from the San Sebastian River, a tidal channel of the Matanzas.

The 600-year-old massacre touched memories still fresh in my own past, and the thought of the doomed Frenchmen pleading for their lives, their ripped and bloody bodies tumbling in the surf, was too painful for me to contemplate. I tried to wipe the unsettling pictures from my mind and finally fell asleep.

Drifting in a current of darkness, the dream returned. Curtains parted inside my head and there she was again, driving with one hand on the steering wheel, the other holding a cell phone to her ear. The camera in my mind zoomed in even closer, and I saw a clearer picture of a young girl with short hair and bright eyes. The girl chatted excitedly, actually taking her hand off the wheel at one point to gesture with an open palm. She laughed, her mouth open, light glinting from the braces across her teeth.

Now my silent movie added a soundtrack, and I heard screeching tires, screams and curses. The light tunneled into a narrow beam outlining a face transforming itself from one of youthful giddiness to a mask of terror.

In my dream, the scene swish-panned from the accident to a peaceful Long Island shoreline. Crunching sounds and screams from the automobile accident gave way to the cries of gulls and waves slapping the beach. I knew what was coming next. My unconscious fought to protect me from the awful pictures of my brother's mutilated body moving in gentle rhythm as the waves washed over his wounds in bloody baptism.

I suddenly felt a giant hand crushing the breath from my chest, and I awoke to find my T-shirt wet and twisted. Sitting up in bed, I pulled the shirt down and did what I did every night. I begged forgiveness.

Four

The tide was out the next morning as I hit the beach for my three mile-run. I headed north passing the Jacksonville Beach Pier where five or six early risers dangled their fishing lines over the side. Bogie, my yellow lab, bounded ten yards ahead of me, tail wagging, streaking left and right to investigate the treasures strewn over the beach. He seemed to take great pride in leading the way, like the high priests going before an Egyptian Pharaoh. Or maybe he thought he was the Egyptian Pharaoh and I was the slave who picked up his poop.

We scattered a few seagulls, and I nodded to the occasional beach-comber searching for sharks' teeth. I made a U-turn at Oleander Street and waited for Bogie to take the point again. He paused a moment and seemed to smile as if to say, "Is that as far as you can run today, O two-legged one?"

As I sprinted over the hard-packed sand, my thoughts returned to the bayonet and the first time I'd seen it at a dinner party at Poe's house two weeks ago.

Poe's culinary skills were amazing. He concocted incredible meals for dinner parties of twelve and fifteen guests at a time when Gail was alive. Months after her death, Poe slowly started cooking again and the process became a catharsis, helping him reconnect with people. These weren't fancy gatherings planned for months in advance, but usually spontaneous calls to a few friends or neighbors to help him share what would have been a lonely meal.

Two weeks ago I received one of those last minute invitations. When I arrived at his house that night, I found the party already in full swing. Through the screen door I heard music and a loud voice I didn't recognize offering a toast in a distinctly Southern accent. "Here's to that monstrosity fallin' down on his head." The words were slightly slurred, but the meaning unmistakable.

I knocked and let myself in. Poe met me in the living room and led me back to the Florida room. Four people were sitting around an oblong table, drinks in their hands. They all turned toward me as we entered the room.

An elderly man held his glass high, tipping it toward me in greeting. His deeply lined face broke into a smile, highlighting the broken capillaries sketched over his nostrils. Next to him sat a woman who would never see seventy again. Deep wrinkles grooved her lips and forehead. Her hair, surprisingly thick for a woman of her age, framed her face with silver curls, and when she looked at me, it seemed her eyes were not quite focused.

Sitting across from the two older guests, with their chairs turned slightly away as though they were fearful of catching the old timers' disease, were two young men. I recognized one of them as Denny Grimes, who had volunteered with me on several of Poe's digs. The other man smiled at me with straight, white teeth. He had short blond hair and a bemused look on his handsome face.

"Quint, I don't think you've met all of these people," Poe said, with a nod toward the table.

"I know Denny. Good to see you again." I stuck out my hand and Grimes gave it more than a friendly squeeze. He was a short man, maybe five-six, who compensated by lifting weights. I remembered that he once worked for the City of St. Augustine, but had left to start his own company. Something to do with website development.

"Hey, Mitchell, how they hanging?" Grimes said, finally releasing my hand.

Poe had me by the elbow and turned me toward the old woman. "This is my neighbor, Eleanor Lawson. She lives across the street and has to look at my pitiful front lawn everyday, so she's definitely entitled to a free dinner or two."

"A pleasure to meet you, Ms. Lawson."

"Please, call me Eleanor."

Her light and reedy voice sounded like it had floated in through the window. High cheekbones, slightly faded brown eyes, a pert little nose. Eleanor must have been a knockout when she was young. No longer young, though, liver spots freckled her face and hands and she drooped in all the usual places.

"I've sent my lawn man over to see Jeffrey, but he prefers to do it himself. When he can find the time," she sniffed.

"I'm sure you know that most any idiot can mow a lawn, but few people can cook like the good doctor here." This came from the man sitting next to Eleanor.

"Thank you for that, Clayton. Quint, meet my good friend and protector, Clayton Henderson."

Henderson put his glass down, grasped the table and pulled himself up with great effort. His face momentarily contorted in pain before he straightened to take my hand. Only then did I notice the cane hooked over the back of his chair, an expensive-looking model with a shiny black shaft and a curved handle tipped with a sterling silver lion's head.

"Don't get up," I said about five seconds too late.

"Young man, I'm not going to use my knee surgery as an excuse for poor manners." His hazel eyes twinkled and his face blossomed with a robust smile. Clean shaven except for a fuzzy patch beneath his lower lip, he laughed and pumped my hand, shaking a wattle of loose skin hanging below his chin.

"Clayton Ford Henderson is a bit of a scoundrel, as you'll soon learn," Poe said. "And Quint Mitchell happens to be a private investigator, Clayton, so watch your step. Let me get you a beer."

"Clayton Ford Henderson? Why does that sound familiar?"

"Ah, you must be a poetry critic as well as a detective," Henderson said after seating himself and picking up his drink.

Poe returned from the kitchen with a beer and handed it to me along with a pilsner glass. He pulled a chair from the corner, pushing it toward the table. Eleanor scooted away from Henderson, making room for the chair.

"Come sit by me. You look like someone I should get to know," she said, rubbing my forearm as I scrunched the chair closer to the table. I couldn't remember the last time I'd been hit on by an eighty-year-old woman.

Poe returned to our conversation. "I'm sure you've heard Clayton's name before. He's well known in literary circles and one of St. Augustine's claims to fame since he's a former Florida Poet Laureate."

"Yes, a legend in my own mind, Mr. Mitchell. And please excuse my boorish manners. I neglected to introduce you to a man who plays a key role in my life right now." Henderson turned and nodded at the blond man who watched us with a coquettish tilt of his head. The bemused smile still pasted on his lips, he struck me as one of those cynics who kept the world at arm's length so he could better mock it.

"This is Jarrod Watts. PI meet PT. Jarrod's a physical therapist and he has the sad duty of putting up with me and my bad habits. I've hired him to not only get me back on my feet, but to act as my caregiver for the next few months."

Watts shook his head in amusement. "How bout it?" he said, hoisting his bottle toward me in greeting. He flashed his dazzling smile once again. I now realized his delicate lips were slightly curved at each end providing the illusion he found the world a humorous place.

I nodded in return to Watts who looked to be twenty-nine or thirty years old, although from the faint etchings around his pale blue eyes I thought he might be older.

"We were just toastin' the demise of the Matanzas Bay project when you arrived, Mr. Mitchell," Henderson said.

"Call me Quint."

"Fine, and you can call me Mr. Poet Laureate." Henderson chortled loudly and whacked my shoulder so hard beer sloshed over the rim of my glass.

"I told you he was a scoundrel," Poe said, handing me a napkin. "But he's serious about his toast. St. Augustine will never be the same if this abortion is allowed to be built." The planes of his face shifted imperceptibly, and I felt all levity from the previous moment exit the room.

"Isn't it a done deal? From what I've heard, the St. Johns Group is breaking ground in a few weeks." Even though Poe worked for the City of St. Augustine, he'd been speaking out against it and making a nuisance of himself at city commission meetings.

"You bet your ass, it's a done deal." Grimes glared at me as though I had challenged him, tilting his head back and jutting out his jaw. He had sloping shoulders, the chest and biceps of someone who made daily pilgrimages to the gym. A scruffy beard covered his wide face. He'd pulled his hair straight back and tied it off in a stringy pony tail. "You know that bastard Marrano has greased this deal and nothing's going to slow it down."

"Yes, but we can always hope more lucid minds will prevail," Henderson said. "I admit it looks like the vice mayor and Kurtis Laurance will surely win this one. Now there's a pair of scoundrels for you. A man preparing to wear the governor's crown and his personal toady on the city commission. Isn't that right, Jeffrey?"

"There's no doubt Marrano's a cheap political hack who'd sell his mother for an extra vote, but Laurance is driving this train," Poe snapped with uncharacteristic bitterness. He pushed himself away from the table. "Excuse me, gentlemen, but I'd better get back to our dinner or we'll be forced to call out for pizza."

"My, my, I seem to have hit a nerve," Henderson said after Poe left. He held his empty glass toward Watts. "Jarrod, nature abhors a vacuum. Please help an old man out, won't you?"

"Hold up, dude, I have to take a whiz." Grimes got up and walked with Watts into the kitchen.

When they left, Henderson turned to me and asked, "You do know about Jeffrey's skirmishes with Mr. Marrano?"

"Oh, do we have to go into that again?" Eleanor dug into a purse and pulled out a pack of cigarettes and a lighter. "I'm going to check on Sir William while you two take turns boring each other. Young man," she said to me, "make sure no one touches my drink." Eleanor's shoulders hunched forward slightly as she stood, like the floor had some magnetic power affecting calcified bones.

"I'll be right back, Jeffrey," she shouted. "I need to check on Sir William." She gave us a puckered smile, flashing yellow teeth, and shuffled away, one hand in front of her as though holding onto an invisible railing.

After she left I asked Henderson, "Sir William? Is that what she calls her husband?"

"She's a widow, but she probably treats her dog better than she did her husband. But back to my question about Marrano and Jeffrey."

I knew Poe and William Marrano had clashed over the real estate development on more than one occasion. At a city commission meeting one night, Poe came close to being fired after he lost his temper and accused the vice mayor and the St. Johns Group of selling out St. Augustine's heritage to increase tax revenues. The three hundred million dollar project had both political and popular support so Poe appeared to be tilting at windmills.

"We've talked about it before and, frankly, this thing is going to happen. In the end, it might even be good for St. Augustine."

"That's what Laurance and Marrano want everyone to think," Henderson retorted. "But if the truth be known, Kurtis Laurance doesn't give a damn about what's good for St. Augustine. He's countin' on another development feather in his cap to help him get elected governor of this fair state of ours."

Both Watts and Grimes returned with fresh drinks.

"You still talking about the Matanzas Bay development?" Grimes asked.

"I was just giving our private eye a refresher course on Florida politics," Henderson said.

"It's all bullshit. Politicians promise you the world when they're campaigning, then stick it to you when they're in office. We should send them all packing." Grimes puffed out his cheeks and blew a mouthful of air toward the ceiling.

"Don't hold back, Dude. Tell us what you really think." Watts said, holding his clenched fist toward Grimes who bumped it with his own.

"Well, you may have a point there, Denny, but I was telling Quint about Kurtis Laurence and his ambitions to be our next governor."

If Henderson was a former Poet Laureate, then Kurtis Laurance should receive *Business Laureate* honors. As CEO of the St. Johns Group, he had offices throughout the South besides his new home office at the World Golf Village outside of St. Augustine.

"You know he's been tapped by the political string-pullers to be our next reigning monarch," Henderson said, referring to the governor's office in Tallahassee. "They need someone to pull their nuts out of the fire after the gambling story hit the papers."

The media had blasted Florida's present governor and key legislators, tying them to illegal contributions from lobbyists who hoped to bring casino gambling to the Sunshine State.

"There's nothin' wrong with a little graft," Henderson continued. "Hell, it's an old American tradition. But we expect our leaders to be discreet and not get caught with their fingers in the honey pot."

"With the smell rising out of Tallahassee these days, Laurance seems to be a pretty good choice to clean things up," I offered.

"That's *bull puckey*, as my grandpaw used to say." Henderson winked at Grimes when he said bull puckey, then leaned in to me, placing a wrinkled hand on my arm. "But you better not let Jeffrey hear you talkin' like that. He's totally against this project and against Kurtis Laurance. You don't want to be sent home without your supper, do you?"

"Actually, he knows where I stand. He agrees the Matanzas Bay project probably makes good economic sense for the city, but, of course, not with a contemporary high rise."

"It will suck the character right out of this city," Poe yelled from the kitchen.

I didn't realize he'd been listening. Attempting to change the subject, I raised my voice and asked Poe, "Do you have any new digs coming up, doc?"

"A small excavation at Trinity Episcopal Parish next week. I could use another hand."

From my previous visits, I knew Poe preferred for his guests to leave him alone while he cooked, but the mouth-watering aroma wafting over us pulled me into the kitchen. "Count me in for a few days," I said, referring to the dig. "God, that smells good. What is it?"

He muscled an oversized cast-iron skillet from the stove to a side table holding four cream-colored bowls. "Gail's Jambalaya. It's the most fantastic thing you ever put in your mouth," he said, spooning steaming heaps into the bowls. "Do me a favor and herd the others into the dining room while I finish what I'm doing."

While I did the herding, Eleanor returned, the smell of smoke trailing after her. "You're just in time," Henderson said. "Our master's voice is beckoning us to dinner."

It turned out to be a New Orleans-themed meal including red beans and rice with beer bread topped off with strawberry beignets and chicory coffee.

After dinner, as we nursed our coffee, I asked Poe if he'd dug up anything interesting lately. Poe's downtown office overflowed with artifacts waiting to be catalogued, and he had a habit of carrying some of the better ones home so they wouldn't be lost or damaged.

Poe's eyes glittered with excitement as he jumped to his feet. "You won't believe what we found."

"Oh, God, Jeffrey. I think I've had enough excitement for one night." Eleanor used Poe's arm to pull herself to her feet. "You're a dear for inviting me, but this old broad needs her rest."

"Are you sure?" Poe asked.

"The meal was delicious. You boys have fun." Eleanor winked at me. "And you, sonny …" She searched for a name. "I'm sorry, my memory isn't what it used to be."

"Quint," I said.

"Quint. Yes. Quint, if I was thirty years younger, I'd be all over your bones." She leaned over and planted a soggy kiss on my lips before departing, looking like a geriatric version of Mrs. Robinson.

Everyone got a charge out of that.

Poe jumped in to help me out. "Do you want to see my new find or not?"

We followed Poe into a spare bedroom lined with wide shelves. The shelves held an assortment of labeled boxes as well as a patchwork of earthenware bowls, buckles, and twisted iron spikes. A warped and scarred workbench stacked with boxes and trays of artifacts dominated the middle of the room. Laid out on the table were pieces of glazed dishes in varying patterns and colors as well as a remarkably intact rust-colored cook pot. Poe put his hand on the pot and beamed.

"We found this at the San Juan del Puerto mission site. Isn't it a beauty?"

Everyone agreed.

Henderson waved his arm at the table full of artifacts. "If I didn't know better, Jeffrey, I'd say you're almost as big a packrat as I am." He'd been drinking heavily the entire evening and his words came out as *Isay yolmos asbigga packra' as I'm.*

The old poet leaned on his cane with one hand and with the other reached toward a second box nearly toppling it from the table. "Hey, this 'ould commin handy for filletin' catfish," he slurred.

Grimes and Poe moved in unison. Grimes grabbed the box before it tumbled to the floor. Poe snatched a wicked-looking dagger from the pile before Henderson could pick it up.

Henderson looked like someone had slapped him in the face. "What's wrong, Jeffrey, you don't want me playing with your toys?" Henderson may have been speaking to Poe, but he put his hand on Grimes' shoulder and pushed him away.

Grimes, who'd been drinking almost as much as Henderson, glared at the old man, his eyes hard and menacing. "Didn't your mother ever tell you drunks shouldn't play with sharp objects?"

Watts stepped toward Grimes, but Poe inserted himself between them still holding the bayonet above his head. "Take a look at this thing." Poe's voice cut through the tension. "This is a real find."

We all turned to look. "Sure is," I said.

Poe beamed, "Yeah, it's one of the better bayonets we've found in the fifteen years I've been in St. Augustine."

"That's unusual for a bayonet, isn't it?" I asked. "The bone handle, I mean. Most of the bayonets I've seen had wood plugs. Or they did before they rotted off."

Poe nodded in agreement. "The military bayonets of that period were very plain, but the later ones, from sixteen-eighty on, had more decorative elements. I've seen them in other collections, but this is a first for us."

He passed it to me for closer inspection and I admired the filigree design and noted the wide, lightning-shaped crack dissecting the bone handle.

"Very nice," I said and handed it to Grimes who gave it back to Poe.

"Now, it's time to put these old things away." Poe replaced the bayonet in the box and looked at Henderson. "I'm afraid that means us old folks, too." He smiled at Watts and me. "And you younger folks, as well."

Henderson sagged against Watts, his eyes half closed.

"Jarrod needs to take you home and put you to bed, Clayton."

"Hell, I'm good for anotha three or four hours," Henderson grumbled.

"You've managed to drink us all under the table again, Mr. Henderson," Watts said, putting an arm around the old man's waist. He gently pulled Henderson toward the door. Watts smiled sheepishly, as if to say, *the old guy's a pistol, isn't he?*

I followed them as Poe turned off the light and closed the door to his storage room. Poe then did an extraordinary thing. Coming up behind me, he tousled my hair and gave me a smile filled with such affection I was taken back to a time when my father would look at me that way.

Poe put his head close to mine and whispered in my ear, "I'm so glad you came tonight, Quint. It means a lot to me."

Five

I finished my run and was back at my place before seven-thirty. I lived on First Street, across from a pizza place and a popular hangout known for the length of its happy hour and the tightness of the waitresses' shorts. People are amazed when they learn I own this building, along with the bank, of course, but they should have seen it fifteen years ago. This end of Jacksonville Beach had deteriorated into a stretch of seedy bars, boarded up storefronts, and a couple of adult book stores.

I'd been based at Mayport Naval Air Station before they shipped me out to the Persian Gulf for the first big blow-up with Saddam. After I returned and later separated from the Navy with a nice amount in my savings account, I looked around for an investment. This old building appealed to me because of its location, its size, and the fact the owner desperately wanted to unload it.

Over the next three years, I converted the four small retail stores on the ground floor to two larger business suites. One of them was now my office, Mitchell Investigative Services; the other I rented to a small graphic design and advertising firm.

Back in my apartment, I fed Bogie and my cat Dudley. Not that Dudley would let me forget. He's developed a habit of pushing against my ankles and yowling loudly to be fed, so I poured a half-cup of hard food into his dish and headed to the shower.

The phone rang as I toweled off, and I padded out to answer it. Surprisingly, William Marrano's name popped up on my digital readout along with a St. Augustine number. "Hello, Quint Mitchell here," I said in my best business voice.

"Mr. Mitchell, this is Erin Marrano." She paused, but before I could respond she said, "William Marrano was my husband."

The statement resonated with a sense of sorrow, but her voice had a soft, hopeful note and an underlying strength. "Yes, Mrs. Marrano, I'm very sorry for your loss. How can I help you?"

"I understand you found his body."

"That's right. I've been working with Dr. Poe as a volunteer on the Trinity Church survey." I prepared myself for another Buck Marrano-style blast against Poe.

"Dr. Poe didn't do this terrible thing." I caught a slight tremor in her voice.

"I'm on your side there, Mrs. Marrano. Jeffrey and I are close friends, and I know he could never murder anyone. But the police seem to have the investigation under control. I'm sure they'll sort it out."

"The police questioned me yesterday, and I had the feeling they've already sorted it out. They're building a case against Dr. Poe."

"It's only natural they start with him because of his differences with your husband. They'll expand the investigation when they realize there's no evidence connecting Jeffrey to your husband's murder." A picture of the Spanish bayonet sticking out of Marrano's chest burst into my head.

"Mr. Mitchell, I've only lived in St. Augustine for seven-and-a-half years, but I've learned there are several versions of justice in this city."

"It's a small town."

"Yes, and your friend needs an advocate. I'd like to hire you to prove his innocence and find the real murderer before they send the wrong man to prison."

The lady knew which buttons to push. "I am his friend, but the police have the equipment and experience to—"

"You are a private investigator?"

"Yes, but murder is more than a few compass points off my usual investigations. I specialize in tracking down people who are lost for one—"

She interrupted me again. "Someone butchered my husband, Mr. Mitchell. Jeffrey Poe is under suspicion only because he stood up for his principles. I want you to find the animal that did this and make sure he's brought to justice."

Her breath seemed to push itself through the phone and my ear tingled with the phantom sensation. "Please, Mr. Mitchell, you have to help me and help your friend."

I tried to put a face to the angry widow who I assumed was in her fifties since William Marrano had been fifty-six when he died. "I'll do what I can," I finally said.

"Good. How soon can you meet with me?"

"My morning is pretty well tied up. How about after lunch? Say, two?"

She gave me her address. I told her I looked forward to meeting her, and I meant it. Her voice had been hypnotic in its intensity. I wanted to see the woman who owned it.

Charla Huggins was already at work when I entered the office. Young and well-organized, Charla ably filled the role of office manager and part-time associate. This morning, though, I hoped to tap into her knowledge of the old city.

Charla's family had lived in St. Augustine for generations, and she seemed to know everyone who was anybody. She greeted me with a broad smile displaying both uppers and lowers. She reminded me a little of Kyra Phillips, the news anchor on CNN.

I told her about my conversation with Erin Marrano.

"I've never met Mrs. Marrano," Charla replied, "but I remember seeing her picture in the paper after they were married. She's a lot younger than he was, maybe twenty years younger."

"What's she look like?"

Charla arched an eyebrow. "You want to know if she's a hottie, don't you?"

"Of course not. I was only wondering what kind of woman marries a man who will be trading his Jockey shorts for Depends before they reach their twentieth anniversary."

She was accustomed to my so-called humor, and shook her head before answering, "I've never seen her in person, but she seemed quite attractive in the newspaper photographs. You can judge for yourself when you meet her."

Unlike what's portrayed on TV shows, a private investigator's life isn't very glamorous. Most of my days are spent on the computer or telephone tracking down people who are trying to avoid their debts. We call them skip traces, and I had one major client who paid me a good monthly retainer to find several hundred of these supposedly missing persons. I spent the rest of my time on background checks for sensitive positions and a growing number of insurance scams. If desperate, I'd been known to accept a few adultery cases, following and photographing wayward husbands and wives.

I paged through the outstanding skip traces, trying to focus, but my mind kept wandering to the dead man in the wicker basket and Jeffrey Poe. I eventually gave up and called Poe to tell him about Erin Marrano.

"She seemed to be a big fan of yours," I said. "She wants to hire me to find her husband's killer."

"She does? That's a surprise." He said this without sounding the least bit surprised.

"You do know her, don't you?"

"I used to speak to her classes when she was teaching, and we've run into each other at some city functions from time to time. That's about it."

"Since I'm coming to St. Augustine to meet with Mrs. Marrano, I was wondering if I might drop by your office first."

"Of course, if you don't mind being seen with a suspected murderer."

I told him I'd be there in an hour or so. I left unasked the key question, not wanting to speak about it on the telephone. When we were face to face, I'd ask him about the bayonet.

My next call was to Serena Howard. I'd been avoiding this task since last Wednesday when she introduced me to her Uncle Walter. The gut-wrenching experience still reverberated in my mind. When Serena and I parted company afterwards, she seemed to close the door on any future we had together. I hoped we might meet for lunch today and perhaps find a way to resolve the growing tension between us. But Serena had other ideas.

"I have a lunch date with a client at noon," she said when I reached her on the phone. I felt a touch of frosty air clinging to her words.

"Earlier then?"

She paused before saying, "How about a quick cup of coffee at eleven-thirty?"

Checking my watch, I swiftly made the mental calculations—travel time, my meeting with Poe at ten-thirty—and agreed.

Poe's office door was open. He stood over an ancient desk that might have been hanging around since Woodrow Wilson's administration. Head down, rummaging through some papers, he didn't see me standing there. His desk was surrounded by shelves of books and a cluttered table in the corner with two mismatched chairs.

Through an open connecting door, I glimpsed what may have once been a conference room, now packed with shelves and low tables overflowing with boxes of artifacts. Stacked on a workbench were trays of human bones spread out like a butcher's display. Bowls of bone fragments balanced precariously atop the trays.

The mess reminded me of his home on Anastasia Island with its spare bedroom storing the growing piles of rubble from earlier civilizations. I knocked on the door jamb and Poe looked up, dark rings evident below his gray-green eyes.

"Quint, come in. Come in." He shuffled a box from one of the chairs and gestured for me to sit before closing the door and sitting in the other chair.

He studied me a moment, a self-conscious look on his tired face. "I have to confess I wasn't totally honest when you called this morning."

"How's that?"

"I knew Mrs. Marrano was going to call you. She phoned last night and told me she didn't believe I killed her husband. A wonderfully supportive thing for her to do. You don't know how much it lifted my spirits."

"And …" I waited for the rest of the story.

"She wanted to know how she could help. I told her you and I were friends. That you were a private investigator."

"I see."

"She asked for your phone number and I gave it to her. I'm sorry if I took advantage of our friendship, Quint. You probably didn't want to get involved in such a messy affair."

"Not at all. You know I'll do whatever I can to help you, and it can't hurt to have the wife of the murder victim on your side. Hopefully, the police will take that into consideration, although Mrs. Marrano seems convinced they've already made up their minds about this case."

He hung his head as if it had suddenly become too heavy to hold erect. When he looked up, he stared directly into my eyes. "You've got to believe me, Quint. I didn't kill him. I admit I let my temper get the best of me. Marrano and the St. Johns Group were about to disembowel St. Augustine with that damned Matanzas Bay project. Hot-headed, yes, but that doesn't make me a murderer."

His eyes glistened with emotion as he spoke. I had no doubt he was telling the truth. But what about the bayonet? "Jeffrey, I have to ask you again about the bayonet."

He nodded slowly, and I knew he'd been anticipating my question.

"You must have checked to see if it was still there when you went home last night." He was still nodding. "Was it?"

The nodding stopped. "No. It wasn't there."

"You understand what this means? The murder weapon was in your possession, and the police will want to know how it ended up in Marrano's chest."

"I was awake all night asking myself the same question. I honestly haven't seen it since our dinner two weeks ago. I don't know what happened to it."

"Have you had any visitors lately?"

He thought a moment before replying. "Had a few neighbors over for coffee and pancakes last Sunday morning." He hesitated, then added, "Oh, one of the city maintenance workers came by last week with something he'd found in the park by Oyster Creek Marina."

"What was that?"

"A piece of pottery. I brought him back to my storeroom to show him some other examples."

"So he was in the room. Did you notice if the bayonet was still there?"

"No. I'm sorry."

"Who else has keys to your house?"

"Several neighbors, but it's not like my house is a bank vault. I don't have any special locks or security. It's a quiet neighborhood, and sometimes I even forget to lock the door."

"Has that happened recently?"

Poe rubbed a thumb over his chin, giving the question some thought. "As a matter of fact, I noticed the back door was unlocked last Thursday morning. I remember it because I'd gone out and done some weeding in the garden after work Wednesday and assumed I'd forgotten to lock it when I came in."

"Was that unusual?"

"As I said, I've left it unlocked before, but ..." Poe paused and scratched his head again. "I guess I'm losing it. Turning into the absent-minded professor."

"You know sooner or later the police will find out you had the bayonet in your possession. Your prints might even be on it."

I saw uncertainty and fear reflected in his eyes. "Do you have a lawyer?" I asked.

"You think I need one?"

"Probably a good idea. It would be best if you came forward with the news about the bayonet rather than waiting for the cops to dig it out. They'd think you were trying to hide it from them."

"God, I don't know what to think. None of this makes any sense."

"Let's go back to your run-ins with Marrano. Did you explain to Chief Conover and his detectives why you were fighting the project?"

"I don't think they understand or even care." He shook his head, and pink circles blossomed on his cheeks. "Lord knows I've watched them put up all kinds of tacky buildings in this town and kept my mouth shut. But this was too much. This so-called Matanzas Bay was going to be huge, totally out of character for St. Augustine."

"But the city commission approved it," I said, as if that explained everything.

"Yes, but that was part of the problem. Half of those commissioners ran for reelection last year. Kurtis Laurance funneled tens of thousands of dollars into their campaign accounts with Marrano pulling in twice as much as the others combined. With all that development money in the trough, do you think they'd vote against it?"

"I suppose they would if they thought it wasn't right for the community."

He gave me the kind of sad smile you might give to a backward child. "Laurance has the commission in his pocket. If he said 'squat,' all you'd hear were butts hitting the floor."

Laurance again. His name kept cropping up.

"You think I'm paranoid, don't you?" Poe asked.

"You know what they say, 'Just because you're paranoid, doesn't mean they're not out to get you.'"

Six

I walked the few blocks from Poe's office to the Casa Monica Hotel at the corner of King and Cordova Streets. While I waited for the light to change, I glanced across the street to admire Flagler College and the statue of Henry Flagler out front. Built in the Spanish Renaissance architectural style, the college began its life as one of Flagler's luxury resort hotels attracting the rich and beautiful to Florida.

As I crossed the street, I caught a brief glimpse of a well-muscled man with dark, curly hair duck into the Lightner Museum on the opposite corner. I didn't get a good look at his face, but my mind filled the void with the snarling visage of Sergeant Buck Marrano.

Shaking it off as the product of an overactive imagination, I entered the dimly lit restaurant of the grand old hotel. Built in 1888, the Casa Monica changed hands the next year when Flagler bought it to add to his growing hotel empire. It thrived for twenty years, but couldn't make it through the Great Depression and the hotel closed its doors. Thirty years later the county purchased it and turned it into a courthouse. Today, the castle-like structure has reverted to a hotel and was the only Triple A-Four Diamond Award-winning hotel in St. Augustine.

I ordered a cup of coffee while I waited for Serena to make her appearance and thought about my conversation with Poe and what he said about the St. Johns Group.

Depending on how you look at it, developers either fuel Florida's economic engine—providing jobs, attracting high-income employees, building communities—or they're responsible for destroying our natural resources and polluting the environment. An argument can be made for both sides. I usually come down in the middle. Let's face it, hundreds of people a day move to Florida for good reason. No state income tax may be high on their list, but the climate and the state's natural beauty are hard to beat. The developers are simply helping to meet the needs of this influx.

Poe implied Laurance had paid off the commissioners. The last time I checked, campaign contributions were still legal, but I made a mental note to pay Mr. Laurance a visit if I could catch up with him between his campaign trips.

Serena stepped into the restaurant, cell phone to her ear, nodding vigorously to her cellular companion. For a moment, an image of another girl with a cell phone flared in my mind. Only a single flash of a horrendous memory, but unless I found a way to re-entomb it in my psychic cemetery, one image would soon cascade into a parade of horrors.

My best tactic for keeping the monsters below the surface was to concentrate on Serena. Without being overly dramatic about it, Serena was one of the most striking women I've ever known. The dozen male eyes riveted to her as she walked across the room reinforced my evaluation.

How many times had I seen men staring at her dark, exotic features, trying to determine her nationality and what fortuitous mixture of genes were responsible for such a stunning woman? The chiseled planes of her face and her tall, shapely figure were like a powerful magnet compelling a man's attention and fueling their fantasies. Their open lust no longer bothered me. Not much, anyway.

If I'm honest with myself, something I try to do from time to time, I'd attribute my feelings for Serena to pheromones and plumbing, the blood rushing to extreme parts of my body and away from my brain. But some deeper attraction tugged at me, which is why our impending break-up seemed so painful and sad.

Seated beside me now, she said goodbye and put away her phone. Without thinking, I leaned over to kiss her, but she adroitly turned her cheek. Serena avoided public displays of affection in the best of circumstances, and our present relationship can't be described as the best of anything. She looked past me, her honey brown eyes sweeping the room.

"What a morning. This is the first time I've stopped to take a breath," she said with a small sigh.

"Breathing is pretty important. You should find time for it whenever possible."

Finally, the hint of a smile lit up a face the color of a mocha latte. She had straight brown hair with a trace of auburn, stylishly short and parted in the middle. "I only have a minute, really," Serena said. "I'm meeting with a representative from an insurance company. They want to hold their next conference here."

"Sounds good."

"A solid two hundred and fifty room nights, plus meeting rooms and banquets."

Serena wore a snug-fitting rose-colored silk suit along with delicate gold filigree hoop earrings and a matching bracelet on her right arm. Her legs were crossed, and I couldn't help but notice the shortness of her skirt and the expanse of thigh it revealed. Surely, this must be one of the devilishly clever marketing tricks she used on insurance executives.

"After you add Mr. Insurance-man to your list of corporate conquests, you might feel the need to relax a bit," I said. "Maybe we can we get together later tonight." I leaned forward and put a hand on top of hers. "I really think we should talk."

She pulled her hand out from under mine. Her eyes seemed to turn darker. "Not tonight, I'm afraid," she said. "Two honchos from corporate are coming in this afternoon for long-range planning sessions, and we won't break up until pretty late. Besides, we're having dinner brought in for us."

"How about tomorrow night? Are you free?"

She took her time before answering. "This week is crazy. Let's make it Friday night at my place."

"Your place? But I wanted to treat you to a nice dinner."

"That's okay. I'd like more privacy so we can talk."

I tried to read the far-away look on her face, but it remained distant and indecipherable.

Seven

Walking from the hotel to my car, I received a call from Charla telling me the senior vice president of Gulf Breeze Insurance wanted to see me at two o'clock. Today. I'd been pursuing their corporate business for six months. Landing this account would punch up my bottom line in a big way, adding another $100,000 to $150,000 to my gross income. I'd be able to hire another investigator and take a pass on those smarmy infidelity cases that left me feeling like I needed a shower.

As I slowly made my way along Castillo Drive toward San Marco Avenue, I checked the clock—11:55. Ahead of me, a horse and buggy conveyed a family of tourists at a ferocious five miles per hour while cars stacked up behind it. I simmered along with the other frustrated drivers, waiting for the buggy to turn onto another street. While I waited, I considered my present dilemma. Erin Marrano expected me at her house at 2:00, the same time as the insurance exec. Despite my amazing talents for detection, I've yet to locate the secret for being in two places at once.

I knew I might not get another chance if I blew off this meeting with Gulf Breeze. I told myself Erin Marrano would understand if I rescheduled our meeting, and kept driving. I passed the Mission of Nombre de Dios where Menendez supposedly knelt to kiss a wooden cross after he came ashore back in 1565. The site is marked by a massive stainless steel cross rising over two hundred feet above the marshes.

I had every intention of continuing north toward Jacksonville, but when I saw Myrtle Street approaching, I whipped the wheel to the right and followed Myrtle to Magnolia Avenue where Erin Marrano lived.

Magnolia was a curving residential street with a canopy of overhanging oak branches. I found the Marrano house and pulled in behind a silver Lexus parked in the driveway. The split-level stucco had a red-tiled roof. Several terra cotta pots filled with hosta and daisies lined the walkway, and I followed them to a handsome front door with frosted, beveled glass inlays. What looked like a handcrafted wreath hung on the door, grapevines stuffed with evergreens, pinecones, and some dried flowers.

I stood there studying the wreath as though I'd written my doctoral thesis on the decorative crafts of the South. I had to keep this short to make my appointment with Gulf Breeze Insurance. Knocking loudly, I stepped to one side expecting Mrs. Marrano to open the door. Instead, a woman's scream jolted me. It came from inside the house and I grabbed the door knob. Locked.

"Mrs. Marrano, are you okay?" I banged on the door with the flat of my hand. Another scream. I ran around the side of the house to my right until I came to a wooden deck and a set of French doors. One of them hung open.

Inside, I saw the form of a woman on the floor half curled in a fetal position, one hand holding the side of her head.

"Help me, please help me." Her hair was wet and she wore what my mother would have called a housecoat, a thin cotton wrap with a bright flowery print. I knelt by her side.

"Are you hurt, Mrs. Marrano? Did you fall?" I placed a hand on her arm.

She jerked at my touch, her eyes wide with terror.

"It's all right. I'm Quint Mitchell. Can you sit up?"

She slowly pushed herself to a sitting position, dropping her hand from her head to grab the robe that gapped open enough for me to see she wasn't wearing anything beneath it. I managed to redirect my eyes to her face and for the first time noticed the red imprint of a hand on her cheek.

"Who hit you?"

She pointed at the open door toward the back yard. "A man ... in the house. He hit me and ran away." Her lower lip trembled, and she touched the side of her face as though feeling the sting of the slap all over again.

I hurried onto the deck, surveying a yard of flagstone paths curving through flower gardens and beneath shade trees. No intruder in sight. A low picket fence surrounded the yard. Not a problem for someone to climb over and make his get-away.

"Whoever it was is long gone," I told her after I returned.

I helped her to one of a pair of matching Queen Anne chairs in front of a tall bookcase. She thanked me and pulled her wrap around her, crossing her legs primly. A petite woman with finely chiseled cheekbones, Erin Marrano had a straight nose, wide mouth, and long dark hair. By any measure, she was an attractive woman, but her frosty blue eyes gave her an alluring, mysterious quality capable of igniting sparks in any man with a heartbeat.

She moved her right arm in a circle and massaged her shoulder.

"Are you okay?"

"I think so. Might have twisted something when I fell."

"You should get it looked at. But now you need to call the police."

"I suppose so, but I've seen enough police to last me a lifetime. And they probably feel the same about me."

Her half-hearted smile brought a lump to my throat. I wondered what would happen if it had been a no-holds-barred, full-voltage smile.

"Thank goodness you ..." A confused look passed over her face and she glanced at a little gold clock sitting on one of the bookshelves.

"Yes, I'm early." I explained why I appeared at her door two hours before our appointment. "Can you tell me what happened?"

"My neighbors have been here most of the morning, and I finally shooed them away so I could shower, have lunch, and get ready for your visit. I'd just finished my shower and was drying myself ..."

She paused and ran her fingers through her still damp hair while an image of a wet, naked widow Marrano snaked into my mind. She must have seen something on my face because she colored and folded her arms across her chest.

"I thought I heard a noise coming from Bill's office," she continued, gesturing at a room to our left. "I called out, 'Who's there,' but no one answered. I put on my robe and went to the office door. And that's where we collided."

"You collided?"

"He rushed from the office and nearly knocked me over. I grabbed onto him to keep from falling and he carried me a few feet toward the door before pushing ... slapping me away. I don't think he meant to harm me, but I was standing between him and the door."

"Did you see what he looked like?"

She shook her head. "He was wearing a gray hooded sweatshirt and jeans. But it all happened so fast. He was big, in a muscular way, not fat. You're what—six-one?"

"About that."

"Well, he was a few inches shorter than you. That's about all I can tell you. I'm sorry."

"You're doing fine. It must have been quite a shock, especially after everything you've endured. Do you think it had anything to do with your husband's death?"

"I doubt it. I've heard about burglars who read the obituary pages to find appropriate targets, checking to see when everyone would be away for the funeral. It was probably poor timing on his part and bad luck on mine."

"I'd say you were very lucky it wasn't more serious. I think you should call the police now, Mrs. Marrano."

She rose from the chair and walked into a large, open kitchen. I listened while she reported the break-in and then returned to the living room. She paused in front of the open doors a moment, the bright sun shining through, and I glimpsed the shadowy outline of her trim body through the thin wrap.

"They'll be here in a few minutes," she said. "If you don't mind waiting, I'm going to get dressed before they arrive."

While she was getting dressed, I peered through the door of the office, trying to figure out what the burglar had been after. Numerous plaques lined the dark mahogany paneled walls. From where I stood I couldn't read any of the inscriptions, but I imagined they were the typical awards civic organizations give to politicians to curry favor and stroke oversized egos.

Mixed in with the plaques were framed photographs of William Marrano with various dignitaries, including the last two governors. In one of the pictures, Marrano and Kurtis Laurance were grinning into the camera and holding golf clubs in the air as though they'd won a playoff with Tiger Woods.

An expensive rosewood desk faced a window overlooking the front lawn. Desk drawers were open with file jackets and papers strewn across the floor. On the desk a computer with a large monitor flickered from columns of characters to a blue screensaver. I glimpsed it briefly before it changed screens. Definitely an email inbox.

A matching hutch behind the desk contained books, a briefcase, and an expensive Nikon SLR digital camera. I'd recently priced the same model and knew it retailed for nearly $2,000. Most burglars snatched money or easily hocked valuables. Jewelry, electronics, cameras. Yet, this dude took the time to rifle Marrano's desk and read his emails, but left the Nikon behind.

"It's a mess, isn't it?"

I hadn't heard Erin Marrano walk up behind me. "Sure is, but it looks like you scared him away before he did any real damage. Tell me, were you using this computer?" I pointed toward the PC. She looked at it and started to enter the office, but I blocked her way. "Better not until the police have a chance to dust for prints."

"That was Bill's office, I seldom go in there. In fact, I have my own computer in the spare bedroom. A new iBook. Why do you ask?"

"Probably nothing more than a nosy burglar, but it seems like he was accessing your husband's email."

"That's strange. Perhaps he—"

The chimes of the front door bell rang through the house, and Erin's eyes flashed with uncertainty. The police had arrived.

Eight

There were lots of *yes ma'ams* and no *ma'ams* as the police took Erin's statement. Detective Horgan accompanied two uniformed officers and a crime scene investigator who dusted all the surfaces for latents. Horgan shot me his version of the hard-ass squint when he saw me. He took my statement, and once again I found myself explaining my role in another crime.

More than an hour had passed, and I knew I'd never make my two o'clock meeting in Jacksonville. While Horgan nosed around, I phoned Charla and asked her to plead my case with the insurance company. She rewarded me with a *tsk, tsk, tsk* like a mother hen, and I returned to watching the police dust the desk and computer for fingerprints. Burglars aren't genetic engineers, but I had a feeling this burglar was too smart to leave his prints behind.

After they left, I asked Erin if she wanted me to come back tomorrow.

"You're probably hungry," she replied. "I'll make us some sandwiches and we can go ahead with our meeting."

She moved efficiently through a large kitchen that looked like it had recently been remodeled with expensive cabinets, granite countertops and brushed aluminum appliances. A large plastic pretzel container half-full of pennies occupied a space next to a built-in wine rack and seemed out of place in the nearly sterile kitchen. Erin picked up a half-dozen pennies sitting on the counter, offered me an embarrassed smile, and dropped them into the jar.

We said little as we ate, but after she cleared the dishes and poured us another glass of tea, I got down to business.

"You told me over the phone that you've lived in St. Augustine for seven-and-a-half years."

"Yes, that's right. I taught school in Huntsville, Alabama for about six years before moving here to accept another teaching job."

"Why St. Augustine?"

"My old college roommate lives nearby in Ponte Vedra Beach. I came for a visit one summer, and she brought me to St. Augustine for lunch. I absolutely fell in love with this quaint old town. On a whim I applied for a job with the St. Johns County School Board. After returning home, I received a letter informing me they had an opening if I was still interested."

"And how did you meet Mr. Marrano?"

She tilted her head back as though it happened in the distant past and she needed to dredge it out of her memory. "I attended a symphony concert at Flagler College with a friend of mine. Bill was there, and my friend introduced us. Back in Huntsville, we'd say he took a shine to me."

"What about you? Did you take a shine to him?"

"Let's say that I was a bit overwhelmed. Bill Marrano had a finger in everything in St. Johns County. He was on the city commission, owned a successful real estate company, and his family had been here for over two-hundred years."

"Did you date long before he proposed?"

"About a year. He took me on a Caribbean cruise and we were strolling the deck after dinner one night when he proposed." She adjusted her skirt, tugging the hem down a fraction.

"Very romantic," I said.

"We were married two months later in the Cathedral."

"When was that?"

"Three years ago next month. Not a very long marriage."

I pressed on. "Any problems with the marriage?"

This is where it can get dicey. I've interviewed dozens of husbands and wives who were screwing around and most will put their individual spin on the facts. Men usually deny they were unfaithful until you lay out the photographs, but most women will 'fess up quickly after they've been caught.

Erin Marrano didn't hesitate. "The first year couldn't have been better. Bill was attentive and we traveled a good bit." A small, dark mole perched below the right corner of her lush mouth like an invitation for closer scrutiny, and I found myself staring at it.

"And after the first year?" I asked, regaining my focus.

"He ran for re-election, won, was appointed vice mayor. Every night he'd go to one meeting or another. He'd come home late and exhausted. You can imagine how that affected our marriage."

I didn't say anything.

"He tried to do his job during the day, but people called him all the time. He and his brother Buck own a camp near Palatka, and he'd drive over there just to get away. Even when it wasn't hunting season."

"It sounds like the honeymoon was over."

"My mother would say, 'The blush was off the rose.'"

"A wise woman, your mother."

"Yes, a cliché for every situation. Let's say things were difficult and it didn't get any better."

She raised a hand to the right side of her face, unconsciously fingering a spot along her cheekbone. A dark blotch was still visible beneath her carefully applied make-up. She'd done a good job concealing the bruise, but not quite good enough. I knew it wasn't from her collision with the intruder since the handprint had been on the left side of her face.

"I believe I get the picture," I said.

She snapped out of her reverie, dropping her hand to her lap.

"Tell me about the last time you saw your husband."

"Saturday night. We were supposed to drive into Jacksonville and have dinner with friends, but he called to say he couldn't make it. Some Republican Club function he needed to attend. He wanted me to go with him, but I decided to go to dinner with our friends. Didn't get back until ten-thirty. Bill was home when I arrived, and had been drinking."

"A lot?"

She shrugged as if to say, *how much is a lot?* "He wasn't knee-walking drunk, if that's what you mean. But he wasn't in a good mood either, and I'm afraid we had an argument."

"What about?"

"Oh, he became rather childish when he'd been drinking. He thought I should have gone with him or stayed home and waited for him. The dutiful wife, don't you know? It didn't occur to him that he was gone almost every night while I sat home alone. I was frankly tired of it and told him so."

"How did he react?"

She touched her cheek again. "He stormed out of the house and said he was going to spend the rest of the weekend at his hunting camp. 'Get it ready for hunting season,' I think is what he said." Looking toward the front door, she shook her head sadly. "That was the last time I saw him."

I waited a beat or two before following up. "Do you have any idea who might have wanted to harm your husband?"

"No, I really don't. I know the police are looking at Dr. Poe, but I can't believe he had anything to do with it."

"How well do you know him?"

"I first met him when he came to speak to one of my classes. He has a remarkable way of making history come alive for the kids, and I made it a point to invite him back as often as possible. I didn't tell my husband this, but I admired Dr. Poe for taking a stand against the Matanzas Bay project."

"Maybe he stood up too often and too loudly."

"Perhaps, but isn't it refreshing to find someone so honest and passionate in defense of their beliefs? Bill was a politician through and through. Very skilled at answering questions without stepping on toes so no one could pin him down on an issue. That's the difference between a politician and someone like Jeffrey Poe who says what he really means."

I couldn't argue with that, but standing up for his principles may have made Poe a target for the police. "Is there anyone else you think I should talk to about this?"

"Clayton Henderson is one of Dr. Poe's closest friends. He also seems to have quite a network of confidants who keep him informed on everything going on in St. Augustine."

"I've met Mr. Henderson. An interesting man. Lives in town, doesn't he?"

"He bought the old Martinez House in the historic district and restored it beautifully."

"What did your husband think about Mr. Henderson?"

She huffed through her nose derisively. "For all his public support for the arts, my husband had an antipathy for intellectuals and academics. Plus Clayton was Dr. Poe's friend."

"Anyone else I should talk to?"

I watched as she rubbed her shoulder, thinking about my question. She finally said, "Not that I know of."

"What about Kurtis Laurance? His name keeps coming up. Aside from being allies on the Matanzas Bay development, he and your husband were pretty close friends, weren't they?" I recalled the photograph of Marrano and Laurance on the golf course. "Do you think he'd know anything about your husband's death?"

"Of course not. He and Kurtis were almost inseparable. Bill was his campaign treasurer, and they've worked closely together to get this development off the ground ever since Kurtis moved to St. Augustine."

Before I could follow-up with another question, her telephone rang. She excused herself and walked to the phone mounted on a nearby wall.

The conversation was one-sided. She listened, keeping her eyes on me, until she said, "Thank you," and hung up. The glow was gone from her face now, the blemish on her cheekbone more pronounced.

Erin Marrano folded her arms below her breasts and took a deep breath before speaking. "That was Chief Conover. He wanted me to know that Jeffrey Poe has been arrested and charged with my husband's murder."

Nine

Even the largest, best-equipped police department normally took more than a day to investigate a murder case. Poe's arrest meant he'd either confessed to the murder, which I didn't believe, or more likely, Conover's detectives had discovered what they believed to be overwhelming evidence. They probably found his prints on the bayonet, but they'd need more than that to make their case stick before a jury.

Knowing Poe's history of depression, I figured he'd take his arrest hard. He needed a friend more than ever. As I drove, I called the County Jail and made an appointment to see him during tonight's visiting hours. Erin Marrano may be my client, but Poe was my friend, and I planned to do everything in my power to clear him. That meant interviewing everyone who might be connected with the case, starting with Clayton Henderson.

I turned onto King Street hunting for a parking place. A white Ford Explorer slipped in behind me. He may have been following me from Erin's house, but I was absorbed in Poe's arrest and hadn't noticed him. He stayed on my tail as I turned into the parking lot behind city hall. I climbed out and fed quarters into the parking meter before turning to find Sergeant Marrano staring at me through his Oakley Ducati's.

"Sergeant, so nice to see you again," I said with what I hoped was the appropriate degree of sarcasm.

He stepped toward me. I reflexively tensed myself in case he blew another valve.

"You've heard the news about Poe?" he asked.

"Didn't take long to wrap it up," I said. "One day. Must be some kind of record, even for a crack investigator like Detective Horgan."

"We have a solid case, and Poe's going to get the needle for what he did." Marrano spoke quietly, under tight control, unlike the raw emotion he displayed yesterday.

"That remains to be seen, sergeant. From my perspective, this is a classic railroad job. The prosecutor will have to hold his nose when he presents the case, and the smell will probably gag the jurors."

Marrano took another step in my direction, and I instinctively tightened my stomach muscles. He responded with a twisted smile. Removing his sunglasses, he said, "You're talking out of your ass, Mitchell. But that's what I'd expect from you. The evidence proves he's the killer. We found his prints on the murder weapon, and—"

"Come on," I broke in. "He must have told you why his prints were on the bayonet. There are three witnesses to back up his story."

"You can think whatever you want, but there's no doubt we have the right man. There is one other thing bothering me, though."

The smug expression on his face didn't waver as he waited for me to respond. Behind him, I spotted the long-neglected statue of Lady Justice standing on a stained pedestal. The statue's arm, which normally held the Scales of Justice, was broken off at the elbow.

When I didn't take the bait, he said, "This is where you say, 'Okay, sergeant, what's bothering you?'"

"I'll bite. What's bothering you?"

"They also found your prints on the murder weapon. That's what bothers me. Be thinking of a good answer because Horgan will want to know when he brings you in today."

"I'll be glad to clear up the mystery for you, as I'm sure Poe did. There'll be a lot of red faces when the truth comes out, sergeant. Not everyone believes you have the right man. In fact, your sister-in-law is one of those people. She's hired me to find her husband's killer since the police seem to have a bad case of tunnel vision."

Marrano replaced his sunglasses. "I'll make you a promise, Mitchell. If it turns out we're wrong about Poe, I'll personally apologize to both of you. But if I find out you had a hand in killing my brother, you're not going to know what hit you."

"You've already demonstrated your investigative techniques," I said, patting my stomach. "But I look forward to your apology, and Mrs. Marrano will look forward to learning who really killed her husband."

"Erin's made a mistake," he said stiffly, his jaw tightening. "Poe killed her husband. There's no question about it, and you should do yourself a favor and back off."

"You may be right, but I'm staying on the case until she tells me it's over."

"And I'm telling you if you don't watch your step you'll be wearing an orange jumpsuit and sharing a cell with your friend." He leaned in close. I smelled stale coffee and fried fish on his breath.

"Listen, sergeant, I know you have a personal interest in this case, but Jeffrey Poe didn't kill your brother. Someone's obviously made a mistake."

"You bastard," he spit out, his rigid control suddenly replaced by a hot fury. "The only person making a mistake is you. And you can't afford to make any more enemies around here."

"What's that supposed to mean?"

His lip curled into a sneer. "You forget where you are, don't you? You're not in Boston or New York. This is St. Augustine."

When I looked at him blankly, he added, "You've already put yourself on some people's shit list by dating that colored girl, Serena Howard. Don't make it any worse on yourself."

I hadn't forgotten where I was, but maybe when I was. Wasn't this the twenty-first century? Hadn't we elected the country's first African-American president? Marrano's brand of ugly racism should have gone the way of those *White* and *Colored* signs once posted on rest rooms and above water fountains. An inner rage bubbled inside me, and I wanted to slam this ignorant redneck against the nearest palm tree and pound some decency into him. But I knew it was a lost cause.

He spun around without another word, got in his car and left me alone with my rage.

Ten

The Martinez House fit nicely into the B & Bs, restaurants, and private homes on Charlotte Street. The fortress-like structure came equipped with an overhanging second floor balcony, recently white-washed walls, and a narrow, shaded front yard. Two Shaker style rockers sat on the porch and a couple of hanging fern baskets filled in the space between the milled posts.

I used the antique knocker to announce my arrival. Jarrod Watts opened the door almost immediately. He greeted me with his familiar bemused smile.

"Good to see you again, Mr. Mitchell," he said, shaking my hand in a crushing grip.

"Hey, Jarrod. I wish you'd call me Quint, I'm not that much older than you." He appeared to be about the age my brother Andrew would be if he were still alive.

He looked at me as though calculating my age before smiling broadly. "Sure, Quint. You here to see Mr. Henderson?"

"Is he home?"

Before Watts answered, a voice behind him boomed, "Jarrod, how long do you intend to stand there with the door open? Either move your ass so I can get a good look at our visitor or pull him inside before he faints from that gawd-awful heat."

Henderson was obviously home.

Watts rolled his eyes at the outburst as if it was something he'd heard many times before, but he moved his ass aside and gestured for me to come in. I stepped into a large open room with exposed wooden beams, a fireplace, polished hardwood flooring, and Clayton Ford Henderson sitting in a Louis XV chateau cane chair next to the stairwell.

"Welcome to Martinez House, Quint. We're pleased to share our humble abode with you."

"You're looking good, Clayton. How's the knee?"

"Still setting off alarms in airports," he said with a chuckle. "Actually it feels pretty good today. I'm only sittin' because Jarrod just put me through a sadistic workout, and I needed to rest for a few minutes." He pushed himself from the chair with a little effort and took a wobbly step forward to shake my hand.

Henderson's wavy white hair was perfectly groomed, and a mischievous twinkle appeared in his watery gray eyes when he smiled. With his

Deep South accent and southern charm, I imagined him in a white linen suit, standing on the veranda of a massive plantation house surrounded by women in ball gowns and servants dispensing mint juleps.

"I was hoping for a few minutes of your time."

"Of course, as much time as you want. Why don't we go upstairs to my study?"

I glanced at the short but steep flight of stairs and back to Henderson. "We can stay down here if it's too much trouble for you."

"Nonsense, I'm fine. Don't you worry about me. Besides, Jarrod keeps telling me I need more exercise." He had one hand on the chair as he waved me off. "You go on up, don't wait for me."

I took four or five steps before pausing to check on his progress. Three steps behind me, Henderson's right hand gripped the railing as he carefully placed his leg on the next step. "What are you waitin' for, Quint? I've climbed up and down these stairs a hundred times since my surgery. In fact, it's been part of my daily—"

His left leg seemed to have other ideas and slipped out from under him. Before I could move Henderson toppled backwards into the waiting arms of Jarrod Watts.

His face paled, but Henderson quickly snapped into character. "Damn, Jarrod, you really are my knight in shining armor, boy. If I'd hit my head and croaked, I guess you'd be out of a job."

"That's why I'm here, boss," Watts said. He held the old man under his arms while Henderson steadied himself and grabbed the banister for extra support.

Watts followed him to the top of the stairs. When we reached the landing, Henderson said, "See, I made it fine, Jarrod. Now stop actin' like a mother hen and make us some Anastasia Island Iced Tea. Care to join me, Quint?"

I raised my eyebrows. "Anastasia Island Iced Tea?"

"Surely you don't think I'd serve anything called Long Island Iced Tea in my house? My dear old granddaddy would send the ghost of Stonewall Jackson to render me a new one."

"I'll have a taste," I said. "Do you need to sit down?"

"My study's right here." He pointed toward an open doorway. "Give me that strong arm of yours, my friend." Henderson squeezed my bicep the way you'd check a melon, and pulled me toward the open door.

We entered a large room with a high ceiling. While the downstairs seemed as immaculate as a model home, stacks of boxes, old newspapers and magazines covered the floor of Henderson's study. We walked along a path cleaved through the middle of the piles of boxes to an open area by a window. Floor to ceiling bookcases lined both sides of the window and along one entire wall. A well-used desk and two chairs were perched between the windows. An old Royal typewriter, probably dating back to the nineteen-thirties or forties, sat on the desk.

Henderson eased himself onto one of the chairs, pointing to the other and waited until I sat. Waving toward the mounds of clutter, he said, "I trust you'll excuse the condition of my study. I'm a hopeless collector, I'm afraid. It drives Jarrod batty."

I smiled. "Reminds me a little of Jeffrey's office. And the storeroom in his home, too, come to think of it."

"Didn't I say as much at dinner that night? Jarrod couldn't believe anybody could be as much of a pack rat as I am. He told me we must have come from the same sperm bank." His smile faded and he licked his thin lips. "Poor Jeffrey. I suppose you've heard he's been arrested?"

"That's why I'm here." I told him Erin Marrano had hired me, of our meeting at her home, omitting the part about the burglary. He listened attentively while I spoke, his eyes never leaving my face. "You and Jeffrey are good friends, and I was hoping you might have some insights into the case. In fact, Mrs. Marrano suggested I should start with you."

He nodded solemnly. "Erin is such a dear. She didn't deserve this. Of course, she shouldn't have married that cretin in the first place, but no one would wish such a dreadful thing on the commissioner, would they?"

Before I could answer, Watts entered the office carrying a tray with two tall glasses and a small dish filled with cookies.

"Ah, Jarrod, your timing is impeccable, as usual. I need this refreshment before launching into my tales."

Watts placed the tray on the desk between us, and with the conspiratorial smile still on his face, retraced his steps through the mass of debris.

Henderson watched him walk away. "I was so fortunate to find Jarrod after my surgery. He has this knack for knowin' just how far to push me."

"Seems like a nice young man," I said.

"Yes, and he likes poetry, believe it or not." He picked up his glass, gestured a symbolic toast my way and downed half the glass in one gulp.

"Ah, that's better," he said, eying my untouched glass. I sipped it to be polite, knowing it would be all booze and no tea.

"You have your work cut out for you, Quint. From what I hear, Chief Conover and the State Attorney have already tried and convicted our friend. But Jeffrey made it easy for them."

"How do you mean?"

"The skirmishes with Marrano at the city commission meetings. The imbroglio over the Matanzas Bay project. The whole pitiful mess. I'm afraid Jeffrey may have lapsed into a bout of temporary insanity."

"But you were against this project, too, weren't you?"

"It is a bit of a monstrosity. Like painting a mustache on the *Mona Lisa*."

"Did you ever accompany Jeffrey to the city commission meetings when he protested the project?"

"One time. That's all." He cast an odd look my way before taking another swallow of the tea. "It was obvious from the start that the development was *a fait accompli*."

"Yet Jeffrey kept butting heads with Marrano. Did he really hate the man?"

"Jeffrey considered Marrano to be a self-serving politician, but I wouldn't say he hated him. No, he saved his hatred for Kurtis Laurance."

"But Marrano pushed it through the city commission."

"If you want to know the truth, Kurtis Laurance may have good reason to celebrate Mr. Marrano's unfortunate demise." He raised one feral eyebrow and fixed me with a look like an exclamation point on his not so subtle accusation.

"I'm a little confused," I said. "From what I've heard, Marrano was leading the charge on this project from the very beginning. How could Laurance benefit by his death?"

"Mr. Marrano's family goes back to the Minorcan settlers here in St. Augustine. You know about them, don't you?"

I indicated that I did. These were a group of indentured servants recruited from the Island of Minorca and elsewhere in the Mediterranean several hundred years ago to help build and work the colony of New Smyrna a hundred miles to the south. Many of them ended up in St. Augustine, and their descendants are influential in the community to this day.

"Despite his other failings," Henderson continued, "and he had many, I believe Marrano truly loved St. Augustine and didn't want to see it harmed. The story I heard is that somewhere along the line, his conscience got the better of him and he had a change of heart about the Matanzas Bay project."

This didn't fit into anything I'd learned about William Marrano. "Wasn't it too late to change his mind? They're breaking ground in four days."

"Never underestimate the power of a reformed vice mayor. Marrano had called a special meeting of the commission for Thursday night, and there were rumors he would try to put the project on hold until he could either kill it or downsize it substantially."

"And you think this is what got him killed?"

"Quint, believe me when I tell you I'm a man who hates clichés, but I'll ask you to do the math. Matanzas Bay is a two hundred and ninety-five million dollar project. Laurance has thirty million of his own money wrapped up in it."

"So?"

"You know he's runnin' flat out for governor. Casting himself as a clear-headed, successful businessman. An alternative to business as usual in Tallahassee. Hell, some people are saying he has his eye on the White House down the line. How would it look if this development goes down in flames and he has to declare bankruptcy?"

I watched him swallow more of the tea and place the glass back on the tray before adding, "Laurance had thirty million reasons to make sure that commission meeting never took place."

Eleven

Afterwards, I returned to my car to discover Detective Horgan waiting for me. Even though Chief Conover took Buck Marrano off the case, I had a feeling the sergeant still pulled the strings and told Horgan where to find me.

"About time you got back, Mitchell. I've been sitting here sweating my ass off for nearly an hour." Horgan squinted through a haze of smoke from the cigarette clamped in the corner of his tight little mouth. "Let's take a ride. We have more questions for you."

Not that I believed Horgan capable of the violence Marrano displayed, but *Let's take a ride* sounded like a line from a bad gangster movie. "Sure, detective, but I'll follow you. Lead the way."

No surprise why they wanted to question me. Had to be the bayonet. But interviews work both ways, and I hoped to learn more about their case. Poe's prints on the murder weapon were easily explained. They might as well release him now if that was all the forensic evidence they had.

Minutes later we arrived at the SAPD on King Street. Horgan steered me through the lobby where the same spectacled receptionist sat behind the desk.

"In here," Horgan said, punching his identification code into the security box next to the door, and pulling it open. We walked along a dim hallway, past the communications center, past a few small offices and stopped in front of a door marked Interview Room. He flipped on the light and nudged me through the door.

A narrow table covered with a faux granite laminate jutted from the wall like the prow of a ship. The table was bolted to the floor and flanked by the same black plastic chairs populating the lobby. Horgan pointed to the chair on the left side of the table so I'd be facing the mirrored observation window. He stood in the doorway a moment before another man joined him. The newcomer appeared to be about forty with a head shaped like a fleshy Idaho potato. With his circular cauliflower ears and flattened nose he reminded me of Mr. Potato Head wearing a buzz cut instead of a derby hat. The man must have been a boxer or wrestler at one time, but his muscles had morphed into soft rolls of fat. He wore a short-sleeved white dress shirt, a narrow striped tie and a perpetual blush that made his face look like a freshly cut carrot.

Both of the men stepped inside before Horgan closed the door and took the seat across from me. The other man plunked a large black storage box on the table between us. I caught the sharp tang of his body odor. "This is Detective Thompson," Horgan grunted.

I nodded to Thompson who ignored me.

"Let's go over how you came to be working with Dr. Poe the other day, and then tell us again about digging up the victim."

"Why don't you look in your little notebook? I already gave you a statement."

"Humor us. Sergeant Thompson wasn't there at the time and he wants to hear the story straight from the horse's mouth. Isn't that right, Dan?"

"Yeah, that's right." Thompson leaned against the wall to the left of the observation window, a wattle of flesh hanging below his crossed arms. He was shorter than Horgan but probably outweighed him by fifty pounds.

"Fine," I said. "I've been a volunteer on Poe's excavations on and off for the past four years."

"What makes a PI want to volunteer to dig ditches?" Horgan asked.

"What makes you want to dig into other's people's dirty laundry?"

"For such a smart guy, you seem to have missed the point of our interview. This is where we ask the questions and you answer them. So answer."

"I took some archaeology courses in college and we were required to take part in a few surveys."

Horgan said, "So, you like digging in the dirt, finding bones and shit."

I ignored his sarcasm. "There's more to it than that. Dr. Poe said each survey is a mystery. We're digging to help solve the mystery, finding clues to how people lived hundreds of years ago." I paused and smiled at the two detectives. "Finding clues. Solving mysteries. Maybe you should try it some time."

"Okay, we get it, smart ass," Thompson said. "Tell us about digging up Sergeant Marrano's brother."

I walked them through the entire afternoon step by step without leaving out anything except my phone call. I told them how we dug the post holes and garbage pits. How each shovel full of dirt is analyzed and recorded. How we discovered the new depression after the weekend rains and added it to the other sites. And finally, how I uncovered the wicker hamper containing Marrano's corpse.

"Did you know Commissioner Marrano?" Thompson asked before squeezing past Horgan to sit at the other chair facing me.

"Not really. A former client introduced us at a restaurant last year. That's the only time I ever saw the man until Monday."

Horgan's eyes flicked down at the box on the table then back to me. "I'm sure you had a good look at Mr. Marrano when you opened up the basket. Did you see anything familiar?"

The preliminaries must be over. Now they were getting around to the real reason they hauled me here. "Familiar? Well, we recognized Marrano, if that's what you mean." I wasn't going to make it easy for them.

"Sure you did. But what else?" Horgan lifted the top from the storage box and reached inside. He withdrew a sealed plastic bag containing the Spanish bayonet. "You've seen this before, haven't you?" He held the bag by one corner and dangled it inches from my face.

"Why play games? I'm sure Poe told you about the dinner at his house two weeks ago. There were six of us there and probably everyone but the old woman touched the bayonet."

"That's what Poe said, but we wanted to hear your version," Thompson said. "Why didn't you mention the bayonet when you gave Detective Horgan your statement?"

I gazed at the stained bayonet in the evidence bag and back to Thompson. "This bayonet is only one of dozens Poe's found."

"But this is the only one used to kill a St. Augustine official and has Poe's fingerprints on it," Horgan said, his voice rising slightly at the end as though he asked a question.

"And, we found partials of your prints, as well," Thompson added.

"That's because we both handled the bayonet that night, damn it." How many ways did I have to tell them the same thing before they understood? "Besides, I couldn't be sure it was the same one. Not like it had a tag on it or anything."

Horgan stared at me, a slight smile playing across his thin lips. "You're not the only history buff around here, Mitchell. We did a little research of our own and learned this was the only bayonet they'd found with a bone handle. So, don't give us this crap about not being able to tell one from the other."

"Okay, it looked familiar, but I couldn't be sure it was the same one. Everything happened so quickly, and then you guys came and chased us away."

"All right, it doesn't look like we're going to get a straight answer from you. Where were you Saturday night, say from ten to two a.m.?" Horgan asked.

"Had pizza with a friend in Jacksonville Beach, and then we went to Pete's Bar and played three or four games of pool. I was home in bed by eleven-thirty."

"Alone?" Thompson asked.

"Afraid so. I guess you could ask Bogie and Dudley, they'll vouch for me."

This caused some confusion before I explained that Bogie and Dudley were my pets. Then Thompson asked for the name and number of my friend and I gave it to him.

The two detectives sat there looking at each other as though they'd run out of questions. They really didn't have anything, I thought, and I couldn't resist sticking it to them.

"Not much of a case, guys. Four witnesses will testify we were there when Poe left his prints on the bayonet. You know the rest is circumstantial. The judge will throw it out before the prosecutor gets his briefcase unpacked."

Horgan shook his head as though stunned by my brilliant argument. "You think so? The prosecutor thought we had a pretty strong case when we told him what we found in Poe's storage shed."

"Yeah, like what?"

For the first time, Thompson's flushed face changed expressions. His lips curled into an ugly version of a smile before he said, "Since you and Poe are such good friends, Mitchell, we'll tell you Poe doesn't have a leg to stand on."

Thompson and Horgan turned to one other and laughed aloud, reminding me of a pair of high school kids telling dirty jokes.

"Right," Horgan added. "Even though we found an extra set squirreled away in his shed."

Twelve

I made a quick stop at the donut shop on San Marco Avenue and picked up a half-dozen Boston cream donuts before driving to the County Jail. Informally known as the lock-up, the place hadn't changed since the last time I was there a few months ago. Not the depressing green walls of the lobby as I entered, nor the skeptical look in Regina Washington's eyes when I told her I was there to see Jeffrey Poe.

"Honey, you might have a cute ass for a white boy, but rules is rules."

Everyone referred to Regina as The Warden, and no one came into the county lock-up without her say-so. An imposing woman with the bulk of a defensive tackle and the smile of a barracuda, she guarded her post ferociously. I felt sorry for anyone who got on her bad side, especially me.

Regina stood from behind her desk, arms folded, daring me to make a move.

"Come on, darling, you know how much I've missed you since my last visit here. I've already called and made an appointment to see him. Why do you always make me beg? Is that what you want? Get down on my knees and beg?" Regina and I go through this charade every time, but it paid to suck-up to The Warden.

"Beggin' is nice, but things have changed since you called, so you won't be talkin' through the glass tonight."

"Changed? What's changed?"

"Poe's lawyer has the next hour blocked off for a face-to-face with the good doctor Poe." She looked at me with a twinkle in her brown eyes that seemed to say *Gothcha*. "Unless your name is Thad Wannaker and you've somehow transformed yourself from lowlife private dick to lowlife defense attorney, then you're goin' nowhere but home."

"That's why I'm here," I lied with a straight face. "I'm part of Poe's defense team, and Wannaker wants me to start questioning Poe because he's running late."

Regina speared me with her skeptical stare once again, but before she could throw me out I held up the bag of donuts.

"Sweets for my sweet."

"Boston cream?"

"Damn right."

Regina snatched the bag from my hand, opened it and inhaled the fresh-baked aroma. "Deep-fried dough is surely one of God's blessings," she said, before pulling one of the donuts out of the bag. She squinted left and right to be sure no one saw her accepting my bribe before biting into the donut. A supreme calmness passed over her as if she'd been invited through the gates of heaven.

"I may be a lowlife private dick," I said as I watched her chew the last bite, "but I take care of my women. You gotta admit that."

"You're so full of shit, Mitchell, I'm surprised you don't choke on it."

Harsh words, but at least she smiled as she said them. She pulled another donut from the bag, but before she raised it to her mouth I coughed.

Regina's brown eyes looked up from her treasure, a smear of cream gracing the corner of her mouth. I tapped on the sign-in log in front of her. "How about it, Regina?"

"You're going to get me fired for sure." She placed the donut on top of the bag, pivoted away from her desk and brushed her hands together. I watched bits of chocolate frosting fall to the floor before she turned back, picked up the phone and punched two numbers.

"Mr. Mitchell here to see prisoner Poe in Visitation Room One." She listened and nodded impatiently before adding, "Don't you think I know his lawyer is meeting him in that room. There's more than one chair, ain't there?"

Shaking her head, she dropped the phone into the cradle. Regina held my stare, waiting to see if I said anything. I knew when to zip it and that's exactly what I did. She extended a finger with a bright red nail protruding a good inch past her finger tip, and pointed to the sign-in log. While I signed, she ran the same finger across the face of the donut, raised the chocolate-covered digit to her mouth and sucked provocatively.

The steel door to my left opened and a Corrections guard stuck his head through it. "Mitchell?"

"That's me." I wanted to thank Regina, but she was fully engaged with her donut.

I followed the silent guard to the Visitation Room. He opened the door and waited until I stepped in before slamming it shut behind me.

Poe stood in one corner of the small room. The baggy orange jumpsuit made him look even more gaunt than usual. Dark crescents bruised his eyes, and he shuffled toward me with the stiff, short steps of a much older man.

"Thanks for coming, Quint. Can you believe this crap?" He grabbed the front of his jumpsuit and pulled it out, shaking his head in disbelief.

We sat at the scarred metal table bolted to the floor and he continued, "You know I'm being framed. Erin Marrano knows it, and my lawyer knows it. Please tell me you found something—anything—that might get me out of here." His voice jumped an octave and broke.

"I'm working on a lot of possibilities. Nothing solid yet." No false hope there. "Heard an interesting rumor, though, that Marrano had changed his mind about the Matanzas Bay development and called a special commission meeting to put it on hold."

His mouth twisted, skepticism on his face. "I can't see Bill Marrano doing that. He and Kurtis Laurance were joined at the hip on this one, or joined at the bank account, I should say."

"You think Marrano took money from Laurance for his support of the project?"

"I can't prove anything, but he raised ten times more money than any other candidate in last year's elections. Most of it from the St. Johns Group's different divisions and key staff members. You know Laurance expected payback for his investment. And he got it with this project."

"I'm afraid the police are using your public dispute with Marrano as a motive. Of course, finding your prints on the bayonet didn't help."

"Godammit, I explained that to them a hundred times, but they're not listening."

"For what it's worth, so did I, but they don't need the bayonet after what they found in your storage shed."

"What do you mean?"

I tried to think of a less painful way of telling him about the discovery of Marrano's legs in his storage shed, but in the end I blurted it out, "Whoever killed Marrano apparently planted his legs in your shed."

Poe's face grew slack, his eyes flicked around the room as though searching for a way out. Getting arrested for this horrible crime was bad enough, now the terrible vision of William Marrano's severed legs would haunt his every waking moment.

He cupped his forehead with one hand. "Why is this happening to me? I'm going to spend the rest of my life in prison, aren't I?" Poe's anger gave way to self-pity. It wouldn't take much to send him spiraling into the same depressive state that consumed him after his wife's death.

"Come on, Jeffrey, you have to hang in there." I gripped his forearm and gave it a little shake. "Someone's obviously framed you, and I'm going to find out who it is and why. But you have to be strong. Don't give up before we even get started."

"Sure," he said without any apparent feeling.

"Hey, who's the best private eye you know?"

Before he could answer, the guard knocked sharply on the door and swung it open. A balding man who looked to be in his early fifties walked in clutching a flat leather briefcase the color of old cognac. He wore tortoise-framed glasses and a bushy salt and pepper mustache that helped to hide his bulbous nose but not the suspicious look he gave me.

Poe jumped from his chair, greeting the man with renewed animation. "Thad. God, I'm glad to see you. What did you find out?"

Dropping the briefcase on the table, the man turned to me and said, "I'm Thad Wannaker, Dr. Poe's attorney." He hovered over me, obviously wondering who I was and why I was sitting here with his client.

"I'm sorry, Thad," Poe said quickly. "This is Quint Mitchell. Quint's a good friend and a private investigator. Mrs. Marrano hired him to find her husband's killer."

I stood, gesturing for him to take my chair. Without a word, he slipped into it, and I retrieved the other one, setting it at the end of the table.

Wannaker's hands played with the clasp on his briefcase. He avoided looking at me when he said, "Jeffrey, I don't think it's a good idea for us to be discussing your case in front of someone else. Particularly an investigator working for the wife of the victim."

"He's probably right, Jeffrey." I pushed my chair back and excused myself.

"No, you sit your butt down," Poe said, the anger flaring up again. "Listen, Thad, Quint and I are old friends, and I trust him with my life. You can feel free to say anything you want in front of him."

"But I have my own investigator," Wannaker countered.

"That's all right. He's not going to get in anyone's way. Besides, we can use all the help we can get."

"You may be right," Wannaker said grudgingly.

"Good. Did you talk with Mrs. Lawson?"

"You bet I did. The old gal was a little unclear about the time, but she remembered seeing you and will back up your story."

"That's wonderful, just wonderful."

Poe must have seen the confusion on my face. "The police told me Marrano was murdered Saturday night between ten p.m. and two a.m. at his hunting camp near Palatka. I was home alone that night, which isn't much of an alibi. But later I remembered the raccoons and I asked Thad to check it out."

"Raccoons?"

"Yeah, I've had a problem with raccoons getting into the garbage cans and sometime after eleven Saturday night I heard a commotion outside. The damn raccoons were at it again, so I went out to chase them away." Poe's face had come alive and his eyes danced with excitement.

"After I cleaned up the mess they'd made, I saw Mrs. Lawson—you remember Eleanor from my little party that night? Anyway, she was walking her dog. We chatted for a couple of minutes about my raccoon problem and the weather before I went back inside."

"There's no way you could have driven to the hunting camp, killed Marrano and been back home at eleven-thirty when Mrs. Lawson saw you," Wannaker said.

"And that doesn't count the time it would have taken to bury him," Poe added.

Wannaker pulled papers from his briefcase. "I have her deposition right here. They'll have to release you when Mrs. Lawson verifies your alibi."

"That's the best news you could have brought me," Poe said, a huge smile of relief flooding his face. "When do you think I can get out?"

"I'm going to talk with the District Attorney first thing in the morning."

I congratulated both of them, but my gut told me it was too early for celebrations.

Thirteen

Instead of returning home, I decided to stop in for a quick one at the Mill Top Tavern. Perched on the second floor of a former grist mill in St. Augustine's historic district, the Mill Top offers an excellent view from its open balcony of tourists parading along St. George Street, and from the other side the Castillo de San Marcos and the bay beyond. Even better, the beer is cheap and they feature live music every night.

Despite Poe's and Wannaker's optimism, I couldn't quell the nagging feeling my friend was in real danger. Maybe they were right and Poe would soon be a free man. But maybe the raccoons, Eleanor Lawson and her dog were just so much smoke and mirrors. And maybe I needed a beer or two to help me put everything in perspective.

As I entered the bar, I heard the booming voice of a female singer. Inside, a throng of drinkers huddled around the tiny raised platform that passed as a stage watching a sweet young thing with multi-colored hair. The vocalist belted out her song while an older man with torn jeans and cornrows accompanied her on a scarred guitar. Her powerful vocals, filled with sorrow and longing, hovered above the beery conversations like a velvet shroud. Her voice reminded me of a young Judy Collins and after I ordered my beer, I leaned against the bar admiring the girl's voice. Her talent was obvious, although I couldn't help noticing her low-rise jeans and her tight middriff shirt exposing a wide swatch of skin.

When the duo took a break, I wandered out to the balcony to get some air. All of the tables were filled with people smoking and talking animatedly, so I eased into an opening along the rail next to one of the whitewashed columns. My bottle was halfway to my mouth when I heard a loud voice from the courtyard below.

"Leave me alone, Jack. You're a whorish shit, and I don't want to see your lying face again."

The girl's strident voice cut through the buzz of conversation, and everyone on the balcony craned their necks to find the source of the editorial comment. Including me. The girl was in her early twenties, wearing shorts, a pale blue tank top, and a very pissed-off expression. Her boyfriend, or more likely her former boyfriend, tried to put a hand on her nicely curved backside, but the girl slapped it away.

"Come on, Tia, you know I love you," the boy whined. "It didn't mean a thing."

Tia ignored him, striding swiftly away. She had undoubtedly had her fill of Jack, but he raced after her, grabbed her arm and pulled her around to face him.

The entire upper balcony took in the scene, and I wagered Jack was well on his way to learning a difficult lesson about the mysterious ways of the fairer sex. I've been there so many times I could teach a graduate level course on it.

"Oh, oh. I think Jack was caught thinking with his small head again."

The voice came from over my shoulder and I turned to see the ever-smiling face of Jarrod Watts.

"Hey, Jarrod. What's up?"

Watts toasted me with his longneck bottle of beer, his face alight with a warm smile. He pointed at the quarreling couple. "That boy's gonna have to eat a lot of shit if he expects to get on the right side of Tia again."

"How true," I said. "How's Clayton doing?"

"Sound asleep, so I thought I'd come out here and see if could find a little action. How about you?"

"The only action I'm looking for is a cool beer and a few songs to help me get my mind off this nasty business with Poe. At least for a little while."

Watts scrunched up his lips and made a sucking sound. "That's bad stuff, man. I can't believe Dr. Poe had anything to do with Marrano's murder."

"He didn't. I'm trying to help him, but things don't look too promising right now."

"Why'd they arrest him?"

"The police have their own theories. I just have to find out what really happened." I didn't want to talk about the case with him, so I changed the subject. "Tell me if it's none of my business, but does Clayton always drink that much?"

Watts gave me a wry smile as he looked from the beer in my hand and back to his own bottle. I caught his not too subtle meaning.

"Yeah," I agreed, "we all drink, but he seems to be more dedicated to the proposition."

"Sure, man. I guess I'm not be talking out of school since everyone knows Mr. Henderson isn't exactly a teetotaler. But he's been drinking more since his surgery, and he has these scary mood swings."

Watts glanced away, an almost embarrassed expression on his face. As a physical therapist, he's probably not legally bound to protect his client's privacy like a doctor or lawyer, but he probably realized it wasn't good business to gossip about his patients.

Conversely, my business demands I acquire information from people even when they refused to part with it. So I asked, "Is this something new, or has he been this way all along?"

He hesitated before answering, choosing his words or possibly deciding whether to answer at all. Finally, he said, "I don't know for sure, but I'd bet the drinking's been going on for years, and probably the mood swings, too. But there's something bothering him."

"What's that?"

"Couldn't say. One minute he's sky high, full of life, bouncing off the walls. Then he falls into a black hole, so depressed it's hard to get him back on track."

Henderson must be an alcoholic, but he still seemed mentally sharp. These mood swings were another matter and might indicate a bipolar disorder. "Do you know if he takes lithium or valproate?"

He shook his head. "Not that I've seen, and I've checked out his medicine cabinet."

I'd hate to see the old guy hurt himself, but each of us has to choose our own path to destruction. And that's what I told Watts.

"He's old enough to make his own choices, but you watch out he doesn't hurt himself."

Watts had been staring down at the old water wheel but now twisted his head around to gaze at me, a look of concern on his youthful features. "I've only worked for Mr. Henderson a few months, but he's become very important to me. Like family." He was speaking softly, then his demeanor abruptly changed and he grinned. "Hell, must be time for another round. I'm buying."

No argument from me. I let him take the two empty bottles with him back to the bar. I thought about the old poet and our conversation earlier this morning. When we spoke, he made a point of implicating Kurtis Laurance. He wanted me to believe that Laurance was somehow involved in Marrano's death, but I didn't buy it. Laurance was a sure bet to be elected Florida's next governor. If the political pundits were right, he'd use that office as a stepping-stone to the White House. No way would a smart politician get on the wrong side of this mess.

"Here's to ya." Watts handed me the beer, and I thanked him.

"Did I miss anything important while I was gone?" He gestured to the couple who had retreated into the shadows next to the water wheel and were wrapped together so tightly I couldn't tell where one ended and the other started.

"That Jack must have some magic beans in his pocket," I said.

Watts shifted his attention away from the two lovebirds. He seemed to be an earnest young man, and I had the feeling he wanted to open up to me about something. I didn't want to talk about Poe's murder case, but Watts was in a good position to hear some choice tidbits from his gossipy employer.

"Has Clayton said anything about Poe and the Marrano murder?"

Watts looked past me, his eyes drifting away into the darkness. My investigator's antennae tingled, and told me Watts knew something.

"Listen, Mr. Henderson is good friends with Dr. Poe, and if you know something that will prove his innocence, then he'd want you to tell me."

"I don't really know if it's anything. It's just ..."

"What?"

He took another slug of beer, licked his lips, and stiffened a bit. "You know that guy Denny who was at Poe's house with us?"

"Denny Grimes."

"Well, last night Mr. Henderson had a few too many, as he usually does. I was helping him to bed when he started talking about Dr. Poe and how he'd been arrested. 'Wasn't right,' he said. Then he said they should be looking at this Denny guy. That he hated Marrano for getting him fired from his job with the city."

"Is that right? Anything else?"

"Nah. He was pretty much out of it by then, but I remembered Denny seemed to have a hard-on about Marrano."

"Certainly worth looking into," I told him. "Thanks."

Watts began looking around nervously. "Listen, don't tell him I told you, huh? He's probably just a loudmouth, and didn't have anything to do with it."

"Don't worry about it." I was always looking for new angles when I worked a case, so I asked him, "Do you think this murder is linked to the Matanzas Bay development."

He snorted as if he thought it was a ridiculous idea.

"What? You don't agree?"

"It's not that, but it's kind of funny when you think about it."

"Funny?"

"I don't see the sense in fighting over a development that everyone seems to want. And what gets me is it's going to be built on the San Sebastian River but they call it Matanzas Bay. What were they thinking? I mean Matanzas Bay is right behind us." He stabbed the air behind him with his thumb.

"When you're right you're right."

"But they got the name from the Matanzas Inlet over by the Fort Matanzas National Monument, and that's fifteen miles away. I don't get it."

"One of the mysteries of marketing," I offered.

"You've been there, haven't you?"

"The Fort Matanzas National Monument? Sure, a couple of years ago."

"I've been there three or four times in the past six months." Watts took a long swig from his beer before continuing. "I find it restful."

"It is quiet, but there's not much to it."

"Guess it reminds me of a place I hung around in when I was a kid. The river flowed through the woods near our house and formed a huge lake. One day when I was maybe seven or eight years old I followed the riverbank and discovered this little bluff hanging over the water. It was surrounded by trees, and I'd sit there on the bluff pretending I was the last person in the world." He smiled sheepishly and finished his beer.

Holding up his empty bottle, he said, "Whoa. I've either had one too many or not enough."

"I can take a hint," I said. "It's my turn to buy."

Fourteen

Back at home that night, I opened a can of clam chowder, poured the entire contents into a large bowl and popped it into the microwave. I carried the steaming soup out to my balcony. While waiting for it to cool, I watched the darkened surf beyond the restaurants and bars across the street. The surf was usually flat in the mornings; the sun dancing on the water as it crawled ashore, leaving streams of foam like the lace hem on a curtain. But tonight I heard restless waves breaking on the shore, and a moody veil of mist had edged across the water and hung gloomily over the shoreline. For a moment, the mist seemed to envelop me, and I visualized myself under water, unable to breathe.

Despite the muggy heat, I shivered, feeling thorny fingers of anxiety scratching my back, prickles of apprehension warning me things were going to get a lot worse before they improved.

I ate the chowder, trying to focus on the other problem weighing me down, letting my thoughts skip back two weeks to a lunch date with Serena Howard, and the time when our relationship hit the rocks.

Things couldn't have been going better between us then, or so I thought, and somewhere in the back of my mind I hoped this lunch meeting would be another step binding us closer together. I still recalled every detail of our lunch date at the restaurant called Stuff of Dreams.

Stuff of Dreams was a cozy café on Aviles Street sitting between a wine shop and one of the many art galleries lining the block. We hadn't eaten there before and I glanced around the restaurant, taking in the old brick fireplace dominating one end of the rectangular room before reading my menu. It listed a half-dozen stuffed calzones along with pita-wrap sandwiches and salads. Each description ended with the phrase *stuffed to perfection*, and I understood where the restaurant's name had originated.

"What a disappointment," I said to Serena, who had this Vanessa Williams thing going on today. Her hair swirled dramatically across her forehead; her earrings, little gold balls dangling from delicate chains.

"You haven't even tasted the food yet."

"No, I'm sure the food is good. I thought it was a tribute to *The Maltese Falcon*."

"The old Humphrey Bogart movie? What does that have to do with the menu disappointing you?"

"Not the menu, the restaurant's name, *Stuff of Dreams*. It's the last line of the film. You know, after Sam Spade has solved the crime, found the missing statue of the falcon, turned the beautiful but murderous Brigid O'Shaughnessy over to the police, he's asked what's so valuable about the statue?"

I put on my best Humphrey Bogart face, snatched an imaginary cigarette from my mouth, blowing the imaginary smoke into her face before proclaiming, "It's the stuff that dreams are made of."

Serena laughed at my impersonation. "Perfect. So Sam Spade reads Shakespeare?"

"Huh?"

"They stole the line from Shakespeare's play, *The Tempest*. Actually, what Prospero said was, 'We are such stuff as dreams are made on.' It worked for him, so I guess it's a good exit line for a sneaky private detective."

She gifted me with one of her dazzling smiles, and I laughed. "Touché! I should learn never to get into a game of literary one-upsmanship with an English Lit major. I'm looking forward to discussing Shakespeare's plays in more detail later tonight, particularly, *All's Well that Ends Well.*"

"Are you sure it won't be *Much Ado About Nothing?*" she retorted.

"Ouch. Maybe *Taming of the Shrew* might better suit you." I had exhausted my knowledge of Shakespeare's plays, but before I could prove it, my cell phone played its little song in my pocket. Still smiling at Serena, I pulled out the phone, flipped it open and read the Caller ID.

Not him again. I stared at the phone wondering what to do. As much as I hated these calls, dreaded the way they left me drained and guilt-ridden, I'd never failed to answer them before. In a strange way, I considered them cathartic therapy for both of us. But his timing couldn't be worse. As I started to power off the phone, Serena asked, "Aren't you going to answer it?"

I shrugged, hesitating, my finger resting on the off button. "No, it can wait. Besides, I don't want to interrupt our precious time together."

"Go ahead, we haven't even ordered lunch yet. It may be important." Serena spent most of her day on the phone and understood the necessity of keeping in touch.

As the phone continued beating out its urgent tone, she looked at me curiously, picking up on the invisible waves of anxiety radiating out from me. "Well?" she asked.

Despite my misgivings, I depressed the talk button and put the phone to my ear, turning slightly away from her. The sound of his breathing greeted me, rasping and rapid. "Do you know what keeps me going?" He didn't expect an answer and I didn't give him one. "Waiting for you to die. If I had the courage, I'd rip your fucking heart out myself, but instead I have to wait." I heard him sniff and waited along with him. "Wait for God to punish you."

I felt the familiar blade slicing into my organs, blood rushing from my head. I glanced at Serena hoping to find her still engrossed in the menu, but she watched me with a puzzled expression.

"Are you there?" the voice screamed into my ear.

"Yes, I'm listening," I managed to say. Serena raised an eyebrow and canted her head toward me.

"You took her away from me. Took away my ...." The sobbing began. "... my little girl." He lost it at this point, and I struggled to keep control.

I listened to the man's wracking sobs for another moment before putting an end to it. "I'm sorry," I said softly and closed the phone. My eyes felt moist and I wiped a hand across my face before looking at Serena.

"Is something wrong?" she asked. "You look terrible." She leaned forward and touched my face.

I'm actually a very good liar. I've found it to be a helpful trait in my line of work, but I have difficulty lying to someone I care about. "It's a long story. I'll tell you about it some other time." I picked up the menu and pretended to examine the calzones.

Serena pulled my menu down. "Who was on the phone?"

I saw clouds of suspicion and doubt slide into her eyes.

"Are you seeing someone else, Quint?"

"No, baby, it's nothing like that, but—"

"But what? Why can't you tell me?"

I let out my breath, met her eyes and told her the story. "Three years ago, I was driving home after a party at a client's house in Jacksonville. It was about one-thirty in the morning, and I went through the green light at an intersection and ..." I halted, seeing the intersection in my mind and fearing what came next. Serena remained quiet.

"I don't remember seeing her car until she turned in front of me."

"Oh, my God," Serena said.

"I was only doing fifty, but it seemed like ... like the world had shifted into hyper-drive. No time to do anything." I reached for the glass of water and swallowed a gulp.

"She was only nineteen years old, I found out later. Coming home from a date and talking to her boy friend on her cell phone."

"Quint, I'm so sorry."

"It's funny what tricks your mind plays, but suddenly we went from moving at warp speed to slow motion. The world froze for a moment in the instant before she saw me. The light from the street lamp caught her face and framed it like a tinted photograph, her head tilted to one side. She was laughing." I had lived through this scene so many times it felt like I was reading from a script.

"The phone was in her right hand, and she turned the steering wheel with the other. Then she saw me closing on her, probably heard my brakes screeching. By then we were only a few yards apart."

Serena had a hand over her mouth, her eyes slightly glazed as though she could see the car bearing down on her.

"I'll never forget her face. The terror. The realization she was going to ..."

"Die?"

I nodded. "It was over quickly, for what it's worth. I couldn't do anything for her."

"Were you charged for her death?"

I shook my head. "I'd only had one drink at the party, and passed a field sobriety test. It turned out the traffic signal wasn't working properly, and we both had green lights. They considered the mechanical failure of the lights, the fact she was distracted by the cell phone and declared it an accident."

"And that phone call?" she pointed at my phone still sitting on the table.

"Her father. The poor guy had a nervous breakdown. He and his wife divorced and he went to pieces. He calls me to ... I don't know, because he doesn't know what else to do."

"He's been calling you since the accident?"

"Only for the past year or so. Sometimes a month will go by between his calls. But now he's calling more frequently."

"What does he say?"

I hesitated, not wanting to repeat the vicious names and gut-wrenching language he used. "You have to remember he believes I killed his only child and got away with murder. "He blames me and wants me dead, let's leave it at that."

"But it was an accident. A horrible accident, true, but he can't hold on to those hateful feelings for the rest of his life." She searched my face wanting, I thought, some reassurance that she was right.

"Maybe, but I've ruined his life, so I figure the least I can do is put up with his phone calls."

Serena shook her head. I realized she was processing what I'd told her and hadn't come to the same conclusion. "It's tragic, Quint, but the man needs professional help. You can't allow him to keep persecuting you for something that wasn't your fault."

Her honey brown eyes glinted like they were imbedded with granite chips. What she said next took me completely by surprise.

"This was a white girl wasn't it?" Her jaw tight, voice low. "You wouldn't put up with this kind of harassment from a black man."

"Serena, this has nothing to do with the girl's race." I reached for her hand. She snatched it away and I felt as though the wind had been knocked out of me, surprised at the ferocity of her feelings. My mind went blank for a moment. It felt like an eternity before I could answer.

"If you must know, the girl was black, and ..." I paused and fumbled for something to say that would erase the anger in her eyes. "And she looked a lot like you."

She appraised me for a long moment before speaking. "This was never about me, was it? It was all about her." The look on her face made my stomach roll over.

Her voice took on a far-away tone, and I strained to hear her. "You're only using me as some sick compensation to assuage your guilt."

"No, you don't understand."

"I understand perfectly. You're reaching out to a local girl of color to make yourself feel better." Serena stood so abruptly her chair tumbled to the floor. "Well, I don't want any part in your therapy sessions."

Heads turned as she bolted from the restaurant.

Fifteen

The scene at Stuff of Dreams still haunted me. We're all products of our culture and environment. Although Serena obviously had a different frame of reference, I never knew her to be conflicted when it came to race. Despite our three-month relationship, huge chunks of her past were unknown to me mostly because I hadn't bothered to probe too deeply.

We'd been seeing each other for nearly a month before our relationship advanced into a more intimate phase. After that first time, lying naked in her bed, I gently rubbed the light sheen of sweat glazing her abs. Serena's eyes were closed, and I let my fingers crawl up toward the swell of her breasts, exploring an erect nipple and tracing the dark tattooed areole surrounding it. She smiled and I heard a low hum, like the purr of a cat, from deep in her throat.

Up to that point, she'd shared only random bits of her life, mostly in answer to my innocuous questions. She told me her father had been born in St. Johns County, moved to Chicago in the sixties, and later married. I learned she had no brothers or sisters, and her parents had divorced when she was three years old. Her mother died of breast cancer several years after the divorce.

Lying in bed together that night, I told her I wished her mother were still alive so I could thank her for having the foresight to give birth to such a beautiful baby. Instead of responding to my offbeat compliment with a smile, a kiss, or, as I hoped, another round of lovemaking, she simply nodded. Without a word, she pulled a framed photograph from the drawer on the nightstand and handed it to me.

I stared at the photo of a couple who were obviously very much in love. A young black man in an army uniform had an arm wrapped around a willowy young woman with long blonde hair. She was nearly as tall as the soldier, smiling into the camera as if posing for the cover of a magazine. The soldier stared at the woman with a look reflecting a fierce and unrestrained love.

"This is your mother and father?"

Serena nodded and took the photo back, gazing at it for a moment before setting it on the night stand.

Obviously, I knew Serena was of mixed parentage, but it wasn't until I saw the photograph of her mother and father that she became defined in my mind as a product of black and white. And as I hit the replay button on our lunch scene, my words came back to me wrapped in layers of guilt and confusion … If you must know, the girl was black … And she looked a lot like you.

Could Serena be right? Was I somehow drawn to her because of my feelings of guilt?

At my office the next morning, I brought up the home site for the St. Augustine newspaper on my computer. I typed *Matanzas Bay Project* into the box to search the story archives and up popped page after page of articles dating back nearly three years. Scanning through them quickly, I verified that the St. Johns Group received the green light to begin construction several months back.

From the beginning, William Marrano was clearly the prime mover behind the project, pushing the mayor and the rest of the commission to sell the city property to the St. Johns Group. One of the articles, dating back six months, reported on a bitter clash between Poe and Marrano at a city commission meeting. Poe addressed the commission, accusing them of *selling St. Augustine's legacy to the developers for 30 pieces of gold.*

Returning to the first page of articles, I pulled up today's story of Poe's arrest. The headline blared, *St. Augustine Archaeologist arrested.* The sub-head told the rest of the story: *Dr. Jeffrey Poe indicted for murder of Vice Mayor Marrano.*

There must be a course in journalism school teaching budding re-porters how to dredge up and list every embarrassing incident in a subject's past no matter how long ago it may have happened. In that fine tradition, the story related Poe's earlier run-ins with Marrano and noted it wasn't the first time his temper had landed him in trouble. According to the article, as a sophomore in college, Poe had been arrested and charged with aggravated assault for attacking a classmate.

I knew Poe had a temper, but aggravated assault was a serious charge involving use of a weapon. My mind rebelled at the thought of Poe as a homicidal maniac, but I knew the prosecutor would jump all over the old aggravated assault charge. Anyone who didn't know the man as I did might conclude from this article that Poe was capable of murder.

I tried to reconcile what I knew about Jeffrey Poe—the man who lovingly nursed his wife during those emotionally draining months of her illness—with the brutal killer who stabbed and mutilated William Marra-no. They were not the same man.

I wondered how a reporter for a St. Augustine newspaper gained access to a thirty-year-old police report? If I had to put money on it, I'd bet Kurtis Laurance or someone else in the St. Johns Group leaked it to the reporter. Laurance had the resources to investigate Poe's background, and the motivation to discredit him.

I printed the newspaper article before shutting down my computer. Sitting at my desk, a picture came to mind of the St. Johns Group in the form of an octopus, slick tentacles worming out in all directions, encircling and suffocating the life out of Jeffrey Poe. Kurtis Laurance's sticky fingers appeared to be all over this case, and I hoped when it was finally over I didn't find myself ensnared in their grip.

Sixteen

At twenty minutes past three, I turned onto International Golf Parkway. I followed the shadowed stretch of country road for five miles until I came to a contemporary three-story building of white concrete. A sign across the top of the building informed me I'd arrived at the offices of the St. Johns Group.

Landing an appointment with Kurtis Laurance hadn't been easy. My calls had been passed to a succession of aides whose main job seemed to be to protect the people's candidate from the people. Frustrated, I asked Erin Marrano to call on my behalf and Laurance finally deigned to speak to me.

"I'm a very busy man," Laurance told me during that phone call. "How about next week, say Thursday?"

I patiently explained that I needed to see him today. "This might have an impact on the Matanzas Bay project," I added. His tone immediately changed, and he told me to be at his office at three-thirty.

A half-hour later, I sat in the lobby squirming uncomfortably on a teardrop-shaped chair probably used in medieval torture chambers. Unable to sit any longer, I rose from my seat and pretended to study the framed photographs along the wall. Each one represented a project the St. Johns Group had built throughout the Southeast. I was looking at a photograph of a shopping mall in West Palm Beach when the door next to the receptionist opened and a tall blonde on stiletto heels surveyed the room. Her face, pinched and aloof as if expecting to find a reeking derelict, transformed itself when I turned toward her. She gave me a surprised smile.

"Mr. Mitchell?"

I flashed her the equivalent of an *Elevated* on my smile-alert system. She returned the smile before extending her hand and saying, "I'm Pamela, Mr. Laurence's executive assistant. I'm sorry for the wait, but he can see you now."

We walked to an elevator whose door glided open at her touch. On the third floor, we stepped through the double doors leading into Laurance's office, a space about the size of a department store in one of his shopping malls. Pamela left me there, closing the doors as she exited.

Laurance sat behind a large executive desk talking on the phone. My attention was immediately drawn to another man in a rumpled dark suit who stood half-turned between me and Laurance, beefy shoulders and thick legs braced to tackle me if I tried anything funny.

With the phone still pressed to his ear, Laurance waved me toward the two chairs at a meeting table across the room. Mr. Rumpled Suit followed as I walked to the chair, positioning his stocky body between us like one of those concrete barriers protecting highway workers from on-coming traffic. He turned his head to stare at me with tiny, hooded eyes the color of watery iced tea bringing to mind an image of a moray eel. Face forward, I now saw a thin scar bisecting his right eyebrow and traversing the corner of his eye. Noting the bulge under his suit coat, I turned back to Laurance who was still talking on the phone.

"Gordon doesn't bother me. Even if he is the Attorney General, how's he going to explain his involvement in that casino gambling business?" He cut his eyes at me and abruptly said, "I have someone waiting for me. We'll talk later."

Laurance approached me with a fluid, athletic stride. In his late fifties or early sixties, he was tan and lean with close-cropped gray hair. He pulled back his cuff-linked sleeve to reveal a yellow gold Patek Philippe watch. Glancing at it before giving me a smile of perfectly even white teeth and offering his hand, he said, "I don't mean to rush you, Mr. Mitchell, but I'm behind schedule as it is."

Before he sat he gestured toward the other man. "Meet Lemuel Tallabois, my security chief. Lem is retired from the New Orleans Police and handles all my security needs."

I nodded to Tallabois who raised a corner of his mouth in a snarky smile. His sideburns were trimmed eye-level in a stark, military cut. Aside from Bourbon Street and beignets, New Orleans was renowned for its corrupt politicians and even more corrupt police. In the wake of Hurricane Katrina, national headlines blazed the news that fifty or sixty police officers were fired for abandoning their posts and stealing, along with a few more serious offenses like beatings and shootings. Lemuel Tallabois may have retired from the New Orleans Police Department, I thought, but probably not of his own accord.

"You may have heard I'm running for governor," Laurance said, sitting down opposite me. "One of my advisers suggested it would be wise to have someone like Lem to watch over me since there are a lot of crazies out there." He smiled again and shrugged, as if he didn't quite buy the sentiment but didn't have a choice.

"You're an important public figure, Mr. Laurance, so it makes sense not to take any chances." I hoped I projected the proper degree of deference. "But rest assured you're safe with me." Laurance grinned broadly, apparently appreciating my little joke, but Tallabois was unmoved.

"I'm sure you're right. Lem, why don't you take a break and get yourself a cup of coffee while Mr. Mitchell and I chat for a few minutes?"

Tallabois squinted at me, the scarred right eye closing completely at the corner, adding to his eel-like look. "Maybe I should check him out to make sure he's not packing." He moved toward me holding out a hand to pat me down.

"I don't think that will be necessary," Laurance said. "Mr. Mitchell looks harmless enough, but I'll give you a call if I need your help."

The muscles along Tallabois' jaw line bunched, and he shot me his creepy stare as a warning before leaving the office.

"Now, what's this all about, Mr. Mitchell? You said something about the Matanzas Bay project."

"First of all, let me thank you for seeing me on such short notice. As Mrs. Marrano probably told you, she's hired me to investigate the circumstances surrounding her husband's murder."

Lines appeared on Laurance's forehead as his smooth face took on an expression of deep sadness. "What a horrible tragedy for Mrs. Marrano and the rest of us. Aside from the loss of a wonderful friend, I hate to see something like this happen in my hometown."

Laurance was either a very good actor or sincerely moved by Marrano's death. Part of his statement surprised me, though. "Your hometown? I thought you were from south Florida."

"I was born and lived here until I was thirteen when my family moved to south Florida. After high school I attended the University of Miami and stayed in the area while learning the real estate development business." He leaned back in his chair and crossed his legs, adjusting the crease in his pants before continuing.

"After working with a couple of companies, I started my own and took advantage of the explosive growth throughout south Florida. But my heart's always been here in St. Johns County. That's why I named my company the St. Johns Group. Later I transferred my main office up here."

"You still have an office in Miami?" Like most politicians, he enjoyed talking about himself, and I wanted him to keep talking.

"Of course, and one in Atlanta and another in Charlotte. I try to spend as much time here as my schedule allows." Laurance looked at his watch again to let me know I needed to get back on track.

"You said Mr. Marrano was a good friend of yours."

"Bill and I developed a close working relationship. I'm happy to say it grew into a deep friendship." He reached across the table and touched me on the arm with a long, delicate finger. "Everyone who knew Bill felt the same way about him. He exuded charisma and had a sincere love for his community. That's why the Matanzas Bay project was so important to him."

"And yet, someone obviously disliked him enough to kill him," I said.

A subtle change flitted across Laurance's features and for a moment the compassion and concern he displayed were gone, replaced by what might have been suspicion and an almost animal-like sense of alertness. The look of concern returned so quickly I thought I might have imagined the change.

"I still have a hard time believing it happened," Laurance said. "Everyone knew Dr. Poe opposed our project, but no one would have guessed he was capable of such a thing."

"Jeffrey Poe may have been arrested for William Marrano's murder, but he hasn't been convicted."

"Of course not, but I hear the police have a very good case against him."

"Mrs. Marrano hired me because she doesn't believe Dr. Poe killed her husband."

"I'm a staunch supporter of our jurisprudence system, Mr. Mitchell. I'm sure the courts will sort everything out, but Mrs. Marrano acted under the strain of her husband's murder before hearing all the evidence. When she does, she'll realize she doesn't require your services any longer."

He held my eyes for a second before looking at his watch again. "I'm not sure how I can help you."

"You obviously think Dr. Poe—"

"It doesn't make any difference what I think." He flicked a hand through the air impatiently. "None of this has anything to do with our project. We've been charged with converting an old waste dump into a jewel for St. Augustine's crown. Everyone will be proud of Matanzas Bay when we're finished."

"Jeffrey Poe didn't consider it to be a jewel."

He snorted. "Poe was obsessive about this development. He was sadly mistaken if he thought he could stop the project by killing Marrano."

"Maybe the point of killing Marrano was not to halt construction, but to insure it went on," I said.

"What the hell does that mean?" Laurance blurted out the words before catching himself, but not before a flush of color reddened his cheeks.

I noted his public mask slipping away, if only momentarily.

"Bill Marrano had been in favor of this project since day one. I'm only sorry he won't be here to see it to completion." Laurance the politician was back in control, smiling and nodding sympathetically.

I had my note pad on the table and flipped through a few pages as though looking for something. Running a finger down one of the pages, I said, "Its come to my attention Mr. Marrano may have had a change of heart. He called a special meeting for Thursday night and some people thought he planned to reverse his position and either delay or halt the project."

Something flashed across his face, and I thought I may have hit a nerve.

"There's absolutely no truth to that," Laurance said, his voice even and confiding. "Marrano knew this project would benefit St. Augustine. He couldn't wait to get it underway. The special meeting wasn't called because he'd changed his mind."

"How much would you stand to lose if this project got shelved?"

All pretenses of affability were suddenly dropped, and Laurance glared at me with narrowed eyes and open hostility.

"Don't think I don't know where you're getting this crap. It's Henderson. The old has-been likes to stick his rummy nose in everybody's business. He plays the part of the village shaman and expects everyone to go along with his game."

I didn't reply.

"Henderson and Poe both tried to stop Matanzas Bay. At least Poe was man enough to go public and do it openly. Let me give you some free advice, Mitchell. Take another look at your poet friend. I mean a good look. He's not the noble creature everyone seems to think he is."

"Are you saying Henderson was involved in Mr. Marrano's death?"

"You're obviously hard of hearing. I said that he's not the noble creature everyone seems to think he is. If that means he also has blood on his hands ..." He let the sentence trail off, holding up both hands as though weighing the implications of his statement. "Maybe the police will get around to questioning him, but since you're a detective, why don't you do your job."

He glared at me a moment before standing. I guessed our meeting was over.

"I'm sorry, but I have to get back to work now." Taking a few steps toward the office door, he called, "Lem."

Tallabois entered immediately, and I wondered if he had his ear pressed against the door, waiting to be summoned. The security chief's right hand hung in the air mid-way toward his holster as though expecting trouble, his moray eel eyes searching the room.

"Mr. Mitchell is finished here. Will you be kind enough to see him out?"

Laurance returned to his desk, and Tallabois gripped my upper arm, pushing me toward the door. I spun around, yanking my arm from his grip and stared into the ruined face of Lemuel Tallabois.

"Thanks, but I think I can find my own way out."

Tallabois sneered and whispered hoarsely, "Watch your ass, pretty boy. I'd hate to see anything happen to it."

Seventeen

Eighteen minutes later I turned off Ponce de Leon Boulevard into the parking lot of the downtown branch of the St. Johns County Public Library. During the ride, I reviewed my interview with Laurance, searching for any clues or discrepancies in his story. He had raised a lot of new questions, but now my head returned to the county jail and Jeffrey Poe.

Wannaker's news about Eleanor Lawson remembering the Saturday night raccoon incident had pulled Poe out of his gloomy mood. I had my doubts the old woman's testimony would offset the grisly evidence the police found in Poe's storage shed. I wondered what the State Attorney had told Wannaker this morning, which was why I asked the elderly Asian woman behind the reference desk for a St. Augustine telephone directory.

Wannaker struck me as one of those attorneys who not only had a full page ad in the yellow pages, but probably advertised on TV as much as the beer companies. I flipped to the section marked Attorneys and wasn't disappointed to find a full page ad with the bold headline, *Your Hometown Criminal Defense Attorney* and Wannaker's stern visage below it. I noted the phone number and address in my notebook and started to leave when the book stacks caught my eye.

Among compilations of the works of James Dickey, Lawrence Ferlinghetti, Sylvia Plath, and Nikki Giovanni, I found four volumes by Clayton Ford Henderson—*Trembling Vision, A Flash of Silence, Waiting for the Other Shoe,* and *Dusty Autumn Daydreams.*

A friend who wrote poetry when she wasn't earning a living as a freelance journalist, once told me very few poets made any money selling books of poetry. Henderson must be the rare exception since he purchased a residence in St. Augustine's historic district and remodeled it top to bottom.

I pulled *A Flash of Silence* from the shelf and studied the slim book wrapped in a muted teal dust jacket. On the back cover, Henderson stared out at me in a three-quarter page black and white photograph probably taken twenty-five years ago. I thumbed through the pages until I came across the title poem and read the first stanza.

A Flash of Silence
Last night's Bordeaux was a teasing

pinch on our tongues,
candles a veil of light that dulled
truth we knew would come.
In the hearth fire rose, a wall
of flames that kindled longing.
Hope drifted away like ashes.

I left Mr. Henderson and his ashes on the shelf and returned to my car, arriving at Wannaker's office in time to see him striding toward a black Cadillac Escalade, shirt sleeves rolled up, tie askew. He carried a folded newspaper instead of his expensive brief case.

"Mr. Wannaker, may I speak to you for a minute?"

He gave me a baleful look. "You're like a bad penny, Mitchell. If you weren't Jeffrey's friend, I'd tell you to make an appointment like everyone else, but ..." He shrugged and I interpreted it to mean he'd break his rigid policies and condescend to a minute's unbilled conversation.

"What's happening with Poe's case? Have you spoken to the State Attorney yet?"

Shaking his head, he said, "Not good news. I was just going down the street for a bite to eat. Come along and I'll fill you in."

During the five minutes it took to reach the sandwich shop, Wannaker remained remarkably quiet. He admitted he'd spoken with the State Attorney, but said he'd tell me more after he had something in his stomach.

Only three bites into my cheese steak sandwich, I watched Wannaker swallow the last of his turkey and ham combo. The man ate faster than anyone I'd ever seen, inhaling great gulps of food seemingly without chewing. Finally, he sucked a long swallow of Dr. Pepper through his straw, wiped his mouth and looked at me.

"Up front, I have to tell you things look rather bleak for Dr. Poe," Wannaker said.

"What about Mrs. Lawson's deposition?"

"I spoke to the State Attorney first thing this morning. He was polite, and said he'd have the SAPD check into Mrs. Lawson's story and get back to me."

"Did he?"

"Oh yes. In fact, he called me back ninety minutes later. Apparently, Chief Conover sent one of his detectives out almost immediately." Wannaker picked up his drink and loudly slurped the last few drops.

"And?"

"It didn't take them long to determine Poe didn't have much of an alibi. By the time the detective finished talking with Mrs. Lawson, she was so confused she couldn't be sure when she saw Poe. Not even what day it was."

I was afraid of that. Even the best witnesses are known to make mistakes, and Mrs. Lawson was a seventy-something woman who admitted her memory wasn't what it once had been. Not exactly a scenario designed to strike fear in the heart of the prosecuting attorney.

"Did you verify this with the witness?"

"Of course I did." He looked at me as though I'd hurt his feelings, picked up a few slivers of turkey remaining on his wrapper and chewed them slowly. "She apologized several times, saying how bad she felt for Poe, and that she'd let him down. At her age, she has trouble keeping track of things and it could have been any day last week. But she did remember seeing him and would be happy to testify if it would help."

I nodded, knowing Mrs. Lawson would never see the witness stand on this case. "What about Jeffrey? Did you tell him?"

"I drove out to the lock-up right away. I thought I should be the one to tell him the bad news."

"How did he take it?"

"Jeffrey said you were his friend. How well do you really know him?"

"I've known him from before his wife died. We're pretty tight."

"Then you won't be surprised when I tell you he fell apart."

"What does that mean?"

"He went ballistic, cursing the police, Mrs. Lawson. When I tried to calm him, tell him it was only a temporary setback, he turned on me. Finally, he shut down."

"This has been an emotional roller coaster for him," I said. "First you tell him Mrs. Lawson was his ticket out of jail. Then he hears this. I'm sure it hit him hard."

"In my business I deal with a lot of emotional types, but this was something else."

"I don't follow you."

"It was like he'd given up all hope. I don't know, he collapsed into himself. Checked out. Gave up." Wannaker took a deep breath and let it out slowly. "I'm not a psychiatrist, Mr. Mitchell, but I'd say my client, your friend, is a manic depressive who might be very close to a nervous breakdown."

I thought back to Poe's behavior following the death of his wife. About how he cut off contact with everyone and fell into a morass of self-pity and depression.

"What can I do to help?"

He appeared to give my question some thought for a moment, using the time to pry the top off his drink cup, and prod the ice into his mouth. After a few crunches, he said, "This is going to be a very short trial if we don't come up with something to offset the county's case. They have the murder weapon with his fingerprints on it. They have motive and opportunity. And they found pieces of the victim in Poe's shed." He reinforced each point by tapping the table, each tap louder than the one before.

"Yes, but—"

He cut me off. "Any first-year assistant prosecutor can sleepwalk through this case and be guaranteed a guilty verdict, but State Attorney Thomas is taking the lead on this one himself."

I looked down at my uneaten cheese steak sandwich, the smell of grilled onions and peppers suddenly rank and sour. "I repeat my question, Mr. Wannaker. What can I do to help?"

"Simple. Find Marrano's killer or your friend is headed to Death Row."

"Is that all?" I said with false bravado. Unbidden, the last line of Henderson's poem flitted across my mind.

Hope drifted away like ashes.

Eighteen

Wannaker dropped me off at his office after our lunch. I climbed into my car and rolled down the windows to let some of the heat out. I sat there sweating and worrying over what the attorney had told me. All the evidence pointed to Poe. No reasonable jury would see it any other way. Hell, if I were on the jury I'd have to vote to convict based on the evidence.

Whoever framed him had done a damn good job, but Wannaker laid it all on my shoulders—unless I found Marrano's murderer, Poe had a one-way ticket to Death Row. Quint Mitchell, super detective and savior of lost and hopeless cases.

I rolled up the windows and turned on the air conditioning. Letting it wash over me, I considered the very real possibility that Jeffrey Poe would be convicted Sure, I had no doubt someone else killed Marrano and framed Poe, but I needed more than gut feelings to convince Conover and Horgan they had the wrong man. Someone knew why Marrano was murdered, and unless I discovered the reason this case would drift away like ashes, again thinking of Henderson's poem.

The flash of Henderson's poem reminded me of Kurtis Laurance's insinuation that Henderson might somehow be involved. What had he said? *He's not the noble creature everyone seems to think he is.*

Henderson and Laurance obviously shared an antipathy for one another, but I chalked it up to a clash of giant egos. Still, a small inner voice whispered to me not to ignore what Laurance said.

I pulled out of the parking lot onto US 1, and for the second time that day visited the downtown library. I found a vacant computer station and Googled Clayton Ford Henderson. As expected, the search engine pulled up hundreds of references, including a fan site with photographs, biography, and snippets of his poetry. I scrolled through pages of old news stories on his appearances, honors won, book reviews, and his appointment as Poet Laureate by former Governor Lawton Chiles.

He was born in Oxford, Mississippi, moved to Huntsville for a brief time and then to Tuscaloosa where he taught at the University of Alabama. While there, he published his second book of poetry and picked up a PhD. He later accepted a position as professor at the University of Florida's Department of English.

Once in Florida, he established himself as one of the nation's foremost poets, winning fellowships and publishing four more books of poetry, including *A Flash of Silence*. Five years ago, he retired and moved to St. Augustine.

I clicked through to more listings of interviews and articles until on the sixth page, near the bottom, I spotted an intriguing item titled *Poet of Death?* The descriptive line beneath the title read *Clayton Ford Henderson's rise to the stratosphere of the poetry heavens began with the mysterious death of ...*

When I clicked on the cached article an old piece from a defunct magazine appeared on the screen. The article's by-line credited Perry Roberts, a name I recognized as belonging to a sleazy shock journalist who'd written four or five controversial and unauthorized biographies of celebrities and presidents. Roberts hadn't built his reputation on unassailable journalism, but he knew how to get headlines.

A black and white photograph, reminding me of a still from an old *noir* movie, accompanied the article. In it, two uniformed police stared into a swimming pool while another talked with a man obviously in a state of shock. The photograph captured a look of disbelief on the man's face. His dark hair was in disarray, a shirt half buttoned as though he'd just woken and hadn't had time to finish dressing. The picture evoked a sense that something monstrous had happened in this tranquil neighborhood.

I recognized the man in the old photo as Clayton Ford Henderson, perhaps forty or forty-five years ago. His grief reached out to touch me. Looking closer at the photograph, I saw the reason for his grief. There, in the pool, floated a woman's body. I began reading the article.

Poet of Death
By Perry Roberts

Clayton Ford Henderson's rise to the stratosphere of the poetry heavens began with the mysterious death of his wife in Oxford, Mississippi in 1970. My investigation into her death shows that the hometown of William Faulkner, one of America's great storytellers, may have been the setting of another literary figure's most deadly creation.

Henderson attended the University of Mississippi where he met and later married Elizabeth Swinton, the only child of Mr. and Mrs. Clyde Swinton. Mr. Swinton, a multi-millionaire industrialist, perished along with his wife when their private plane crashed during a thunderstorm. This left Elizabeth sole heir to an enormous fortune.

The courtship and marriage had all the trappings of a storybook romance for the Henderson's. But the story didn't have a happy ending for

Mrs. Henderson who was found floating in the couple's backyard swimming pool sixteen months later.

The drowning caused more than a few to raise their eyebrows since, as a student, Elizabeth Swinton had set several Southeast Conference records as captain of the women's swim team. While the Oxford police wouldn't admit Henderson was a suspect, my sources tell me he was questioned for days and remained under constant surveillance until the case was officially closed and labeled an accident.

This fit the pattern of Roberts' smear jobs. He dug into a person's background looking for any peccadillo or weakness, hacked away at it, weaving rumors and gossip in such a way even the pope would be hard-pressed to defend himself. I made a few notes and continued reading.

The poet told police he had stayed up late working on his new book of poetry and had fallen asleep at his desk. When he awoke it was nearly 6:00 a.m. and he went to the kitchen to make coffee. At that point, according to Henderson, the children began crying and he went to check on them. He called for his wife to help him, but she didn't answer. Not finding her in bed, he began searching the house, calling her name.

Eventually, he went outside and found his wife's body in the pool. Elizabeth Henderson had a cut on her forehead, and the medical examiner testified it might have come from her falling and hitting her head against the side of the pool. After his wife's death was officially declared an accident, Henderson became the sole recipient of the Swinton millions.

A year later he sold the Oxford house and moved to Huntsville, Alabama with his two children.

Questions still remain about the drowning death of a swimming champion, and the poet who inherited $8 million. Could it be that Clayton Ford Henderson planned and carried out the perfect crime? He certainly had the rhyme and reason for it.

The story continued with two more pages of wild speculation, but I didn't have the stomach to finish it. It seemed to me that Henderson had grounds for a solid libel suit. Still, something didn't feel right, and tiny lights began to flash in my head.

Nineteen

Leaving the cool, tranquil atmosphere of the library, I walked to my car through a series of lengthening afternoon shadows. Sergeant Buck Marrano fell into step beside me.

"Don't you have anything better to do than follow me around town?" Counting our initial confrontation at the church, this was the third time Marrano had surprised me in a parking lot. Our first encounter left me doubled over, sucking wind, and the last time he shocked me with his racist tirade. Even considering the impact of his brother's murder, Buck Marrano struck me as a bully with a vicious streak. Certainly not the kind of person who should be carrying a badge for the City of St. Augustine.

"Ah, man, you better be careful or you'll hurt my feelings." Marrano's face broke into a surprisingly engaging lopsided grin, his sunglasses glinting in the sunlight. "I thought you'd be happy to see a member of the criminal justice system since we're sworn to serve and protect."

"Are you telling me it's a coincidence you bumped into me? Maybe you're here to pay an overdue fine on your coloring book?"

"Funny guy. No, it's not a coincidence. The Chief sent me to give you a message about your friend Poe."

I doubted Chief Conover would ask Buck to deliver messages for him since he's not supposed to be working the case. Horgan probably told his Detective Commander about Eleanor Lawson changing her story, and now Buck wanted to rub my nose in it.

I ignored him, walking the last few steps to my car. The sergeant silently tagged along like one of the shadows dappling the parking lot.

"Okay, let me have it," I said, hoping to rid myself of the gloating detective as quickly as possible. "You want me to know Poe's alibi didn't hold up, and poor Mrs. Lawson was dazed and confused."

"I don't know what the hell you're talking about, Mitchell. It sounds like you're the one who's dazed and confused." He turned his head away and spit on the ground.

"Then what's your message?"

Marrano removed his sunglasses and made a show of taking out a handkerchief and wiping the lenses. Holding them up to the light, he spent another half a minute inspecting them while I fumed, my internal temperature rising by the second.

Finally, he turned to me, still holding the glasses in his hand. "I thought you'd want to know your buddy Poe tried to commit suicide this afternoon."

His statement stunned me. He said the words with little inflection, no emotion. I sagged against the car remembering Wannaker's warning.

"Is he ... did he?"

"Nah, he's not dead, if that's what you're trying to say. Tried to strangle himself, but screwed it up. He tied one of his pant legs around his neck and the other to the top of his bunk. One of the guards heard him thrashing around and got him down before much damage was done."

"Where's he now?"

"They took him to the emergency room to be checked out, but he's back in his cell on suicide watch."

"I'd like to see him."

"You know the rules. No visitors until seven tonight."

I slammed my palm against the car's fender. "Damn it, Marrano, Jeffrey's in bad shape. He needs to see a friendly face."

"Who the hell do you think you are? Poe's a gutless murderer. Are we supposed to change the rules because your friend couldn't live with himself? Too bad he didn't finish the job."

Marrano put on his sunglasses and said, "Guess my job is done. You can take it from here, hoss." After flicking me a mock salute, he turned and walked away.

I sucked in several deep breaths of humid air. Banal thoughts of suicide being a permanent solution to a temporary problem flashed through my head. I closed my eyes for a moment picturing Jeffrey Poe struggling against the knot tightening around his neck. I couldn't imagine the desperation he must have felt, the feeling of total isolation and abandonment. Fortunately he failed, but I knew I had to do something before he tried again.

Twenty

While waiting for the light to turn green at the corner of San Carlos and San Marcos Avenues, I spotted a black Buick LaCrosse swing out from the electronics shop across the street. It pulled into line two cars behind me. I turned away, my mind still rehashing Marrano's revelation about Poe's suicide attempt.

I wanted to reach out and assure Poe he still had the confidence of his friends. That he shouldn't give up. Easy for me to say, but I wasn't the one wearing the orange jumpsuit or sleeping in a jail cell.

I couldn't even imagine a solution to his problems, so I decided to check in with my client. I called Erin Marrano as I drove slowly along Castillo Drive, passing the new Pirate & Treasure Museum. Her phone rang eight or ten times before her recorded voice asked me to leave a message. I didn't want to break the news of Poe's attempted suicide on the phone, so I said I wanted to talk with her and would check back later.

By now I'd passed the statue of Ponce de Leon and turned right onto King Street. Checking my rearview mirror, I noticed the same Buick still behind me. Coincidence? Possibly.

I crept along Charlotte Street hoping to find a parking place close to Henderson's house. St. Augustine's parking situation could cause a nun to swear, but I did my best to concentrate on avoiding exchanging paint with the lines of cars parked on both sides of the narrow street. I passed Henderson's restored home, turned on Bravo Lane and eased into an open parking place in front of a small frame house badly in need of a coat of paint. As I climbed out of my car, the black Buick slid by me so close I saw the driver clearly through the tinted glass. He turned his head away from me as if looking for an address across the street, but I'd have to be blind not to recognize Lem Tallabois.

The man may have been a former New Orleans Police officer, but he knew diddly-squat about moving surveillance. I watched him drive to the end of the street and turn onto Aviles without signaling. Had Laurance sent his boy to keep an eye on me after our conversation in his office?

Suppressing my growing aggravation with the heavy-handed Tallabois, I walked to Henderson's house. Henderson answered the door himself, greeting me enthusiastically, grabbing my arm, and pulling me inside. "Just when I feel like I've been abandoned, what with Jarrod going off, I open my door and find my own gentleman caller. Do you bring me truth in the guise of illusion?"

I looked at him wondering how many of those Anastasia Island Teas he'd sampled. We walked through the hallway arch past a formal dining room with a massive table replete with twelve place settings as if I'd arrived for a dinner party. Although he still used the cane, he didn't seem to have any problems walking.

A small alcove with a fireplace framed the other side of the dining room. Several of Henderson's books of poetry were stacked on the mantle. He gestured for me to sit in one of two vintage chairs covered in gold brocade. A small pedestal table perched between us.

"I'd offer you something to drink, but Jarrod's taken a few days off to visit his uncle in Destin, and I'm shamblin' along as best I can on my own."

"You seem to be doing better."

"It's been a good day. But what brings you back? Have you learned anything that will help Jeffrey?"

He wore a short sleeve, linen guayabera the color of oatmeal and leaned forward on the table as though expecting a kiss.

"Afraid I'm the bearer of bad news."

"What could be worse than finding Bill Marrano's legs and a bloody hacksaw in Jeffrey's shed?"

Hacksaw? I hadn't heard that tidbit before. Henderson could teach the CIA a thing or two about uncovering secrets. I answered Henderson's question simply by saying, "I just learned Jeffrey tried to commit suicide."

His face twisted into a mask of pain, and he hung his head for a moment. "Oh, God. That poor, poor man. He must be utterly crushed to try to end his life. Is he going to be all right?"

"Physically. They got to him before he hurt himself, but knowing Jeffrey, I'm sure he's slipped into a pretty deep funk. It would help if you visited him this week."

"Yes, yes, of course. Anything I can do." Henderson pulled at the patch of hair below his lip before pushing himself out of his chair. "I need a drink. Can I get you something?"

"No, thanks."

He shuffled around the corner without his cane, and returned a few minutes later with two cognac glasses containing a generous amount of liquor. He placed one of the glasses in front of me, but I ignored it.

"I also wanted you to know I visited Kurtis Laurance as you suggested," I told him after he'd settled.

"And were you as taken with him as he is with himself?"

"He's quite a chameleon, full of charm and personality one minute, cold and arrogant the next. But he denied any knowledge of Marrano's death."

"Of course."

"And he seemed to find the idea that Marrano had changed his mind about the project somewhat preposterous."

"You're the detective here, Quint, but would you expect him to say anything else?"

"Funny thing though, Erin, Mrs. Marrano, didn't say anything about her husband changing his mind when I interviewed her yesterday. Said he and Laurance were tight and worked closely together on the project."

Henderson paused, his glass halfway to his lips, and I thought I saw uncertainty creep over his features. He recovered quickly and said, "Guess Bill kept things from the missus. I understand the two of them were sleeping in separate beds." He offered me a droll smile.

"Mrs. Marrano seemed to think her husband didn't care for you very much. Why is that?"

"You're familiar with Hans Christian Andersen?"

"Fairy tales?"

"*The Emperor's New Clothes*. Marrano may have fooled everyone else, but he came from trash and it clung to him like stink on a hound dog."

"That's pretty harsh," I said. "Marrano was a successful businessman and popular enough to be elected to the city commission."

Henderson stared at me, a patronizing smile pasted on his wrinkled face.

"You can be excused for not knowing the man's family history," Henderson said.

"So, enlighten me."

"I take it you've met Brother Buck?"

I nodded.

"I'd say the Marrano family offers ample proof man evolved from apes, but such a statement would be disrespectful of that noble primate species. The Marrano gene pool is rather shallow, and both Buck and Bill took after their grandfather, the infamous *Bat* Marrano."

"I've heard of Bat Marrano."

Henderson took another sip of the cognac, and smacked his lips before continuing. "Our fair city has a storied past, as you know. I'm not talking about the Spanish in the fifteen-hundreds, but our own civil rights' struggles in the nineteen-sixties."

Serena's uncle recently gave me a blow-by-blow account of how those struggles nearly crippled him.

"Unfortunately, St. Augustine became a battleground between blacks and whites," Henderson said. "One side fighting to hold on to an ignominious way of life, the other trying to pull themselves out of the pit of oppression."

"Didn't Martin Luther King come here in nineteen sixty-four?"

"Yes, the summer of St. Augustine's discontent. A time of demonstrations and violence. Not St. Augustine's finest hour, I'm afraid. I wasn't here then, of course, but I understand there were citizens of a more progressive attitude working to cool things down, to give the demonstrators their rights. Unfortunately, other voices were louder. Bigots from far and near were taking a stand for our dear southern values."

"It happened all over the South," I added. "Selma, Birmingham, Atlanta."

"It did. And St. Augustine had more than enough home-grown trouble-makers to roil the waters. Bat Marrano was the worst."

Henderson shifted in his chair and eyed the untouched glass sitting in front of me. I pushed it toward him.

"Do you know how he got his nickname?"

I shook my head indicating I didn't.

"Seems he played semi-pro baseball for a summer or two. Later, as a sheriff's deputy he carved a club from the branch of a water oak, sanded it down to look like a miniature baseball bat. Used it to break heads."

"Charming."

"That's not the half of it. Bat and the other red-neck deputies agitated the citizenry during the sit-ins, the swim-ins, and the Freedom Marches."

"Anything else?"

"He was also a Klan member, and they held rallies at his hunting camp in Palatka. I've been told he was such a good family man he'd bring his grandsons to the rallies. During that summer of nineteen sixty-four, he and his gang of thugs hunted for quarry of the two-legged variety."

While he drained his glass, my mind darted back to Serena and her uncle. Last week, a few days after our disastrous lunch at Stuff of Dreams, she invited me to her apartment and introduced me to her uncle. Walter Howard told me a wrenching story of his involvement in the civil rights struggle of the sixties, how the Klan almost killed him. Henderson's tale of Bat Marrano and his grandsons shed more light on that tragic episode.

"Do you think Erin knew any of this when she married Marrano?"

Henderson's lined face appraised mine for a moment before glancing away. His voice had a brittle edge to it when he answered. "All I know is she married into a family of trailer trash and her husband was murdered. She's better off without him."

I recalled the article I read implicating Henderson for the death of his wife. This might be a good time to rattle his cage and see what fell out. "I guess if we look hard and search deep enough, we can find skeletons in most of our closets."

Understanding sparked in his gray eyes. "Skeletons are natural, aren't they? We all have them," he said. "I would hope that as God's creatures we can forgive an errant sin, but there is no redemption for the violently ignorant and intolerant among us. What was it Doctor King said? 'There's nothing more dangerous than sincere ignorance and conscientious stupidity?'"

I didn't think I'd get much more from him and stood. "Thank you for your time, Clayton. I have a few more stops to make before I visit Jeffrey tonight."

Henderson scraped his chair back, reaching up to the fireplace mantle to steady himself. As he did, he knocked one of the poetry books to the floor.

"Let me." I bent over to pick up *A Flash of Silence*. When I handed it to him he opened it to the page with the title poem. "Have you read any of my poetry, Quint?"

"I have. That one" I pointed to the one where his finger rested.

"I'm afraid I was in a somber mood when I wrote this one." Henderson began to read the second stanza of *A Flash of Silence*.

Now your parting look crowds
this room. I hear
the click of a lock
and the hollow tick of a clock,
long sounds chilling my limbs,
freezing my breath.

He laughed suddenly and gripped my arm. "This could have been titled *Old Man Contemplating Sobriety*. Here, let me offer you a gift." Henderson pulled a pen from his shirt pocket, signed the title page, and handed it to me.

"That's very kind of you."

"Nonsense. I appreciate what you're doing to assist Mrs. Marrano. And Jeffrey, too, of course," he added, as we ambled toward the front door. He paused in the large anteroom and gestured toward a painting of the St. Augustine Lighthouse.

"Have you visited our wonderful lighthouse yet?"

"It's been a while."

"Oh, you really must see what they've done lately. I'd love to give you a personal tour."

I examined the painting closely and noticed the small plaque at the bottom with the inscription *To Clayton Ford Henderson in grateful appreciation of his generous support.*

He watched me read the inscription and laughed. "I'm utterly shameless. I gave the Lighthouse Foundation an obscene amount of money and they practically made me the lighthouse keeper. Gave me my own key." He patted his pocket and I heard the jingle of keys and coins.

"I'd enjoy a tour."

"You'd make an old man very happy." He smiled broadly, dazzling me with yellowed teeth and pink gums.

I thought of something and asked him, "What do you know about Denny Grimes? I heard that Bill Marrano had him fired from his city job."

"Do you think he had something to do with the murder?"

"Anything's a possibility at this point, but I'm just looking for answers."

Henderson shifted his weight onto his good leg, leaning against the doorjamb. "Here's what I know. Grimes supervised the IT department for the City of St. Augustine. Not much of a department really, four or five people. But he must have rubbed the vice mayor the wrong way because he convinced the rest of the city commission that some of the department heads were overpaid and unnecessary. Of course, he meant Grimes, and when they asked him to take a salary cut, Grimes refused and they let him go."

"Huh. And you know the vice mayor was behind this?"

"Everyone knew, especially Grimes."

"Did he do or say anything," I asked.

"There was talk that he made a few threats, but Grimes is a nasty drunk, as you might have guessed, and he tends to talk bigger than he is."

I thanked Henderson for his help and said goodbye.

Pausing outside Henderson's front door, I checked the street in both directions. Sure enough, I spotted my tail. Tallabois had backed into a driveway across the street about three houses away. The driver's window was down and he had his face in a magazine. I slipped around the corner of Henderson's house and cut through a hedge, circled behind his neighbor's house onto Marine Street, and walked quickly around the block.

Tallabois still had his nose buried in the magazine when I edged along the side of the old house. From my angle at the corner of a wraparound porch, I watched him flip through the pages of a *Penthouse* magazine, peering past it at Henderson's house before turning the magazine sideways to get a good look at the pin-up. When he did, I slipped next to the open window.

"Quite a view you have there." I snatched the magazine from his hand and tossed it on to the passenger seat.

"Hey," Tallabois sputtered as he reached for the magazine. I stuck my arm through the window and pulled the keys out of the ignition.

"You make a piss-poor spy, Lem." I held the keys up while he pushed against the door, but I leaned all my weight on it and listened to him curse.

"You sonnuvabitch."

Tallabois' swarthy face reddened and he reared back and threw his shoulder against the door. I stepped aside as he hit the door full force. The door flew open followed by his bulky body. He rolled out of the car awkwardly, his shoulder hitting the paved driveway before he slid forward onto his hands and forearms.

He raised his head to look at me while I dangled the keys above him. "You might need these when you drive back and tell your boss how you screwed up the assignment."

I threw the keys into a clump of azalea bushes in the next yard and ran to my car. At the corner, I turned to see Tallabois searching through the bushes for his keys.

Twenty-One

Serena surprised me with her call last week. After she ran out of the restaurant leaving me confused and angry, I tried vainly to talk with her. She wouldn't return my calls, and she even closed the door in my face when I showed up at her office. Over a beer one night—okay, maybe more than a single beer—I accepted the fact that we'd had some good times, but it was over.

Then came her call inviting me to her apartment the next morning. I arrived ten minutes early. She greeted me at the door with a shy smile, barefoot, dressed in a pale blue blouse and black jeans.

"Thanks for coming, Quint."

She shepherded me into the kitchen where a kettle whistled on the stove, and a glazed navy blue coffee mug sat on the counter. "Would you like some tea?"

"No, I'm fine. Thanks."

I knew she didn't invite me over for tea, and waited for her to get to the point. After a moment, she reached out and touched my arm. "There's someone I'd like you to meet. But first let me tell you a little about my family background. It might help you understand why I reacted the way I did at the restaurant."

"You don't have to explain any—"

"It's important to me," she interrupted. "There's an amazing man in the living room waiting to tell you his story. He's my Uncle Walter, my father's brother."

She went on to tell me both her father and uncle had grown up in St. Augustine, but they moved after her uncle suffered a terrible experience. I tried to get more details, but she put me off, saying, "You'll hear it all from him in a minute. But I wanted you to know the background. After what happened to Uncle Walter, my father left St. Augustine and moved up north."

Eight years younger than his brother, Serena's father moved to Chicago while still in his early twenties. He joined the army and later met Helen Nilsen. He'd been smitten by the lithe blond who seemed like a door into another world to the young man from the segregated South. Her parents had been very much in love, but she said the marriage was doomed from the start. They brought with them a clash of cultures that seemed dangerously romantic at first, but quickly moved into a dark stalemate of quiet bitterness.

Serena grew up not fully accepted by either world. "As a girl, I felt caught in the grip of a cultural tornado. Things were a lot different back then. You have to remember that this was before Tiger Woods and Barak Obama shifted America's view of African-Americans. I tried to cope with attitudes and judgments shaped by something beyond my control."

I pondered that as she pulled a tea bag from a ceramic bowl with a cork stopper, put it in the coffee mug, and poured steaming water over it. I finally said, "It's easy to forget what happened below the Mason-Dixon Line when you grow up in the white bread world of the Connecticut suburbs like I did."

She didn't respond, instead dribbled a long stream of honey into the mug from a plastic container shaped like a bear.

"That's pretty much it for the family history," she told me. "Dad and I moved back to St. Augustine, and shortly after that I went off to college. I returned to St. Augustine after graduating, but it took some time to grow up and accept myself."

We walked into her living room, an open area with a creamy leather couch, a matching wing back chair, and a low coffee table. On the wall over the couch was a triptych painting alive with swirling colors and long-necked birds that never flew anywhere except in the artist's imagination. Sunlight from a pair of sliding glass doors filled the room. An elderly man stood silhouetted in front of the doors, one hand resting on the leather chair. Although his back was to me, judging by his small frame and stooped shoulders, I'd guess he was in his mid- eighties.

She placed the tea on the coffee table before moving behind the old man and tapping him on the shoulder. "Uncle Walter," Serena said, raising her voice and bending close to his ear. "This is Quint Mitchell. The man I told you about."

He turned slowly, pivoting from the waist as though his neck was fused. He smiled shyly at Serena before turning his attention to me through thick lenses and cloudy dark eyes that held mine for a full thirty seconds. The old man's skin had the texture and color of an over-ripe eggplant. A strange discoloring covered the left side of his creased and crinkled face. Pale yellow patches, like bleach dribbled onto a dark towel, spattered his cheek, trickled along his neck, and disappeared under his collar.

I held out my hand, and Walter Howard grasped it tentatively. His hand had the feel of ancient parchment.

"Let's sit down, please." She helped her uncle who hobbled slowly, one hand gripping the chair, the other on Serena's arm. After he sat down and Serena and I were seated on the couch, she turned toward me.

"Quint, I wanted you to hear my uncle's story. He doesn't like to talk about the things he endured while fighting for our people's freedom, but he's doing it as a favor for me." She reached across and laid a reassuring hand on his knee.

Howard's left hand trembled as he lifted it from the arm of the chair and placed it atop his niece's. He licked his lips before speaking. "My name is Walter Howard," he began in a quiet, dignified voice. "I fought for my country in Korea before coming home and teaching school."

Behind the thick glasses, Howard's eyes blazed with the vision of distant memories. "I was young and filled with a hunger for justice. We would gather together in our homes and in our churches to listen to Dr. King telling us change was coming. Dr. King knew our suffering, and we listened when he said our people had been imprisoned for too long. That freedom would wash over us like a giant wave."

Howard slowly bent to pick up the cup of tea with both trembling hands and brought it to his lips.

"Uncle Walter was elected president of the NAACP in nineteen-sixty-three," Serena added.

"It was time for the white folks to give us our rights," Howard said. "St. Augustine still had a plantation mentality. I knew if we didn't demand our rights, these people would never give them to us." He paused and stared at me, possibly wondering if this white man had any idea what he was talking about.

"Back then, the Association was filled with scared old folks who didn't want to rock the boat. The young people were ready, though. They knew what was happening across the south, and didn't want to wait any longer. I pushed the others into taking action."

Throughout 1964, he told me, they organized demonstrations outside McCrory's and Woolworth's stores. Then the sit-ins began, and fifteen, sixteen, and seventeen year olds were dragged from their seats and taken to jail. This led to marches in the heart of the old city, fiery speeches, and swim-ins at white-only beaches.

"We made the national news and got Dr. King's attention. He came here to help us. Sat down with the mayor and the other white leaders and they did a lot of talking. But when Dr. King went home, nothing had changed." Howard paused in his story and looked at his niece. "Nothing had changed," he repeated.

Things got so bad, Howard told us, that he sent his family to live in Daytona Beach to protect them from the hate-mongers. His gaze drifted toward the triptych, tracing the flight of the exotic birds. I guessed he was thinking back to those days. Thinking back, as he would tell me, to how his life had changed abruptly one summer night in 1964.

In a quiet voice, Walter Howard recounted how he returned home from his meeting that night, locked the door on his 1959 Bel Air sedan, and glanced in both directions. He remembered Washington Street as a quiet residential area with modest one-story homes. Most of the homes were already dark, and he didn't notice any strange cars parked along the street. He had promised his wife Aletia that he'd be careful, although he knew there wasn't much he could do if the Klan decided to make him their next target.

As he stood in front of the boarded-up windows of his home and fumbled for the door key, he thought of how his little girl had been nearly killed the night his house was shotgunned. I listened as his memories took him back and he told me about the oppressive humidity on that July night, and a star-filled sky flickering with far-away heat lightning. He remembered the sweet scent of night blooming jasmine and then hearing footsteps pounding the walk behind him.

He said he turned to see four hooded men. The closest one, a man with huge forearms and a massive chest, held a club resembling a miniature baseball bat. The club flew toward his head, and he instinctively jerked away. While he avoided a solid blow, the bat bounced off the side of his head, stunning him, sending flashes of pain coursing through his skull.

Everything happened so fast after that, he said. "One of the men forced a coarse sack over my head. Someone clamped a hand on my mouth, and they dragged me to their car."

"I can't imagine what you went through," I said.

"I did a lot of praying. I knew if they got me into that back seat it would be the last ride I ever took. I tried to fight back. I kicked out at them and managed to put one foot against the doorframe hoping to fight them off. But it was four against one. Next thing I knew, something hit my shin, probably the club, and I was inside the car."

He said they drove for about thirty minutes before the car stopped, and he heard doors opening and felt hands clutching his arms and legs.

They threw him to the ground and pulled the sack from his head. "I expected to see a tree and a rope waiting for me. Instead, I was in a plowed-up field, rows and rows of black soil." In the moonlight, he saw a stand of pines ringing the field. Nearby, he saw a pick-up truck and an old Ford sedan, its back doors hanging open.

"They'd tied my hands together and I couldn't do anything to protect myself. When I started to scream one of the men grabbed me by the neck and forced a dirty rag into my mouth. It smelled of gasoline, so powerful it made me gag." He stopped and held a hand to his mouth. I thought he would be sick.

"Uncle Walter, you don't have to keep talking if it's too painful for you." She rose and put a protective arm around her uncle.

"That's all right, child. I want to tell the story."

Serena retreated to the couch as he continued.

His eyes watering from the gasoline fumes, he blinked away the tears and stared at the men in the white hoods. "I remember thinking that the glow of the moon made the men in their hoods look like the bellies of dead fish," he said.

"And that's when the big man with the bat stepped toward me. He might have had his Klan hood on, but I knew it was that racist deputy sheriff. The one they called Bat Marrano. He gave me a little push with the end of the bat and said, 'You've been shooting your mouth off all summer, nigger. Don't you have nothing to say now?'"

Howard licked his lips and held the mug in both hands, taking comfort, I hoped, from the warmth of the tea.

"I tried to answer him, but with the gag in my mouth I could only grunt. That made them all laugh. One of them called me a monkey and kicked me in the side. After that, they took turns kicking and punching me until I passed out."

I heard quiet sobs coming from Serena. She sat with one hand over her mouth, shaking slightly. I wanted to comfort her. Wanted to say something to her uncle that would bring him relief, but I remained mute, muzzled by my own state of shock.

This time Howard offered solace to his niece. He reached out and patted her knee. "S'alright, girl. It was a long time ago. All them men are dead now, but I'm still here. The Lord does indeed move in mysterious ways."

Serena nodded and offered him a brave smile.

"What happened then?" I asked.

"They woke me up by throwing whiskey in my face. Deputy Marrano was slapping that bat into his hand. He said, 'You know you've got this coming, don't you, boy?'"

"I couldn't answer him, only stare at the club. He tapped it against his shoe like a baseball player knocking dirt from his cleats. I could see he was getting ready to hurt me."

"Oh, God," I murmured. "I'm so sorry."

Howard looked up at me for the first time since he began telling his story. "Even though I knew good men like Medgar Evers had been killed fighting for their rights, I didn't believe it would ever happen to me. I wanted to hold my wife and daughter again, tell them I loved them. I didn't want to die."

He told me he looked at the four men clustered around him, searching for a shred of humanity. But there was no humanity or help to be found. "As I looked at these men, I saw movement behind them. My heart jumped thinking maybe someone had come to save me, but what I saw was two boys back in the shadows near the truck."

"Boys?" I couldn't believe they'd bring children to a lynching.

Howard nodded. "One of the boys was only about six years old. The other one, he might have been twelve or thirteen. The older boy was tall and skinny with long wavy hair growing over his ears. He was bouncing from one foot to the other like he'd been touched by the spirit."

Howard gazed at his niece. "You know what I mean, Serena. Like some of those church ladies carried away by the preacher's sermon?"

She told him she did.

"What happened then?" I asked.

"Bat Marrano saw me looking at the boys, and he waved his club at them. I thought he was chasing them away. But instead he said, 'Which of you boys want to take the first swing?'"

Howard cleared his throat and let his gaze settle between Serena and me. "As soon as Marrano said that, the older boy ran toward us. He stuck his hand out. Marrano gave him the bat and pointed at my left knee.

"I tried to scream, but nothing came out. I watched the boy raise the bat while I shook my head, thinking this child couldn't do such a thing, not even to a black man. I closed my eyes before it hit, but ..."

Howard's voice trailed off, and he placed a hand on his knee as if the pain of that night still haunted him. I suspected that it did.

"When I opened my eyes," Howard continued, "I saw the younger boy, who'd been right behind his older brother, if that's who he was, staring at me like he'd been the one hit in the knee. His eyes were wide, and I almost felt sorry for him. He squawked something I couldn't make out and climbed into the pick-up truck.

"The pain was almost too much to bear," Howard said. "I screamed and cried for Jesus to help me. Of course, my misery made them laugh even harder. I was twisting and rolling when Marrano kicked me in the back. He bent down close to me and said, 'Can you still hear me, Mr. NAACP President? Consider yourself lucky.' He told me they thought about burning me alive or hanging me from a tree, 'But we wanted you to remember this night for the rest of your life.'"

"I knew that was the one true thing he'd said all night. I'd never forget it. Then he said, 'I promise you'll remember us every time you even think about making trouble for your betters.' He lifted the club and swung it down against my other knee."

Howard looked directly at me, his watery stare gnawing at my gut. "I passed out." Then he began sobbing quietly. Serena moved to the arm of the chair and tenderly embraced the frail old man. She held him like a mother holds her child, his head against her breast, a warm reassuring word in his ear.

Twenty-Two

A few minutes later, I thanked Walter Howard for sharing his story with me and said goodbye. Serena walked me to the front door. Her apartment was on the second floor, and I stepped outside onto the long walkway overlooking the parking lot and a circle of palm trees. She sagged against the doorframe, her right hand gripping the knob.

"Thanks for coming."

"Will he be all right?"

She nodded. "It's taken a lot out of him, but he's stronger than he looks."

I wanted to hold her in my arms and tell her how important she was to me. Tell her I understood what she'd gone through and how her family's experiences had impacted her. Warm words of compassion darted erratically in and out of my brain, eluding my tongue and leaving me grasping for the right words.

"Serena, I don't know what to say."

"It's okay," she said. "Listen, I have to drive him home and then get to work."

"Sure. I'll give you a call later."

She hesitated for a moment and it seemed her face stiffened before she answered. "This is going to be a crazy week for me. Lots of meetings. I won't have any time to talk until next week."

I nodded dumbly, searching for confirmation I'd be given another chance to set things straight between us, but she had already closed the door.

Later, I sat in my car and watched Serena and her uncle drive away. The clear skies had clouded over since I arrived and a brisk northeast breeze riffled through the palm fronds overhead. I had the feeling this morning somehow marked the end of a chapter. With the telling of her uncle's violent experience, a page had been turned in whatever story Serena and I were writing together. As she drove away, it felt like we'd written our last page and closed the book.

Until Serena's eruption at the restaurant, I thought that despite our different backgrounds and races, our relationship was growing into something very special. Even as Howard recited his agonizing tale, I let myself believe she'd arranged this meeting because she really cared about me, and perhaps with this new knowledge we might form a stronger bond between us.

Now, as I turned the key in the ignition, I realized I'd been deceiving myself. Our relationship, like so many I'd had in recent years, was over. I've become quite good at reading body language, how to decipher the true meaning hiding beneath a person's carefully parsed words. A look or an unconscious gesture gives them away, and my instincts told me her hidden message was simply, *goodbye, loser*. Howard's story, I saw now, had been shared not to help me understand her better, but because it provided an excuse to end this reckless relationship with her white boyfriend.

At that precise moment, while my head crackled with self-destructive images and echoes of what might have been, my cell phone rang. I turned off the ignition and snatched the phone from the pocket between the seats where I'd dropped it.

"This is Quint," I snapped, without looking at the Caller ID.

A deep rasping breath greeted me. He was back again.

"Listen—" I started to say.

"You listen. Is that too much to ask of the man who ... No, you're not a man. If you were a man you would have done the right thing long ago and blown your goddamn head off." His voice sounded like a rusted nut being wrenched from its bolt. "You're not a man, you're just a thing. A murdering thing that killed my daughter."

Filled with guilt and remorse, I had listened patiently to this sad man's tortured rantings over the past year. His name was Samuel Parks, and before his daughter died he was a vice president with an insurance company in Jacksonville. Now, he only had her memory and his hatred to keep him alive. The phone calls, the bitterness and bile he spewed at me, hadn't brought his daughter back nor brought healing to either of us.

"Listen to me, Mr. Parks, because this is the last time we'll have one of these conversations. I'm sorry your daughter is dead. And I'm sorry I was the one driving the car that night. But get it through your sick head that it was an accident. The police said it was an accident." I felt beads of sweat popping out on my forehead, and realized I was shouting into the phone.

"Calling me every day isn't going to bring your daughter back. Wishing me dead might make you feel better, but it doesn't solve your problems."

"But, why—" He tried to cut in.

"Why?" I growled at him. "Don't you think I ask myself that every day? Why was the light not working? Why couldn't I have left five minutes later or earlier? Why did she have to be on the phone instead of paying attention to the traffic?"

"You have all kinds of excuses, don't you?"

"I don't have any excuses. Can't you see it doesn't help to beat on me? We can't change what happened that night. I've listened to your demented ravings for the last time. It's coming to a stop. Right now! Do you hear me?"

I paused waiting to see what he'd say, but he remained silent, probably stunned by my outburst. But I had more to say.

"Find yourself another therapist because I won't listen to your miserable whining anymore. I've got my own fucking life to lead. Get your own." I slammed the phone closed and threw it on the seat beside me.

I gasped as though I'd sprinted the final lap of a 400-meter race, my chest heaving, sweat pouring from my face. Before pulling away from Serena's, I glanced into the rearview mirror, hardly recognizing the pair of haunted eyes staring back at me.

Twenty-Three

After leaving Tallabois searching for his car keys, I drove across town to Magnolia Avenue hoping to find Erin Marrano at home. The radio was tuned to a Jacksonville classic hits station, and Jimmy Buffet had just realized it was his damn fault he was wasting away in *Margaritaville*. I pulled into Erin's driveway as her silver Lexus came to a stop. Her car door opened and she emerged, turning quickly as she heard my car behind her.

"Mr. Mitchell, I was hoping to hear from you today." There was that smile again, adding heat to the 90-degree day.

Inside her home, we sat in the same pair of Queen Anne chairs. Only this time I faced the bookcases. Three slim volumes were stacked at one end of a middle shelf, and I immediately recognized the distinctive teal book jacket of Henderson's *A Flash of Silence*. A number of framed photographs occupied the shelves. Erin and Bill Marrano in various poses and locales, holding hands, smiling at the camera. Obviously in happier times.

We were nearly knee-to-knee in the two arm chairs, and I caught the musky scent of her perfume. Erin's makeup had been carefully applied, and although the red outline of the hand had faded, there were still traces of the purple bruise on her other cheekbone.

"How's your shoulder?" I asked.

She rotated it slowly, making a tiny pout with her lips. "Still hurts a little, but you didn't come here to talk about my ailments, I'm sure."

"No, I'm afraid I have some bad news."

Her eyes grew wide. "What?"

"Dr. Poe attempted suicide this morning. He tried to hang himself."

"Oh, sweet Jesus."

"Your brother-in-law said the doctors checked him out and he's going to be fine," I said, trying to offset the bad news.

"Have you seen him yet?"

"No visitors until seven, but I plan on going by tonight."

The tip of her tongue slipped hesitantly from between her lips, circling them and leaving a trail of shimmering dampness. I stared, caught in the moment like a rabbit in the glare of an automobile's headlights. She extended a hand, grabbing my fingers tightly and I felt an electric shock course along my arm.

"Tell him something for me, please."

"Of course. Anything."

"Tell him I believe in him. Don't let him give up because I know he'll be found innocent." She said it with such conviction I was almost convinced she could see the future.

"I'm sure it will mean a lot to him, but the evidence is stacking up."

She pulled her hand away. "He's being framed." Again, she seemed so sure.

"We agree on that. But so far all the evidence points to Jeffrey."

"And you haven't found any other possible suspects?"

"There's a man named Denny Grimes who got fired from his job with the city. Some say he blamed your husband."

"Have you talked to him?"

"Not yet, but I'm going to swing by his place today or tomorrow."

She didn't seem too impressed, and asked me, "Anything else?"

"There've been a few interesting theories thrown out, but nothing substantial." I searched for something positive to report. "Mr. Henderson seems to think that Kurtis Laurance might have something to do with it."

Erin shook her head and a strand of hair fell over one eye. She brushed it back. "I don't see how that's possible. Kurtis and Bill were so close."

"Did your husband ever indicate he had second thoughts about Matanzas Bay? Maybe changed his mind?"

"You'd have to know my husband to understand just how stubborn he could be. Once he made up his mind that was the end of it. Where did you hear that?"

"Henderson. He said your husband had called a special meeting to put the project on hold. Suggested Laurance had too much on the line, both politically and financially, so he might have had something to do with your husband's death. Of course, Laurance denied the whole thing."

She didn't respond to Henderson's claim, instead she said, "So, you were able to see Kurtis."

"Thanks to your call. The man has a lot of balls in the air, but he took a few minutes to set me straight on a few things."

"Oh, like what?"

I debated whether to share with her Laurance's implication that Henderson might somehow be involved or what I learned about the old man's past. At this point, I couldn't see how the death of his wife forty years ago had any bearing on Marrano's murder. But I didn't have anything else to go on so I said, "Laurance seems to share your husband's dislike of Mr. Henderson."

"I'm not surprised. Clayton has made his feelings known about the project, and publicly supported Jeffrey on several occasions."

"That's what I thought, but I did a little research on our poet laureate and he seems to have a few skeletons in his closet."

Her face tightened and the blue eyes skewered me. "I don't see what that has to do with my husband's murder."

"Probably nothing. But let's say Henderson was trying to hide something, to protect his legacy—"

"His legacy doesn't need protecting," she snapped.

"And if your husband learned about these … uhmm … improprieties, and threatened to reveal them, then we have a motive for murder." I was making this up as I went along, but it sounded feasible.

Her face colored, and an angry storm front settled over her. "That doesn't make any more sense than Jeffrey killing Bill because of the Matanzas Bay project. I'm sure you're wrong."

"You're probably right, but I want you to know I'm following up on every lead. We'll see where it takes me."

The storm clouds passed as quickly as they appeared. Her face softened, and a hint of a smile formed on her lovely lips. "I'm sorry if I sounded ungrateful. Jeffrey spoke very highly of your abilities. I have complete faith you'll find out what really happened." She placed her hand on mine again, but only for a moment.

Erin looked at her watch. "I'm sorry, but we're having Bill's visitation tonight and I have a few things to take care of before I go."

The scent of her fragrance drifted over her shoulder as she walked toward the front door, distracting me for a moment. When she turned toward me, her breasts brushed across my chest. I stepped back awkwardly. Erin smiled and held out her hand. I gripped it, losing myself in her dazzling eyes and warm smile for a moment.

"Please don't forget to give my regards to Dr. Poe when you see him tonight."

"You can count on it."

I returned to my car with the memory of those warm fingers still tingling against my skin.

Twenty-Four

I still had some time before visiting hours began at the jail. I considered looking up Denny Grimes, but my grumbling stomach directed me back into town. Driving into the old city, I turned onto Cathedral Place just as a car pulled out of a space by the plaza. I slipped into the vacated spot, locked up, and walked across the street to A1A Ale Works.

Sipping on one of their homemade brews, I waited for my burger, and dissected my earlier conversation with Erin Marrano. Something didn't add up. Erin believed Poe was innocent, but she scoffed at any connection with Laurance or Henderson. In fact, she became defensive when I hinted that Henderson might be trying to hide something.

Recalling the slanderous old article about Henderson, I couldn't help but wonder if it had any bearing on my case. It seemed like ancient history—decades ago, hundreds of miles away in Oxford, Mississippi. That's when I thought of Jack Fuller. Fuller was one of my instructors at the DEA Training Center in Quantico, Virginia. I worked out of the Jacksonville District Office for three years before I decided to strike off on my own and earned my PI license.

I liked Fuller from the first time I met him. He had huge, hulking shoulders and looked like he could run a mile with a mule on his back. From his unfortunate overbite and country boy twang many were tempted to write him off as just another hayseed from the sticks. But that would be a mistake. Fuller had a first rate brain, and more than once I saw him spear a wise guy trainee to the wall with a well-aimed tirade.

Fuller now served as Deputy Director of the Mississippi Bureau of Investigation's Special Ops Unit. I checked my watch. 6:05 here but an hour earlier in Mississippi. I stepped out onto the balcony, pulled out my cell phone and called him.

"Special Ops. This is Fuller," he drawled.

"Hey, you old mule-skinner, how they hanging? This is Quint Mitchell."

"Damn, boy, I didn't know you were still alive. Figured one of those cheatin' husbands you snoop after would have carved you up by now."

"So far I've managed to keep my skin intact. How about you? Still chasing after those hog rustlers?" Once we finished the warm-up act, I got down to business.

"I'm working a murder case, Jack, and I've turned up a possible connection to someone who once lived in Mississippi. I thought you might know something about it or check into it for me."

"Who's that?"

"Clayton Ford Henderson. His wife drowned in the family pool about thirty-five or forty years ago. Do you remember?"

"Believe it or not, Quinton, that's before my time." He took great delight in using my given name. "But I do remember my old captain talking about it. He was lead investigator on the case back in the day, and it still gnawed at his behind that they weren't able to pin anything on Henderson."

I told him about meeting Henderson and how he fit into the case. "I read something online about Henderson leaving Oxford with his two children and eight million dollars."

"Went to Huntsville," Fuller replied. "I recall the captain saying Henderson only stayed there long enough to unload the kids."

"What do you mean?" I hadn't read anything about his kids in Roberts' story.

"It was pretty hush-hush, so it took some time before it got back to us. The captain told me Henderson left his kids with an old aunt outside Huntsville. He apparently felt parenthood and poetry didn't mix, and six months later, the aunt passes and the twins wind up with an adoption attorney in Huntsville."

"Christ! He abandoned his own kids?"

"From what the captain said, they were better off without him."

I must confess that in my younger days I spent too much time in arcades watching the little silver balls bounce from bumper to bumper while lights flashed and electronic noises signaled my mounting score. These days, I sometimes felt the insightful flashes of neurons making connections like the silver ball hitting a target. One of those flashes was striking its target now, but I had no idea what it meant.

"Jack, any chance you can find out what happened to his kids?"

"Well, let me check tomorrow's schedule." He took his time and I heard pages being rustled. "No stagecoach robberies needing my attention, so you're in luck. I probably have time to make a few calls. I'll get back to you."

Regina Washington greeted me with an expression so sour I knew we'd passed the donut stage. This called for some serious ass-kissing.

"You got your nerve showing up here again."

"What? I'm here to see my client. You remember, Dr. Poe?"

Regina narrowed her dark eyes, slowly shaking her head. Her black braids fanned out like flower petals around her face. "I shoulda' known better than trust you. Bribin' me with those donuts, and lyin' to my face like I was some junkie in the street."

"But Regina, honey—"

"Don't you go *honeyin'* me, boy. I got a good notion to slap you across the head. You almost got me in trouble with your last trick. That lawyer complained to me after your visit with Poe. Said you weren't part of his defense team and had no reason for being in the Visitation Room."

She had me dead to rights, and I knew it wouldn't do any good to deny it. I hung my head, giving her my little boy look, throwing myself on her mercy. "Jeez, Regina, I'm sorry. Hope I didn't cause too many problems for you."

She held her tongue for a time, and I tried to guess what caliber gun she had in her drawer. Finally, she said, "I talked him down from his pissed-off perch, otherwise the Chief might have chewed on my ass six ways from Sunday." She smiled as if to say, *Yeah, that would happen.*

"I'm sorry, Regina. I promise I'll be straight with you from now on. I owe you Boston creams for life."

"You owe me more than that. So, what you want?"

"I need to see Dr. Poe. He's in bad shape, and needs a friend."

"I should throw you out on your scrawny ass, but you got twenty minutes."

"Great! You're the best."

"Who don't know that? This time, we do it by the book, though, you hear. It's through the glass, like the rule book says."

Five minutes later, a guard with a broad face the color of the beer I'd recently consumed escorted me to the visiting area. Sections of tempered glass bisected the long narrow room. A plywood shelf ran along the length of the window, and a pair of black phones sat on either side of the glass. I waited for Poe to arrive.

Jeffrey Poe entered through the door on the other side of the glass and waved half-heartedly before sitting. We picked up our phones.

"How are you feeling?" What do you say to a person who just tried to hang himself?

"You know that famous medical phrase the doctors are fond of using in place of the truth? About as well as can be expected." His voice rasped as though forced through a long tunnel lined with shards of glass.

I smiled at his attempt to make a joke out of what must have been a horrific experience, and fumbled for something reassuring to say. "I've just left Erin Marrano and she wants you to know she still believes in you. We all do."

Poe's eyes glistened and he brushed them with his free hand. "I'm sorry if I let you down, Quint. You must think I'm a real nut case."

"Not at all. You're under a lot of pressure, I—"

"Pressure," he snorted. "Is that what you call it? You're looking at a man who's been proven guilty without a trial. The only thing I have to live for is five years of appeals before they execute me. I can't live that way. I'd rather end it now." His skin looked nearly yellow under the fluorescent lights. His left eye ticked nervously.

I tried to imagine myself in his position. One day the respected city archaeologist, doing his job, preserving St. Augustine's history, and the next indicted as a psychotic killer.

"Jeffrey, you're not alone. Wannaker is still working hard on your case, and I'm out there following every lead I can."

His eyes were closed, his forehead resting against the glass.

"Someone's gone to a lot of trouble to frame you, but nothing can convince me you killed Marrano."

Poe wet his lips, and his head bobbed up and down, the muscle below his eye still ticking. "That means a lot to me. I appreciate it. Have you found anything yet? Anything at all?"

"I've been busy interviewing people and doing my homework. Unfortunately, it's going to take some time, but don't give up. I know something will break."

"Sure, something will turn up."

"Listen, Jeffrey, I know you were counting on Mrs. Lawson's testimony to back up your story, but it probably wouldn't have helped."

Poe raised a hand as though about to gesture or rub his face and I waited for him to say something. The hand hung in the air for a moment, fingers trembling slightly, before it dropped in his lap.

"Before the prosecutor finished with her, the poor woman would be so confused she'd have zero credibility with the jury. I'm sorry, but that's the way these things work."

"I guess you're right, but wouldn't you think that after all the years I've lived here and devoted myself to this city ... wouldn't you think it would count for something?"

"It does, and in the end a lot of people will have to apologize to you. But right now—"

"Right now it doesn't look too good."

"Yeah. And they're doing their best to paint you as someone with extreme anger management issues."

"That's bullshit."

"You and I know that, but when the general public reads you were once arrested for aggravated assault they may wonder."

"Aggravated assault? You mean that old charge from my college days? That was a load of crap."

"So, there's nothing to it?"

Poe's eyes grew wide, the ticking even more noticeable now. "You're goddamn right there's nothing to it." He slammed a palm against the glass, and the guard stepped forward, his hand moving toward the baton on his belt.

I waved off the guard, indicating everything was okay.

"Relax, Jeffrey or he'll take you back to your cell." He shifted his eyes toward the guard and raised a palm to show he meant no harm. The guard shuffled back to his spot by the door.

"It happened at a fraternity party in college. A couple of drunks got into a fight, and one of them hit the other with a beer bottle. I tried to break it up and got into the middle of a free-for-all." Poe blinked twice trying to stop the tick that had moved into high gear.

"The police came and arrested everyone, and I was initially charged with the others. It was a big mistake and they eventually dropped the charge after hearing from all the witnesses. I can't believe they dredged up that old story."

I shrugged my shoulders as if to say, *what do you expect?* "I'm glad you cleared that up. I'll pass it along to Wannaker and he'll make sure it doesn't pop up in any more stories."

"Is there anything else?" Poe asked.

"I'm planning to attend tomorrow night's special city commission meeting."

"What for?" For the first time his eyes flickered with life.

"Henderson seems to think Marrano called the meeting because he'd changed his mind about the Matanzas Bay project. I know there's probably nothing to it, but I'd like to hear what they have to say."

Poe stared through the glass as though waiting for me to continue, to offer him some possibility of hope. When I didn't add anything, he sighed deeply and let his forehead fall against the glass again.

Twenty-Five

The next morning I spent some time in the office trying to whittle down the stack of skip traces piling up. Charla was at the county courthouse prowling through public records on a couple of cases, while I held down the fort. I made good progress, working steadily for three hours, before taking a break to pour myself another cup of coffee. That's when the phone rang.

"Mitchell Investigative Services."

"Shit, son, that sounds real official."

"Hello, Jack. One day you need to get out here and I'll show you how a real investigative agency works."

Fuller brayed into my ear. "You need to take that routine on the road, boy."

"Have anything new for me?"

"Like I told you before, Henderson left the twins with his aunt and before the year was out the kids were up for adoption. He apparently signed them over to a shyster by the name of Sternwald. Lester Sternwald. At one time, Sternwald was legit, although small time. He handled adoption cases, but somewhere along the line he ran up a huge gambling debt. The bookies threatened to realign his spine and he decided to make some quick money with an adoption scam."

"Hmm. I take it he didn't get away with it."

"Ended up wearing a state-issued jumpsuit."

"So, what happened to Henderson's kids?"

"It looks like his daughter, Amelia Faye was her name on the birth certificate, was adopted by a couple in the area."

"And the son?"

"Christopher Henderson didn't make it. A note in the file said Sternwald reported the boy died of ..." I heard pages being turned, "... complications from scarlet fever when he was eighteen months old."

I still found it hard to believe Henderson cast away his children like giving his old clothes to Good Will. "Henderson doesn't strike me as that kind of person," I said.

"Yeah?"

"You have to meet him to understand. He's a charming old guy filled with personality. Great storyteller. The kind of guy you'd want to have a few beers with."

"Sounds like you two hit it off. Be sure to send me a card when you announce the engagement."

"I mean, there must have been something else going on. Maybe he had a nervous breakdown after his wife died and couldn't take care of them."

Silence greeted me for almost twenty seconds before he responded. "Sure, or maybe he didn't give a rat's ass for the twins. He had his wife's eight million. The two kids were just extra weight."

"I don't know," I said. "How much time did Sternwald get?"

"He served sixteen months and got time off for good behavior. Then he went back to Huntsville and did some small time paralegal stuff since he lost his bar license."

"Is he still around? I'd like to talk with him."

Fuller snorted. "Funny you should ask. The world's a better place with one less lawyer. Mr. Sternwald was beaten to death behind a strip club about a year ago."

Later that day I returned to St. Augustine under a darkening sky. A nasty weather front was rapidly approaching from the northeast, and dark circles of threatening thunderclouds were forming like a mob of vigilantes in a vicious mood.

Fuller's conversation flitted through my head as I drove. Sternwald must have been a sleaze ball of the first order. Any number of people must have celebrated the news of his passing. Still, I wondered if his death had any connection with Henderson.

What if Henderson had a late-life conversion and wanted to make amends for his daughter and deceased son? Perhaps a twisted sense of guilt caused him to blame Sternwald and he had the attorney killed to even the score. Maybe there lurked an evil streak beneath his aura of charm and genteel sophistication. The links to Henderson may be coincidence, but coincidence can only be pushed so far in my mind and too many trails seemed to be leading me back to the old poet.

Henderson's connection was only speculation at this point, but Denny Grimes was another story. He apparently had a strong motive for killing Marrano, and he struck me as a hot head with a mean streak. I'd looked up Grimes' phone number and address before leaving the office. I called him and asked if it would be okay to drop by and talk a little business. I may have given him the impression that I was interested in setting up a website, and he told me to come over.

Grimes lived in an old two-story house near De Haven Street, just south of the historic district. At his front door, I listened as heavy metal shook the windows. Metallica, maybe. The image of Poe's near-death experience returned, and for a moment I saw him hanging from his bunk, orange jumpsuit coiled around his neck, squeezing the life out of him as he jerked to the raucous rhythms of the band. Let Grimes be the one, I told myself before knocking on his door.

After a minute I knocked again. Louder. The music faded away and the door opened.

"Hey, dude. Didn't take you long to get here. Come on in."

Grimes wore a pair of blue running shorts and an orange polo shirt hanging loosely over his hips. We entered a spacious living room with a twelve-foot high ceiling. It was surprisingly neat, although the furniture was dated. I'm not into antiques, but several pieces looked like they may have some value.

"This used to be my mother's house," he said. "She died a few years back, and I moved in. You want to see my office?"

He padded away before I could respond. I followed him into a long hallway with several rooms on either side. We passed an open door and I spotted a large four-poster bed. Another room was bare except for some plastic storage tubs and a set of weights. His office was a dimly lit twelve by twelve room with a threadbare oriental rug covering the hardwood floor. Three computers, two Dell PCs and an iMac with a large monitor, were lined up on an eight-foot folding table; their power cords neatly bundled with plastic ties. Along with two filing cabinets and a bookcase, the room had four speakers mounted in each corner connected to a compact audio system. A tall rack of cd's hovered over the components.

"This is where the magic happens," he said with a sweep of his arm. "I already have some great ideas for your website. Man, you'll be amazed what this will do for your business. Quint Mitchell, super PI."

Grimes grinned and spread his arms over his head as though unveiling a banner advertising my business. I almost hated to tell him why I was really there. Almost.

"Denny, I'm not here to talk about a new website."

"You're not? But I thought you said—"

"Maybe I misled you. I needed to talk to you about William Marrano's murder."

He stiffened, his mouth working like a fish out of water. "What the hell," he sputtered. "What the hell, man. Do you think I had something to do with that jerk-off's death?"

"I didn't say that, Denny. I'm just following up on all possibilities. That includes talking to people who might have had a motive for—"

"You're full of shit if you think I had anything to with killing Marrano. Poe's the man, isn't he?"

"I don't believe Poe killed Marrano, and neither does Marrano's wife. She hired me to help find who did it."

"You can believe what you want, but you're not laying this on me."

Grimes' arms were at his side, fists clenched. His knees were slightly bent, making him even shorter, and I eased one leg behind the other, adjusting my body weight, in case he charged me. He may have been eight inches shorter than me, but he was compact and muscular. I'd seen the damage some of these small guys could do when you pissed them off.

"Cool down, Denny. No one's accusing you of anything. I've been talking with a lot of people. Someone is framing Jeffrey Poe and I'm just looking for leads."

"I should lead you out the front door. After I kick your ass for lying to me." He scratched at his bearded chin, and I heard him inhale, his chest rising and falling.

"Hey, I'm sorry about lying. I just want to talk."

Some of the tension seemed to leave his body. "So let's talk."

We returned to the living room where he dropped into a large easy chair. I sat facing him on a high-backed couch covered with a faded floral design and matching pillows.

"Sure, I had a hard-on for Marrano," he said. "The prick got me fired. I'd been with the city for twelve years. Worked my way up to head of the IT Department."

"Why did he have you fired?"

"You want the official reason? Gross insubordination. Failure to follow city guidelines. Fucking goats on city time. You name it. It was all bullshit." Grimes glared at me, all the while pressing one hand down against his other hand, doing some kind of isometric exercise while he talked. The muscles in his forearms bunched and corded like strands of steel cable.

"So tell me the real reason."

He thought about it for a few seconds, his face going slack. "I'm not sure. Guess the piss ant just didn't like me."

"Come on," I said, "there must be more to it than that. What was the last thing you worked on?"

"Marrano asked me to pull together everything in our system on a piece of property the city owned."

"You mean the property the St. Johns Group bought?"

"No, I'm talking about Ripley's Believe It or Not. What the hell do you think?"

I ignored his sarcasm and asked, "What did he want to know?"

"How long had the city owned it. How much we paid for it. Other real estate surrounding the city's property. He wanted to know the entire history of the site, whether any toxic chemicals had been stored there. What had been on the property before we bought it? Like I said, everything I could find."

"This doesn't sound like a job for IT."

His eyes met mine, narrowed. His shoulders hunched as he leaned forward. "You think I'm just some button pusher? All hardware and no software? I have lots of smarts, asshole. Probably a higher IQ than you." The tone of his voice told me this was one of Denny's hot buttons. *Poor little man, underestimated and underappreciated.*

"Sorry, I didn't mean to imply anything," I said.

"My job was more than showing screw-ups how to use their email or loading new software into the computers. Before I took over the IT department, I coordinated a project to gather information files from every department and construct a central database. It took us almost three years."

He puffed out his chest and thrust his jaw up in the same defiant gesture I'd seen at Poe's house.

"That was it? You ran a report on the old motor pool property and they fired you?"

"Pretty much. Remember this was before the city announced they were going to sell the property, but I'd heard the scuttlebutt. Hard to keep secrets in city hall. I figured Marrano's a real estate guy, right? He was probably looking for a way to cash in. He knew the area would take off after the developers began turning dirt."

"Seems like Marrano could have found this out himself since that's his business."

"That's what I thought, so I asked him."

"What did he say?"

"Asshole gets all huffy with me. Tells me it's none of my business. I might have said a few things back to him in my defense. Next thing I know, Mayor Hal comes to me and says they're cutting my budget and I have to take a twenty-five percent pay cut."

"That's pretty steep."

"You think? They weren't paying me a hell of a lot to start with. I told them to go fuck themselves. Well, not in those words, of course. Next thing I know, I'm out on my ass." Grimes released his hands and settled back in the chair, his legs dangling inches above the floor.

"Sounds like you got royally shafted," I said. "Are you sure Marrano instigated your early retirement?"

"Had to be. So, yeah, I didn't exactly grieve when I heard the news Poe had killed him. He did us all a favor."

"Except Poe didn't do it."

Grimes attempted to stare a hole in my face before breaking into a lopsided smirk. "Loyalty is one thing, Mitchell, but you're setting yourself up for a big disappointment."

"How so?"

"I'm just saying that Poe's the man, whether you want to believe it or not."

I've interviewed hundreds of people in my job. Maybe thousands. After listening to so many people, hearing their excuses, absurd alibis, and bald-face lies, I've developed a pretty good bullshit detector. Most liars are easy to spot. Body language, facial expressions, even eye movements give them away. Grimes was telling the truth.

"You seem pretty sure that Poe killed him. Almost like you know something."

Grimes folded his arms across his chest and remained silent. I saw his face shift imperceptibly, lips pursing as though running a search program through his head, finding the data he was seeking, and deciding whether to tell me or not.

After a minute of silence, he finally said, "I'm an insomniac, okay. Sleep about three hours a night. Helps me get a lot of work done while the rest of the world is sleeping."

"Okay," I said, not sure where this was leading.

"When I get tired of playing with my computers I run. You probably didn't know it, but I've run a few marathons; even did a triathalon last April."

Grimes knew how to milk the moment, build the suspense. "Go ahead," I said.

"I love to run through the old city in the middle of the night. No sun. No traffic. I hardly ever see anyone, but Sunday morning I did."

He held my gaze, expecting a response from me. I didn't disappoint. "You saw someone Sunday morning. What time and where?"

"I like to vary my route. Makes it interesting," he said, ignoring my questions. "Sometimes I run along the bay front all the way up to the Visitor's Center and back. That's a great run. Sometimes I run through the center of the district, right in the middle of the street, not having to worry about traffic or those damn horse carriages."

I tried again. "And on Sunday morning?"

He nodded to let me know he was getting to it. "The moon was nearly full, made it easier to see, which was why I selected the historic run, turning and twisting through the side streets instead of the main thoroughfares. It was about three-thirty in the morning and I was running full out along Cordova, not another soul around. I turned right onto Hypolita down by Scarlet O'Hara's, raced through St. George Street, then Cathedral Place, my breathing steady and—."

"I get the picture, Denny. You're one running stud. Get to the point."

Grimes jumped off the chair, and I thought he was going to do something foolish. I was right.

"Hey, watch this," he said.

Grimes dropped to the floor and proceeded to do one-armed push-ups. He did fifteen of them before standing and displaying his bicep to me. "I can do that all day," he said.

"Very impressive. Let's go back to why you believe Poe killed Marrano."

He smiled, all of his facial muscles stretching. A liar has a hard time with facial expressions. Their muscles tense up and a smile is obviously forced, using just their mouth rather than the entire face.

"Right. You know where Artillery Lane intersects with St. George?"

"Sure."

"There's the Parish Hall, a parking lot, and that fenced in area."

"Uh huh."

"Here's the part you've been waiting for. I was hoofing it past the fenced area, heading toward the bay when I saw him."

"Saw who?"

"Poe. Haven't you been following me?"

"Back up a minute. Where was he exactly and how do you know it was Poe?"

"He was behind the wall walking away from me toward your survey site. He probably heard my feet pounding the street, but he kept walking. A tall guy, carrying a shovel. One of the long-handled kind." Grimes' head bobbed a few times, and he shrugged as if that was the end of it.

"Let me see if I understand this. You're hoofing it behind the church and you see a tall man walking away from you carrying a shovel. It's the middle of the night. You don't even see his face, but you know it's Poe. Do I have it right?"

Grimes did his jaw-jutting trick again. "Glad to see you've been paying attention. Sure it was the middle of the night, but like I said, there was a moon and there are street lamps every hundred feet or so. And yes, I know it was Poe."

"What makes you so sure if you didn't see his face?"

"You know that big, floppy hat Poe always wears at his digs?"

I nodded, fearful of what he would say next.

"He had it on that night. No mistaking it. And I've never seen anybody else with a hat like that."

Twenty-Six

Standing on Grimes' front porch I listened as the heavy metal music resumed, an amped up guitar and gruff voice blasted from the house. I wondered if Grimes was doing his one-armed pushups again.

Across the street, a neighbor watered a leggy hibiscus while a pair of Yorkies ran along the edge of his lawn yammering in my direction. The man cut his eyes toward me and back to the hibiscus.

I felt sick to my stomach. Pain shot through my abdomen as I thought about what Grimes had told me. Could I have been so wrong about Poe? Had he been playing me for a fool this entire time? Maybe Buck Marrano was right about why Poe tried to kill himself.

I thought about all the dead ends I'd been pursuing, wondering why I couldn't find evidence of anyone else's involvement when the answer might have been sitting in a jail cell the whole time. Once again, I let my mind scroll through the details of Grimes' eyewitness account. He may not have been lying, but that didn't mean Poe was the man he saw. Grimes made an assumption based on seeing a tall guy wearing a hat similar to Poe's. Poe is an inch or so shorter than me, but Grimes is five-foot six. To him, most men might seem tall.

I decided I should trust my own instincts and not give up on my friend. It would take more than Grimes' early morning sighting to convince me Jeffrey Poe was a murderer. And I still wanted to question Henderson about his connection with Sternwald, the adoption attorney. But I made a mental note to ask Poe about the hat next time I saw him.

My meeting with Denny Grimes put me behind schedule. The St. Augustine City Commission meeting had already started. I drove through the historic district searching for a parking place before I found one around the corner from city hall. I ducked inside just as the first raindrops began falling. Upstairs, in the Alcazar Room where the St. Augustine City Commission held their meetings, I located a seat in the back near the door and gazed around the crowded room until I spotted Lemuel Tallabois staring at me. Tallabois leaned against the wall near the railing separating the commissioners from the common folk. His eyes were glued on mine and one corner of his mouth curled upwards in a smirk. As I watched, he slowly raised his right arm and pointed his forefinger at me, cocking his thumb like the hammer on a pistol.

I ignored Laurance's thug and turned my attention to the meeting, which had already started. The commission normally met on the second and fourth Mondays of the month, but William Marrano apparently called this special meeting the week before his death. Henderson seemed to be the only one who thought Marrano had a change of heart about Matanzas Bay, but I was still curious about tonight's meeting.

"Vice Mayor Marrano will be missed by all of us for his passion to make our city a great place to live," Mayor Hal Cameron intoned. Cameron, a rotund, florid-faced man with a dark thatch of hair that did everything but scream *toupee*, wore a string tie over his navy blue polo shirt. He squinted at his notes. "Bill realized we were taking a radical departure from the way things had been done in the past and he called this special meeting, with my blessing, to reinforce the commission's decision backing the St. Johns Group and the Matanzas Bay project."

He paused and turned to the other commission members. Receiving confirming nods, he continued. "This commission has the utmost confidence in the St. Johns Group. Matanzas Bay will be a lasting tribute to the vision of William Marrano."

Cameron looked up from his notes and stared into the audience. I followed his gaze, and for the first time saw Kurtis Laurance sitting in the front row several seats from where Tallabois stood.

"Now, I believe Mr. Laurance has an announcement he'd like to make," the mayor said. "Please step up to the lectern, Mr. Laurance. We all know who the next governor of Florida will be and where he lives, but state law dictates you must identify yourself for the record."

Polite laughter and applause greeted Cameron's remark as Laurance walked to the lectern. After stating his name and address for the record, he said, "Mr. Mayor, commissioners, thank you for this opportunity to speak to you and all of the citizens here tonight."

"First, I want to thank the commissioners for their confidence in the St. Johns Group, and assure you Matanzas Bay will make everyone proud they live in St. Augustine. Like you, I am deeply troubled and saddened by the death of Mr. Marrano. I considered him as more than a visionary and a true community servant. He was a friend, and he will be sorely missed."

He waited while the commissioners nodded their agreement and the murmurs of assent faded behind him. "Mayor Cameron and I spoke earlier today, and he has graciously allowed me to make this announcement."

Cameron smiled boyishly and made a kind of *aw shucks* head bob.

"As you know, the St. Johns Group is constructing a riverwalk as part of Matanzas Bay. In tribute to the passion and persistence the vice mayor demonstrated in his support of this project, I am proud to announce it will officially be named the William A. Marrano Riverwalk."

The entire audience and the commissioners jumped to their feet and applauded Laurance's announcement. Even the reporters from the St. Augustine and Jacksonville media followed suit. After the celebration died down, the mayor thanked Laurance, practically bowing before him, and plugged Saturday's groundbreaking ceremony.

"Everyone is invited to the Malaga Street site for the groundbreaking this Saturday morning at ten. The St. Augustine High Jazz Band will perform and we'll have free refreshments. Of course, you'll have to listen to a few speeches first, but we'll keep it short since Mr. Laurance is itching to get started."

Outside, the wind rattled the windowpanes and I heard the muffled rumbling of thunder in the distance. Mayor Cameron glanced up at the high ceiling and then back to his constituents with a grin. "Surely, that's Bill Marrano giving his enthusiastic blessing to this project."

After they adjourned, I waited while the crowd filed out of the room. Sitting there, I thought about what I'd just witnessed. It had been nothing more than a public proclamation of support for Laurance, along with a fond farewell for Marrano. Thinking the evening had been a waste of my time, I prepared to exit the room only to find Tallabois blocking my way.

"Hoped I'd run into you again. Just didn't think it would be so soon," Tallabois said, his scarred face inches from mine.

I held my ground. "Figured you'd still be rooting through the azaleas hunting for your keys."

"Boy, you better rethink your attitude or you're in for some serious aggravation." He jabbed a finger into my chest to make his point.

"Don't do that," I told him.

"You're out of your league here, and I'm only giving you this one last warning." Tallabois' nose almost touched my own, and he poked his stubby finger into my chest again.

I thrust my hand up before he had a chance to remove his finger. With my thumb braced against his metacarpal joint, I pulled his finger back. This forced Tallabois to twist away trying to alleviate the pressure on his finger.

"I told you not to do that again."

"You're breaking it," he managed to gasp through contorted lips.

"Did you know there are twenty-seven bones in your hand, and it takes four to six weeks for a fractured finger to heal?" I increased the pressure and Tallabois went down on one knee.

"Boys, this isn't the time or place to be playing your macho games." Kurtis Laurance tapped me on the shoulder. "Let him go, Mitchell, I want to talk with you for a minute."

I released Tallabois' finger and stepped back. Clutching his hand, Laurance's security chief got to his feet. Nostrils wide, face flushed, he attempted to rush me, but Laurance put a hand on his arm and stopped him. Several members of Laurance's entourage stood to the side, their eyes wide with shock.

"Lem, let's say this game was rained out and call it a night. Go down and bring my car around for me."

Tallabois ignored Laurance, edging toward me, his jaw muscles working furiously.

"I mean it, Lem. Go get the car." Laurance barked out the order with an angry edge to his voice. He turned to the other two men standing nearby. "Why don't you go down with Lem? I want to have a word with Mr. Mitchell here."

Tallabois brushed my shoulder as he passed. The others followed him out of the room.

"I'm sorry about that," Laurance said after Tallabois had left. "Lem sometimes lets his testosterone overcome his common sense, I'm afraid."

"You might want to keep a tighter leash on your dog."

"You may be right. Walk with me to the elevator, won't you, please, Quint."

"That was quite a love-in for your company," I said, referring to the meeting.

"It must be apparent to you by now that you were the victim of bad information."

"Apparently."

"I tried to tell you Bill Marrano would never renege on a deal, particularly this one. Matanzas Bay was as much his concept for the future of St. Augustine as it was mine. Whoever told you he'd changed his mind was feeding you a load of crap. Probably self-serving crap."

"Maybe."

"I've lived in St. Augustine off and on for many years, Mr. Mitchell. Like all small towns, we have our share of good people who only wish the best for their community and act accordingly. Human nature being what it is, unfortunately, there are others who seem to delight in sowing the seeds of discontent."

We paused in front of the elevator. He pushed the button for the first floor and turned toward me, his dark eyes twinkling under the overhead fluorescents. "And sometimes it's difficult to tell one from the other."

"I wonder why they wanted me to believe Marrano had changed his mind?"

The elevator door slid open, but Laurance wasn't moving. He answered my question with one of his own. "Have you been to the Matanzas Bay construction site yet?"

"I've driven by, but I haven't given it a white glove inspection if that's what you mean."

"Do me a favor and walk around it before our ground-breaking ceremony Saturday. I want you to pay special attention to the property outside the construction fence."

I wasn't sure what he meant by this strange request. Laurance must have sensed my puzzlement because he said, "Humor me. After you have a chance to visit the site, we'll talk again. I'm interested in your impressions, plus I've been thinking about what you said concerning Tallabois." He shook his head as though he'd changed his mind about sharing something with me. "We'll talk later," he said, and we entered the elevator.

I emerged from city hall to a persistent rain. The black skies told me the storm front had settled in for the night. I sprinted through the downpour to my car parked around the corner, watching the drops splash on the brick-lined sidewalks. Above me, overhead arc lamps cast a saffron hue over the city.

Once inside my car, I used a handkerchief to wipe my dripping face, then pulled the phone from my coat pocket. I had turned it off before entering the city commission meeting, and when I powered it up, the phone beeped twice indicating I had a message. I retrieved the message and listened to Henderson's strained voice.

"Quint, meet me at the lighthouse at seven tonight. Please, it's important."

There was none of Henderson's gentleman-of-the-manor Southern charm in the message. Instead, I detected a sense of urgency. Possibly even fear. Then again, Henderson might be setting me up. If my paranoid theories were correct, and Henderson was somehow involved in Marrano's and Sternwald's murders, he might be afraid I was close to uncovering the truth about his role in all of this.

It was nearly eight, and I figured Henderson was long gone. Or perhaps he was waiting to ambush me. I weighed the odds on my Mitchell Risk-Taking Scale and decided to take the risk.

Twenty-Seven

I made several wrong turns on the narrow roads as I approached the St. Augustine lighthouse, my eyes scanning the muddy sky for the telltale beacon flashing every thirty seconds. The drenching shower that greeted me when I left city hall had erupted into a full-blown thunderstorm with fiery spider webs of lightning fracturing the night sky. Florida leads the nation in deaths and injuries caused by lightning. Knowing this didn't give me much solace as I parked my car under the trees next to the visitor's center and watched the pounding rain turn the unpaved parking area into a swamp.

The museum and lighthouse normally closed at six, and I seemed to be alone in the parking lot. I flashed my high beams and peered through the fogged windshield hoping to see Henderson on the porch of the visitor's center. No sign of life anywhere. Instead of mucking around in the storm, I circled the parking lot until my lights reflected off a gray Passat GLX half hidden behind a giant philodendron.

Someone parked the Volkswagen next to an exit path leading from the lighthouse to the parking lot. I surveyed the empty Passat before turning my attention to the rain-cloaked lighthouse, the top half draped in storm clouds and nearly invisible. Every thirty seconds the fixed flash illuminated the entire structure and I had a perfect view of the barber-striped tower.

I tapped the car horn twice not expecting a response and not getting any. If the Passat belonged to Henderson he may be inside the lighthouse where he couldn't see or hear me. I slipped off the expensive sport coat I'd worn to the commission meeting and tossed it into the back seat. Unlocking the glove box, I pulled out the Maglite and noticed the Smith & Wesson I kept there for emergencies. It was a standard issue Model 10 service revolver with a four-inch barrel.

There had been many times during my career as a private investigator that I'd rather forget. Unpleasant cases, emotional clients, and uncomfortable surveillances. But except for a California case where a maniac off his meds attacked me, I've never felt personally threatened. I'm not anti-gun, but I rarely carry one.

Thinking back to what I learned about Henderson's past, of Sternwald's and Marrano's murders, I figured it was better to be safe than dead. I pulled the revolver from the glove box and tucked it into my waistband.

Taking a deep breath, I pushed the door open, ran to the Volkswagen, and shined the flashlight through the windows. Inside, I saw a stack of papers cluttering the back seat. It reminded me of the mess in his office. In case there was any doubt, Henderson's black walking cane with the sterling silver lion's head handle lay on top of the pile of papers.

Turning toward the open gate, I yelled, "Clayton, are you here?"

Along with the rain, the wind had picked up, sweeping in across Salt Run and carrying with it a sour odor of rotting foliage and swamp gas. My shirt and pants quickly soaked through, and water seeped into my shoes. A shiver coursed up my back and along my arms even though the temperature probably hovered in the mid-eighties.

With the drumbeat of thunder echoing in the distance, Henderson's poem came to mind. I mumbled the last lines of the second stanza as water flowed down my face.

"... long sounds chilling my limbs,
freezing my breath."

Pushing through the gate, I swept the Maglite in an arc ahead of me to be sure I didn't trip over anything. Every thirty seconds the lighthouse flashed its nightmark, stabbing orange horizontal beams across the sky like the cross arms of a radiant crucifix. In the beam's glow, I saw the red-topped lens room and the observation deck below it.

"Clayton, it's Quint," I bellowed as I approached the base of the tower. A small cottage-like structure served as the entrance to the lighthouse. Half of it was once the lightkeeper's office and the other half used to store the lard and kerosene fueling the old lamps before electricity and automation took over.

A low wall of red brick surrounded the lighthouse grounds, and on the other side a thicket of live oaks and pines cast gloomy shadows each time the nightmark flashed. I hurried toward the entrance, rain whipping my eyes with each step. A cyanic shaft of light split the sky and disappeared into the trees, followed immediately by an explosive crack of thunder. My ears rang from the blast and my heart pounded in my chest from the near miss.

I paused at the door leading into the tower's spiral staircase. Henderson told me he'd been given the key to the lighthouse. If it was locked he probably had come and gone. Perhaps he met someone else here and left with them, which would account for his car still sitting in the lot. He may have thought it important to meet me here, but I couldn't imagine him still waiting for me in this weather, especially since I was an hour late.

The lighthouse door was unlocked. I unlatched it and shouldered it open, shining the light inside. "Hello," I called out, pointing the Maglite up the stairs. "Is anyone here?"

Wind whipped through the trees. The clatter of rain slapping against the roof of the lightkeeper's office made it difficult to hear, but I thought I heard a far-away sound like a muffled groan.

Stepping onto the staircase, I yelled out in frustration, "Clayton, where the hell are you?"

My words reverberated around the tower. Listening again for a reply and hearing only the storm's fury, I guessed the noise I heard must have been the wind sweeping through the top of the tower. I briefly considered climbing to the top, but what was the point? Henderson wouldn't be playing hide and seek games. Besides, I couldn't see him climbing those stairs so soon after his knee operation.

I called his name once more. Still no reply. Frustrated and dripping wet, I decided to call it a night. If it was so damn important he could track me down tomorrow.

Opening the lighthouse door, I peered into the gloom, preparing to dash into the torrential downpour. I only made it to the bottom of the steps when a lightning bolt cracked loudly thirty feet away in the copse of trees behind the lighthouse. "Christ," I sputtered as my heart jumped into high gear.

I edged along the side of the tower drawn by the lightning bolt. I stepped out into the rain, staring at the dark patch of trees behind the tower, wondering which of them had been struck. We had an old hickory tree in our backyard in Connecticut. I remember how my father had rigged a swing to its branches when my brother came along. He enjoyed that swing for nearly a year before the tree was blasted by lightning during a storm and died soon after.

A squawking noise above me caught my attention. Looking up just as the nightmark flung its ghostly ochre light across the murky sky, I saw a dark form hurtling toward me. Arms outstretched, legs flailing wildly, Clayton Ford Henderson plowed into the ground just a few feet from where I stood.

I gaped from the broken figure crumpled at my feet up to the vacant observation deck and back to Henderson's body. Henderson's arms were tucked beneath his body as if he tried to break his fall, and one leg pointed toward his head like a contortionist's trick.

I edged closer, my Maglite sweeping over him. The left side of his face was imbedded in the soggy dirt. His guayabera shirt, the same one he wore when I last saw him, blossomed with an ever-growing pool of blood spreading out from his body and soaking into the ground below him.

As I bent over Henderson's body, my imagination conjured the sound of mournful prayers and the gleam of candlelight dancing in the trees. His body seemed to twitch in the rain, and I half expected him to sit up and quote me another line of poetry. But I knew it was all illusion. Clayton Ford Henderson had written his last poem.

What were his final thoughts? He must have wrestled with inner demons too fierce to live with. Maybe the knowledge of how he'd treated his two children was too much for him to bear. I'd never know.

A wave of guilt swamped over me. If I hadn't gone to the city commission meeting I would have received Henderson's call. If only I'd been here earlier, I might have prevented this.

I'm not sure how long I knelt over his body, the rain pounding my back, before I came to my senses and realized I should call the police to report Henderson's death. Thinking about the police finding the fastidious old poet in such a state made me want to clean the mud and blood from his face and comb his hair. Instead I walked toward my car to retrieve my cell phone.

Near my car, still absorbed in Henderson's horrific fall, something caused me to turn around. My eyesight was nearly perfect in good conditions, but the gloomy night and drenching rain provided zero visibility. Squinting into the shadows, I thought I saw a figure dash behind the lighthouse and disappear into the tree line. Or did I? Was my imagination playing tricks on me again?

I rubbed the rain from my eyes, remembering my earlier vision of candlelight and ghostly moans. "Hey," I yelled after the apparition. No one answered, and I ran toward the lighthouse.

I hit a muddy patch of grass and one foot slid out from under me. I tottered on one leg momentarily trying to regain my balance before my legs split in different directions and I fell on my ass in a puddle. Getting to my feet, I rushed to the brick wall and stared into the darkness. Nothing. No sound except the rain. No one here except one sodden private eye and the ruined body of Clayton Ford Henderson.

Twenty-Eight

The police black and white arrived ten minutes after my call followed quickly by the now familiar white SUV. Sergeant Buck Marrano always seemed available when the Bat Signal went up. He looked at me curiously as I told him about Henderson's message, and then seeing the old man drop to his death. He listened to the phone message, and made a few notes.

"This is becoming a habit for you," Marrano said.

"What is?"

"Finding dead people. I hope it's a habit you can break because I'm getting tired of it."

"You and me both. But I know one thing for sure."

"What's that?"

"You can't blame this on Poe. Not unless he knows the secret of walking through walls."

"No problem there. Unless we find anything to the contrary, this looks like a clear case of suicide."

The storm hadn't lost any of its intensity, and we were standing under the back porch of the Lighthouse Museum while waiting for the Crime Scene Unit from the St. Johns County Sheriff's Office to arrive. One of the deputies had placed a blue tarp over Henderson's body and the surrounding area, but the rain had surely washed away any meaningful trace evidence.

I'd already told the sergeant I thought I'd seen someone running away. "Maybe it's not suicide," I said.

Marrano's dubious expression made it clear he'd already made up his mind. "From what I've seen, everything points to suicide. I'm not saying you dreamed up this mystery man, but you know the conditions are less than ideal, and you admit your imagination may have been playing tricks on you." Marrano cut his eyes away from me dismissively and stared into the woods.

"I was pretty shook up," I agreed, "but it sure looked like someone running into the woods."

Marrano returned his gaze to me and nodded the way a pre-occupied father might after hearing his four-year-old tell a fanciful story about an imaginary friend. "Looked like someone? Maybe it was Henderson's ghost."

My jaw muscles tightened and I barked out, "Why the hell would I make up something like that?"

"Hey, I didn't mean to upset you." Marrano flipped to the page in his notebook where he'd written my earlier statement. "Let's go over it again. You say you were heading to your car to call the police when you *thought you heard* a sound like someone running and *maybe you saw* a guy run into the woods?"

"That's right." I'd walked him through it twice already, showing him the path the man took.

"How far away were you?"

I shifted my eyes toward the path leading from the lighthouse to the parking lot. "About twenty yards."

"Uh huh. Then you ran after him, slipped and fell. And he just disappeared into the woods back there."

"Yeah."

"And you can't describe him."

"I told you it happened so quickly I only got a glimpse of him. Dark clothes, maybe a ball cap."

Marrano looked up from his notes. "Here's what we know for sure. It's darker than crap back there. It's raining like a sunnuvabitch, and you were probably still in a state of shock from Henderson nearly hammering you into the ground."

"So you think I imagined it?"

"I'm saying the mind can play funny tricks on us." He peered into the dark again, gesturing with his chin toward the spot where I'd seen the man run away. "The thing is that we didn't find any foot prints and no sign of anyone else up on the observation deck."

I was too tired to spend the night arguing about it. "Do you need anything else from me?"

Marrano tucked his notebook into an inside pocket of his rain jacket. "I'll tell you what, Mitchell. Why don't you sit down while I take care of a few things? Then we'll go to my office. Maybe you'll remember something else by then."

He walked toward the two men who had just arrived wearing yellow rain suits with Crime Scene Unit stenciled on the back. I watched while Marrano reviewed the scene with them, pointing to the top of the lighthouse and then to the misshapen heap beneath the blue tarp that used to be Clayton Henderson.

Nearly an hour later, Marrano steered me into the interrogation room at the SAPD. I was still wet, and the temperature in the room had to be in the mid-sixties. I began shivering, and Marrano excused himself. I glanced around the sterile, little room at the observation window and back to the table top. The words *Life sucks* were carved in the corner of the table next to my elbow. Fitting, I thought.

Marrano returned with a cup of coffee and a dry SAPD windbreaker. "Here, this should help. I can't vouch for the coffee, though, probably's been sitting there a while."

"Thanks." I tasted it and made a face.

"Don't say I didn't warn you. There's something—"

A sharp rap on the door interrupted him.

"Come on in," Marrano called.

Detective Horgan entered the room carrying a large manila envelope. He was wearing latex gloves. They huddled for a moment, their voices low, before Marrano turned to me. "Detective Horgan's just returned from Henderson's house. He found something I think you should see."

Horgan opened the envelope and with a gloved hand pulled out a slim book with a teal dust jacket.

"*A Flash of Silence*," I said. "Henderson must have a thousand copies of that book lying around his house. He even gave me one."

"We found it on the foyer table opened to this page." Marrano nodded toward Horgan, and the detective opened the book to the title poem.

Giving it a brief glance, I said, "Okay. That's kind of his trademark poem. No big deal."

"Take another look," Marrano said.

The second stanza of the poem had been circled in pencil, and in the margin were the words, *no more ticks of the clock left for me—good bye.*

"What do you think of that?"

A flurry of confused thoughts flickered through my mind. Maybe he wrote it in a fit of depression. Maybe it was an idea for another poem. Maybe he didn't write it. "I don't know. Are you sure it's his handwriting?"

Horgan and Marrano exchanged glances before the detective answered, "We'll have to do more tests, of course, but it sure looks like his writing."

Turning to Horgan, Marrano said, "Thanks, George. I'll take it from here."

Horgan returned the book to the envelope, and after he left, Marrano sat in the chair opposite me. He was quiet for a long time, probably waiting for my reaction. When I didn't say anything, he finally spoke, "You and Henderson were friends, weren't you?"

"Friends? No, I wouldn't say that. I met him at Poe's house a few weeks ago for the first time. They were good friends. Poe and Henderson. Since then I spoke to him twice trying to learn more about Poe's involvement with this Matanzas Bay project and your brother's death. That's about it."

"You know, as a cop I have to go to these educational workshops from time to time and read stuff about behavioral problems."

"Is this where I get the mental health lecture?"

Marrano rubbed his eyes and I could see exhaustion on his face. "Hear me out, you might learn something. Suicide's the eighth leading cause of death in this country and it's highest in old people."

"Henderson didn't strike me as someone who was thinking of killing himself."

"How many times have you heard friends or relatives say, 'we didn't have any idea so-and-so would do something like this?' That's the sad part, most of the time they don't know until it's too late."

I remembered what Watts told me about the old man's mood swings, and how something seemed to be bothering him.

"One other thing that plays into this is alcoholism. Henderson was a boozer, wasn't he?"

"Yeah, he might have been," I agreed, "but I don't think—"

"The suicide rate among alcoholics is three or four times the average." He let that sink in for a moment before adding, "Everything points to suicide—his state of mind, his drinking, his age. Hell, he even left a suicide note. And he had his own key to the lighthouse."

This was a side of Marrano I hadn't seen before. Serious, concerned. "I admit it makes a lot of sense."

"So maybe your eyes were playing tricks on you and you only thought you saw someone running away."

The events of the past few hours had taken their toll on me. I felt like an oxygen-deprived diver drifting toward sleep, wanting nothing more than to close my eyes and forget about everything else. With great effort, I replayed the lighthouse scene in my head. The shock of Henderson plunging to the ground. His broken and bleeding body washed by the downpour while I searched for ghosts amidst the lightning strikes. Perhaps Marrano was right and I imagined the whole thing.

I sipped the bitter coffee before saying, "I don't know, maybe you're right."

"Are you aware of anything else that might push him to take his life?"

I'd already told him about dropping by Henderson's house earlier in the week. I gave him all the details of our final discussion, leaving out Henderson's tirade about the Marrano family. Now I considered whether to tell the sergeant about Henderson's early history, the death of his wife, and the abandonment of his twins. But besmirching the dead poet's reputation seemed petty and pointless.

"Not really. You seem to have dug up all the usual suspects—old age, depression, alcoholism."

Marrano gazed at me then down at his notes. "What about his call to you? Do you think it might have been a cry for help? Maybe he wanted you to talk him out of it."

That idea had flashed through my head more than once. I wondered what would have happened if I'd arrived an hour earlier. "Could be," I said, feeling goose bumps shuttle across my shoulders and down my arms. "Any more coffee?" I pushed the empty cup toward him.

I waited another five minutes before the sergeant returned with two steaming cups. "I made some fresh," he said, and handed me one of the cups.

I sipped it cautiously. It tasted like it may have been brewed this morning instead of last week. Looking up, I noticed Marrano staring at me.

"I think we can put this thing to bed. Henderson, for whatever reason, obviously jumped."

I started to protest, but he ignored me. "I want to give you the benefit of the doubt, but your story about a third person just doesn't hold water. There's no way it's anything but a suicide."

"Maybe someone encouraged him to jump."

"We'll see what the coroner says." He stood and I did the same. Leaving the coffee cup and the windbreaker in the room, I followed Marrano down the narrow hallway past dark and empty offices toward the front entrance. Before we got there, he stopped and leaned against the wall.

"Listen," he said, looking down at the coffee cup still in his hand. "I may have come on a bit strong the other day with my comments about Serena." He avoided my eyes, his face a blank screen.

"You think?" I snapped, reliving the sting of his racist remark. After hours of listening to Marrano do everything but call me a liar, now I had to listen to his half-assed apology. "I wouldn't expect anything less from a redneck cop whose grandfather was a Klan leader."

His conciliatory attitude evaporated, and his eyes narrowed. "Yeah, we're all a bunch of bigots, aren't we?" His face had colored, crimson highlights tinting his cheeks.

I recalled Walter Howard's sad story. The pain and humiliation he suffered at the hands of Bat Marrano. Pain that haunted him to this day. Two boys watched the beating; one of them even took the first whack at Howard's knee. It may have happened forty years ago, but Marrano needed to know actions had consequences.

"I don't know if you're all bigots," I told him, watching to see how he reacted to my next statement. "By the way, I met Serena's uncle last week."

He didn't reply so I went on. "Walter Howard, the old NAACP president who was beaten by the Klan back in the sixties."

"It must be serious between you two if she's introducing you to her family, but why should I care?"

"You've lived in St. Augustine all your life and I thought you might have made Mr. Howard's acquaintance at some time. Maybe years ago during all that civil rights stuff back in the sixties."

"Can't say that I have, hoss. I would have been a little kid back then."

I let it hang there while he sipped his coffee. "Yes, that's what I thought. Besides, why would Bat Marrano's grandson hobnob with a civil rights leader?"

Twenty-Nine

Back at my apartment, I stepped into the shower, hoping to wash away the weariness and painful visions parading through my head. I rolled into bed bone-tired wanting nothing more than a good night's sleep. About the time my head hit the pillow Dudley jumped on the bed, placed his paws on my chest and meowed in my face.

Dudley is a smallish gray and white cat I brought home from a case that took me to California last year. He sat patiently staring into my face as if waiting for me to answer some unasked question. When the only answer he got was a grunt, Dudley meowed again and gave my arm a headbutt. I knew he wanted me to move, make room for him to spread out. The queen-sized bed had enough space for a herd of cats to my right, but this cat preferred to sleep on my left side, and he wouldn't let me rest unless I complied. It was like having a wife, but with none of the fringe benefits.

I scratched Dudley's head and lightly rubbed along his jaw line. He closed his yellowish-green eyes, momentarily lost in feline bliss while his purring motor cranked into high gear. I let him lick my fingers a few times before shifting over to give him space to snuggle beside me.

The story of how Dudley came to be living with me is complex and almost too incredible to believe. The funny thing, though, is that I'd never owned a cat before. Dogs were my thing. I had two or three of them growing up in Connecticut, and Bogie, my yellow lab, has been with me for eight years.

After I rescued the cat, I named him Dudley after Andrew's big Maine Coon. Andrew came along as a surprise package to my parents who were both in their mid-forties at the time. My sister, Marlie, seemed a bit embarrassed by mom's pregnancy, but as the only boy in the family I thought it might be nice to have a younger brother.

Dad's law practice kept him working long hours and weekends when I was growing up. He didn't have a lot of time for me, but I understood and had my own life with my own friends. Andrew was a different story. Dad seemed to reconnect with his own childhood with Andrew, finding time in his busy schedule to attend many of his soccer games and swim meets.

My own hedonistic lifestyle didn't leave much room for jealousy. I was a junior in high school the year Andrew turned eight, quarterback on my football team, and working my way through the cheerleading squad.

Let's say I had different priorities. Besides, Andrew's winning personality, quick wit and 1,000-watt smile made it nearly impossible to dislike the kid.

Dudley sighed as though understanding he was no longer the center of attention. He butted my arm again until I lifted it and allowed him to squeeze in next to me. Andrew named his cat Dudley after the cartoon character *Dudley Do-Right of the Mounties* on the old *Rocky and Bullwinkle* show. I stroked Dudley's soft fur and thought about my brother and the events leading up to his death. Reflexively, I raised a hand to my throat and felt the cool silver chain. Running two fingers along the links, I touched the smooth surface of the medallion, traced the arc of its back from the blunt point at one end to the fanned tail.

Andrew's swim team was named the Dolphins, and the sponsor, a local jewelry store, gave each of the swimmers a bracelet with a sterling silver dolphin after they won the conference title. Andrew wore the bracelet proudly for a few months before putting it aside after his friends teased him, saying it made him look like a sissy.

I found the bracelet after Andrew died and took it without telling my parents. Before I went off to the Gulf War I had the dolphin added to a silver chain. It's remained around my neck ever since as a constant reminder of my brother.

"Sorry to disturb you," I said aloud to the cat, and slid over to the other side of the bed. Dudley eased back on his haunches, eyeing me suspiciously. "Don't worry, I'll be back."

I turned on the lamp and pulled a small photo album with a red, green and black plaid cover out of the drawer of the bedside table. I sat with my legs hanging over the bed, the album cradled in two hands like a holy scroll, and willed myself to open it. Dudley left the warm spot on the other side of the bed and padded over to me. He sat by my side, back straight, eyes moist and golden in the lamp light.

While Dudley watched, I opened the album to a picture of my brother and me in front of my first car. Andrew Mitchell held his cat in his arms. I stood next to him in the photograph, one hand resting casually on his shoulder while Andrew's head craned up at me, a huge smile on his face.

I remember my mother had received a new Canon SLR for her birthday and was irritating everyone with her zeal to record our family's every waking moment. That day, I was in the driveway washing my treasured Trans Am, which I'd recently bought secondhand from a friend. It was a warm Saturday afternoon in May, and I was shirtless, wearing a pair of old shorts and holding a soapy sponge in one hand. I recall mom took forever to get the f-stops right and frame each shot as if she was on assignment for *Life Magazine*. While she fiddled with the camera, Andrew ran from the house carrying the unhappy Maine Coon. He slid in beside me and I placed a wet hand on his shoulder. He smiled up at me just as mom snapped the shutter.

Looking at that picture of Andrew, sunlight splashed across his face, there was no hint of the traumatic events that would irretrievably alter our family. The photo was a cruel reminder that life deals the cards blindly. To anyone else, there is nothing exceptional in the family photo, just an eight-year-old boy holding a cat and looking admirably at his big brother. But if you knew Andrew, you'd see the sweetness in his face, the intelligence in his eyes, the potential that comes with good genes and social and financial advantages, and an inner strength that was obvious even at his young age.

As he smiled at me, his eyes had a light of expectation in them; filled with the knowledge his big brother would always be there to protect him. Two months later, Andrew was dead.

Quint pulled Jillian LeBlanc as close to him as the sport seats in his 1980 Pontiac Trans Am allowed. They were parked in the driveway of her parents' Tudor-style mansion after taking in the summer's big hit, *Back to the Future*. While they kissed, Quint's hand found her knee and slowly inched north toward the promised land.

The Mitchells and the LeBlancs were close family friends when Jillian and Quint were younger, even taking a few vacations together, but the families had eventually drifted apart. Jillian and Quint discovered one another again near the end of the school year, both of them rising seniors. They'd been dating for less than a month, but to his growing frustration, Jillian successfully managed to keep him at arms length— away from the hot zones, as she put it. Now her right hand clamped down on his just as he was within reach of his goal. She pushed him back with surprising strength for a girl whose idea of exercise was carrying shopping bags from the mall to her car.

"My parents won't be back from their cruise until Wednesday," she said in a throaty whisper. "I was thinking maybe we could drive over to our beach house this weekend. Just you and me."

He fell back against the door, dramatically clutching his chest.

"I don't believe it," he said, before quickly adding, "Why wait? If they're away, let's play tonight." He pointed toward the big house where spotlights illuminated the shrubbery and driveway.

"I'm sure my sister will appreciate that," Jillian said. She was the youngest of four girls—two of them were married, and one in college, but now home for the summer. "Besides, the beach house is private and so much more romantic, don't you think?"

Atmosphere wasn't a top priority for Quint at the moment. Any bedroom would accommodate the fantasies he'd been conjuring the past few weeks.

"Well, are you interested or not?"

"What do you think?" he said, trying to slide his hand under her skirt. "How about a preview of coming attractions?"

Jillian pushed his hand away and crossed her legs, pulling the skirt primly over her knees. "Not now. We don't want to spoil the big moment, do we?" Jillian patted his hand as she might placate a pouting child.

Quint liked this girl, but he wanted to tell her she was driving him crazy. Instead he said, "Sure, I was only kidding. What time shall I pick you up?"

"Will your parents let you go if—you know? Spend the weekend alone with me."

"My parents are busy people. I don't like to bother them with every little detail."

Jillian leaned over and kissed him lightly on the mouth. "That's good. You can pick me up at nine Saturday." She slipped out of the car and walked to the front door of her house.

Quint watched her walk away, admiring the curve of her calf and the delicious bounce of her hips. Each step she took rocketed bolts of testosterone into his teenage bloodstream, and he knew this weekend would be the best in his young life.

At home that night, Quint told his mother and father about Jillian's invitation to spend the weekend with her parents at their Guilford beach house on Long Island Sound. Bending the truth this way gave Quint a slight twinge of guilt, but parents didn't need to know everything their kids did or they'd never allow them out of their sight.

"Got a problem, son," his father said, closing the legal file he'd been reading. Robert Mitchell, still called Bobby by most of his friends and business associates, took off his reading glasses and stood. He was a big man with an athlete's build that had softened over the past few years as his hairline receded and his waistline thickened

Quint shifted his eyes from his father to his mother. "What's the problem?"

His father moved several steps to the settee where Quint's mother sat. "Your mother has decided to accompany me to New York City for my conference this weekend." He placed a hand on his wife's shoulder and rubbed it affectionately.

Quint remembered his father mentioning the conference at dinner last week, but this was the first he'd heard about his mother going along.

"That's cool," Quint said, "but what's the problem?"

"Have you forgotten your brother? Someone needs to take care of Andrew."

Quint had forgotten. His mind raced, searching for a way around the roadblock his father had thrown in his path to orgasmic heaven.

"Maybe he can go with you. You know, a nice family outing, see the Empire State Building and Statue of Liberty."

His father and mother exchanged glances before his father shook his head. "Sorry, big guy, not this time."

"What about Marlie? She can come home for the weekend, can't she?" His sister was in summer session at college, and hadn't been home in more than a month.

His mother spoke up, "Marlie needs to study for a couple of tests. I spoke with her earlier today and she's pretty stressed out about her economics mid-term."

"Can't she come home and study?" Quint's dreams of a fantasy weekend were crumbling before his eyes. "I do it all the time."

His mother smiled at Quint's desperation. "Think about it, son. She'd have to be on the road for more than seven hours coming and going. That's seven hours she could be studying."

He couldn't think of an answer for that and hung his head, trying to imagine what he would tell Jillian.

"I've got an idea," his father said.

Quint wasn't sure he wanted to hear his father's idea. "What?"

"Why don't you take Andrew with you? It's a huge house and Andrew will enjoy a weekend at the shore. I'm sure Sam and Betsy won't mind."

Quint toed a mauve flower on the Oriental rug wondering what to say next. He wished he never had this conversation in the first place, but now he didn't have a choice. "I don't know," he managed to say. "Maybe they're having some of their friends over, and—"

Bobby Mitchell smiled at his son. "Come on. I know you think he's going to get in the way of your fun with Jillian, but there are plenty of things to keep him occupied. It won't be a problem."

"Why don't I call Betsy in the morning and make sure it's all right?" Quint's mother chimed in.

"No, that's okay," Quint said quickly. "I'm sure it won't be a problem. I'll talk with Jillian later and she can clear it with her parents."

The LeBlanc's beach house was located at the end of a quiet road on one of the exclusive fingers of land poking into Long Island Sound. The house had all the amenities of the good life, a private beach, swimming pool, boat dock and spectacular views of the water. While he'd enjoyed all of it in past visits, none of these currently held any interest for Quint who had his eye on the four bedrooms.

Jillian had been put off when he called to tell her about his younger brother, but he explained that there was plenty to keep Andrew busy outside while they rested inside. Plus, after Andrew fell asleep Saturday night, they'd have a good six or seven hours to do whatever they wanted. More than enough time to work out his frustrations.

"Man, this place is cool," Andrew announced after romping through all of the rooms. He found a stack of games on a bookshelf next to the color television set, and began rooting through them. "Look, Dudley, they have Monopoly." Andrew had insisted on taking the giant cat with him. Dudley was ensconced on the back of the couch keeping a sharp eye out for anything that looked like food.

"Yeah, bud, maybe we'll play a few games later tonight," Quint said. "Did you put your suitcase away in the bedroom?"

"Uh huh."

Andrew had close-cropped straw-colored hair, their mother's tiny turned-up nose, and dark brown eyes that twinkled like they held the key to a storehouse of mischief. Losing interest in the games, Andrew ran to the bay window and stared at the blue waters dotted with sailboats. A Sunfish with red and blue sails was anchored on the beach next to the house. A kayak perched beside it.

"Do you think we can go sailing?" Andrew asked, looking hopefully at his brother.

"Maybe after lunch. Jillian has a couple of bikes in the storage shed, and there are some neat trails if you'd like to go exploring later." A protected land trust surrounded the home, warding off encroachment by developers, and offering picturesque hiking and biking trails through the woods and along the shore. Quint remembered hiking the trails with Jillian when they were only a few years older than Andrew.

"That would be cool. Will you show me?"

"We'll see," he said to Andrew. "I was up late last night and might want to take a nap after lunch." Quint and Jillian exchanged glances. She shrugged and eyed him coolly. Her displeasure with him wasn't making this any easier. Neither was her outfit. Jillian had on a pair of shorts so short and so tight he wondered why the button didn't pop off. She'd tied her loose-fitting T-shirt into a knot exposing her navel and Quint thought about the drive to the beach house when he'd drifted onto the shoulder of the road because he couldn't take his eyes off her crotch.

"How about a peanut butter and jelly sandwich?" Jillian asked, moving toward the kitchen.

Andrew whirled away from the window and ran after her. "Sure, and do you have any Oreo's? I love Oreo's." He stopped suddenly, trotted back to the living room and grabbed Dudley from the top of the couch. The cat's copper eyes lasered its displeasure and a low growl rumbled in its throat. Dudley weighed nearly a third of Andrew's sixty-five pounds, and the boy's arms encircled the cat's middle clutching it against his chest.

He stopped in front of a family portrait of the LeBlancs that included Jillian and her three sisters. "Hey, when are your parents getting here?" Andrew yelled after Jillian who was already in the kitchen."

Jillian hurried back into the living room, shooting a deadly glare at Quint that would have made Dudley proud. "They were held up and won't arrive until tomorrow," she said.

"That's right," Quint added, prodding his brother in the back. "Now get in there and wash your hands. You've got a big day ahead of you and you'll need your energy." He smiled at Jillian hoping this held true for him as well.

The day didn't go entirely the way Quint had envisioned. After lunch, Andrew headed for the sailboat. Knowing it might consume two or three hours of his afternoon, Quint put him off, promising they'd go later. Instead, they splashed through ten games of Marco Polo in the LeBlanc's swimming pool.

Jillian's lime-colored bikini covered only the bare essentials and Quint slid his hands over her smooth skin while Andrew paddled around with his eyes closed yelling *Marco*. Each time Quint groped her, she would laugh, yell *Polo* and dunk him. After the tenth game Quint was so horny he thought he was going to burst. He climbed out of the pool, quickly pulling a towel around his waist.

"That's enough for me," Quint said, flopping on his belly on one of the lounges by the pool.

"Aw c'mon. Just one more game," Andrew called from poolside, palming a spray of water at his big brother.

"Don't you think you can get it up for one more game?" Jillian teased, and joined Andrew in splashing Quint.

In the end, Quint acquiesced. After another game he boosted himself out of the pool and announced, "Andrew, you've got too much energy for me. You're the world champ of Marco Polo. Now I'm going to take a nap." He gazed at Jillian, who had lifted herself onto the ledge, leaning forward on her tanned and willowy arms. The afternoon sun glinted off the water streaming over her full breasts compressed between her arms, and Quint ached to be with her.

"Well, I don't want to take a nap." Andrew's mouth began to shape itself into a pout.

"Of course not," Jillian said. Quint grabbed her outstretched hand and pulled her out of the pool. "This would be a good time for you to check out that hiking path Quint told you about earlier." She handed Andrew a towel. "Here, wipe off and put on your sneakers. Then I'll show you where the path starts."

She pointed to a wooded patch behind the house. "Once you're past those trees the path curves back along the shoreline. You'll see a cave cut into the rocks at Pelican Point, and a small beach where the seals hang out in the winter. If you're lucky you might be able to spot a heron or some egrets or maybe osprey hunting for fish."

"Cool. Are you coming with me?"

Jillian smiled at Andrew, reached out and rubbed his stubbly head. "You know, I was about your age the first time I explored the path by myself. I thought I was so grown up."

Andrew nodded enthusiastically. "I can do that. How long will it take?"

"It depends on how much you want to explore, but I'd say a little over an hour. When you get back, Quint will take you sailing, and then we're going to my favorite restaurant in Guilford for dinner."

Andrew laced up his shoes and took off toward the woods. "Take your time," Quint called after him, "and be careful around the rocks."

Jillian and Quint exchanged looks as Andrew disappeared into the tree line. "Alone at last." Jillian bent toward him and ran her tongue lightly around his ear. She let her fingers trail over his chest and down his solid abs until she got to the band of his bathing suit. One finger stroked his lower abdomen under the band and his muscles contracted. She laughed at his involuntary intake of breath.

"Why don't you follow me, big boy?" she said, gripping the top of his suit and pulling him toward the house.

Sixty-five minutes later, a sated and still smiling Quint emerged from the shower. He'd dressed in a clean pair of shorts, slipped on a white knit Lacoste polo shirt, and walked barefoot into the kitchen where Jillian sat drinking a Coke. She swallowed a large mouthful, and licked her lips.

"That tastes good," she said.

He leaned over and kissed Jillian on the mouth, his tongue separating her lips. "Uhmm, I'd have to agree," he said when he came up for air.

Quint dropped onto one of the stools beside her. "Heard anything from Marco Polo the explorer?"

Jillian glanced at the kitchen clock over the stove. "Not yet, but he should be along pretty soon."

"Maybe he'll be too tired to go sailing this afternoon. I know I am," Quint said.

"Don't think you're going to get much rest tonight, mister. I have plans for you."

He groaned theatrically, squeezing his eyes shut, his shoulders sagging. "What is it they say, be careful what you wish for?"

"As if you weren't about to die before you got me alone in there," she said, cocking her head toward the bedroom.

He popped off the stool and wrapped his arms around Jillian, who had changed into a yellow sundress with skinny shoulder straps. "And I'm ready for another round right now if it wouldn't scare the hell out of Andrew."

She laughed and pushed him away. "I'll remind you of that at three-thirty in the morning when you're begging me to let you sleep."

In the living room, Quint turned on the TV and ran the channels until he found a baseball game. The Mets were in the middle of a three-game home series with the Red Sox and the Sox were leading 3-0 in the fourth inning. Quint leaned back thinking the Mets were going to get slaughtered. The next thing he remembered was Jillian shaking him awake.

"Quint, Andrew isn't back yet."

Quint rubbed the sleep out of his eyes. "How long's he been gone?" He was having a hard time waking up.

"Over two hours. The trail isn't that long, ninety minutes max, and that's if you were walking at my grandmother's pace and stopped to pick up every rock." Jillian stood over Quint, a worried look on her face.

"Andrew's a real social person. He probably met another kid and they're playing at his house or on the beach." He looked at the television and saw that the score was now 9-2 at the top of the eighth inning.

"I think we need to look for him," Jillian said.

"Okay, you're right." He forced himself off the couch and found his flip-flops. "Why don't you go along the shore and I'll backtrack through the woods? We'll meet somewhere near Pelican Point. I'm sure we'll find him pretty quickly."

The temperature had been a warm 83 degrees when they'd been playing in the pool earlier in the afternoon, but four hours later, in the shadows of the woods, Quint wished he'd worn long pants. A shiver ran over his arms, and he hurried through the thicket of black oak and white birch along the narrow hiking path.

"Andrew, where are you hiding?" Quint yelled, not really believing his brother was still on this stretch of trail.

Ten minutes later he passed through the last of the trees and followed the path past a patch of waving grasses and small shrubs. A cool breeze carried the crisp smell of the ocean, and he heard the cry of gulls overhead.

"Quit playing games, Andrew," Quint yelled, his frustration rising with every step. Quint pictured his brother playing at another kid's house, lost in his own world with no idea of the time or the fact that Andrew and Jillian were looking for him.

Then he remembered the many times he'd disappeared at supper time, his mother calling for him. Now he knew how she felt, and he wanted to take Andrew by the shoulders and shake some sense into him. He also realized he was responsible for his brother, and pin pricks of heat flushed his cheeks as he thought about how he'd deceived his parents.

Quint skirted a cluster of rocks known to the locals as Pelican Point, disturbing a gull tearing apart a small fish it must have found washed up on the shore. The gull shrieked its displeasure at Quint, and flew away with a ragged and bloody strip of flesh still in its beak. He yelled for Andrew once more, hearing only the cry of the gull in response.

The sun glinted across the still waters of the sound and Quint stared at the sailboats to see if any of them carried an eight-year-old boy as a passenger. He told himself there was nothing to worry about. Jillian and her sisters had played on this little peninsula since they were younger than Andrew. It was a perfectly safe playground for kids. Despite that, Quint's heartbeat increased as a feeling of unease swept over him.

Where the hell are you, Andrew?

One hundred yards away, Quint spotted a figure walking in his direction. He recognized Jillian's sundress even from that distance, and a hot sensation warmed his groin as he recalled their afternoon couplings. He waved at her, but Jillian kept walking and Quint figured she must not have seen him. When she started running along the beach, Quint thought she was running to greet him.

Jillian stopped alongside a miniature inlet cut into the shoreline, her head down, hands on her knees. He didn't have time to consider what she might be staring at before Jillian screamed. The anguished cry knifed through the stillness of what had been a perfect summer's day. Quint felt a cold hand grip his heart, ripping his breath away as Jillian's scream continued to build and she fell to her knees, holding her face in both hands.

With great effort Quint willed his legs to move, and he began running toward the spot where Jillian had fallen. His athlete's legs took control and he ran like an opposing lineman was chasing him, legs pumping, arms churning. He told himself there were any number of reasons why Jillian had screamed, but he couldn't imagine what they were as he concentrated on putting one foot in front of the other. His flip-flops had flown off his feet after a few steps and his toes dug into the sand. He kept running, cutting the distance down to seventy-five yards, then fifty.

At about thirty-five yards he looked up and spotted something lying in the water beside Jillian.

Quint couldn't quite make out the pale form at Jillian's feet. Perhaps his mind wouldn't allow him to recognize what his thudding heart already knew. He ran faster, whipped by an icy fear. Ten feet away he skidded to a stop.

He tried to convince himself those weren't the purple baggy shorts his brother had worn when he last saw him. They couldn't be, especially since they were pulled down, bunched up around the ankles. It couldn't be Andrew.

Jillian had stopped screaming, one hand to her mouth, one hand caressing the boy's straw-colored hair. Quint attempted to move but his legs refused to go any farther. He stared at his brother with complete disbelief. A terrible taste flooded into his mouth and he thought he would vomit. He felt blood pulsing in his ears, a cruel drummer marching through his head.

Bloody bands crisscrossed Andrew's chest and abdomen. With a massive effort of will Quint forced himself to move closer. One step then another until he realized the curved bands of blood covering his brother were actually gaping wounds exposing muscles and organs as though Andrew had been caught in the blades of some giant blender. Perhaps his brother had been run over by a motorboat, he thought, but then he noticed the thin line of crimson beneath Andrew's chin. His throat had been cut.

Quint fell to his knees and grabbed his little brother in his arms. "No," he mouthed to the boy. "No, you can't be dead."

He didn't know how long he sat clutching Andrew's savaged body before Jillian shook his arm. "Quint, you have to put him down." One of Jillian's sisters was with the state attorney's office and she knew a body shouldn't be moved.

"We need to call the police."

Quint looked at her as if she'd been speaking in tongues. He rocked back and forth with his brother's body, trying to comprehend how such a thing had happened.

"And," she said, "we have to call your parents."

Thirty

Closing the photo album, I returned it to the nightstand drawer. Dudley purred and rubbed against me, trying to push me back into bed. But sleep was not an option for me now as my mind relived the awful telephone call to my father's hotel room in New York City. To this day it was the single worst moment of my life, aside from finding Andrew's body.

My father never forgave me for my deception, blaming me for my brother's death. At first he verbally flayed me with a fury I never thought possible. I accepted it as my rightful penance. I may not have wielded the weapon, but we both knew my deceit was responsible for the horrible things visited upon Andrew. His fury eventually cooled and solidified into an impenetrable stone wall keeping me at bay.

I tried numerous times to break through my father's seething anger and resentment, but the pain was too intense, his anguish too deep. I finally stopped trying. There was no going back for either of us, and in the past dozen years we've not spoken more than ten words to each other.

Recently, my mother let me know that my father, now in his late seventies, would be open to reconciliation. She urged me to call him, but the twin obstacles of time and guilt prevented me from picking up the phone. The fact that Andrew's murder remained unsolved only added fuel to the smoldering fires burning between us. As much as I wished it could be otherwise, the gap had grown too wide to bridge. Like acid leaking out of a battery, corroding vital contacts, all sparks of connectivity between us dissolved after Andrew's death.

At my office the next morning, I sorted the stack of mail, tossed the obvious garbage in the trash, put the bills aside to be paid later, and picked up the new edition of *PI Magazine*. When I lifted the magazine, I uncovered a small manila envelope with a St. Augustine postmark but no return address.

Slitting it open, I pulled out a photocopy of a legal document. At the top were typed the words:

CODICIL TO:
Last Will and Testament

OF

CLAYTON F. HENDERSON

I inspected the envelope again to see if I'd missed a cover letter, but saw only the legal document. The three pages contained a restatement of Article III of Henderson's will declaring the distribution of his Tangible Personal Property along with his Residuary Estate. A list of real estate holdings, cash bequests, and assorted articles of art and furniture followed.

My eyes returned to the top paragraph where I noted the execution date six months earlier on February 10th. Why, I wondered, would someone send me a copy of Henderson's codicil unless it had something to do with his death?

I sat down and read from the top.

I, CLAYTON FORD HENDERSON, a resident of St. Johns County, Florida, and a citizen of the United States, make, publish and declare this codicil to my Last Will and Testament, executed by me on the 10th day of February 2006.

I. I hereby restate Article III of my Last Will and Testament as follows:

ARTICLE III

Tangible Personal Property

I give and devise certain items of my tangible personal items to the persons named in the last dated writing signed by me and in existence at the time of my death.

The rest of the paragraph went on to list his personal representatives and how his remaining property should be divided. I quickly scanned through the list of property and cash bequests ranging from $5,000 to $100,000 to be given to various entities, including the St. Augustine Lighthouse Foundation and Flagler College.

I turned the page and a couple of items jumped out at me. Tucked between bequests to the University of Florida English Department and a few area charities was the name Jarrod Watts. According to the codicil, Watts was to receive $75,000 upon Henderson's death and allowed to live in the Martinez House for one year, although the house had been deeded to the St. Augustine Historical Association. Henderson liked and appreciated Watts, so I understood why he might want to reward him for his services.

The next beneficiary was Erin Marrano. Henderson had willed her some real estate in the historic district along with the sum of one million dollars.

Watts I could understand, but why Erin Marrano? Why gift her with a million dollars if they were only passing acquaintances? It didn't make any sense to me. What was the connection between them?

Lights flashed in my brain and pieces began to fall into place.

According to Jack Fuller, Henderson turned his twins over to a crooked adoption attorney in Huntsville, Alabama. Erin told me she taught in Huntsville before moving to St. Augustine. Could she be the poet's daughter? And what if Henderson followed her to St. Augustine to be close to her? It made a lot of sense. I could see a man of Henderson's sensibilities stewing in his homemade gumbo of guilt and remorse. Seeing the end of his life approaching in the rearview mirror, I imagined the old man might try to set things right with the child he abandoned.

Looking at the codicil, I wondered if he ever revealed their kinship to Erin. I doubted it, although Henderson seemed upbeat when I visited him before his death. Maybe he planned to tell her. I followed that assumption with another thought. What if he did tell her and she rebuffed him? Rejection has provided the motive for everything from murder to suicide, and it might have literally pushed him over the edge. If so, then Buck Marrano's contention that Henderson committed suicide made even more sense.

I was making some wild-ass guesses now, but I thought about father and daughter discovering each other after all these years. He must have followed her to St. Augustine. If the two of them were able to overcome the past then Henderson's final years might have brought him peace and comfort. Too bad his remaining time had been cut short.

One hour later, I pulled into Erin Marrano's driveway and turned off the ignition. I had called from my office and she was expecting me. I trailed her to a sunny room looking out on a well-landscaped back yard. A long, narrow flowerbed bisected the yard with blooming rose bushes and hydrangeas. Flagstones led to a small pond with a terraced waterfall to the left of the bed, and to several smaller gardens on the right where doves, woodpeckers and jays swooped in to the bird feeders spotted throughout the gardens.

"Would you like something to drink?"

When I said no she sat across from me at the round, glass-topped table. "You must be making progress, Mr. Mitchell. You said you had some new information." Sunlight streaming through the windows danced across her blue eyes, which at the moment were staring hypnotically into my own. I looked at the manila envelope in my hands to break the spell.

Erin followed my gaze to the envelope and pointed to it. "Does that have something to do with my husband's murder?"

"I'm not sure."

She gave me one of those *you're not making any sense* looks, so I jumped right in. "This came to my office today." I placed the envelope on the table.

She glanced at it then back to me. "Yes."

I pulled the codicil out of the envelope and showed it to her. "Have you seen this before?"

Her eyebrows shot up and she shook her head slowly. "No, why would you think I've seen it?"

"I may have mentioned at one of our other meetings that Mr. Henderson had some baggage in his past. There was no reason to go into detail with you at the time."

"And now?"

"If I'm right about this, it explains why you're a beneficiary in Clayton Henderson's will."

"He included me in his will?"

I told her about Henderson's marriage to the only child of a wealthy Mississippi industrialist. How his wife inherited a fortune after her parents were killed in a plane crash, and how she later drowned in the family swimming pool.

Erin listened quietly to my tale of the sad family saga, how Henderson had been a suspect in his wife's death, but later cleared for lack of evidence.

"Shortly after his wife's death he moved to Huntsville with his infant twins, a boy and a girl. He gave them up for adoption."

I could see her mind working behind those azure eyes. I picked up Henderson's codicil and flipped to the second page. Pushing it toward her, I pointed to the section with her bequest. "This is why I thought you needed to know about Henderson's children."

She lifted the codicil off the table and studied it for a full minute before looking at me and asking, "You think I'm his daughter?" Erin

Marrano's voice trembled with emotion and a shimmering film glazed her eyes.

"You told me you were from Huntsville. A year after you moved to St. Augustine, Henderson retired from his position at the University of Florida and bought the Martinez House."

A single tear tumbled from her left eye and trickled down her cheek.

I tapped the codicil with my forefinger. "I believe this was his mea culpa. I'm guessing he would have told you the truth if he hadn't died."

Erin remained silent, the tears dripping from her face and onto the table.

"You didn't know?" I asked her.

"How could I? We were acquaintances, but he never told me he was my father."

She stared at the document, and I tried to imagine her thoughts at the moment. Was she cursing Henderson for abandoning her? Or was she sorry for all the years they never had together? The shock of a million-dollar bequest would only add to the swirling emotions she must be feeling.

Tears cut tracks through her make-up, and she sniffed loudly before asking, "My brother, what happened to him?"

"He died of scarlet fever when he was eighteen months old. I'm sorry."

Erin pushed her chair back from the table and stood. For a second I thought she might bolt from the room, but she stared at the codicil then at me with wounded eyes, tears streaming down her face.

Her anguish reached out to me. In the last forty-eight hours this woman's world had collapsed. Her husband murdered, house burgled, and now she learned her father abandoned her along with a twin brother she never knew she had. Without thinking, I moved around the table behind her, and held her. Her shoulders sagged against my chest.

If I tried to objectively analyze my actions at that moment I'd probably tell myself I was only offering solace to a person in need of human comfort. But when she turned to face me, it became more difficult to focus on anything but the intoxicating scent of her perfume and the heat of her body against mine.

Objectivity flew out the window. Her eyes sought mine, our heads came together and my mouth found hers. For a long moment we lost ourselves in that kiss, tongues probing, the fullness of her breasts against my chest. I held my breath as we clung together until sanity at last returned, and we stepped away from each other.

"I'm sorry," I gasped breathlessly. "That was inappropriate and unprofessional."

She shook her head and offered a wan smile I couldn't decipher. "There's no need to apologize, but you should probably go now."

"You're right," I said, and started for the door.

The kiss had left me both excited and confused. I stopped at the front door, my head still buzzing. "You'll probably hear from Henderson's attorney about the will," I said.

"And where do we go from here?"

Her words seemed so innocent, but left me groping for a deeper meaning. Was she referring to my investigation, her inheritance, or the kiss? How should I answer her? "I'll keep plugging away," I said. "Something will turn up."

She nodded, the enigmatic smile still on her face.

Thirty-One

I hoped my visit with Erin would help clarify the murkiness surrounding this case, but as I drove away from her house I felt like I'd
walked through a revolving door into a hall of mirrors.

The impression of her lips on mine still tingled. Despite the confusion blurring my brain, I had a sneaky grin on my face like a teen-ager
who copped his first feel. Grow up. She'd been carried away by the
emotional news I'd brought her. Our kiss meant nothing more than one
human reaching out to another. One moment of human weakness. That's
all it was.

I returned the grin to its proper resting place and drove into the heart
of historic St. Augustine. It occurred to me that the groundbreaking
ceremony for the Matanzas Bay project was scheduled for tomorrow
morning. Later, I'd visit Poe, and tell him about the death of his friend.
Then, there was the little matter of the tall man with the floppy hat. I
hated to bring more bad news to Poe, but decided he should hear it from
me before the police heard about it.

Instead of driving straight to Malaga Street, I detoured along Avenida
Menendez, hooked a right on Bridge Street and a left on Marine. I had a
morbid reason for this side trip and it involved an infamous piece of local
history. About the same time I celebrated my 7h birthday in January of
1974, a former New York City model and actress had been hacked to
death in St. Augustine.

The grisly murder ranked as one of the most notorious crimes in the
nation's oldest city, and it happened in the victim's front yard on Marine
Street. I'd read a true crime paperback about the grisly murder, and I
always wanted to see where it took place.

All the evidence pointed to the victim's next door neighbor, the
county manager. For some reason, the woman had taken an instant
dislike to the man. She berated him at county meetings for his lack of
qualifications. Her letters calling for his replacement as county manager
appeared frequently in the St. Augustine newspaper.

After a long investigation, the manager was finally arrested and tried
for her death. Despite all the incriminating evidence pointing to the
defendant, including bloodstained clothing and a bloody machete, the
jury only deliberated ninety minutes before returning a *Not Guilty* verdict.
Maybe this was the kind of St. Johns County justice Erin Marrano was
worried about.

As I drove by the modest bungalow where the brutal murder happened, I thought about the obvious parallels between that case and Marrano's death. Both involved well known, highly visible members of the community; one an elected official, the other appointed. In both cases a nasty public feud might have provided the motive for a murderous act. While the county manager had been acquitted, I feared if Jeffrey Poe's case went to trial he wouldn't be so lucky.

I parked near the San Sebastian Winery and walked to the construction site on Malaga Street. A chain link fence surrounded the entire 15 acres. A billboard with the architectural rendering of Matanzas Bay provided a vivid picture of what this site would look like 18 months from now. Currently, it resembled a giant's sand box, complete with bulldozers, stacks of reinforced concrete pipes, and a mountain of fill dirt. I closed my eyes and attempted to match the artist's rendering to the massive patch of ground, sketching in the red-tiled roof of the hotel, the balconied condos looking out on a marina filled with boats. The image sparked brightly for a moment before fading away.

When I opened my eyes, I saw a crew of workers busily erecting a huge tent by the waterfront in preparation for Saturday's groundbreaking festivities. The ramshackle warehouses had been razed, and the damp dirt seemed barren and cold. Still, the enormous potential in this piece of land was apparent. No doubt both Kurtis Laurance and Mayor Cameron would invoke Marrano's name when they made their speeches in the morning. Marrano may have been a visionary as Laurance had said, but I couldn't help thinking what a tremendous price he'd paid by crawling into bed with Laurance.

That thought brought to mind Laurance's strange comment suggesting I take a look at the parcels of land outside the Matanzas Bay property line. What the hell had he meant by that? Only one way to find out.

I walked south past the fence onto a large weed-filled lot about a quarter the size of the fenced-in area construction site. The remains of what looked like an old garage sat a hundred feet back from the road. Three large garage doors were covered with ancient dirt and more recent graffiti. Plywood with No Trespassing signs covered the windows of the concrete block structure. Several padlocked storage sheds were clumped behind the garage. A dozen or more cars and pick-up trucks lined the side of the property nearest to the fence. They probably belonged to the construction workers, I guessed.

Walking north to the end of the block, I counted 280 steps from one side to the other and estimated it was at least as deep. I wondered why Laurance hadn't bought the property to add to the Matanzas Bay project.

To the east of the development site was a block of dilapidated shops. I wasn't sure if this was part of the property Laurance wanted me to inspect, but I walked to the other end to examine it. What looked to be the original prototype strip shopping center snaked along the intersection of Malaga and Lorida Streets. Five ancient concrete block stores, low-slung and desperately in need of a coat of paint. Three of them were obviously vacant with For Rent signs taped to the windows. One of the other two contained a storefront chapel. The hand-painted banner over the window proclaimed, *Christ died for your sins*. The other store advertised *Laser Hair Removal. Now under new management.*

The thought of these desolate parcels of land sitting next to a multi-million dollar development like Matanzas Bay made no sense. Someone could make a nice profit by selling to the St. Johns Group, and I again wondered why the construction fence didn't extend around both of these pieces of property. This must be what Laurance wanted me to see.

Satisfied I'd found the source of Laurance's cryptic statement, if not the answer to the mystery, I started back to where I parked my car. Before I reached the Camry, I spotted a familiar figure leaning against a familiar black car. Lem Tallabois stood as I approached, arms stiff, fists clenched, storm clouds scudding across his face.

"You keep stickin' your nose where it don't belong and you might lose it."

I smiled at him and raised an eyebrow in mock surprise. "If it ain't the New Orleans boogey man. How's your finger?"

Tallabois answered me with a different finger, but didn't try to stop me when I kept walking toward my car.

"You're pushin' your luck, PI man." He stepped forward, his thick body and scarred face combining to give him the look of a thuggish street enforcer. "Don't say you ain't been warned, boy." Tallabois slid the lapel of his jacket back to show me the gun tucked under his arm.

I ignored him and climbed into the car, slammed the door and sped away.

Twenty minutes later, I arrived at the County Jail. Someone called my name as I walked toward the entrance, and I turned to see Chief Milo Conover hustling toward me.

Despite the humidity and the excess weight he carried, Conover looked fresh and cool. "I'm glad I ran into you, Mr. Mitchell."

"How's that, Chief?" There may be any number of reasons why the St. Augustine Police Chief was happy to see me, but I couldn't think of any at the moment

"Henderson's death has been officially ruled a suicide by the ME. That little note he wrote in his poetry book pretty well nailed it." He moved closer to me and I smelled the sweet scent of peppermint on his breath.

I said nothing and he reminded me, "No more clicks of the clock left for me."

"Uh huh." I tried to recall the image of the man running away from the lighthouse the night Henderson plunged to his death, but nothing came to mind.

"We spoke to his physical therapist. He confirmed that Mr. Henderson had been drinking a great deal and seemed to be depressed about something. Henderson wouldn't talk to him about it, just kept drinking. Do you think it was the knee surgery?"

"He seemed to be coping with the surgery rather well."

"I suspect Henderson was an alcoholic," Conover said. "Who knows what goes through their heads when they're deep in the bottle. Anyway, I thought you'd like to know we've put this one to bed and you won't have to testify. Of course, we may need to question you more about the other case."

"When the time comes, I suspect you'll know where to find me."

We walked together into the lobby. "You're here to see Mr. Poe."

It wasn't a question. I simply nodded, and he disappeared through a door marked Employees Only.

Jeffrey Poe quietly considered the news I gave him about Henderson. He sat on the other side of the reinforced glass drumming the fingers of his left hand against the plywood shelf. His fingernails were gnawed to the quick. A scab had formed at the edge of one bloody cuticle. He noticed me looking at his hand and the drumming ceased.

"Sorry, Quint. Guess I'm wound up pretty tight," he mumbled into the phone.

"That's all right. What do you think about Clayton?"

"I can't believe he's dead."

"It was a shock for me, too."

"He loved that old lighthouse, so I guess it's a fitting way for him to end it. Still ..." He paused as though he'd run out of words and chewed at a cuticle on his little finger.

"Don't know if it had anything to do with it, but Henderson had a lot of baggage," I said.

"How do you mean?"

"Did you know about his two kids?"

"He had kids?"

"Twins. But he gave them up for adoption back in Alabama when they were still infants."

"He never mentioned it."

"That's not the sort of thing you discuss over a glass of port." The more I thought about it, the more convinced I became that Henderson's drinking and mood swings revolved around those two kids he'd abandoned, not his knee surgery as Chief Conover suggested.

"Maybe that played into his depression," I said. "Not to be too philosophical about it, but there comes a time when we look back on the things we've done and it weighs heavily on us."

His fingers rapped the wood again before he caught himself and stopped.

I continued. "Some people build inner calluses or perhaps they're missing a conscience, so it doesn't bother them. Henderson wasn't like that, and I suspect he still felt the pain of his actions. Anyway, I'm sorry to bring you more depressing news."

Poe's eyes had taken on the disconnected look I associated with a doomed animal. In the wild, predators feed on the weak and the cycle of death and survival goes on. After a brief struggle, when a lion chased down a wildebeest or a fox snagged a rabbit, the prey understood its time had come. If you've watched any of the *animals in the wild* documentaries on the National Geographic or Animal Planet channels, you've seen what happened next. All struggles cease and their eyes took on a glazed look of acceptance. Jeffrey Poe had that same hollow-eyed look.

"I've made some inquiries about your attorney. Wannaker is extremely well respected. I know he's been busy taking depositions, and I'm sure between us we'll uncover something. You can't give up."

His fingers started drumming again. I heard him sigh, his head bobbing as though in rhythm to his finger percussion.

"Jeffrey, listen to me. There's something else I have to tell you. I went to see Denny Grimes today thinking he might be a suspect."

Poe jerked to attention. The drumming ceased, a spark of life returning to his eyes.

"I'd forgotten that Marrano had him fired. Denny probably hated him more than I did."

"That's what I thought. He had motive and opportunity and not a very good alibi. But he said he saw you at the Trinity Parish site the morning of the murder. You were carrying a shovel."

"That's ridiculous. I was home in bed. Do you think he's part of the frame-up?"

"I don't think so. And I don't believe it was you he saw, but he saw someone."

"Why did he think it was me?"

"He said the man was wearing a hat like the one you wear at the digs. You must still have the hat since you were wearing it Monday."

Poe stared at me a moment, his eyes searching mine.

"You do have it?"

"I have it, but ..." He put a hand to his forehead.

"But what?"

"I always loop it over the doorknob of the door of my artifact room."

Now I remembered seeing it there the night of the dinner party.

"But it wasn't there when I looked for it Monday. I looked everywhere in the house and couldn't find it." He started chewing on another cuticle.

"But you were wearing it at the dig," I said.

"I finally gave up looking. As I left the house, I almost tripped over the hat. It was lying on the ground by the front door."

"I can't see you leaving your hat on the ground. It's more likely that whoever stole the bayonet also borrowed your hat and returned it when he planted the evidence in your storage shed."

Thinking I should change the subject, I told him, "I went by the Malaga Street construction site before I came by to see you. The groundbreaking is in the morning."

"That's it, then."

"What?"

"Once they break ground it's all over."

"What do you mean?"

"They want this case over and done with. The city commissioners. The police. Everybody. Once they start construction it will be the same as writing my death warrant. No embarrassing loose ends left over."

"You're going to get a fair trial. Wannaker will see to that."

He stared at me for a moment, his eyes moist. "It doesn't matter if I'm innocent, they need a scapegoat. When those bulldozers start moving dirt you might as well order my casket."

Thirty-Two

My cell phone rang as I left the jail. I thought it might be Jack Fuller with the information I'd asked for, but when I flipped it open *Casa Monica Hotel* was displayed on my Caller ID. Probably Serena breaking our dinner date.

"I only have a minute, Quint," she said without preamble, "but I wanted you to know I'm still expecting you for dinner tonight."

"You are?" I'm sure I sounded incredulous.

"We have a lot to talk about."

I would have jumped at the chance to salvage our relationship if this call had come last week, but now I wasn't sure if that's what I wanted. My mind flashed back to an image of Erin Marrano, my arms around her, our bodies pressed together, the sweet taste of her mouth on mine.

I said, "Yeah, you're right. What time?"

"Our sales meeting will run until about six. Why don't you come over around eight? I'll fix dinner. Nothing fancy."

After our disastrous lunch date last week when everything turned to shit, I desperately wished for another chance to make things right. Like a character in H. G. Wells' *The Time Machine*, I pictured myself zipping back in time and changing the outcome of that hour. Given another chance, I would have turned off my phone. I certainly wouldn't have told her she looked like the dead girl.

But that was last week. Now I only wanted to get on with my life. Besides, if I really had a time machine there were more important things in my life I'd change. And they would begin with a trip back to my seventeenth year. I touched the dolphin medallion and my mind flashed to an image of Andrew's bleeding corpse, only to be replaced by my father's anguished face.

In the parking lot outside the jail, I spotted a yellow piece of paper tucked beneath my windshield wiper. A parking ticket? That didn't make any sense since there were no parking meters in the county lot. I pulled the slip of paper out and realized it had been torn from a sheet of yellow lined paper. Unfolding it, I read the handwritten note before looking around. Only a few people were in the lot and none of them paid me any attention. I returned to the note, reading it once again.

I have information that will clear Jeffrey Poe and help you find William Marrano's murderer. Meet me at the Alligator Farm tonight at 10PM. Come alone. Park in front by Conservation Center to the right of the main entrance. Wait for me.

Thirty-Three

I watched as Serena stir-fried the vegetables and shrimp in an oily wok. She tossed a dash of cumin and a tablespoon of Szechwan sauce into the mix before turning down the burner and covering the wok with the top to an aluminum pot.

"I think we're about ready," she said, taking a sip of the chardonnay I brought with me. "Do you mind putting the rice on the table? And pour yourself some more wine while I take care of the stir-fry."

I carried the rice to the table in the dining area adjoining the kitchen. While I poured my wine, Serena joined me with the platter of steaming shrimp and vegetables.

"Thanks for bringing the wine, but it wasn't necessary."

"Never let it be said that Quint Mitchell is a boorish dinner guest." I flushed as I remembered how my boorish remark caused her to run out of the restaurant.

We ate in silence for the next fifteen minutes, neither of us prepared to wade into the dark swamp separating us. When we were finished, I put down my fork, and broke the silence.

"Serena, I—"

"There's no easy—"

We both spoke together, laughing in embarrassment. "You go ahead," I said.

"First of all, I want to apologize for the way I acted at the restaurant."

I tried to tell her she had no reason to apologize, but she plunged ahead.

"No, I over-reacted, and it wasn't fair to you. Now that you've met my uncle and heard his story, though, you probably have a better idea of who I am and why I might have these conflicted feelings." Serena gazed toward the plush leather chair where Walter Howard had sat as if checking to see if he was still there.

"It took a lot of courage to tell his story to a stranger."

She nodded in agreement. "The truth is he's kept it pretty much to himself. I never heard his story until a year or so after I returned from college."

I looked at her with raised eyebrows.

"He had moved to Daytona Beach with his family after it happened. My father moved to Chicago, and we lived there through high school." She paused and took a sip of wine.

"After we returned to St. Augustine, and I went off to college, dad persuaded Uncle Walter to move in with him. His wife, my Aunt Aletia, had died, and his daughter had married and moved to Atlanta. There was nothing keeping him in Daytona."

"But didn't your father tell you what had happened?"

"Not exactly. He told me his brother had been part of the civil rights movement in the sixties, and hadn't been treated well by some of the racists in the community. Then I returned home from college filled with myself, thinking this nearly white girl could do or be anything she wanted. I even dated a white man for a while until my father told me Uncle Walter had something he wanted to share with me. That was the first time I heard the complete story about his beating at the hands of Bat Marrano and the Klan."

I reached over and placed a hand on hers. She didn't move away, but slowly looked up at me.

"You can't imagine how I felt when you told me you were working for Mrs. Marrano. She's part of this family of ... of racist dogs who almost killed my uncle, and you were working to find her husband's killer."

Her eyes glistened, her emotional turmoil churning my stomach.

"You heard what my uncle said about the two boys. Who do you think they were?"

I recalled what Henderson had told me about Bat Marrano taking his grandsons to the Klan rallies. "Bill and Buck Marrano."

She pulled her hand from under mine as though an electric shock had passed between us. "Buck and Bill." The names exploded from her mouth. "Your client's husband jumped at the chance to beat on a helpless nigger."

"But that was such a long time ago," I replied. "You can't blame Erin for what her husband might have done as a kid. Besides, you never said anything to me about this when I took the case."

"I should have," she admitted. "Anyway, you were the first white man I've dated in twelve years. I hadn't intended to get involved, but you grew on me." She offered me a hint of a smile before turning her head away, maybe hoping I hadn't seen it. Too late.

"The thing is, I still have feelings for you."

I came here tonight convinced our relationship was beyond resuscitation. In my mind we were here for only one reason—to sign the death certificate and make it official. But if I was reading her right, a faint heartbeat still existed.

I stared at Serena who seemed to be waiting for me to pick up on her cue. Her honey brown eyes sparkled, but for a moment I saw bright blues and pictured myself kissing Erin Marrano. I wanted to tell Serena it was too late for second acts. Tell her I couldn't handle the kind of emotional heartburn that would surely come with a renewed relationship. Instead I said, "Hey, I have feelings for you, too."

Thinking I should learn to keep my big mouth shut, I leaned over to kiss her. At least I tried to kiss her.

Serena pushed me away. "No, Quint. I'm telling you this just won't work." She read the confusion on my face and added, "I'm sorry."

We eventually sorted things out, confirming our friendship for one another and promising to stay in touch. All the insincere things men and women say to each other when they break up. At her door, I kissed her on the cheek and she offered me a sad smile and a pat on the back. Jamming my hand into my jeans, I pulled out my car keys and the yellow piece of paper fluttered to the floor.

"What's this?" Serena bent to pick it up.

"Nothing." I held out my hand but she was already reading the anonymous note.

"When did you get this?"

"This afternoon. I'm on my way over there now."

"You don't even know if it's legitimate. Someone could be fooling with you." Serena gave me the note and I stuffed it back into my pocket.

"You're right, but I can't ignore it. What if it's legit?"

"Maybe you should call the police and let them handle it."

"No, that would screw everything up. The note said to come alone. Someone has to know something about Marrano's murder. This could be the break I've been looking for."

She held my eyes for a long time before saying, "I'd feel better if you called me after the meeting."

"You don't have to worry. Like you said, it's probably someone's nasty idea of a joke and I'll find myself alone with the alligators."

"Quint, promise me that you'll call."

I shook my head as if to say she was a big worrywart, but secretly I was pleased to know she cared. "Fine, I promise I'll call you as soon as I find out what this guy has to say. One way or the other, I should be on my way home by ten-thirty or so."

"Get out of here," she pushed me through the door into the hallway. "And Quint …"

I turned around. "Yeah."

"Be careful."

Thirty-Four

The Alligator Farm was bathed in shadows as I turned off Anastasia Boulevard into the darkened parking lot. Scaly and beaked creatures of all sizes and dispositions were sequestered behind a high wooden fence flanking the perimeter of the zoological attraction.

One of Florida's oldest tourist spots, the Alligator Farm began its life over a hundred years ago as a scam, a place of *burning waters*. The owners figured if people would pay to see oil burning in a pond they might pay to see alligators, which in those days were so common you might trip over one on your way to the privy. Today, St. Augustine's Alligator Farm is part of the American Association of Zoological Parks and Aquariums with a diverse collection of animals and one of the largest wild bird rookeries in the State of Florida.

By day, the palm trees and scrub oaks dotting the parking area formed a pleasant enough environment for the visiting tourists, but the attraction closed at six and now an uncomfortable air of apprehension hung over it. Dark and foreboding, the shadowed fence loomed like a malignant organism lying in wait to pounce on any unwary creature unlucky enough to wander too close.

Standing next to my car, waiting for my vision to adjust to the darkness, I felt the smothering presence of the elongated shadows. There were no other cars in the parking lot even though it was five minutes past the ten o'clock meeting time. I wondered if Serena was right, and someone was messing with me. She had woman's intuition on her side, but maybe, just maybe, this was the lucky break I'd been searching for.

I walked around to the passenger side, opened the door and reached into the glove box. Retrieving my revolver, I slid it into the waistband of my jeans. This might be a harmless meeting where a name was the only surprise thrown at me, but I wasn't taking any chances.

I tried to imagine who my mystery informant might be—a secret witness to Marrano's murder. Possibly a disgruntled girlfriend hoping to get even. Could it be someone I knew? No face appeared in my mind's eye, and I still had no clue who left the note on my windshield. It didn't matter, I told myself. With Poe's attempted suicide, the pressure mounted. Find the evidence to free him. Find it quickly, or I feared Poe's fragile mental underpinnings would collapse.

I walked to the corner of Anastasia Boulevard and Old Quarry Road hoping to see someone waiting for me. No one in sight. In the distance a dog barked and a twinkle of light appeared. Soon the barking stopped and the light winked out.

Trudging to the front of the attraction, I heard night calls of birds and the huffing and grunts of what I assumed were either alligators or crocodiles on the other side of the fence. From a previous visit, I knew the Alligator Farm had an impressive collection of crocodilians, including one monster they called Maximo, a 15-foot, twelve hundred and fifty pound saltwater crocodile from Australia.

During that visit, I'd watched in fascination as the massive creatures swarmed toward a feeding perch, clawing and leaping at chunks of raw meat dropped into their midst. Perhaps these night noises I heard were a crocodilian version of Morse Code, a signal that fresh prey was approaching.

A thick hedge of pittosporum fronted the fence surrounding the Alligator Farm. For the first time I noticed a service door cut into the fence to the left of the conservation center. I pulled at the metal handle on the door. Locked.

A slash of light slithered past me and I turned to watch a car driving along Anastasia Boulevard. The gloom returned as the car faded into the distance. Ten minutes had passed since I arrived, and I feared Serena may be right.

Patience, I reminded myself. I owed it to Poe to stay the course, to solve the puzzles surrounding this case. I'd always been good at solving puzzles, and it got me to thinking that I'd been treating the case as another puzzle in search of a solution. Not placing enough emphasis on the potential for danger.

We're all familiar with those insipid movies where the moronic teen in her bra and panties creeps down the stairs into a darkened basement despite everything, including the ominous music, warning her to run in the other direction. Of course, she gets what she deserves when the crazed killer takes her head off with a machete. I've always laughed at those scenes and knew I'd recognize a dangerous situation with or without the portentous soundtrack in the background.

Before I had a chance to worry about a man with a machete, the dog down the street began barking again. I stared in the direction of the racket, wondering if a stranger lurking in the shadows had triggered the dog's response. Reflexively, I grasped the handle of the Smith & Wesson.

Something crashed to the ground in the parking lot near my car and I spun around feeling goose bumps erupt on the back of my neck. I pulled the revolver from my jeans, prepared to defend myself.

The weak light spilling from the spots on the front of the building illuminated a palm frond lying near the front of my car. It hadn't been there when I'd parked. I took a deep breath and let it out slowly, lowering the gun to my side. Smiling at my jumpiness, I told myself life wasn't like a bad horror movie.

As I turned away from my car, the gun still in my hand, I heard a rustle in the hedge behind me. Out of the corner of my eye I spotted a dark shape rise up from behind the thick foliage. My muscles tensed. Adrenaline spiked into my system. I pivoted toward the hedge, raising the gun as I turned, but the looming figure had already moved and something smashed into my right temple. My legs buckled. The gun slipped from my hand. A battery of brilliant tangerine-colored sparks burst through my head, and I fell into a black, crystalline sea.

Consciousness played fickle games with me, and I remembered hearing what must have been the door in the fence scraping open. I seemed to be floating in a thick fog, unable to move, but I forced myself to open my eyes. A stocky man dressed in dark clothes, his head covered by a hood, pulled the door closed. My head throbbed and my stomach lurched, the sour taste of shrimp stir fry paying me a return visit. Feebly, I reached out with my right arm and attempted to grab his leg. The man in black easily eluded my grasping fingers and a heavy work boot shot out toward my head.

More pain before blessed blackness carted me away.

Minutes later—or perhaps hours—I emerged from my stupor only to wish for the sanctuary of sleep as a roaring filled my ears and crushing pain reverberated through my skull. I pictured myself tied to a railroad track, my head resting on one of the tracks, and a train engine rolling over it. Then backing up and doing it again.

Through the fog of misery, I felt myself dragged roughly by the feet, my head bouncing along the ground. The grunts of large animals filtered through my dazed brain. I heard water splashing, and knew this night would end horribly for me if I didn't do something.

I recalled the feeding frenzy I witnessed during my last visit to the Alligator Farm—dozens of prehistoric creatures clawing over each other to snatch a piece of raw rodent dropped from above. Powerful jaws snapping, the water boiling with whipping tails and probing snouts. If they put on such a show for a piece of goddamn rat, I thought, what would they do for a real hunk of meat?

I grabbed at the weeds and swamp grass trying desperately to slow my rush to extinction. They slid through my hands, leaving them raw and bleeding. Finally, I managed to wrap a hand around a small bush. The bush held and I caught my breath, trying to lift my head to see the person on the other end of my legs.

Strong hands tugged furiously at my ankles, trying to loosen my grip on the bush. I clenched it tighter, digging my other hand into the muddy ground, hoping to find some purchase there.

"What do you want?" I managed to quake, but received no response as my grip on the bush slipped. The pressure on my legs suddenly eased and I renewed my handhold on the bush. I turned my head to get a better look seeing only the dim outline of his legs in the dark. As I watched, I saw one thick leg rise over me before crashing into my stomach. All the air rushed from my lungs and I gagged. I also let go of the bush. The bouncing and scraping began again.

Gasping for breath, fighting the dizzying pain in my head, I again attempted to yank myself free. My legs suddenly flipped upwards in a tight embrace against the man's chest. He hoisted me off the ground like I was chained to a pulley, and drove my head against the ground. I passed out again.

I awoke with a crash to find myself on the other side of a fence. Face down in a patch of damp earth, fetid smells assaulting my senses, I lay there feeling the throbbing pain radiating from my temple down through my arms and chest. All around me I heard the feral sounds of the denizens of the Alligator Farm. The shrieks of birds awakened by our intrusion into their sanctuary mixed with the grunts and cries of larger, more dangerous animals.

Afraid my tormenter would return, I rolled away from the fence. Pain coursed through my body with each movement, but I kept rolling over the marshy ground until I banged into a tree. I lay there holding my breath, praying he wouldn't return to put me out of my misery.

My body worked against me, and I lost consciousness again. I awoke confused, wondering where I was. My head throbbed, white spots danced before my eyes. The sounds of the swamp brought all the painful memories back to me. I heard unnerving slithering nearby, the swishing of underbrush, a bubbling of water.

It took all my will power to raise my head, to concentrate on the shadows in the swamp edging closer and closer. Staring into the darkness, my vision shifted in and out of focus but I saw a beam of light tracking toward me. He was returning to finish me off.

I lay still hoping he wouldn't see me by the tree. The flashlight beam swept the ground in front of me lighting up a small section of my world. Peering into the night, trying desperately not to make a sound, I saw multiple pairs of red eyes reflected in the passing light.

Urgent steps scurried in my direction, while ahead of me the swishing of powerful strokes sliced through the water. Dazed and shocked, I drifted into unconsciousness, unable to face the approaching beast— either the two-legged or four-legged variety.

A sound, perhaps a word, suddenly split the air, and in the haze enveloping me I struggled to decipher it. Again it reverberated, rising above the pounding in my head. A single word rang out, and filtered through into my battered brain.

"Quint."

The voice belonged to my brother, summoning me. Andrew, is it really you? I wanted to touch the dolphin charm hanging around my neck, rub it like a talisman, pray it would whisk me away from danger. But I couldn't move.

Something clamped down on my arm, yanking me roughly across the ground. The pain became unbearable and I groaned. For a moment, an image from the feeding frenzy returned to me. I saw much too clearly the open jaws of a twelve-foot alligator snapping over the raw meat, swallowing it whole. But this time the massive jaws were biting into my arm, pulling me deeper into the nightmare waters.

Mercifully, I lost consciousness again.

Thirty-Five

In my nightmare, I saw myself dragged naked through the streets of St. Augustine. With one leg roped to the rear bumper of a pick-up truck driven by Bat Marrano, I skidded and scraped along the cobblestone lanes of the ancient city.

The old Klansman leaned out of the pick-up's window and asked, "How you feeling there, hoss?"

Eyes open, head pounding. Still alive? I remembered being eaten by the alligators. Then the nightmare ride, and now Bat Marrano wanted to know how I felt. Squinting at a blurry shape floating above me, I shook my head to clear my fuzzy vision. Bad idea. Spasms of pain burst through my sinus cavity into my right temple.

"Oh, shit." I closed my eyes, praying for sleep to return.

"Easy there."

The voice was familiar, but in my woozy condition recognition hung just out of reach. I doubted Bat Marrano had returned from the grave to haunt me. Still, my pummeled brain wouldn't make the connection.

"I'll go find the nurse and let her know you've awakened from your nap."

Nap? This clown had a real sense of humor. I groaned again, raising a hand to my head to tenderly finger a knot the size of a small plum beside my right ear. Gawd, my skull felt shattered.

"Welcome back to the land of the living, Mr. Mitchell," said a cheery voice.

I turned toward a large, round-faced woman with coppery-red hair pulled into a small bun on the back of her head. "It's good to be back," I managed to say.

She inspected my face for a long moment before picking up my wrist to feel my pulse. I lay there waiting to see if she found one.

"You're a lucky man. If it hadn't been for Sergeant Marrano here, I understand you'd be marinating in the digestive juices of some alligator's stomach instead of enjoying our hospitality." She seemed to find this more than a little amusing, and laughed aloud at her witticism.

"Where am I?"

"Flagler Hospital. I'm Nurse Wren, and you've had yourself quite a night." She leaned in and gingerly lifted my eyelid. On her left cheek, a granulated mole, pale in the middle and rosy at the edges, caught the light like a third eye. Hovering over Nurse Wren's shoulder, the blurry form of Sergeant Buck Marrano finally took shape.

I started to raise my hand to acknowledge Marrano's presence and for the first time noticed the IV line in my arm.

"You've suffered a pretty nasty trauma, Mr. Mitchell," the nurse said, pushing my arm back on to the bed. "The doctors were worried you may have a fracture or subdural hematoma," she continued. "You don't remember it, but you've already had a CT scan and fortunately it didn't show signs of a TBI."

I must have looked even more confused because she explained it for me.

"Traumatic Brain Injury. You have some bruising on your arms and chest, nothing serious, and several blunt traumas to the head." She ran a finger over the lump by my eye and I jerked back.

"That one is definitely the worst, but you have another on this side of your head." She touched it and I winced. "Bet they hurt like the dickens," she said, flaunting her grasp of the medical lexicon.

"Hurts like hell."

"Well, the doctor thinks you have a concussion so we need to watch you overnight. We gave you a quick sponge bath, but you'll want to take a shower in the morning after we release you. But now I'm going to give you some Tylenol for the pain and drops for your eye."

"I'm fi—" I started to say I'm fine and tried to sit up, but a wave of nausea gripped me and I closed my eyes, dropping back on to the cool pillow.

"Better listen to her, hoss. You don't look so hot." This time, there was no mistaking Marrano's cracker twang.

I swallowed the tablets Nurse Wren gave me and let her place drops in my eye. When she left, Marrano eased himself onto the side of my bed.

"I guess I need to thank you for saving my life."

"Kinda galls you, I'll bet."

"How'd you happen to be there?"

He hesitated a moment before answering, "You can thank your girl-friend."

"Serena?"

"Do you have another girlfriend? Of course, it was Serena. When you didn't phone by ten-thirty, she got worried and called." He gazed over my shoulder as if he'd sighted a bug crawling up the wall. Turning back to me, he said, "I happened to be available and not too far from the

Alligator Farm. Lucky for you I got there when I did. Saw your car in the parking lot, and spotted the door hanging open, so I came looking for you."

I remembered hearing my name called. "That must have been you yelling for me."

"Yeah, but you didn't bother to answer so I kept looking. Had my flashlight with me so I wouldn't step into a nest of critters."

Marrano studied my face, turning his head from side to side apparently examining my injuries. "You look like pure-n-tee shit," he finally said.

"Thanks. That's how I feel, too."

"Anyway, I found you spread out like the main course on a cruise ship buffet. Whoever did this must have had some muscle, cause he lifted you over a fence and dropped you into the Alligator Lagoon. I'm not saying I got there in the nick of time, but them ol' boys were drawing straws to see who got the first helping. I almost felt bad taking away their midnight snack."

"Sorry if I upset the balance of nature."

"Feel like answering some questions?"

"I don't remember much, to be honest, and I'm not sure how long I'll be able to stay awake."

"We'll keep it short, but I have to ask if you have any idea who did this. You know the drill by now."

I told him about finding the note on my windshield. How I arrived to an empty parking lot and waited for someone to make an appearance. "He must have been hiding behind the hedge. Sorry, I didn't get a look at his face. Dark clothes, hoodie. He creamed me fast and I went out. I remember being dragged, but that's about it."

Marrano stared at my eye again. "Could be a sap."

"I was definitely a sap for going out there alone."

"Not that kind of sap." Marrano smiled in amusement. "A blackjack. Leather-covered weapon filled with lead shot. Delivers a blow that will take a man out and leave a nasty lump. Some of the old lawmen carried them, but that was before we became more concerned about the criminal's rights than the victim's. Now, anyone can buy them online."

"Well, I got sapped in the eye, and then kicked in the head and stomach for good measure." I didn't bother to mention the pile driver trick.

"What about the note?"

"The note?"

"Do you still have the note he left on your car?"

I reached toward my pocket before realizing I was wearing a hospital gown. "In my jeans. Left front pocket."

Marrano went to the closet and pulled out a pair of mud-encrusted jeans. He dug around in the left pocket, and then the right. After searching all of the pockets, he tossed the jeans back into the closet. "Note's gone. Perp must have taken it before he scooted."

"Sorry I can't be of more help," I mumbled, feeling myself slipping away. Then I remembered my revolver. "Did you find my gun in the parking lot?"

"No. What kind was it?"

"Smith and Wesson thirty-eight, Model 40. Guess he took that, too."

"Probably, but I'll go back in the morning and see what I can find."

Marrano peered at me with an indecipherable expression. Was he hiding something?

"I'll check on you tomorrow," he said. "Maybe you'll remember something after you get some rest. Oh, I had one of the patrolmen drive your car over. It's downstairs in the lot. Keys are in the nightstand drawer."

I drifted in and out of a restless sleep over the next three hours. Nurse Wren awakened me twice to be sure I was still breathing, and I lapsed into a serial dream involving playing hide-and-seek with dozens of predatory red eyes. They lurched forward, surrounding me, moving closer and closer. I awoke with a thundering headache and a terrible urge to piss. Both needed instant relief, but I decided to tend to my bladder first. Carefully easing myself toward the edge of the bed, I grabbed the IV stand and pulled myself to my feet. I rolled the stand toward the open door of the bathroom, my gown flapping open behind me.

My tongue tasted like I'd licked the scum from the bottom of the alligator's pond. After relieving myself, I dipped handfuls of water from the tap and swished it around in my mouth. Slowly, I raised my head and stared at my reflection in the mirror. Not a pretty sight. Streaks of red oozed from the outside corner of my right eye and marched across the sclera in shaky lines. The puffy lid displayed the dark beginnings of a black eye.

Returning to the bed, I pulled the covers over me, suddenly cold, my arms and legs going numb. I hugged myself trying to warm my limbs, stop the shivering shaking my body. I didn't need to be a psych major to know the shivers had nothing to do with the hospital's air conditioning. They were a result of my near-death experience.

I had no idea why someone tried to kill me. Sure, I'd been poking around and asking a lot of questions, but few answers had been forthcoming. At least nothing particularly germane to Marrano's death. Somehow, though, I must have hit a nerve and came too close, but too close to who? Too close to what?

Sometimes there were no answers to the violence that's become an unfortunate fact of life these days. Daily headlines bring frightening stories of random violence and the sad state of the human species. Terrorists plotting another 9/11 style attack was one thing, but today's violence was even scarier. It didn't seem to matter where you were—church, school, mall, or even in a court room—there was no safe haven.

Instead of dwelling on those unsettling images, I turned my thoughts to Serena. She called the police and Buck Marrano came to the rescue. They saved my life, and even if Marrano called her back, I knew she must be worried sick.

I sat up and ran a hand behind me until I found a cord for the fluorescent light above the bed. Turning it on, I ripped the adhesive from my arm and extracted the IV needle before checking the bedside table for my watch and car keys. I grabbed them both, slipping on the watch and noting the time—3:42. This probably wasn't the smartest decision I'd ever made, but something urged me toward the closet where I pulled out my dirty clothes and put them on.

"Where do you think you're going?" Nurse Wren must have seen the light in my room. Her sturdy form blocked the door, bulky arms entwined across her chest, daring me to make a move.

"I appreciate everything you've done for me, but I have to get going now."

"Mr. Mitchell, the doctor will be making rounds in a few hours, why don't you wait until he releases you? A concussion is not to be taken lightly. You need rest, and we need to monitor your symptoms to be sure—"

"Really, I'm fine." Headache's gone," I lied. "You said I needed rest, and I'll rest better in my own bed."

She stared at me, her dark eyes narrowing, trying to will me back into the bed. I slipped on my muddy deck shoes, jiggled the car keys and she stepped aside.

"I can't force you to stay here, but you have to sign a release before you can leave."

"No problem."

She continued staring as though she wanted to take me over her knee and whack away until I came to my senses. "I'm going to find my supervisor who will bring the release for you to sign. You wait right here until we return. You hear me?"

I agreed to wait and she gave me two more Tylenol before walking away. At the door, she turned back to me. "One more thing, if you feel nauseous or dizzy you better get your skinny ass back here at once. And you'll want to put an ice pack on that eye to keep the swelling down."

Five minutes later, I'd signed the release form and made my way down the hall to the elevator. I felt Nurse Wren's eyes on me all the way, but managed not to trip and fall on my face.

Thirty-Six

I wasn't lying when I told Nurse Wren I'd rest better in my own bed. My plan had been to drive myself home and call Serena along the way to reassure her I was still among the living. But when I contemplated the long drive home and the serious pounding in my head, I found myself turning back toward St. Augustine Beach and Serena's apartment.

As I drove, I fought battles with myself about the wisdom of showing up at her door in my condition at four in the morning.

Look in the mirror, asshole. You're not thinking straight. What is she going to think when she opens that door and finds her big lug of an ex-boyfriend beaten to a pulp?

One side of the argument bounced around in my aching skull and I looked in the rearview mirror confirming Mr. Negative's assessment. But then, the other voice piped up.

You're in no condition to drive home. You need some TLC. If you had a choice, and you do, where would you rather look for solace and bed rest, at home with your dog or with Serena?

Couldn't deny the logic in the second argument, so I continued on to Serena's apartment.

Instead of banging on her front door and scaring the hell out of her, I decided to call. After three rings she answered with a sleepy hello, and moments later the door swung open. Serena was dressed only in an oversized pink T-shirt. Her eyes sparked briefly with annoyance until she saw my face.

"Oh, my God, Quint. Are you all right?"

"Can I come in?"

"Of course. I'm sorry." She pulled me gently inside and closed the door behind me.

She flipped on lights as we moved through the apartment into the kitchen. Sitting me down at the kitchen table, she studied my face under the overhead fluorescents, holding my chin and turning it from one side to the other.

"Sergeant Marrano called to let me know he'd found you, but he didn't ... I had no idea." I gave her an edited version of my night at the Alligator Farm and how I awakened at Flagler Hospital. "The nurse said I should use ice packs to bring down the swelling, and I remembered you had an ice maker."

Serena grabbed a plastic storage bag from a drawer and filled it with ice cubes, wrapped it in a towel and pressed it carefully against my eye. "When I didn't hear from you I got worried and called ..." she hesitated a moment before finishing her sentence. "I called the police."

"It's a good thing you did and that Buck Marrano happened to be in neighborhood. I know you're not crazy about the Marrano family, but Buck saved my ass. I don't know why, but he did, and I owe him."

Her hand rested gently on the back of my neck. "Can I get you anything? I think I have some aspirin."

"Took some before I left the hospital. What I need is to lie down."

Serena helped me to my feet and together we walked into the bedroom.

She touched my muddy shirt and wrinkled her nose. "You should get out of these clothes. Do you feel up to taking a shower?"

I told her a shower sounded good, and we moved slowly toward the bathroom where she helped me out of my shirt and blue jeans. Naked, with the ice pack pressed against my face, I waited as Serena tested the water with her fingers. When she was satisfied, she took the ice pack and nudged me into the shower enclosure.

"You soak for a while, and I'll throw your clothes into the washer."

Warm and gentle spray washed over me. I let the water sluice over my bruised head and face. Slowly, I shampooed and scrubbed myself, washing away the stench of the alligator pond from my hair and body. Little by little, life returned to my aching limbs.

When I finished, I carefully climbed out of the shower and onto the mat. Serena handed me a clean towel and I began drying myself. When I reached around to wipe my back, hot rivets of pain shot through my shoulders. I groaned loudly.

"Here, I'll do that." She took the towel from my hands and stepped behind me. I felt the thick material gently easing over aching muscles, her fingers kneading my shoulders before sliding down my spine to my lower back.

"God, that feels good." I turned around and Serena gazed sadly at my wounded face.

She reached up and ran a finger around my eye before taking my head in both hands. With only the slightest of pressure she pulled me to her and tenderly kissed my injured eye. Her lips eased down my cheek to my mouth.

As I responded to her touch, to her kisses, to the suppleness of her body against mine, a strange blend of emotions engulfed me. Swept up in a sudden joy bordering on rapture, I embraced Serena yet somehow felt isolated, as though watching through a window. I saw myself peering at the scene with a deepening melancholy, a grim awareness of my own mortality. How close had I come to never feeling Serena's touch again—to sharing the same fate as my brother's?

Shaking off the shroud of gloom, I ran a hand under Serena's T-shirt, over her smooth skin. She raised her arms and I tugged the shirt up over her head, letting it drop to the floor next to the towel. Hungrily, I kissed her, my hands caressing her breasts, cupping her buttocks and pulling her against me. I felt an urgency to lose myself inside her unlike anything I'd ever felt before.

Sensing my need, Serena led me into the bedroom. She lowered herself onto the bed, then pulled me gently onto her. Electricity charged my skin, sending sparks of pleasure coursing through my body. The tingling grew as our bodies met and melted into one another. Serena shifted under me, moving up, lifting her legs. I followed, pushing forward.

She stroked the back of my head, my shoulders, murmuring indistinct words in my ear. I moved by instinct, all raw emotion. Feeling the heat of our bodies as we shifted and slid against one another, tasting her sweetness, I wanted to possess every part of her. Unconsciously, I wanted to erase the memories of my close call and celebrate the fact I'd been given one more chance at life. My hands wandered over her smooth body: clutching a breast, palming her nipples, trailing trembling fingers down her sides, pushing them beneath her thighs and lifting them higher as I plunged deeper.

Our breathing seemed to be synchronized. Faster, shorter breaths. Our hips moved as one in the ancient rhythms of love until finally, with animal cries and our sweaty fingers interlaced, I collapsed with a moan.

"Oh, God."

"It's all right," she whispered. "It's all right."

Thirty-Seven

I awoke to find myself the lone passenger in Serena's bed. Sitting up, I stretched my arms out, forgetting the hellish beating I'd endured at the Alligator Farm. Immediately, pockets of pain hammered up my spine and I envisioned a miniature mountain climber scaling my back and wedging his chocks deep within the fissures of my backbone. On the plus side, the sharp pangs, which now ascended vertebrae by vertebrae towards my neck, made me forget my aching head for the moment.

The pounding in my temple returned soon enough, and I applied pressure with the heel of my hand hoping to suppress the torment. I shut my eyes thinking that no job was worth this kind of punishment. Then I remembered Jeffrey Poe. He was depending on me. Any career changes would have to wait.

I rolled over and buried my face in the pillow, inhaling the scent of last night's lovemaking still clinging to the rumpled bedclothes. My frustrations and self-pity vanished as memories of Serena flooded through me. Listening intently, I swore I could still hear tiny outbursts of pleasure burbling up from deep in her throat.

From the doorway, Serena asked, "How are you feeling?"

Surprised, I turned over and sat up too quickly. Dizziness forced me back to the bed. "Great. I feel great."

"Sure you do. Should I hire a nurse to look after you?"

I used my elbows to force myself into a sitting position. "There's nothing wrong with me that a little breakfast and a lot of coffee won't cure." I patted the bed beside me. "And maybe a little encore of last night's show."

Serena shook her head. "Better save your strength if you expect to make it through the day. Do you know what time it is?"

I looked around the room for a clock.

"It's almost one-thirty. I'll make you some coffee and scramble some eggs, but I want to talk with you first."

"One-thirty? Gawd, I've got to get moving." I swung my legs around, planting my feet on the floor. Noticing my naked thighs, I asked, "Clothes?"

Serena lowered herself onto the bed next to me, an outstretched arm across my legs keeping me from getting up. "I have your clothes, but first I have to tell you something."

I tried to read her face, but she wouldn't meet my eyes. "What is it?"

"I haven't been entirely truthful with you."

I waited for her to continue.

"I told you I called the police last night, and—"

"And you saved my life."

"Only because I called Buck Marrano."

"I know, he told me you called the SAPD and he responded to the call."

She shook her head. "No, Quint, you're not listening. I didn't call the police department, I called Buck Marrano at home and begged him to find you."

Knowing Buck's grandfather had crippled her uncle, I couldn't imagine Serena asking help from any of the Marrano clan, particularly a closet racist like Buck.

"You're saying you have Buck's home number? You know him personally?"

She surveyed my ruined face for a moment before telling me, "In college, I discovered white men were as attracted to me as black men. When I returned home to St. Augustine, I opened myself up to the possibility that I could rise above the stereotypes. Help bring St. Augustine into the twentieth century."

"And Buck helped you do that?"

"I thought so. For all his brashness and occasional arrogance, Buck has a surprisingly sensitive core."

I snorted.

"I'll admit he keeps it well hidden."

"So you, what? Dated?"

"For a brief time. You have to remember this was twelve years ago. I was young, and I hadn't heard Uncle Walter's story yet. Someone told my father I was dating a Marrano, and he had Uncle Walter tell me how Bat Marrano and his grandson crippled him. I broke it off with Buck the very same day."

This explained Marrano's hostility toward me from the outset, and perhaps his less than forthcoming behavior at the hospital. I reminded myself that Serena's life before she met me was her own business, and attempted to dismiss the graphic pictures of Buck and Serena flitting through my head.

"Thanks for telling me, but like you said, it's ancient history." I wrapped my arms around her and kissed her. "Today is what counts, and after last night, who knows."

"Quint, you're the first white man I've dated since Buck Marrano. I wanted you to know that. I do care for you, but last night was mostly a reaction to the trauma you suffered mixed with my own guilt."

"Guilt? Guilt for what?"

"Guilt comes with the territory, I guess. What I'm trying to say is we should take this one day at a time and not jump to any *happily ever after* conclusions. Besides, I don't want to worry about whether someone is going to kill you every time you go to work."

"I know this doesn't look good," I said, pointing to my eye, "but it won't happen again. Believe me."

"How can you be sure? I'm sorry, but I can't live with something like this hanging over my head all the time."

Maybe last night's lovemaking was exactly what she said it was—a visceral reaction to my trauma, but there must have been more to it than the sex. A connection had been made on a level I'd never experienced before. But then, near-death experiences probably have that affect.

Confused, I sputtered, "Fine, whatever you say. We'll take it one day at a time. Now, can I get dressed?"

While Serena fixed me breakfast, I made a quick call to Charla and asked her to run by my apartment and take care of Dudley and Bogie. Next I visited the bathroom. Flicking on the light, I stared at the battered face in the mirror. It reminded me of a boxer after enduring ten-rounds of punishment with a young Mike Tyson. Last night, a small platoon of red had made inroads across the white of my eye. This morning, the red army had clearly won the battle. My entire eye was bathed in what looked like fresh blood, so thick I imagined it spilling out of the socket and pouring down my face. Dark, purplish bruises decorated both eyes and I wondered how Serena allowed such a creature into her bed.

"I have to run to the office for an hour or so," Serena said when I entered the kitchen. "Breakfast is on the table. Take your time and we'll talk later." She kissed me before leaving.

While swallowing my last bite of eggs, the morbid thought struck me that if not for Buck Marrano's heroics, I'd have ended my days as a crocodilian midnight snack. Dead as Clayton Ford Henderson.

That fleeting neural reminder of the dead poet sparked a quirky switcheroo in my line of thinking. Henderson must be involved with this puzzle. I didn't know how or why, but like a giant wheel, the spokes all pointed in his direction. I thought about his abandoned children. About how he left them with Lester Sternwald, the sleazebag attorney, and turned his back on them forever. Jack Fuller told me only the barest details of the lawyer's involvement with Henderson's twins. Now I wondered if they played any part in the adoption scam leading to his arrest. Taking a chance Fuller might be in his office on a Saturday, I made the call. He picked up on the second ring.

After our greetings, I said, "Jack, you told me Lester Sternwald had served some time for an adoption scam."

"Uh huh. In the Limestone Correctional Facility, as I recall."

"What kind of scam was he working?"

"Sternwald had a source inside one of the adoption agencies who told him when couples were rejected for one reason or another. He'd contact them and say he represented an unwed mother looking to place her child in a good home. He showed them pictures of some of the babies he'd placed—"

"Wait, do you think he might have used the Henderson babies?"

"He could have."

"So what happened?"

"He strung these poor folks along, sucking them dry for phony medical expenses, for food and board. Hell, I think he even got money for plane tickets so they could fly the mother in for a visit. Of course, in the end the mother had a change of heart and they were left with nothing but empty promises that he'd find another baby for them."

"And these people didn't complain?"

"Think how desperate they must have been. They'd tried all the legitimate avenues only to be told they weren't suitable parents. This was before people flew all over the world adopting Chinese, Russian and Vietnamese babies. Legitimate agencies had turned them down, and even if they suspected something shady, Sternwald was their last hope. I'd heard he had a girlfriend who posed as the unwed mother when the couples insisted on meeting the girl. They even had a baby to show them, but, of course, they never got to keep the kid."

"How many times did he pull this stunt?"

"Not sure. At least a half-dozen times before someone went to the authorities."

"Did he use the same baby?"

"I still have the file on my desk. Give me a minute." He returned shortly. "Doesn't say. Is that important?"

"I don't know. Does the report say what happened to the baby he used as bait?"

"No. He probably had more than one."

"Do me a favor, Jack. Check Christopher Henderson's death certificate and see when he died."

"You think he was one of the babies Sternwald used in the scam?"

"Could be."

"Makes sense. And when the kid died, Sternwald probably found himself another one. I'll check on it and let you know if I find anything."

"There's another thing. See if you can dig up some background on Amelia Faye—his sister. Including anything you can find on the adopted family."

"Boy, you're really straining our friendship," he grumbled. "How about some professional courtesy for all this work I'm doing for you?"

"Sure. Whatever you need."

"Cynthia and I are taking the grand-kids to Disney World in a few weeks and we thought we'd spend a day in St. Augustine."

"That's great. Dinner is on me. Just let me know when you're coming in."

"Well, actually, I was hoping you'd be able to get us some passes to the Alligator Farm. Scotty has this thing about gators and I promised him a visit."

Thirty-Eight

Fortified by another cup of coffee, I decided to take care of a few things in St. Augustine before returning home. My call to Fuller had further triggered my curiosity about Henderson's past. If Erin Marrano was his daughter, as I suspected, I wondered if the old man had kept any ties to his past. Perhaps somewhere in that landfill he called an office I'd find the adoption papers he signed when he turned the twins over to Sternwald.

After a few knocks on the door of the Martinez House, Watts opened it and greeted me with a perplexed look.

"What the hell happened to your face?"

"Careless accident. Mind if I come in?"

"Of course not." His blond hair was spiked haphazardly. He wore a pair of cut-off Levis and a red tank top exposing solid shoulders and arms ripped with muscles.

Inside, I offered my condolences on Henderson's death. He hung his head for a moment before looking at me, his pale blue eyes gleaming with emotion.

"Thanks. I appreciate that. Guess I was all he had left in this world. Why did I have to pick that day to visit my cousin in Tampa? I should have been here for him when he needed me most."

"Don't beat yourself up over it. I know he appreciated your friendship these last few months of his life. I understand he left you some money and the use of his home."

Watts nodded.

"Have you done any cleaning?" I poked my trigger finger toward the ceiling.

"As a matter of fact, I'm already working on the housecleaning. You want to help?

"Not really, but I'd like to check on something."

Watts had made quite a dent in the piles of boxes and old newspapers that littered the room. I commended him on his housekeeping skills.

"Mr. Henderson had a hard time throwing things away," Watts said.

"Did you find anything of value?"

"Not unless you consider ten years worth of old magazines and newspapers valuable. He had boxes of his poetry books, too. Take some, if you want. I plan to donate them to the library and local schools."

"Do you mind if I look through the desk?"

He raised an eyebrow. "Looking for anything in particular?"

I didn't want to tell him too much about Henderson's less than commendable past as a father figure, or that I thought my client was the dead man's daughter. "I honestly don't know. It's a long shot, but I wondered if his suicide had any connection with Commissioner Marrano's death."

"You're kidding, right?"

"I said it was a long shot. But stranger things have happened."

"Go ahead if it'll satisfy your curiosity. But his attorney's already been here along with one of the police detectives. I don't think you're going to find much of anything."

He was right. I rummaged through stacks of bills, old correspondence, the usual assortment of office supplies, and a drawer reflecting his obsessive-compulsive habits. It overflowed with paperclips, rubber bands, pencils, some worn down to the nub. I found markers, rulers and scraps of papers with odd phrases that might have been ideas for poems, but no adoption papers.

I thanked Watts for letting me snoop around and wished him well. "What's next for you?" I asked him at the front door.

"I'll see if the hospital needs anyone on their rehab staff. There's always private work with people like Mr. Henderson who need personal therapy. Might as well hang around. At least I don't have to pay any rent for the next year."

Walking to my car, my internal pinball machine began flashing again telling me I'd missed something. I waited for a spark of inspiration, but nothing surfaced in my battered brain.

I left my car parked near Henderson's house after pulling out my sunglasses. I was going to walk to the SAPD on King Street to see Marrano and I didn't want to scare any young children. Besides, the light hurt my eyes, even though the sky was overcast.

I owed Buck Marrano my life, but more than that he was another of the central figures in this case. William Marrano was Buck's brother, which made him Erin's brother-in-law. He was also the first cop on the scene after Henderson's death, and now I learned he and Serena had once been an item. I wondered where the coincidences stopped and conspiracy began.

My head reeled with the interlacing connections. After last night, I could relate even more with Walter Howard's savage beating in 1964. Bat Marrano had brought his grandsons along to watch the Klan deliver white justice to the NAACP leader. In their own way, the two Marrano brothers made their mark on St. Augustine. One of them would become a Detective Commander in the St. Augustine Police Department, while his older brother, the dead vice mayor, a successful realtor and politician. In my mind, there was no question that William Marrano was the eager boy who took the first whack at Howard.

Unless I misread the signals, Marrano knew a lot more than he'd shared with me. I asked for him at the front desk. In less than a minute, he walked into the lobby pulling sunglasses from his shirt pocket. He studied my face for a moment, but said nothing, only shaking his head

"I haven't eaten yet. Do you want to grab a sandwich next door?"

"Sure, I can eat."

We walked to Flavor's Eatery, a little sandwich shop on the corner of King and Riberia Streets. Taking our baskets outside, we sat at one of the umbrella-covered tables. A dump truck rumbled along King Street, grinding through gears as we chewed our sandwiches.

"Anything on my assault?" I asked him.

"Apparently, the lock on the service door had been picked. No fingerprints, but we got some partial footprints. I don't think they'll come to anything." He slurped a large sweet tea through a straw and wiped his mouth.

"Doesn't sound very hopeful," I said.

"Not unless something else pops up. We didn't find the note or your piece. Sorry."

"I have a spare, but I hate to think this asshole's still walking around loose."

"I don't like this sort of thing happening in my city, either. Makes us look bad."

Sometimes first impressions are difficult to overcome. Buck Marrano made the worst kind of impression on me from the moment he jumped all over Jeffrey Poe, sucker-punched me, and later accosted me in the parking lot. After that, I had him pegged as a racist bully. Yet Serena had been smitten with him at one time. And let's not forget the man saved my life.

"Listen, Buck, I want to thank you again for saving my ass. It took a lot of balls to go into that alligator pen in the middle of the night."

He colored and seemed genuinely embarrassed by my remarks.

"Part of the job. I'm glad I was around when Ms. Howard called." He rubbed a finger over his nose and gazed away, taking a sudden interest in the Methodist Church across the street

"Uh huh, part of the job. Serena told me about dating you a while back."

"She did?"

"Yeah, she did."

"Damn, I would've liked to seen your face. Surprised?"

"You have to admit you're not exactly the poster boy for racial harmony."

"We were a lot younger then, and it didn't last very long before we went our separate ways."

We both knew the reason for their break-up. Walter Howard. Did he really think he could date Howard's niece without having to face the ugly legacy left behind by his grandfather? Curious to hear what he'd say about Howard, I asked him, "This doesn't have anything to do with the case, but you remember me telling you I'd met Serena's uncle?"

"The N-double-A-CP guy?"

"That's him. You know, he told me two kids were there when your grandfather crippled him. One of the boys even took part in the beating."

Marrano stayed silent, gnawing at his lower lip. When he spoke again, his voice wavered and I strained to hear him. "He shouldn't have done that."

Was he talking about his brother? About Walter Howard? Or Bat Marrano? "Howard didn't have much choice in the matter, if that's what you mean. They tied him up and took him to a field where some maniacs crushed his knees with a club."

Marrano's eyes seemed to cloud over. Had his thoughts returned to that night in 1964? His memories must be filled with frightening bogeymen. But these monsters didn't live under his bed or in the closet of his childhood imagination. One of them was his grandfather and the other his dead brother.

Thirty-Nine

My cell phone drummed to life as I drove north on US 1 toward my Jacksonville Beach apartment. I expected to hear Fuller's voice when I said *Hello*. Instead, another familiar voice said, "Mr. Mitchell, this is Pamela, Mr. Laurance's executive assistant." Voice clipped. All business.

"Yes, how can I help you?"

"Please hold for Mr. Laurance." The line went dead and I held for Mr. Laurance.

Thirty seconds later, there was Kurtis Laurance's unctuous voice. "How are you feeling, Mr. Mitchell? I understand you had a close call last night at the Alligator Farm."

"That's right, but I'm still above ground. I doubt if you're really interested in my health, though, so why don't you get to the point."

"I'm sorry if we got off to a bad start. My life's been a blur lately. Keeping up with my campaign schedule and shepherding all the construction details for Matanzas Bay hasn't been easy. That's no excuse for rude behavior, but there's something important I'd like to discuss with you. If you're feeling up to it, that is."

Laurence had slipped into his politician's persona, his voice ingratiating and appealing. "What is it?" I asked, letting my irritation show.

"Not on the phone. Can you come by my office?"

"Now?"

"If it's not too much trouble."

I was only six miles from his office. "I can be there in fifteen minutes."

Unlike my last visit, Laurance's assistant was waiting for me when I entered the lobby. She ushered me into his office suite and closed the door behind her. Laurance rose from behind his ostentatious desk to greet me. He gripped my hand tightly, his other hand grasping my forearm. I expected to see Tallabois lurking in the background, but Laurance's security chief was noticeably absent.

He examined my battered face. "Are you sure you're all right? I have an excellent specialist I can recommend."

"It looks a lot worse than it is. I'll be back to my old handsome self in a few weeks."

"Good." He still clutched my hand. "Good," he repeated, and we walked to the chairs by the window.

"I know you must be wondering why I called."

"You might say that."

"I felt bad after the little scene with Lem at the commission meeting. Also, I said some cruel things about Clayton Henderson and then the poor man commits suicide." He shook his head and opened his hands as if to say, *who knew this would happen.* "It's certainly been an eventful week for you."

"Hasn't it?"

"I wanted to apologize for Lem's belligerence. He means well, but sometimes his sense of duty leads him astray."

"Sounds like the definition of a loose cannon."

"Perhaps, but that's one of the reasons why I wanted to speak with you."

Lifting the top folder from a stack lying on the table, Laurance held it a moment as though judging its weight. "This contains the latest poll figures from a survey taken last week. Although the first primary is more than a month away, it shows me twenty points ahead of the Attorney General, my most serious challenger, and nearly thirty points ahead of the Democratic candidates."

"Congratulations."

"I'm quite pleased, as you may gather, but a lot can change between now and November."

"Sounds like you're in the driver's seat, so I doubt you invited me here to give you political advice."

The broad smile spread across his face again. "In a way, Quint—you don't mind if I call you Quint? In a way, you could be very helpful."

"How so?"

"I've taken too much time away from campaigning tending to business matters. By-the-way, we missed you at the groundbreaking ceremony this morning."

I pointed at my bruised face. "I was otherwise detained. Everything go well?"

"Couldn't be better. As I was saying, I've taken time away from campaigning to make sure Matanzas Bay and some other projects stayed on track. Monday, I return to the campaign fulltime. I'll be making five, six stops a day all over the state. Republican Club meetings, civic organizations, town hall meetings, fundraisers, you name it. Wherever my staff can find a few hands for me to pump."

His expression implied he was a reluctant participant in the three-ring circus of big-scale, high-budget political campaigns, but I felt he relished every moment of it. "Exciting times ahead for you," I offered.

"Non-stop. Everything is planned to the second. Once we're underway I can't afford a potential loose cannon, as you said, creating problems for me."

Any number of issues might pop up before the elections, but Laurance seemed to have everything going for him. His chief competitors were longtime politicians, many of them bumped from office due to term limit restrictions. Most political insiders believed the recent gambling scandals had set the stage for Laurance to win going away.

"Here's the point, Quint. I've always prided myself on finding the best people to work for me and then giving them the authority to do their jobs. It's the secret to my success. That and the fact I'm just plain brilliant."

He laughed heartily at his little joke, and I found his good humor contagious despite myself.

Laurance turned off his laugh and said, "Unfortunately, I didn't follow my own rules and hired Tallabois at the urging of one of the party hacks in the panhandle."

"The man does have a few rough edges."

"True, but don't judge him too harshly. He's had a tough time of it recently. His wife is in a cancer ward in Baton Rouge, and he's been spending every cent I pay him on her medical care. I feel for him, but it's time to move on. I'm hiring another security chief and you're the man I want."

Blame my head trauma, but I never saw it coming. "Me?"

"Don't look so shocked, Quint. I told you I always look for professionals."

I could think of a dozen reasons why he had tagged the wrong man. "I'm flattered, but as governor you'll have your pick of anyone in the Highway Patrol or the FDLE."

"Yes, but I've been a private businessman all my life and I want someone without any ties to the state bureaucracy. Someone who understands the way business works, as well as having a good head for security and investigation."

It seemed to make sense when he explained it that way, but still I asked, "Why me? There are probably a hundred people within fifty miles of here with better resumes."

"Don't be so modest." He pulled another folder from the stack and opened it. Inside were a dozen or so sheets of paper and he lifted out the first document. "Quinton Logan Mitchell, you actually have a very impressive track record. Good family background. Good education. You achieved Master-at-Arms ranking in the Navy, and your service during the first Gulf War was exemplary. Some people might even call you a hero."

He was referring to the commendation I received for my part in putting down a prison rebellion by Republican Guard soldiers that left three people dead.

"You did solid work with the DEA before forming your own investigation business. You have hands on experience with law enforcement and private enterprise. My sources tell me you are a well-respected professional in your field." He set the report on the table between us and folded his hands on top of it.

"Admit it; you're head and shoulders above Lem Tallabois. Your expertise is wasted as a private investigator. With me, you'll have a much larger stage."

"Politics has never been my game."

"I'm not talking about politics. You'll be point man for all security operations for me as governor, and for the St. Johns Group. You'll tell the Highway Patrol what to do as it relates to my protection, and when I leave office you continue as security head for my company. How does that sound?"

Serena's words rushed through my head. *I don't want to worry about whether someone is going to kill you every time you go to work.* If I wanted it, Kurtis Laurance was offering me the perfect solution.

"This is all a bit overwhelming, and totally unexpected."

"I consider myself a good judge of people and even though we didn't get off on the right foot at our first meeting, I believe you're the man for the job."

"I don't know what to say."

"Maybe this will help you make up your mind. I won't embarrass you by asking what your annual take home might be as a private investigator, but I'm offering you a starting salary of two hundred thousand dollars."

I attempted to get my head around the number of zeros. "Per year?"

"Yes, of course." He smiled at my incredulousness before turning serious. "Here's the thing, though. I'm flying to Tallahassee in the morning for a planning session with party officials before my campaign swing starts on Monday. We'll be taking the corporate jet, and I wanted you to come along if possible. You'll have the opportunity to meet some of my campaign advisors and give me your impressions. Of course, I'd also like you to travel with me Monday for my campaign swing."

"I don't know, I have a pretty full plate right now."

"It's not a deal breaker, by any means. I know this has all been sudden and you have to get your other affairs in order."

"I don't see how I can drop everything and—"

"That's perfectly understandable, but I do want your answer by nine tonight." He tapped his index finger on the folder. "I need to have everything in order before we start, and knowing you're on my team will put my mind to rest. Of course, if your answer is no I'll have to make alternate plans."

He gave me his cell phone number and I promised to call. As he walked me toward the door, one hand on my shoulder, he asked, "By-the-way, did you ever take a look at the property around my Matanzas Bay development?"

"As a matter-of-fact, I did. Were you referring to the large vacant lot and run down stores adjoining the project?"

"That's right. Would you care to guess who owns both of those parcels?"

"I haven't the foggiest."

"Well, it doesn't matter now, but they belonged to Henderson."

"Henderson?" The codicil that mysteriously appeared in my mail itemized two parcels of real estate along with a million dollars as a bequest to Erin Marrano.

"Yes, Henderson owns, or I should say owned, both of those parcels. More than four acres between the two parcels. They'd fit nicely into the second stage of development."

"Didn't you try to purchase them?"

"Of course. My real estate people offered him a fair price."

"I guess he didn't take you up on your offer?"

"Henderson laughed at us and said it was worth five times what we'd offered. He was jockeying for more money, so I met with him personally. Increased the offer to five hundred thousand dollars. Very generous, I thought."

"He didn't take it."

"No, he wanted a million-and-a-half dollars. When I refused, he told me he would do his best to stop Matanzas Bay from getting built. Shortly afterwards, Poe began ranting about the project at the city commission meetings."

It wasn't much of a stretch to believe Henderson had fueled Poe's passions and caused him to go public with his feelings.

"Anyway, Henderson was only playing for time, hoping to keep me distracted until I increased my offer."

"And would you? Increase the offer?"

After a long pause, he finally said, "Yes. I spoke with Bill Marrano a few days before he was killed and told him I'd be willing to go as high as one million dollars."

"What did Marrano say?"

"He thought it was too much money."

"Huh."

"Bill suggested another more cost-efficient route. Eminent domain." Laurance paused for a few beats while I processed the information. "I couldn't say anything when you mentioned you'd heard Bill had called a special meeting of the city commission. You thought it was because he'd changed his mind about Matanzas Bay."

"So, the meeting was to—"

"That's right. We were going to begin legal proceedings to acquire Henderson's property. Obviously, he didn't want to alert Henderson by advertising his intentions. After Bill's murder, Mayor Cameron decided to put it off until later."

Now I wondered where Henderson picked up the story about Marrano changing his mind.

"Ironic, isn't it?" Laurance said.

"What's that?"

"If Henderson hadn't taken that plunge off the top of the lighthouse, and the city decided not to invoke eminent domain, he probably could have pushed me to a million dollars. But now I should be able to snap up that property for even less than my original offer."

Forty

Back at my apartment, I walked Bogie and fed both animals before pulling a handful of ice cubes from the freezer and dropping them into a freezer bag. Pressing the ice pack against my throbbing head with one hand, I grabbed a beer with the other and walked out to the balcony hoping to make some sense of the last few hours.

This day had not turned out the way I thought it would. Hell, the entire week was like something out of the *Wizard of Oz*. The only things missing were the flying monkeys, and there was still time for them to show up. A rumble of thunder rolled over the traffic sounds below me on First Street. I dropped into a rocker to work my way through Laurance's surprising offer.

Here I was in the middle of a murder case. Perhaps two murders if Henderson's death wasn't a suicide, and maybe three if Buck Marrano hadn't come to my rescue. Of course, I wouldn't be sitting here musing over the perplexities of life and death if the gators were a bit faster. If all of this wasn't confusing enough, out of the blue Kurtis Laurance announces he wants me on his team. Another coincidence? Maybe I'm becoming too cynical for my own good.

Laurance definitely made a poor decision by hiring Tallabois. It didn't take a genius to see the ex-cop was out of his league for such a high profile position. What about me? I spent most of my time tracking down deadbeats and investigating white collar criminals. Did I honestly think I could slip into the big money corporate world as head of security for a billion-dollar company?

Yes, I guess I did. But was that what I wanted? I'd always been the independent type. The Navy had more than its share of rules and regulations, but the DEA was a bureaucratic nightmare. I left to become my own boss. I decided what cases to accept and when to take a day off to volunteer with Poe's archaeological surveys. On the flip side, I hated the constant pressure to keep the business afloat, dealing with unsavory clients, and the boredom of what was often no more challenging than a clerk's job. And I wasn't forgetting my recent brush with death.

There's an old joke about a circus worker who cleans up after the elephants and constantly complains about his nasty job. When he's asked why he doesn't quit and find another job, he responds with, *what, and leave show business?* Maybe I was like that circus worker.

Laurance's offer had a lot of appeal, but I couldn't drop everything and climb aboard his jet in the morning. I owed it to Poe and Erin Marrano to see this case to the end. My internal alarm system told me I was close. But close to what? Close to who? If I forced myself to write a progress report it would be filled with gaping holes and wild speculation.

I chugged the last swallow of beer and set the bottle down. Spatters of rain pelted the nearly empty sidewalks of First Street. I looked at my watch. 7:10. Less than two hours before I had to call Laurance and give him my answer.

My intentions were to drink at least one more beer while I pondered the pros and cons of hitching up with Florida's next governor. Before I could return for a second bottle, my phone rang.

"Hello, Jack," I answered after checking the Caller ID. "Did you dig up anything else?"

"Your hunch was right, sailor," Fuller said in his Mississippi accent. I listened carefully as he gave me his report. I followed up with a few questions before thanking him for his efforts.

I pulled my spare .38 from the top shelf of my closet. Fifteen minutes later I was on my way back to St. Augustine.

Rain peppered my windshield with fat, oily drops that flattened and scurried to the side like roaches hiding from the light. The weather forecast called for the storm to break later, but I saw no sign of a let-up as I drove along A1A.

I used my handkerchief to clear the condensation accumulating on the inside of my windshield. The sky looked as bruised as my face. Thunder rumbled in from the south as the rain fell even harder.

Fuller's research had uncovered a missing piece to the puzzle, and in my head I heard the sweet sound of the silver ball hitting its target. Still, there were questions to be answered and motives deciphered. But the more I thought about it, the more sense it made—in a perverted sort of way.

Some of the pieces would have to wait until later, but now I saw how I'd been led astray by Marrano's and Poe's feud over the condo and hotel project.

I stopped at the traffic signal on San Marco, the lights from the merry-go-round across the street glowing lurid and spectral through my rain-streaked windshield. While I waited for the light to change, I called the St. Augustine Police Department and asked for Sergeant Marrano.

"I'm sorry," a nasally voice answered, "but he's on his dinner break. Do you want his voice mail?"

"Can you give me his cell phone number?"

"No, we can't give out that information."

I thought about asking for Horgan, but after Marrano saved my life I felt he should be the first one to know who killed his brother. I left him a message telling him I was on my way to Henderson's house, and to call me as soon as possible.

If I'd known what the evening had in store for me, I would have waited for Marrano to call.

Outside lights shimmered through the pouring rain, but the interior of Henderson's house was dark. I sat in my car for a moment trying to decide what to do. Should I wait for Marrano to call me back or take some action on my own? Finally, I grabbed the .38 and stuck it into my waistband under my water-repellent windbreaker. Running through the rain to the welcome relief of the overhang, I banged on the door, hollering, "Jarrod, its Quint."

No answer.

I twisted the door handle. Locked. I continued knocking and calling for Watts. Either he wasn't home or didn't want company. Back in my car, I watched the house for a minute or two more. Rain dripped from my body, blending with my sweat and soaking the seat. I stared at the console clock unsure of what to do next, willing Buck Marrano to call. This was stupid. Buck had been clinging to me like a cold sore for the past week, but when I needed him most he goes AWOL.

Patience had never been my strong suit. I kept telling myself a few more minutes wouldn't hurt and I should sit tight. Acting rashly could have deadly consequences. Let the police handle it. Good advice, but someone else might be in danger if I did nothing.

I flipped open my phone and tapped in Erin Marrano's number. The phone rang once, twice, three times.

"Come on. You have to be home on this gawd-awful night," I muttered to myself. After the fourth ring, I heard the hand-set fumbled as though she may have dropped it. I waited for Erin to say 'hello' and apologize for dropping the phone, but instead heard a muffled scream before the line abruptly went dead.

In my mind, I pictured Erin Marrano, her scorching blue eyes now cauterized with fear. I closed the phone and dropped it on the seat between my legs so I could grab it quickly if Marrano called. I cranked up the Toyota and turned off onto King by the statue of Ponce de Leon. There I joined a procession of cars crawling along Avenida Menendez.

I cursed the traffic and winced as a flash of lightning illuminated the Bayfront, swabbing a pair of sailboats anchored near the bridge with a ghostly light. When I saw a slight break in the traffic, I took a chance and swerved around two cars in front of me. Ignoring the angry gestures and honking horns, I fishtailed onto Myrtle Street and then Magnolia.

The street was dark and overhead the huge oak branches seemed to flail out at each other forming a shadowy and forbidding canopy. Closing on her house, I spotted a dirty brown pick-up truck backed into Erin Marrano's driveway, driver's door open, lights on. Fifty feet up the street, my headlights swept across Lem Tallabois' car parked beneath the drooping branches of a weeping willow. Dark splotches stippled the windshield making it difficult to see into the front seat, but I saw the outline of a man and wondered why Laurance's security chief was parked in front of Erin Marrano's house.

Two people moved briskly from the house to the truck. I was still half a block away, but recognized one of the figures as Erin. The other person had his back to me as he dragged her toward the pick-up and pushed her into the front seat. I didn't get a good look at his face, but there was no doubt it was Jarrod Watts—Erin's twin brother.

Erin kicked him and scrambled partly out of the vehicle. Screeching to a stop directly behind the truck, I saw Watts punch Erin in the face. She staggered and he pushed her back inside the pick-up and slammed the door. He ran around to the driver's side just as I jumped out to intercept him.

"Watts," I yelled, grabbing at him with my right hand. My fingers grazed his rock-hard shoulder searching for something to hold onto. Leaning into the truck, already off balance, I didn't expect his next move. Instead of pushing me away, Watts grabbed my wrist and pulled me forward as he accelerated. I lost my balance, slipping on the wet driveway and bouncing off the side of the truck.

Watts twisted the steering wheel to the right onto Erin's front lawn. The truck's rear wheels swerved toward my head. I rolled away and jumped to my feet watching the pick-up lurch crazily across Erin's front yard, tires carving twin furrows in the St. Augustine grass as he bounced over the curb and onto the street, barely missing Tallabois' Buick.

He turned toward me briefly as he roared away, and in the glare of my headlights I saw the finely chiseled features of Jarrod Watts smiling at me.

Forty-One

The tires on Watt's truck spun and squealed as he drove south on Magnolia toward the Myrtle Street intersection. I raced to my car and followed the glow of the retreating taillights. The truck's brake lights flickered momentarily at the stop sign before fishtailing around the corner onto San Marco.

A near-by street lamp cast a yellowish pallor over the scene, and as I passed the Buick on my left, I confirmed that Tallabois was inside the vehicle. I also recognized the spatter across his windshield as blood. The dirty red specks matched the thin trickle flowing from the neat hole in his forehead.

It was too late to help Tallabois but not Erin. Turning the corner, I spotted the pick-up truck on San Marco. Together, we headed east over the Bridge of Lions and onto Anastasia Boulevard where the traffic thinned considerably.

Watts increased his speed and I accelerated to keep him in sight. He cranked a hard left at State Road 312 where the road squeezed from four lanes to two. We swept through St. Augustine Beach past restaurants, motels, banks and condominiums.

Surprised I hadn't heard from Buck Marrano yet, I reached for my cell phone in the pocket between the seats where I normally kept it. When I couldn't find it, I scraped my hand across the passenger seat, keeping one eye on the road. Then I remembered dropping it between my legs after I called Erin's house. I boosted my butt off the seat, and felt beneath me. Nothing but damp fabric. My eyes raked the floor before I figured it out. When I jumped out of the car to stop Watts, I must have dropped the phone, and now it was lying in a puddle in the street.

Shit! I'd lose Watts if I stopped to make a phone call, so I kept his taillights in sight, wondering where the hell he was headed. Minutes later he made another turn to the left, passed the Oasis Restaurant and entered a stretch with gated residential communities on both sides. A1A widened to four lanes again. The speed limit increased to forty-five, and Watts bumped it up to seventy.

Like a somber gray curtain, the rain sucked up the headlights of the other vehicles until they broke through in garish splashes of orange and gold. I concentrated on the road and mentally kicked myself for not suspecting Watts earlier. There were clues, but I'd been so focused on the St. Johns Group's development that I hadn't connected the dots.

The lights on my internal pinball game didn't begin flashing until Jack Fuller told me about Sternwald's adoption scam. It struck me Sternwald may have used Christopher Henderson as bait. Of course, the infant's death report threw me off track, but now I knew it was only another of Sternwald's lies.

There were other clues, including the cold blue eyes Watts' and Erin shared. And when I saw him this afternoon he said something that slipped by me at first. He said he wished he hadn't been away visiting his cousin in Tampa when Henderson committed suicide. Later, I remembered Henderson told me Watts had gone to visit an uncle in Destin. Both of them were lies. Watts stayed in town to murder his father.

Of course, it took Jack Fuller's digging to put it all together for me. Keeping one eye on the pick-up's tail lights, I recalled how Fuller, through his research and questioning, had reconstructed the sad and sordid story of Christopher Henderson's young life.

According to Fuller, Christopher Henderson had been one of the babies used in the lawyer's cruel shell game. After baby Christopher became sick with what was first diagnosed as scarlet fever, Sternwald put a note in his file along with a forged death certificate. Then he gave the toddler to his girlfriend, Anita Watts, a hooker from Delmar, Alabama.

Fuller tracked down Anita Watts and learned of her relationship with Sternwald. He learned she had posed as the unwed mother in a few of his scams. In return, Sternwald, who probably thought Christopher was going to die, had given her the baby. The baby recovered, but Anita's crack addiction made it impossible for her to be a proper mother. After two years, she turned herself in to social services and voluntarily gave up the boy she'd renamed Jarrod Watts.

Watts spent his childhood bouncing from one foster home to another. The small and pale child often found himself bullied by older boys sharing crowded rooms. He learned to hide from them, but he also learned to fear the adults as much as his peers.

At age seven he landed in the home of foster parents Mr. and Mrs. Thomas Rindale. Authorities later learned the couple had never been married, and Rindale, who had changed his name, was a convicted pedophile from Texas. For nearly two years Rindale sexually abused the boy with the icy blue eyes and angelic face.

Despite his shame and fear, the boy eventually told a teacher, and they placed him in a state shelter. But the damage had already been done, and Christopher Henderson, now known as Jarrod Watts, became an abuser and bully before seemingly putting his life in order.

Along with Anita Watts, Fuller interviewed officials from the state shelter. He told me Watts graduated from high school and attended a junior college where he entered a pre-nursing program. Later he completed a physical therapy internship at a Huntsville hospital, but then dropped out of sight.

"Funny thing, though," Fuller told me in his telephone call. "About two years ago there was a break-in at that shelter where Watts grew up. Someone made a mess of their records."

"Did those records have details of his connection to Anita Watts?" I'd asked.

"You bet. Anita told me the boy visited her around that time. She wanted to unload herself of all the guilt she felt, so she told him the whole sordid story of his birth parents and how she and Sternwald had used him."

"So that's how he found out about Henderson and Sternwald?"

"Yep, and a few months later, Mr. Sternwald turned up dead."

"Damn."

"Yeah, and that's not all. This Rindale character—"

"The pedophile?"

"Uh-huh. He was a Vietnam vet who came home without his legs."

Forty-Two

As I followed the siblings along the rain-soaked highway, I understood Christopher Henderson's tragic childhood must have wreaked horrible psychic damage. Through his intelligence, charm and coping skills, he nearly straightened out his life to overcome the abuse he'd suffered as a child. Everything changed after he learned the circumstances of his adoption, about his twin sister and how Clayton Ford Henderson had abandoned them.

I could definitely see him wanting revenge against Sternwald and Henderson. But why had he snatched his sister? And what triggered him to kill William Marrano?

The rain had eased leaving a welcome break in the dark storm clouds. We passed Butler Beach and then Crescent Beach when I remembered our conversation at the Mill Top Tavern. Less than a mile ahead on the right was the Ft. Matanzas National Monument. Watts had talked about it as a place of refuge, comparing it to a hide-away he favored as a child. Now I realized that childhood refuge must have been where he went to get away from Rindale, trying to forget the terrible things he did to him.

The glow of the low fuel light interrupted my reverie. Shit. I should be okay for another twenty or thirty miles, which worked if Watts turned into the Ft. Matanzas National Monument. But if he kept driving south I'd be forced to stop for gas. Then what?

I edged closer to Watts' rear bumper, weighing my options. I had his license plate number and I could call the police once I found a phone. Maybe I should stop at the next restaurant or service station and make the call.

Watts stared at me in his rearview mirror as though sensing my indecision. He lifted his right hand, giving me the middle finger salute. Without thinking, I stomped on the gas pedal and swung into the other lane. I pulled along side the truck and Watts rewarded me with a grin. Instead of flipping me a bird this time, he held up a pistol.

Directly ahead I saw the sign for the Ft. Matanzas National Monument. Not waiting for him to get off a good shot at me, I surged past the pick-up, whipped the wheel to the right, tearing his bumper loose, and carrying him with me off the road. Together, we bounced along a short access lane on a path leading directly into a concrete monument sign marking the entrance to the Ft. Matanzas National Monument. Braking hard, I stopped within inches of the sign. Watts threw the truck into reverse, his dangling front bumper scraping the pavement, sending up sparks.

A wooden barrier blocked the road leading into the park. I half expected Watts to return to A1A. Instead, he blasted through the barrier and stormed into the park. I followed his trail of sparks. Watts skidded around the island of live oaks and picnic benches, bounced up on the curb in front of the squat visitor's center and came to a stop with his front right tire on the sidewalk. I hung back, parking thirty feet away and waited for him to exit the truck.

It occurred to me that following him here might not be the most intelligent thing I'd ever done. I was within spitting distance of a man who'd killed at least three people, and probably was responsible for my new alligator phobia and throbbing headache.

I watched Watts gesticulating wildly while Erin cowered against her door. Above them a slice of moon appeared through a break in the clouds, and the dim light shimmered in the wet oaks towering over the visitor's center.

Erin pushed open her door, but Watts grabbed her by the arm, dragging her across the seat and out on the sidewalk.

I impulsively jumped from my car. "Watts, let her go," I shouted.

Still holding onto Erin's arm, he half turned and in one motion raised the pistol and fired. It felt like a slow motion sequence in a movie, but as his arm came up I dove through the open door of the vehicle. The bullet passed through the driver's window where I'd been standing only a moment before. Just a lucky shot, I told myself, but I knew I was the lucky one.

With my head on the car seat, I stared directly at the dashboard panel and noted the clock. For the first time since I chased after Watts, I thought about the deadline Kurtis Laurance gave me. He said I needed to respond to his offer by 9:00 p.m. I only had ten minutes left to give him an answer. At the moment, his offer and the $200,000 per year salary sounded more tempting than ever. But in life, timing was everything, and I had more important matters to think about. Like saving my ass, and, hopefully, Erin Marrano's.

I slowly sat up, sneaking a look over the dash. Watts was dragging Erin up a leaf-strewn hillock to the left of the visitor's center. She wasn't going easily, struggling, slapping at her brother. One strap of her pink tank top slipped from her shoulder. In a panic, she turned to look in my direction.

A rush of adrenalin coursed through my bloodstream. My heart rate jumped and I felt beads of sweat on the back of my neck. A saner person would drive away. Find the nearest telephone. Call Sergeant Marrano and let him deal with Watts. The next call should be to Laurance, telling him to save me a seat on the plane.

Even while those thoughts thrashed through my head, I knew it wouldn't go down like that. Not after the way Erin looked at me. Her wild blue eyes glowed with a feral fear so intense I felt it pass between us.

"Help me," she screamed as Watts dragged her over the top of the little hill.

Images bombarded me. Images of William Marrano's corpse. Of Jeffrey Poe on suicide watch. Of Henderson's body lying at the foot of the lighthouse, broken and bleeding. I saw again the look of horror on Serena's face when she first saw my injuries.

There would be no call to Laurance tonight. He'd have to fly to Tallahassee without me. Sucking down a deep gulp of air, I pulled the Smith & Wesson from my belt and leaped from the car. I folowed the path to the top of the grassy hillock, careful not to slip on the slick, leaf-covered grass. As Watts and Erin disappeared over the other side, I ducked behind the trunk of a huge oak, yelling, "Jarrod, don't do this. We can talk it out."

He stopped near the bottom of the hill leading to the inlet and turned to face me. He held Erin in front of him with one arm, and with his gun hand gestured at me to turn back. A slash of moonlight cut diagonally across one side of his face giving his cheek the appearance of bleached bone.

"Get out of here while you can, Mitchell. This is no concern of yours."

"I know that Henderson was your father, and Erin your sister."

"You think you have it all figured out, don't you?" Without waiting for an answer, he raised the pistol and fired.

The round thwacked into the tree, sending chips of bark flying. I stayed hidden behind the oak for a minute and waited while my pulse decelerated to something closer to normal. Cautiously, I peered around the tree and spotted them at the bottom of the hill. Nearby, a narrow walkway extended over the inlet to a dock where several small boats were tied up. From a previous visit, I knew these boats were used to ferry people across Matanzas Inlet to the barrier island housing the fort. Watts stood staring at the boats as if weighing his chances of using one of them to get away.

"Watts, listen to me," I shouted. "Rindale did terrible things to you, but don't take it out on Erin. She's your sister, for God's sake. Let her go."

He whirled around, still using her as a shield. "Yes, she's my sister, and we're more alike than you'll ever know." His arm tightened around her throat.

"Show yourself or I'll put a bullet through her head." He raised the pistol, which I now recognized as a Glock 22, which takes a hefty 40 caliber round. He placed the barrel to her head.

Without a clear shot I didn't have much choice. I tucked the .38 into my waistband in the small of my back, stepped out from behind the tree and raised my hands. "Okay, Watts, I'm coming down. Don't hurt her."

With the Glock still pressed against Erin's right temple, he watched me approach.

"You tossed Henderson off the lighthouse, didn't you?" I hoped to get him talking, distract him until I was close enough to disarm him.

"That was sweet." His frigid blue eyes gleamed unnaturally in the moonlight and he smiled at the memory. "He squealed like a little girl, begging me not to hurt him. To give him another chance. Do you believe that? Now he wanted to be my daddy. After what he did to me, he's lucky it ended so quickly."

I took several more steps toward him. "A jury would take your terrible childhood into consideration, and—"

"Don't try to shit me, Mitchell. We both know there won't be any jury trial for me. Not after tonight." He twisted his hand in Erin's hair and pulled her head back. She gasped and clawed at his hand. "I like you Quint, but if you come any closer I swear I'll kill you along with this lying bitch."

I backed up a step and held out my hands to calm him down. "Okay, okay. Tell me something, Jarrod. Why'd you kill William Marrano?"

He seemed to be working through my question. "Henderson showed me his will," Watts finally said. "He actually told me he was fond of me and wanted to take care of me. What a laugh."

"But he did like you."

"The old fart willed his property to my sweet sister. I'd heard him talking on the phone to Laurance and knew it was worth more than a million dollars. When I asked him why he gave so much money and property to Erin Marrano he started blubbering like a baby. He was drunk as usual, and admitted he'd left his twins behind in Alabama. Said his poor son Christopher had died, but he would make it up to his daughter."

"He didn't know you were his son?"

"The old fool was blind to everything except my sis here. Of course, I told him who I was before dropping him from the top of the light-house."

"So you didn't know Erin was your sister?"

He smiled his choirboy smile and shook his head as though I completely missed the point. "I went to see her again that night after Henderson showed me the will to ... I don't know, to be closer to her." Watts still held Erin's hair, but he'd relaxed his grip, and she stood quietly as he relived the night her husband died.

"I watched them through the back window. They were arguing. She said something I couldn't hear and he slapped her. Almost knocked her down." Watts returned to the present for a moment, gazing at his sister.

"A few minutes later he drove off and I followed him. I knew about Marrano because Henderson and Poe would sit and moan about how the vice mayor was ruining St. Augustine. I didn't care about any of that crap, but when I saw him slap Erin ..." He stopped, his face softening as he looked at Erin.

"So you followed him to his hunting camp."

"He made the mistake of putting his hands on me," Watts said. "Asshole called me a little pussy and laughed at me. I hit him with the handle of the bayonet before sticking it into his ugly heart."

"So you stole the bayonet from Poe's house?"

"Poe has a bad habit of leaving his back door open and I slipped in there one day last week and helped myself."

"You took his hat, too."

"I was going to keep the hat, but after I killed Marrano, I figured if anyone saw me, they'd remember the hat."

"Why'd you bury him at the survey site?"

Watts smiled broadly as if I'd praised him for some extraordinary accomplishment.

"Why not? The cops arrested Poe, didn't they? I planted the shovel in Poe's shed along with ..." He stopped suddenly, and twisted Erin's hair tighter. "That's enough reminiscing," he snapped.

Watts eyed the path cut into the line of scrub oak and red bay leading to the water. Slowly he backed down the path, pulling his sister along with him until they stood on the narrow spit of beach next to the overhead walkway.

I followed him onto the sand. I started to reach for my gun, but he aimed the Glock directly at my chest.

"Don't do anything stupid, Watts." I was still five feet from him and needed to close the distance to have any chance of disarming him.

He solved that problem by snarling, "Shut up and get over here." Watts gestured with the pistol. "Hands behind your head."

I did as he said.

He backed up, little wavelets lapping at his shoes. Over his shoulder moonlight silhouetted the outline of Ft. Matanzas, its thirty-foot tower standing guard over the ghosts from past massacres.

Watts pushed his sister aside. She stumbled and fell on the beach. He grabbed the front of my shirt and pulled me forward. "On your knees," he commanded, shoving me down at his feet. "I gave you a chance, but you wanted to play hero. Keep your hands behind your head, and put your face in the sand."

I pressed my forehead into the damp sand listening to the croaky serenade of frogs and insects. The odor of brackish water intermingled with the putrefying remains of dead fish. For some reason, Watts hadn't shot me. If I played along, I might be able to do something. Not sure what, but I refused to end up on this beach like those Frenchmen the Spanish put to the sword—or like my brother.

Once again, an image of Andrew slipped into my head. My brother, slashed and bleeding on a Long Island shore. Jillian bent over him screaming.

Watts pressed the Glock to the back of my head and I instinctively flinched. Keeping the pistol aimed at my head, he ran his other hand over my chest, under my arms and around my waist.

"What's this?"

He pulled the revolver from my belt.

"Well looky here. The big, bad private eye's packing."

Watts swiped the revolver's snub nose across my scalp, whipping up a froth of blue green stars exploding behind my eyes. Nauseating pain radiated through my skull.

"You won't need this anymore," he said and I heard the gun hit the beach twenty feet away.

Lying in the wet sand, head pounding, hands behind my back, I weighed my odds. I might reach out blindly and attempt to trip him, but that was such a long shot it almost guaranteed a bullet to the brain or at least another whack to the skull. I felt as impotent as Henderson must have been when Watts pushed him off the top of the lighthouse.

"You're a real knight in shining armor, aren't you, Mitchell? Too bad you stuck your— Shit."

Watts stumbled backwards. I took a chance and lifted my head. He held a hand to his cheek where Erin had scratched him. He must have hit her with the gun because she was sprawled in the shallows, her legs splayed.

Digging my feet into the sand, I propelled myself toward Watts, using my head as a battering ram. I collided with his crotch and he gasped as my skull smashed his tender parts.

He staggered back with a cry of pain, and I jumped to my feet. Barreling forward and wrapping my arms around him, I drove him backwards. Watts staggered, trying to catch his balance. He pounded the Glock against my kidney as I struggled to hold his arms down. I ignored the blows. A greater fury had taken control of me.

All of my pent-up stress and anger erupted in a vicious frenzy. With a primal scream, I swung a loopy right against Watts' temple and dragged him into the water.

I grasped his gun hand, digging my thumb into the soft tissue of his wrist. Watts grunted and flailed at me with his other hand. I covered his body with my own. He stopped beating on me and for an instant it looked like he'd given up. Instead, he snatched a fistful of hair and yanked savagely. Stars burst in the periphery of my sight. Still holding his wrist, I grabbed his throat with my right hand and let the black rage carry me away. My fingers compressed his windpipe until he released my hair. I wanted to crush the life out of him, but Watts was strong and slippery.

He gyrated beneath me and we shifted and thrashed together, rolling in the shallow water until we were beneath the walkway. As we struggled, he forced his gun hand upwards, inching closer to my head. I pushed against his arm with every ounce of strength I had. The hand holding the Glock crashed roughly against the side of my head. Tears blurred my vision, but I whipped his gun hand and the gun tumbled into the water.

Jackhammers banged away inside my skull. Dizziness and nausea swept through me. Watts flipped me over until I was face down in the tepid waters of Matanzas Inlet.

One of Watts' knees pressed into my back, and he pushed my face into the slimy silt of the bay. The water was only two or three inches deep at this point, but deep enough. Salt water oozed into my mouth and nose. I held my breath, chest aching, lungs burning. Reaching back, hoping to find an eye to poke or anything to grab, but he stayed out of reach, and I thrashed helplessly.

My chest ached from lack of oxygen, my lungs felt like they'd explode if I didn't take a breath. It couldn't end like this, I told myself. I kicked and bucked in a futile attempt to shake him off, but he stayed on top, holding my head down with one hand while the other snaked around my throat. I jerked violently with my last ounce of energy and his hand tore at my shirt as I twisted away. I felt a sharp tug at the back of my neck and realized Watts had pulled the chain from my neck when he tore my shirt.

The dolphin medallion. My link to Andrew was gone. With a blackness born of desperation, I pulled my knees under me and rocketed my head back into the bridge of his nose.

Screaming obscenities, furious heat pulsating through my cheeks, I turned, ramming my head against his face over and over. A manic howling roared through me as our heads collided. I heard the satisfying crunch of cartilage and pulled back. A bright flume of blood poured from Watts' broken nose. He sprawled backwards in the water, stunned, eyes glazed.

Still on my knees, I gasped for air, the taste of blood filling my mouth. Watts lay back in the water. Blood poured from his nostrils and he had a nasty gash in his forehead. My hands pushed against my thighs as I struggled to stand. My arms shook uncontrollably and my vision rolled in and out of focus.

Watts wasn't finished.

He sat up and shook his head, droplets of blood flying to either side. One muscular arm rose from the water and I saw the silver chain wrapped around his index finger, the dolphin medallion glinting in the moonlight.

He groped in the shallows by his knee with his free hand. His fingers dug beneath him as though trying to pull his leg from out of a hole. When he raised his hand it held the Glock. I wanted to throw myself to the side, hoping he'd miss, but all of my reserves had been burned. As he pointed the pistol at me, its ugly black snout dripping water, I let myself fall back, closing my eyes against the inevitable.

A pop sounded at the edge of my consciousness. I expected to feel something, even momentary pain. Maybe a wrenching white light as the bullet passed through my brain. Nothing. Opening my eyes, I saw Erin Marrano standing over her brother's body.

He lay on his side in the water like he'd curled up for a nap. The bullet had stamped a dark hole into his left temple and a line of blood the color of rose petals trailed down the side of his face. I stared at Erin and for the first time noticed my Smith & Wesson in her hand.

Forty-Three

It seemed like a night at Disney World with flashing lights from four police cars and an emergency rescue vehicle. Apparently, when Watts crashed through the front gate, it triggered an alarm. A park ranger investigated and quickly called the local authorities from nearby Crescent Beach. They, in turn, called for an emergency medical unit and put in a call to both the St. Johns County Sheriff's Office and the City of St. Augustine Police Department.

An emergency medical technician had already tended to my many contusions and given me a pain killer. Peering into my eye, he advised me to have my head examined. Too late for that.

After conversations with officers from the different jurisdictions, I now focused on the familiar face of Sergeant Buck Marrano. Erin and I were sitting on either side of a picnic table in the middle of the park. Marrano stood at the head of the table taking notes as I gave him the details.

"Let me get this straight." Marrano's expression told me he wasn't totally buying the story. "This guy Watts was Henderson's son and Erin is Watts' twin sister? Henderson's daughter?" He turned towards Erin with a raised eyebrow.

"After his wife died, Henderson put the twins up for adoption," I said for the third time.

Erin shivered despite the oppressive humidity and a temperature hovering close to eighty. She had a wide bandage on her forehead and one of the EMTs had given her a light blanket. She wrapped her arms around herself, grasping the blanket as though expecting a heavy wind. She nodded in response to my statement.

The confused look still lingered on Marrano's face. "Why would he kill his own father?"

I gave him some of the back story I'd learned from Jack Fuller—the adoption scam, the foster homes, the abuse Watts endured. "Somewhere along the line, the abused kid turned into an abuser and then a killer," I added.

"You think he tracked down his father intending to knock him off?"

"That's what it looks like," I said with a little shake of my head. I gritted my teeth against the torrents of pain cascading through my brain. I wanted to lie down and let the drugs do their work. "Listen, can we take care of this later? Both of us could use some rest."

"Just a few more questions." Marrano turned to Erin. "Did you know about all this—Watts and Henderson?"

She glanced at me for a moment before answering. "I knew I was adopted, but had no idea Henderson was my father when I moved to St. Augustine. I didn't know anything about my birth parents or if I had any siblings." She shivered again and pulled the blanket tighter around her. "Mr. Mitchell informed me yesterday about my twin brother, but said he'd died of scarlet fever."

She looked away, gazing between us in the direction of the inlet. "No, I didn't know Jarrod Watts was my twin brother until tonight."

Her face was unreadable in the flashing lights. It reminded me of the statue behind the courthouse, stark and distant, a study in alabaster indifference. I noticed she hadn't mentioned Henderson's will or the money she and her brother would have inherited.

"I had my suspicions, but didn't put it all together until earlier today," I added.

Buck Marrano still looked puzzled, trying to make sense of the strange aggregation of events that began with his brother's death. I'd already told him what Watts said about following William Marrano to the hunting camp and killing him in a fit of rage. How he later buried Buck's brother at the excavation site, and planted the evidence in Jeffrey Poe's storage shed.

He ran a hand through his curly hair. "I don't know. You're telling me Watts killed my brother? He gives his father the heave-ho from the lighthouse, and then tries to kill his twin sister?"

"Don't forget Lem Tallabois." Marrano had already told us they found Tallabois in front of Erin's house.

"Right. Tallabois. The kid was a freaking killing machine."

"And he almost fed me to the alligators."

Marrano stared at me for a moment, lips twisted as though he'd bit into a rancid peach. He scribbled something in his notebook and closed it. "Okay. I guess that's enough for now. Come in to the station tomorrow and write out your statements." He moved behind Erin, putting his hands on her shoulders and helping her up. "I'll give you a ride home," he said to Erin. "How about you?"

"I'm fine to drive," I answered. "I just want to put some distance between me and this place."

Together we walked through the curtain of strobing lights toward our cars.

Forty-Four

Sergeant Marrano had already taken Erin's statement by the time I arrived at police headquarters late the next morning. He met me in the lobby and walked me down the hall to his office. After sitting in the chair next to his desk, Marrano handed me a white legal pad and a ballpoint pen, saying, "Write down everything that happened last night. Anything you think might be helpful to us."

I clicked the pen a few times, looked at him and asked, "What about Jeffrey Poe?"

Marrano inhaled and let it out slowly through his nose before answering. "We released him. The chief offered him the apologies of the department and wished him well."

I could see he was struggling to keep his emotions under control. I waited. He sighed and said, "And I apologized, too." The desk seemed to hold some fascination for him. He stared fixedly at it and finally said the words I was hoping to hear. "I'm sorry, Quint. You were right and I was wrong." He looked at me and I nodded.

Thirty minutes later, I finished my statement, signed and dated it.

"You might want to touch base with a man named Jack Fuller," I said. "He's the Deputy Director of the Mississippi Bureau of Investigation's Special Ops Unit, and the man who helped me get the goods on Watts. I wrote his name and number down for you."

"Good."

I started to get up.

"There's another thing you should know," Marrano said.

I sat back down. "What's that?"

"That night Walter Howard ..." He paused and cleared his throat. "When the Klan beat him up."

"Yeah, what about it?"

"I was there."

I remained silent. Marrano licked his lips and continued.

"Everyone knew my grandfather was in the Klan. He was proud of it. To his mind, there was an accepted order of things and he was protecting that order. Know what I mean?" His shoulders were slumped and fatigue etched his face.

I waited for him to continue.

"He'd written my father off as a loser, but he liked having me and Bill around. We got to ride in his deputy car from time to time. He took us hunting, and to a few Klan rallies."

His chin rested in his hand, his eyes fixed on the floor. I had the feeling he may never have spoken of that night with anyone. He lifted his head, letting his arm drop and looked me in the eye. "People think there's a lot of my grandfather in me, but I never had the stomach for his kind of white supremacy hatred and violence. When I saw that club come down on Howard's knee it made me sick to my stomach."

Silence smothered the office for a minute before I asked him, "But your brother enjoyed it, didn't he? Couldn't wait to take the first swing at Howard."

Marrano shook his head. "That's the thing. Bill wasn't there that night. He was home sick with mono."

"Come on, Howard saw both of you. He's dead. Why protect him now?"

"It wasn't Bill."

"You expect me to believe that?"

He hesitated, and I sensed a shift in his expression as though a great weight had been lifted from him.

"It was Kurtis Laurance."

"What the hell are you talking about?"

"Laurance is my cousin. He and Bill were about the same age and pretty tight when we were kids. He used to come to some of the Klan rallies with us, and my grandfather brought him along that night to show us 'how they dealt with troublemakers and niggers,' is how he put it."

"Laurance is your cousin? This isn't public knowledge, is it?"

He shrugged. "His family moved away when he was thirteen or so, and Laurance didn't move back fulltime until four or five years ago. Naturally, he didn't want to publicize his family connection to Bill after they began working together on the Matanzas Bay project. Conflict of interest is how it would look."

"I'll be damned."

"When you told me you'd met Serena's uncle I thought you might find out who those two kids were." His eyes shifted away from mine then back. "I told Kurtis about it."

"You told him?"

"He's family, so I figured I owed it to him. But only to give him a heads-up in case of any bad publicity."

While my brain scrambled to link together the implications in Marrano's admission, he jumped in again.

"I'm afraid that's what provoked your attack at the Alligator Farm. It wasn't Watts, it was—"

"Tallabois. Laurance sent Tallabois after me?"

"I don't think Kurtis put him up to it. Anyway, we can't prove anything, and Kurtis denies it all. He does admit telling Tallabois you were becoming a problem."

"But killing me seems like a radical solution to the problem."

Marrano picked up a stack of papers and tapped them against the desk, evening the edges, before laying them back down. "I went to his house last night after I left you and we had a long talk. Kurtis swears he had no idea Tallabois would attempt to kill you. He said Tallabois hated you and took it on himself after they talked."

"Do you believe him?"

"Doesn't matter what I think. There's no way I can prove Kurtis is linked to the attempt on your life. Hell, I'm not sure I could prove Tallabois did it."

Laurence's job offer now made a lot of sense. Tallabois botched the job, so Laurance figured he'd buy me off the case.

"I checked out Tallabois with the New Orleans Police Department and he had a reputation for running his own games and playing outside the rules," Marrano said.

I still wasn't convinced Tallabois had acted on his own. "What about the burglary at Erin's house?"

"Kurtis said he and Bill had exchanged correspondence about the Matanzas Bay project, including emails, which might prove compromising if they were misinterpreted, is what he told me. So ..."

"So, Tallabois to the rescue."

Marrano nodded.

"Of course, Laurance knew nothing about that, either, did he?"

"It was all Tallabois' idea. Told me the guy couldn't control his temper, and he was sorry he'd ever hired him."

"Did Tallabois find the letters?"

"I don't know, but I think not. Probably why he went back last night. Bad timing. Watts shows up and maybe thinks Tallabois is the police or a private bodyguard and kills him."

"So what happens now? With Tallabois out of the way and no proof of Laurance's involvement, I guess he has a clear road to the governor's mansion."

Marrano stood and I did the same. "You probably don't believe this, but I think he'll make one hell of a governor."

"Sure, like Hitler was one hell of a Chancellor."

He walked me down the hall. "Thanks for everything," I said, and left him standing in the lobby.

I pulled into Jeffrey Poe's driveway later that afternoon. He was mowing the front lawn, but killed the engine when he saw me. He wiped his face with the front of a ragged T-shirt that looked like it might have come from his collections of ancient artifacts. Instead of his trademark wide-brimmed hat, he wore a Michigan Wolverines ball cap. A shadow fell across the top of his face masking his eyes.

I climbed out of my car and walked over to him. "How you doing, Jeffrey?"

"Much better today. I understand I have you to thank for getting me out of jail."

"Erin Marrano should get the credit," I said. "She's the one who saved me from the embarrassment of having to explain how I got myself killed."

Poe smiled at my sorry attempt at humor displaying the gap in his front teeth. "How 'bout a beer?"

We sat on his screened porch while a ceiling fan spun overhead in wobbly circles and made hard clicking noises. I hoisted the bottle toward him and we clinked. "Here's to what doesn't kill us, making us stronger," I said, and took a long swallow.

He peered at my injured face. "You seem to have taken the brunt of the damage, Quint. I'm sorry, but I do appreciate everything you've done for me. You were one of the few people who believed in my innocence. You and Erin Marrano."

"It probably would have worked out even if I hadn't been involved." I looked at the half-mown lawn and gestured toward the mower. "I hope you're going to take a few days off before heading back to work."

A faint smile appeared on his face. "Taking a lot of days off," he said. "I'm tendering my resignation in the morning. Figured I'd go ahead and do it before they fired me."

"They wouldn't fire you. Not after what you've been through."

"It's all right. I've overstayed my welcome in St. Augustine. It would always be awkward, and I'd rather put this whole mess behind me. This gives me a chance to find someplace where I can do some real research."

We sipped our beers, only the clicking of the fan breaking the silence. Poe had taken off his cap, and his fleshy cheeks glowed a cheery pink. "Any idea where you'll go?" I asked him.

"I have a lot of friends in the field. Maybe I'll head southwest. They're making some intriguing discoveries of the Anasazi people out there. Rewriting the history books." A glint of excitement flashed in his eyes.

"Sounds like something you'd really enjoy. Just remember your old pal if you need a volunteer."

Later that afternoon, I sat in my car in the shade of an old oak bearded with Spanish moss. The dark skies and heavy rains of the past few days had evaporated, and the sun had returned in full force. I knew there were more questions needing answers.

This case began with Elizabeth Henderson's drowning in Oxford, Mississippi. It erupted again decades later. Most families remain together long enough to learn how to cope with the stress that builds and distorts the bedrock of their lives. Henderson's decision to abandon his twins created invisible seismic waves in his family, erupting with disastrous consequences generations later.

I approached the house, knocking on the door with the decorative wreath. Erin Marrano seemed surprised to see me, but she stepped aside and invited me into her home. I followed her to a breakfast nook off the kitchen where several manila folders lay beside a partially empty glass of what looked like iced tea.

"Sorry to interrupt you," I said. She'd combed her dark locks of hair into improvised bangs covering most of the bandage on her forehead. Her makeup couldn't cover the ugly bruise on her cheekbone where Watts had punched her. Otherwise she seemed to be in good spirits.

"No problem." She pushed the folders aside. "How about a glass of tea?"

"Thanks."

She busied herself getting a glass from the cabinet and a pitcher of tea from the refrigerator. Considering everything she'd been through over the past week, she carried herself with a surprising grace and confidence.

She placed the tea on the table and sat down across from me. "How's your head?" she asked.

"Healing. It looks a lot worse than it feels."

"I'm glad to hear that because it looks terrible."

"Yeah, actually it hurts like hell."

She laughed loudly, the sound bubbling up from her throat. "An honest man. How refreshing." Erin waited until I took a drink of my tea before asking, "So, what brings you here today? Delivering my bill for your services?"

"Actually, there are a couple of things I was wondering about."

She picked up her glass and took a dainty sip. A glint of moisture sparkled on her upper lip like a sliver of glass next to the dark red lips. "What's that?"

"How long did it take you to put Henderson and Watts together?"

Surprise danced across her face. Her eyes hardened. No more pretenses of vulnerability. No signs of the affection she'd displayed during my other visits.

"What are you talking about?"

"I think you know. You sent me Henderson's codicil, didn't you?"

"No, I—"

"Let's not play games, Erin. Somewhere along the line, Henderson admitted he was your father. Surely, he confessed everything to you, about your twin brother and how he'd followed you here to St. Augustine. He probably gave you the codicil to his will, which means you were in a position to copy it and send it to me."

She folded her arms across her chest and stared while I waited for her reply. A moment later, she relaxed, letting her arms drop.

"I first met Clayton at a poetry reading at the library a few years ago. He called me several days later and invited me to lunch. He said something about us being kindred spirits living in a cultural desert. That we should get to know one another better. We talked for two hours. Clayton shared stories of his career, people he knew, gossip about the fine citizens of St. Augustine."

"Is that when he told you he was your father?"

"No, it wasn't until months later. We'd meet for lunch or he'd take me to a concert when Bill had a late night meeting. We enjoyed each other's company. Bill was gone all the time and I was lonely. Clayton seemed to like me and I appreciated having someone to talk with. I guess he was probably building up his nerve to tell me. When he finally did, I had a hard time believing him."

"You knew you were adopted."

"Of course, but the idea of finding my birth father in St. Augustine, hundreds of miles from home, seemed too much of a coincidence."

"But it wasn't a coincidence, was it?"

"No. He said he'd hired a private investigator to find me, and then moved here to be close to me. That he regretted what he'd done and wanted to set things right."

"And the will?"

"The bequest was his way of making amends for my brother's death, for waiting so long to reenter my life." She picked up the glass of tea, started to drink, but put it down again.

"Clayton sent me a letter with the will asking me not to make it public. At least while he was still alive. He was very protective of his reputation, and didn't want the world to know he'd put his children up for adoption."

I compared her words with my own scenario of this bizarre and sad chronicle. She seemed to be telling the truth—up to a point. "When did you figure out Watts was your brother?"

Her eyes reminded me of blue calcite tumbled and polished by a lapidary's wheel—beautiful, but cold and unfeeling. "Clayton told me my brother died. You said the same thing. So why would I think he was my brother?"

"The family resemblance," I said. "A psychic bond. Maybe he approached you."

"After Clayton's knee operation, Watts appeared out of nowhere. They were always together, more than just a patient and a physical therapist. I thought it strange." She looked at me with one questioning eyebrow raised. "I'll admit Jarrod bothered me, but I never had any inkling we were related. And neither did Clayton."

"What happened then?"

"I noticed the way Jarrod always seemed to be hovering around Clayton like a protective hen. After Clayton's death, I re-read the will and wondered if Watts had anything to do with it. After all, he didn't have much and if Clayton died he'd inherit a lot of money—at least it was a lot of money for someone in his position."

"So you sent me the codicil?"

She inhaled deeply before answering. "Yes. I thought you might see a connection there and find out if Jarrod was involved."

"Of course, it didn't have anything to do with getting Watts out of the way so you'd be sole beneficiary of Henderson's estate?"

"Not at all." The words erupted from her mouth as harsh pellets of sound. "I didn't care about Clayton's money. Bill left me quite comfortable."

I studied her for a few seconds, the indignation mirrored on her face, the tilt of her chin, the eyes holding mine for a moment then skidding past my shoulder. I leaned in to get her attention before saying, "You put me on the case to get rid of Watts."

"You truly are hallucinating, Mr. Mitchell. That blow to the head must have caused amnesia."

"How so?"

"Have you forgotten Jarrod wanted to kill me? He was the one who wanted to inherit."

"Perhaps. Or maybe he came to your house to reconnect with his family and you turned him away."

"Jarrod Watts was a sadistic sociopath who murdered my husband, killed his own father, and, if I hadn't shot him, would have killed you." She glared at me, adding, "You haven't forgotten that, have you?"

She had a point, but as much as she denied it, I knew the answers to this puzzle were more basic than the emotional attachments of a long lost father and daughter. That's why I'd asked Jack Fuller to not only check out Christopher Henderson, but his sister, Amelia Faye, and her family background.

"Your brother may have been a sociopath, but I don't think he was crazy. There are a lot of reasons why we do the things we do. Jarrod was surely influenced by his horrible childhood. How about you, Mrs. Marrano?"

"Me? I had a perfectly normal childhood."

"Not quite true. I understand your father had an accident when you were young."

Her eyes narrowed and the brittleness returned to her face. "He fell off the roof of our house and broke his back."

"The accident left him crippled, unable to work. In fact, he needed constant medical attention."

Erin Marrano remained silent, her clasped hands resting on the table.

"Your father's medical bills demolished the family savings, and your mother was forced to sell the house. For several years, your family lived on welfare and you moved from one low rent apartment to the next."

"What's your point?"

"You were what, eight years old when your adopted father had his accident? Living on welfare, wearing hand-me-downs, seeing your mother humiliated taking money from family members she knew she'd never be able to repay. That sort of thing has an impact on an impressionable child." I glanced over at the large pretzel container half-filled with pennies.

"It might even be the reason a young, attractive woman marries a successful man twenty years her senior."

"You're out of your depth, Mr. Mitchell." She pulled her hands apart and pressed them against the table. "I don't need any pop psychology lessons from a second-rate private detective."

"When Henderson died, you'd inherit the Malaga Street property. And you knew the value would skyrocket once the St. Johns Group began the Matanzas Bay project."

"Ridiculous. I didn't know anything about the property until Henderson showed me the codicil."

"No? Your husband had a city employee research that property months ago. He knew who owned it. I'm guessing he told you."

She glared at me, one hand gripping the glass so hard her knuckles whitened.

"And there were a few other things that never added up in this case. Like your husband calling a special meeting to announce he'd changed his mind about supporting the Matanzas Bay project. You said there was nothing to it. Laurance told me the same thing. Yet Henderson seemed convinced the vice mayor had changed his mind. Where would he get such an idea if not from you?"

"I told you the truth when I said my husband wouldn't have changed his mind."

"You're right. Your husband hadn't changed his mind. He called that meeting to push the city into taking Henderson's property by eminent domain. But you told Henderson your husband had second thoughts about supporting the project and would put it on hold at the special city commission meeting."

"Why would I tell him that?"

"That's what I wondered. It didn't seem to make any sense until Kurtis Laurance told me Henderson owned several large pieces of property adjacent to his new development. I finally made the connection between Laurance's disclosure and the generous gift Henderson left you in his will. The same property."

"So what?"

"Laurance also told me he'd discussed Henderson's demands with your husband and would be willing to raise his offer for the property to maybe a million dollars. Your husband told you all of this. Of course, he had no way of knowing Henderson was your father or that you'd inherit the property after Henderson's death."

Erin's nostrils flared and I watched a flush of red spread across her cheeks. "Pure fiction," she said.

"Is it? When your husband told you they were going to take the property by eminent domain, you realized you'd lose much of the value of that land and you panicked. Henderson had to die before the city took action."

She shook her head in denial.

"By this time, you and your brother had connected. Watts wasn't stupid. I'm guessing he figured out why Henderson had been paying so much attention to you. He learned he had a twin sister after he broke into the record center of child services back in Huntsville. Do you remember what Watts said last night? He came to see you *again* after Henderson showed him the will. Again. And he called you a 'lying bitch.' What did he mean by that?"

"Just a crazy man's rantings."

"I don't think so. I'm betting he told you about growing up in foster homes, the abuse he suffered, and his plan to kill Henderson."

"This is preposterous."

"Is it? What kind of deal did you make? Offer Watts half of the money from the sale of the real estate if he moved up his timetable to do away with dear old dad? Maybe you even told him Bill Marrano abused you, hoping—"

"No, I wouldn't do that," she screamed at me.

"You told Henderson a fairy tale about your husband changing his mind about Matanzas Bay so he'd think Laurance would no longer have any interest in purchasing his property. In the meantime, you waited for Jarrod to do the deed."

She started to get up, but I pushed her down. "I'm almost finished," I said, "so hear me out." She sat back in her chair and glared at me.

"The final piece slipped into place for you when poor Clayton committed suicide. Wasn't it ironic that the city commission met on the same evening to praise your husband instead of asking the city attorney to invoke eminent domain? It was more than you could have hoped for. You knew the city wouldn't pursue eminent domain against the vice mayor's widow, and you could work out your own deal with Laurance."

I waited to see if she had anything to say before adding, "Of course, you never intended to share the money with Jarrod, and probably told him so last night. Which is when he went ballistic."

Instead of erupting at my charges, a cryptic smile appeared on Erin's face. "Have you seen today's paper? Front page story about how poor Mrs. Marrano, after losing her husband, and then, sadly, her father, was nearly murdered by a deranged serial killer. Wouldn't you say I'm the victim here?"

The tip of her tongue explored her lips as she closely watched my reaction. "Do you actually expect anyone to believe these paranoid delusions of yours, Mr. Mitchell?"

Erin Marrano abruptly pushed herself away from the table. "I hope that answers all your questions. Now I must get ready for another appointment." She walked out of the kitchen without waiting to see if I was following her.

At the front door she, said. "Thank you for your help. I trust you'll send me your bill." For a moment, her eyes filled with a mocking exultation, and she gave me a fleeting smile with more than a hint of triumph. In that smile, I recognized a reflection of Jarrod Watts, her ever-grinning tragic twin.

She closed the door and I retreated to my car. No doubt I'd been a pawn in Erin Marrano's little game. She was right when she said she would be viewed as the victim. Within one week, her husband murdered, her birth father and twin brother equally dead. This left her as the sole heir of a fortune totaling several million dollars.

All of us are the product of gene pools contributing more than a sequence of chromosomes. I wondered about the Henderson gene pool. Erin Marrano seemed to be an intelligent and insightful person. Supposedly, she'd been a caring and dedicated teacher. Still, I couldn't shake the feeling any answers would be found deep below the surface. Like my work at archaeological surveys, the deeper we dug, the more soil we turned over and screened, the more likely we were to discover hidden artifacts from the past.

Clayton Ford Henderson was a complicated man who abandoned his children and possibly killed his wife. His son used the abuse he suffered as a child as an excuse for murder.

And Erin Marrano?

If scientists examined the Henderson genome I wondered what they might find. Perhaps under their electron microscopes, they'd discover Erin Marrano was the smartest, most devious of them all.

Forty-Five

A month later, I wangled an invitation to a reception at the University of North Florida's Young Republican Club. The guest of honor was Kurtis Laurance and he was meeting with his VIP supporters prior to his speech at the University's Fine Arts Center. Over a hundred people were crowded into the meeting room, and I stood in the back holding a glass of red wine waiting for Florida's next governor to make his appearance.

After twenty minutes, he entered through a back door along with his entourage of campaign workers and local politicos. He worked the room like an old pro, shaking hands with everyone, making small talk, cracking jokes. He finally made his way along the perimeter and, while talking with several elderly women, spotted me hovering nearby. Laurance turned away, concentrating instead on the two women and their concerns about homeowner's insurance.

One of his aides came over and whispered in Laurance's ear. The candidate offered apologies to the women and moved to the front of the room. Taking a bottle of water one of his aides handed him, he swallowed a mouthful before addressing the throng of supporters.

"Friends, I want to thank you for coming out today and helping us eat these hors d'oeurves. I was afraid we'd have to carry them back to our plane with us, and I really don't need any more calories." He chuckled and patted his flat stomach while the rest of the room echoed his laughter.

He spent ten minutes ticking off the major planks in his campaign platform, the same talking points he'd repeated five and six times a day at stump speeches throughout the state for the last two months. When he finished condemning corruption in the previous administration, the need to cut taxes and bring more jobs to Florida, Laurance answered a few questions. Then he thanked everyone again, asking for their vote in Tuesday's primary election, and said, "Ya'll better hurry and get yourselves a good seat. You don't want to miss hearing my speech again."

Everyone laughed and applauded Kurtis Laurance as his aides hustled him toward the rear door. While the rest of the crowd hurried in the other direction to find their seats for his speech, I made my way toward Laurance's retreating figure.

Laurance and his entourage moved along a narrow corridor. I called out to him, "Mr. Laurance."

They all stopped, turning toward me. "I wonder if I could have a minute of your time."

My face had mostly healed, but there were still a few faint bruises around my eyes. I must have looked suspicious because several of his aides immediately moved in front of Laurance, shielding him from any potential trouble. A Florida Highway Patrolman stepped forward to block my approach.

"No, it's okay," Laurance said. "Mr. Mitchell and I are old friends."

He broke away from the others and strode rapidly toward me, a swagger in his step. If anything, he appeared even more confident than the man I met four weeks ago. All the polls showed an overwhelming victory for his ticket, and he wore the mantle of success as an invisible cloak. "You're looking good, Quint." He extended a hand, but I ignored it.

"I heard about what happened with you and Erin. Terrible. Just terrible."

"Looks like nothing can stop the Laurance bandwagon now."

"That's up to the voters," he said, looking at his watch. "I really have to go. I'm already a half-hour behind schedule."

"I know you sent Tallabois after me."

"Ridiculous. Lem was a loose cannon. You said it yourself. Heaven knows I couldn't control him. That's why I offered you his job. Whatever he did, he did entirely on his own. And the truth is the police don't have any proof he did anything, except get himself killed by that maniac." He turned to wave at an aide waiting impatiently at the end of the hall, tapping on his watch.

"I'm sorry you got caught up in the middle of this, Quint, but I had nothing to with it."

"I guess you didn't have anything to do with Walter Howard having his knees smashed either."

Laurance edged closer, bending toward me. Lowering his voice to almost a whisper, he said, "For God's sake, Mitchell, I was a kid. I can't tell you how sorry I am for what happened back then. But people change. I was twelve years old. People change," he repeated.

People do change, but my few encounters with the man told me that for all his success, despite his charisma and beneath the smooth veneer, Laurance was a manipulative and ruthless bully who'd do almost anything to get his way. Perhaps the voters believed those were strong leadership traits, but I wasn't convinced.

"What do you think the voters would say if they knew you played a part in crippling a civil rights leader?"

Laurance seemed taken aback and regarded me through wide eyes as though I'd suddenly popped into the corridor in a cloud of smoke from another dimension. He straightened, slipping back into the confident pose of the CEO of the St. Johns Group and Florida's next governor.

"Hell, Mitchell, this is Florida. If that gets out, it might even bump my numbers up a few percentage points."

With that, he turned his back on me and walked away.

The moon perched above the cluster of low buildings forming St. Augustine's horizon. Down below, the tiny San Sebastian River, no more than a tributary of the Matanzas River, flared with amber highlights. I couldn't help thinking about how the landscape would soon change, drastically altered by the condos and hotel of the Matanzas Bay development going up across the street. St. Augustine, with its bloody yet proud past, seemed to be one of those places where change was a reluctant visitor. Yet the town was changing despite itself.

Serena and I sat on the roof of the San Sebastian Winery, sipping a glass of their Castillo Red. A local blues band had completed a rowdy set, and we were enjoying the stillness of the night.

"Here's to a positively lovely evening," Serena said, holding her glass toward the full moon, and then to me.

We tapped glasses and sipped. Around us, clusters of locals and tourists were talking and celebrating their own personal victories. Five weeks had passed since my battle with Jarrod Watts, and all of the purple bruises, headaches and bloodshot eyes had finally disappeared. Serena agreed with me that this was worth celebrating.

"Any time of the day or night is lovely if you're around," I said with a straight face.

Serena laughed, but seemed to appreciate the compliment. "Maybe you should get hit in the head more often," she said. "You're turning into Mr. Sensitivity."

"Let's keep that between us. Okay? I don't think it'd be good for my business."

Streams of moonlight reflected across the rooftop, and Serena's face glowed with an inner radiance. She reached out and ran her fingers over my cheek. "Good to have the old Quint back."

"Good to be back."

She smiled, but I saw apprehension in her eyes. "You aren't giving this up, are you? Next time you might not be so lucky."

"Hey, I'm fine. Nothing that a few more nights with you won't clear up." I brought her hand to my mouth and nibbled at her fingertips.

"You're impossible," she scolded, pulling her hand back, "and you're trying to change the subject."

"Listen to me, baby. My profession doesn't even make the top ten most dangerous jobs list. Commercial fishermen and lumberjacks are far more likely to have a serious accident than private investigators."

Her expression said, *you're full of beans.*

"Hey, it's true. My job is usually boring and no more dangerous than yours." I pointed at my face. "Believe me, this private eye is done with murder cases. I'm only chasing after old women with walkers from now on."

I'm not sure she bought it, but some of the tension slipped from her face. "I just don't want to worry about you all the time."

"Don't worry," I said. "I'll be here to take it one day at a time, if that's the way you want it."

She squeezed my hand, and we sat in the glow of a citrine-colored moon while we finished our wine. I caught our server's eye and asked for the check.

"While you take care of that, I'm going to the little girl's room. I had a wonderful time tonight. Thanks."

"The night doesn't have to end here. There are a couple of four-legged creatures in Jacksonville Beach jumping at the chance to deposit hair on your dress."

"I'll think about it," she said, and walked toward the rest rooms.

While I waited for the check, I studied the moon and thought about the twists and turns my life had taken since I uncovered William Marrano's body. I'd settled back into my old routines at Mitchell Investigative Services, tracking down skip traces and uncovering insurance scams. The publicity from the Watts case even helped me land the Gulf Breeze Insurance account.

Everything had worked out for Kurtis Laurance, too. The news hounds were describing his overwhelming primary victory in terms usually saved for Nobel Prize Laureates and rock stars. Laurance still had to win the general election in November, but the pundits were already speculating on his upcoming administration, comparing him to other southern governors who made the leap to the White House.

I thought about Erin Marrano and her part in Henderson's, and perhaps her husband's, death. Maybe I should have pursued it more vigorously, but like she told me, I had no real evidence. Only my paranoid theories. I considered going to Buck Marrano with my suspicions, but in the end decided against it. There was no way the state attorney or a grand jury would bring charges against William Marrano's widow. Not on my gut feelings.

Hundreds of years from now, these mysteries will still be waiting for an archaeologist's spade, but what interested me at the moment was the more immediate future. I couldn't change the past, but tonight, for some reason, the future seemed alive with possibility.

I checked to see if Serena was on her way back to the table before pulling my cell phone from my pocket. I stared at it as though sensing it held the answer to a great enigma. I hadn't heard from Samuel Parks since that afternoon I exploded and told him to find another therapist. His daughter's tragic death would always lie heavy upon both of us, but I hoped he found a way to achieve some peace.

Without thinking, my hand reached up to the medallion hanging around my neck. I had retrieved it from Watts' dead fingers and it now hung from a new silver chain. My finger slipped between the top two buttons of my shirt, and I felt the smooth figure of the dolphin. In the past, touching the cold metal was a way to connect with my brother and reinforce the guilt I carried with me as a constant reminder of my failure. Now, as I touched the hammered stainless steel, I pictured the acrobatic leaps and smiling snout of a living creature.

My past had become part of my internal structure as much as the blood pumping through my body. But on this night, I felt the past had controlled me for too long. It couldn't be changed, but perhaps the future might. Taking a deep breath, I flipped open my cell and pulled the old numbers out of my head. I punched them carefully into the phone and hesitated a moment, my finger shaking slightly, before pressing the green Send button.

The ring caught me by surprise, and I almost changed my mind. I listened as it rang again, wondering what I'd say. With any luck, no one would be home. The voice on the other end startled me. It had been so long. Finally, I said, "Hello dad, it's me. It's Quint."

The End

While *Matanzas Bay* is a work of fiction, it should be noted that St. Augustine played a major role in the Civil Rights Movement. Throughout 1963-1964, blacks picketed segregated establishments, conducted sit-ins, and marches. Dr. Robert B. Hayling, a local dentist and Air Force veteran who led the movement, was viciously beaten by the Klan during this period. This was the genesis of Walter Howard's story.

Carl Halbirt has been the City Archaeologist of St. Augustine since 1988. Working with a cadre of volunteers he's helped to recruit and train through the St. Augustine Archaeological Association, Mr. Halbirt has salvaged and preserved remnants of the old city's storied past. I'm grateful to him for allowing me to observe one of his surveys, and for the important work he's doing.

Thanks also to my friend Kay Day for contributing "Clayton Henderson's" poem, *A Flash of Silence*, which added greatly to the story.

Readers familiar with St. Augustine will recognize the various landmarks mentioned in the book. The St. Augustine Lighthouse and Alligator Farm, for example, are popular destinations for visitors and, to my knowledge, no acts of violence have taken place there. Other places depicted in the story, like the Stuff of Dreams restaurant, are fictional. Everything else is true, except the parts I made up.

Keep reading for an excerpt from the next Quint Mitchell Mystery, *Bring Down the Furies*.

Bring Down the Furies

Quint Mitchell is on the move again. The private investigator tracks the "Heart Throb Bandit" to the tiny hamlet of Allendale, South Carolina on behalf of a client. In another time, Allendale felt the wrath of General Sherman's troops as they blazed a fiery path through Georgia and Carolina during the Civil War.

There's another conflagration brewing today fueled by a serial arsonist and an ugly confrontation between an ultra-conservative minister and the scientist responsible for a renowned archaeological survey known as the Topper Site, which has uncovered proof of the oldest humans ever found in North America.

Mitchell is pulled into the growing violence, working with the sheriff's department to calm the growing storm as a media frenzy leads to massive demonstrations, and arson turns to murder. Caught in the middle, Mitchell becomes a target for the arsonist, and must save himself while helping to save the town from being destroyed for the second time.

Enjoy this advance look at *Bring Down the Furies*

BRING DOWN THE FURIES
by Parker Francis

PROLOGUE

Flames flickered, then flared brightly. Within minutes, the fire was visible throughout the interior of the handsome plantation. The moon had slipped behind a bank of black clouds as if unable to face the inevitable destruction, but the growing inferno illuminated the night with a devilish hue.

Glaughtner's men had already foraged through the deserted mansion, dumping foodstuffs left behind by the fleeing residents of the stately home into an abandoned wagon they'd found in the barn. Hams and sweet potatoes were piled along with greens, preserves, oil paintings, and bottles of wine. He felt sure the wine wouldn't survive the forty-mile journey back to camp.

He watched his men cheer as the fire sizzled and popped its way into the entry hall and dining room beyond. Rippling shadows sidled over the yard. Flames blossomed, sending out torrents of heat. Glaughtner's face flushed, but he welcomed the heat. The night had grown increasingly frigid, a light rain only adding to their misery.

He stood mesmerized, watching the flames consume curtains and furniture, the smoke billowing through broken windows. Something exploded inside the house, sending fragments flying in all directions. Glaughtner stepped back several paces, unwilling or unable to turn his back on the conflagration. Not yet. Not before the first flames broke through the roof of the three-storied mansion.

When it finally did, the small band of men cheered even louder. Some of them singing and dancing their little jigs. Bottles of wine were passed from hand to hand. It didn't take them long to break into the spoils, he thought, but they had earned their rewards.

The wind shifted direction once again. Sparks and soot and pieces of burning debris flew through the night air. The acrid stench of smoke assaulted his senses. A nearby pine tree suddenly burst into flames, adding to the unholy spectacle.

Glaughtner remained fixed on what he'd created, his eyes glowing red in the reflected light of the fire. "Oh, lord," he murmured to himself. "Forgive me. I do love it so." A rush of pleasure shot tendrils of heat through his body, warming his limbs, his very loins.

"Captain, the men are going to drink themselves to sleep if we don't move on."

The speaker was a sergeant from Pennsylvania.

"You're right, sergeant. I think we've done more than enough damage here," Glaughtner said.

The sergeant nodded in agreement. "These Carolina bastards won't forget us for a long time, that's for sure. We left our mark on them."

Glaughtner gazed one last time at the flames devouring the house before turning away. "Gather the men and let's ride," he told the sergeant. "I think Uncle Billy will be proud of our work here tonight."

CHAPTER ONE

Allendale, SC – Day One

The pass flew over the receiver's outstretched hands, hit the defender in the back of the head, and bounced crazily away.

"You dummy," one of the players screamed at the defender. "That could have been an interception. How many times do I have to tell you to turn around and find the ball?"

The defender, a boy of no more than twelve years old, grinned and flipped his teammate off before retreating to his position behind the defensive line.

The offensive team huddled up, listening intently to the quarterback who punctuated his play calling with hand gestures toward the opposing team. As I watched the play unfold, I kept an eye on the motel across the street, watching for the familiar white Cadillac and the man I'd trailed to Allendale.

"Hup one. Hup two. Hike," the quarterback yelled.

I guessed he was one of the oldest players on the field, possibly thirteen or fourteen. He stepped back from the center, the ball in his left hand where he made a convincing pump fake to a freckle-faced boy streaking down the right sideline. When the defenders turned to look for the pass, he tucked the ball under his arm and squirted through the line. He feinted right, causing one defender to collide with his teammate. He cut to his left, broke an arm tackle and raced down the field to the makeshift end zone.

Watching the young quarterback brought back memories of my high school glory days. The cheering crowd rocking the wooden stands. My teammates pounding me on the back. The rush of adrenaline and the feelings of triumph that engulfed my seventeen-year-old brain. I led my team to the state finals in my senior year, throwing for over 1,200 yards and running for eleven touchdowns. Of course, I was lucky to have a future Pro Bowler as a receiver, but like the young speedster, I always had a good set of wheels. Even in college, I was one of the fastest guys on my team, even though I ended up playing defensive back.

But you still have it, Mitchell, I thought to myself. And if DeAngelis decides to make a run for it, he doesn't stand a chance. Because I'm still fast. Also because Ricardo DeAngelis is nearly sixty years old.

At that moment, the Cadillac pulled into the motel parking lot. I turned back to the field where the celebration was still in progress, clapping my hands like a proud parent, one eye watching the Caddy.

From my position on the far side of the field, I had a direct view of the front of the Allendale Budget Lodge. The motel looked like it may have been built in the fifties or sixties. A faded pole sign advertised AIR CONDITIONING – TV IN EVERY ROOM. A single row of eighteen rooms faced South Main and the field across the street. The Caddy had parked at the far end in front of number eighteen.

I watched the car door open. A tall man unfolded himself from the vehicle. Ricardo DeAngelis, who preferred to be called Ricky, stood six-foot-four-and-a-half. He was lean and in very good shape for his age. I couldn't see his green eyes from where I stood, but most of the women he'd bilked described them as glowing with an inner light. That sounded like romantic bullshit to me, but something must have blinded them to the man's devious intentions. The media had crowned DeAngelis the Heart Throb Bandit, and he'd made a career out of separating lonely rich women from their bank accounts. I'd been hired to find him.

I watched him scan the parking lot, glancing in all directions before unlocking the door to his room. He stepped inside, surveying the lot once more, then closed the door.

Running the length of the ball field, I left the pick-up game behind, surely impressing the kids with my speed as I ran. There was little traffic on South Main Street and I hurried across, moving to the right of the motel where several dozen used RVs sat in diagonal rows. A sign out front announced Bargain Prices for Road-Ready Class A Motorhomes.

Roberta Nesbitt had hired me to find DeAngelis and bring back her grandmother's broach. Nesbitt was a crusty old broad who started out selling shrimp on the side of the road. Her husband had been a shrimper based in Mayport, outside of Jacksonville. So she knew shrimp, but obviously didn't know much about men. Her husband left her with two kids and mortgages on the house and shrimp boat. It took her thirty years, but now she owned one of the largest wholesale seafood houses in the Southeast.

Unmarried since husband number one, Nesbitt fell for Ricky's line, hook, rod, and shrimp net. She even paid for her own two carat engagement ring, spotted him a twenty-thousand dollar loan, and arrived home one afternoon to find her jewelry cleaned out and her white Caddy missing—along with DeAngelis.

She told me she'd like to cut off his balls, but what she really wanted was her grandmother's broach. I told her I'd find him and see that he did some time, but there was no guarantee he hadn't already fenced the jewelry. That didn't make her happy.

Nesbitt had bought DeAngelis an iPhone, which was GPS enabled. Through a contact in the Jacksonville Sheriff's Office, I received tracking reports from the cellular network carrier, which led me through Georgia to Allendale, South Carolina.

As a private investigator from another state, I had no legal justification for apprehending a wanted man. Hell, even a PI living in Allendale couldn't arrest anyone. Wrong kind of badge. My intention had been to locate DeAngelis, which I had, then call the sheriff. Let the locals deal with him. Nesbitt's attorney was prepared to alert the local police and have the Heart Throb Bandit extradited to Florida.

That was still my plan until the door to room eighteen swung open and DeAngelis stepped out. He carried an overnight bag and a slim aluminum briefcase, which he locked in the trunk before returning to the room. I hugged the outside wall of his room weighing my options. I could dash back to my car and follow him. But he might give me the slip. I could tackle him in the parking lot when he returned to his car. Too public. I'd rather do this quietly. Taking him in his room seemed to be the best option.

Nothing in DeAngelis' file indicated he was violent. All of his crimes had been of the passive variety, walking away with his victim's savings, leaving behind broken hearts. Even so, I'd tucked my Smith & Wesson into the waistband of my jeans as a precaution. My shirt hung out, long tails covering the gun.

Quickly forming Plan B in my head, I decided to confront him before he returned to the car and detain him until the law arrived. Although he seemed to be in good shape for his age, I didn't think he'd fight. Everything I'd read about DeAngelis described him as gentle and well mannered. He might try to sweet-talk his way past me, but I wasn't a gullible old woman. Maybe he'd make a break for it and try to out-run me. Like that would happen. No, he wouldn't argue with a thirty-eight in his face. Then I'd call the local constabulary and hope they understood why I took the law in my own hands.

Stepping up to the door, I knocked sharply and waited for it to open.

"Just a minute," a voice called out from inside the room. I'd have to agree he sounded gentle and well mannered.

A few seconds later, I heard footsteps approaching the door and the click of the lock. The door swung open and I instinctively looked up a few inches expecting to see the refined features of the Heart Throb Bandit smiling at me. One hand was on my hip, ready to pull out the revolver.

Through the open door I saw a darkened room; a double bed looking like it hadn't been slept in, an ugly floor lamp sitting next to a green easy chair with a matching hassock. What I didn't see was Ricardo DeAngelis.

I heard a soft whoosh before a blinding pain exploded across my knee. My knee buckled under me as the pain burst into pinpoints of light in the back of my retina. I rolled on the sidewalk clutching my knee. Cursing my stupidity. Cursing DeAngelis.

DeAngelis rose from behind the wall next to the door where he'd been kneeling. Through my pain I heard him say, "Sorry about that, my friend."

He held a length of pipe in one hand and his car keys in the other. DeAngelis stepped over my writhing body and sprinted to Roberta Nesbitt's Cadillac. I attempted to stand, reaching for my revolver at the same time, but I lost my balance and landed on my ass.

Lying in front of the open motel door, like a discarded pizza box, I watched helplessly while DeAngelis fired up the Caddy and roared away.

Look for *Bring Down the Furies*, coming soon

CPSIA information can be obtained at www.ICGtesting.com
Printed in the USA
240539LV00002B/67/P